JAMIE HOLLAND

one thing leads
to another

HarperCollins*Publishers*

HarperCollins*Publishers*
77–85 Fulham Palace Road,
Hammersmith, London w6 8jb

www.**fire**and**water**.com

Published by HarperCollins*Publishers* 2000
1 3 5 7 9 8 6 4 2

A catalogue record for this book
is available from the British Library

ISBN 0 00 651415 4

Set in Minion
Typeset by Rowland Phototypesetting Ltd
Bury St Edmunds, Suffolk

Printed and bound in Great Britain by
Omnia Books Limited, Glasgow

Acknowledgements

Lots of people have given me help and advice with this, and I would like to thank in particular Susan Watt, Victoria Routledge, Annabel Hardman, Vicky Edwards and Patrick Walsh. I must also thank the Bell family for owning Drumnacarf in Scotland and for inviting me up there on several occasions, and Stuart Mills for his invaluable insight into the IT world. I also want to thank my parents for all their support and for raising me in such a beautiful part of the world. Special thanks go to Bro and Sado whose patience and good advice have gone way beyond what could reasonably be expected from a brother and sister-in-law. And finally, I would like to thank my precious Rachel for her forbearance and for simply being wonderful.

For Rachel

PART ONE

summer

chapter one

The Beginning of Summer
and a Pact is Made

Outside in the pub garden, it was still light, and surprisingly warm. It was the first time they had been able to sit outside that year, and the three of them were making the most of summer's arrival.

'OK then,' said Jessica, laying her hands decisively on the table and looking at Flin and Geordie in turn, 'we're agreed. Yes?'

Geordie looked at Flin, nodded, and looked back at Jessica. 'Agreed.'

'Great. At last.' Jessica smiled, and stood up. 'I'll ring the landlord straight away.' She took her mobile phone out of her bag and walked away from their table.

It had been a trying few weeks. Initially the prospect of finding a new house had seemed quite exciting, but after sacrificing two Saturdays and several evenings trudging round gloomy, soiled houses, all three of them had become extremely disenchanted with the whole procedure. Nothing they'd seen had ever quite fitted the bill; even the house they'd finally agreed on wasn't perfect, but for a year, they'd decided, it would certainly do. And the location – Barons Court near to the west road out of town – was certainly a big point in its favour.

'Give it a lick of paint and it might look really quite nice,' Geordie suggested hopefully.

3

'Sure, it'll look great,' Flin agreed.

'And I could easily put up a few shelves and bring a few bits and pieces up from home.'

'Brilliant,' said Flin. Geordie's enthusiastic DIY-talk was cheering him up. He really wanted their new house to be as homely as possible and not like the down-at-heel digs he had lived in before; after all, they weren't students any more.

Jessica switched off her phone and walked back over to them. 'Ninety-three Turneville Road is ours.' She grinned triumphantly. 'We've got to sign next week and then we can move in the week after next.' She kissed them both happily. 'I can't wait – it's going to be such fun, the three of us.'

'And Geordie's already got great plans for improving the place,' put in Flin.

'Brilliant, darling – what a little DIY king you are. I honestly don't know where we'd be without you.' Jessica gave Geordie another kiss. Their decision had cheered her enormously and she felt suddenly more affectionate towards her two friends.

'And you two are going to help,' Geordie added, sternly.

'Yeah, yeah, yeah,' said Flin flippantly, then reminded Geordie it was his round.

Having returned with more drinks, Geordie sat down and lit himself a cigarette. 'Thank God this is sorted out. Moving in will be fun. I need a bit of excitement in my life.'

'Me too,' added Flin.

'Not much going on otherwise. Same old job, still no girlfriend,' Geordie continued.

'We'll be a house of singletons,' put in Jessica brightly. Flin and Geordie both glanced up from their pints dubiously.

'Whoopee,' said Flin.

Jessica tucked a strand of her newly shortened hair behind her ear and said, 'OK, I've got an idea. We move in on the twenty-fourth of May and we've got the house for a year. By the same date next year we should all make sure we have better jobs and are in steady relationships. We should make it a special goal.'

'But that's always my aim,' said Geordie. 'I spend my whole time wishing my work wasn't so boring and yearning for a girlfriend.'

'We should make it a competition though,' added Flin, warming to Jessica's notion. 'I mean, I'm obviously in more or less the same boat as you, Geordie, but if we had a definite time-scale to work to, then perhaps it would make us try harder.'

'Exactly,' said Jessica, 'we should make a proper pact, right here, right now.'

'I s'pose we could,' said Geordie glumly, 'although you two have such a head start. Jessica, you nearly always have a boy-friend.'

'Nonsense – they're just flings. I haven't been out with any-one properly for ages, and anyway, I've never, ever been in love. By next May,' she announced emphatically, 'I want to be head over heels.'

'And Flin's always in love *and* he has a great job,' continued Geordie.

'Rubbish,' said Flin. 'Firstly, Claire and I split up nearly four months ago, and secondly I wasn't really in love with her anyway. And film PR might seem fun to you, but the pay is dismal.' He grinned at them both. 'By next May, I want some-one to be in love with me, and I want to be better paid, so at last I'll be able to keep up with you two.'

'And I want to be promoted too,' said Jessica, 'and working on much more exciting accounts, not just low-fat microwave meals.'

'OK,' said Geordie resignedly, 'I don't mind going along with this, although ideally I'd like to be doing a job I enjoy and both be in love and have someone love me by the end of next week.'

'Pressure's on already,' laughed Flin.

'That's the whole point, darling,' said Jessica, 'it'll focus our minds.'

'And a bit of competition never hurt anyone,' continued Flin, slapping Geordie heartily on the back.

'What's the prize?' said Geordie dejectedly. 'If it's a competition, then there's got to be a prize.'

'All right,' said Jessica, 'the prize is free drinks all night. On May the twenty-fourth next year, we meet back here, at the Atlas, and whoever hasn't fallen in love or been promoted has to buy the other two drinks all night. I think that's fair enough, don't you?'

'What happens if none of us wins?' added Geordie.

'Then we still meet here, but everyone buys their own and we discuss what we've been doing wrong.' Jessica looked at her two friends and raised her glass. 'A pact has been made and we've got our house at last. Cheers to that, darlings.'

And two and a half weeks later, the three of them moved in. Flin managed to persuade Geordie to pick him and his belongings up from his sister's house (where he had been staying temporarily for free), and Jessica and Geordie successfully transferred their belongings from their tiny two-bed flat in Hammersmith. It was a beautiful early summer's day. The trees in the street were full-bodied with fresh deep-green leaves, lending an air of calm serenity to their new home. Inside, the sunshine brightened the whole house, and all three felt a renewed sense of expectation for the year ahead. It was going to be a good year.

That evening, with bags and boxes all around them, they once again toasted the challenge they had set themselves. They were in buoyant moods, the ordeal of moving house finally over. The early summer sun and new home helped create a creeping sense of confidence. It was as though by merely agreeing to the pact, they were sure to achieve their goals.

chapter two

A Promising Encounter on
the Piccadilly Line

Flin thought it the most wonderful serendipity bumping into
Poppy again. They had been at primary school together and
hadn't seen each other for – yes, they agreed, it must be –
sixteen years. In fact, it had been she who had recognized him
as they stood wedged up against each other on the Piccadilly
Line. It had taken Flin a moment to place her, but he felt
justified in that: it seemed scarcely possible that the haughty
girl who'd been his childhood object of hate could have blos-
somed into someone so ... well, gorgeous. A carriageload of
silent commuters shared their reunion. Oblivious to the glances
and raised eyebrows, Poppy asked him a barrage of questions.
What was he up to? Where was he living? Were his parents
still in Wiltshire? It was so good to see him – and after all this
time, he hadn't changed a bit; she'd recognized him at once.
Well, she certainly had changed, Flin thought to himself, and
very much for the better. As the train pulled into Leicester
Square, Flin moved to leave her.

'I think it's brilliant having found you again after all these
years.' She beamed at him, bright teeth and full, luscious lips.
'Will you come to my party? It's in Sussex.'

'I'd love to.' Flin meant it. She kissed him goodbye.

'You *must* come,' she cooed as the doors closed.

As he stood on the escalator well-I-nevering to himself, he

supposed her invite was nothing more than conversational gush, and assumed he'd be lucky if he saw her again before another sixteen years had gone by. But much to his delight, that very same afternoon as he was writing up some production notes, she called.

'Poppy! Hi!' he exclaimed, startled. 'How did you find me?'

'Easy as pie!' she told him triumphantly. 'You told me who you worked for and there aren't any other film companies with that name.'

This time they exchanged numbers and addresses properly. 'Actually, I've just moved in,' he told her, 'last weekend, and you're the first person I've given my new address to.'

'I'm honoured,' she replied, laughing. 'Invite me to supper and I can be the first person to see it too.'

'OK,' Flin said, 'as soon as we've made it respectable, you're on.'

In the meantime, she told him, she was going to put an invite to her party in the post immediately. 'And you must promise me you'll come,' she insisted once more.

'I promise,' he assured her, leaning back in his chair and smiling. What an encouraging start to the competition. He needed this excitement in his life and was fantasizing as to where it might lead when Tiffany put her head round his cubicle.

'Daydreaming again, Flin?'

'Hm? Yes, well, something funny's happened. I was just thinking about it.'

'Oh yeah? Let's hear it.'

Flin told her. 'What d'you think?' he asked.

'Play your cards right – who knows? Sounds to me like she's making a hit on you though.'

'You reckon?'

'Yeah, I reckon. Anyway, keep me posted.'

Flin liked Tiffany. She'd only recently come over from Australia, but already he considered her his best friend in the

8

department. He got on well with the others, but they all seemed a bit neurotic, especially his boss Martina, who, Flin had once been told, even put her shrink on expenses. There was no side to Tiffany though – or at least none that he'd seen. And they gossiped about everything: Flin told her all about his friends and the various dramas in his life, and she told him about hers.

It was good to be in their house at last and now with Poppy suddenly reappearing things seemed to be looking up. He had a good feeling about it – almost as though fate was lending a hand: new house, new girlfriend; it simply had to happen. Living with his sister had been very restricting. Both Sam and her boyfriend Will were very easy-going about Flin staying, and he adored his older sister, but however welcoming she and Will might be, Flin was conscious that it was *their* house and that he was nothing more than a guest there. And now he'd moved in with Jessica and Geordie, his oldest friends – it was going to be such fun, just like the old days when they were living near each other at home and spending all their time together. And so much better than his last house. He'd had a lucky escape there: the lease had originally been for a year, but when Eddie had decided to get married, they'd all agreed to move out after six months. It had been such a relief. Flin liked Eddie a lot, but his friend Bomber – well, just thinking about him made him wince. Putting Bomber immediately out of his mind, Flin punched in Geordie's mobile number.

With only four or five miles to go, Geordie knew it might take him another hour to get home. It was nearly four o'clock and he could not understand why narrowing the M4 from three lanes to two should, at this time of day, cause the traffic to grind to a standstill. Each time this happened, he felt an overwhelming sense of frustration descend upon him. It was such a waste of his life. He had begun the journey in Manchester and from thirty miles north of Birmingham to thirty miles on its other side the motorway had been one huge contraflow. Those sixty miles had taken him the best part of three hours; the whole journey, so far, six hours. Ridiculous. He whacked his hand on the steering wheel. In the car next to him was a man in a light grey suit picking his nose, blankly devoid of emotion.

Geordie was not a great fan of London. He knew this was largely because he was still comparatively new to the place, but everyone seemed so rude. He hated being shouted at by overly aggressive cabbies, carved up by monstrous buses and jostled and accosted on the streets; he liked to be able to walk in a straight line along the pavement. Right now, in the throes of yet another hold-up on the roads, he was feeling particularly disgruntled. London may have been voted the coolest city in the world, but this did little to sway Geordie – he preferred a country pub to a London bar any day.

None the less, most of his friends seemed to live there, and although there was so much about the capital that he disliked, he knew he was basically quite happy and that it was too early to move out. That could wait, although he did have some sense of a grand plan: he would continue to work in London for another year or two, obtain some crucial experience in the IT industry, and then get the hell out into a business of his own. Working for Burt Kwang at FDU might be boring, but Geordie knew he had to put up with it: give his presentations, visit clients, learn about the industry and not let Burt's indifference to him get him down. It was a case of going through the motions until the right opportunity appeared. In the meantime, he had the new house to think about. He needed to borrow some tools from his father to make the shelves and get the place painted. And he needed to sign up to a new tennis club now that the rugby season was over. He might be tall and fairly thin at the moment, but too much sitting about in his car without exercise would soon change that. Anyway, he liked feeling healthy.

After successfully blocking out an aggressive-looking BMW

from cutting in ahead of him, Geordie flicked back a lock of his drooping blond mop and then looked in his mirror. At least he was ahead of the massive queue behind him. He glanced down at his phone, and was wondering whether he should call someone when it rang.

'Guess what?' said Flin in muffled tones from the hands-free microphone.

'What?'

'I've bumped into a gorgeous old friend from home and she's invited me to her place for the weekend.'

'Bastard! How'd you manage that?'

Flin told the story of his encounter for the second time.

'Bastard!' Geordie said again. 'I knew you'd be first off the mark. And we've only been in the house half a week.'

'Well, yes, obviously the pressure's really on for you now.'

'This better not stop you from helping out with painting the house.'

'Course not, but if you think I'm going to turn down a weekend in the country because you want me to do DIY, think again.'

Flin's upbeat mood did nothing to improve Geordie's. What was wrong with him? Why this lean patch? If anything, it used to be the other way round: he was constantly going out with someone while Flin less frequently did. This was because Flin was nearly always chasing after people who were completely unobtainable. Whenever Geordie pointed this out, Flin would invariably reply, 'But I'm in love, and I can't help how I feel.' It had been the same at school, Geordie remembered. Flin had been madly in love with a girl in the year above who simply wasn't interested. Meanwhile, Kate Rodgers had been desperate for him. Flin had forever had plenty of girls after him: after all, he was a popular person, always had been. Geordie felt ever so slightly jealous of his oldest friend's easy charm and ability to be liked by just about everyone. Even when they'd been little, Flin had been that little bit more popular than him, and nothing had changed since. Still, it had been great coming

11

back from travelling into an even wider circle of friends, and for that he largely had Flin to thank.

Geordie had never really thought about being in love. He supposed he had been; certainly he'd told previous girlfriends he was. It had seemed the right thing to say. At any rate, he'd enjoyed a steady string of sleeping partners: Alex and Sophie in his first year, then Susannah for over a year, and finally Nell, whom he only split up with because he was going travelling and he didn't want to have to feel guilty if he met anyone else. But since coming back, nothing.

Catching his own face in the mirror, he suddenly noticed a line had developed down one side of his face, etched between his nose and the corner of his mouth. Where had that come from? He was sure it hadn't been there last time he looked. Had he really already reached that stage in life where the ageing process was beginning to set in? And his spindly round glasses were smudged and getting loose. This was too much: he was twenty-five, stuck in a traffic jam on the M4 and wrinkling. How had he let his life lead him onto this course? What had he been thinking when he left university? The truth was: Not a lot. The options open to a graduate with a lower second in zoology had seemed a bit limited, and since he had a bit of family money, he'd decided he might as well delay the career for a year or two and explore a bit more of the world instead. He flew east first, to Thailand and then on to Australia and New Zealand, where he skiied and surfed and hung out, and then worked for a bit in a bar. From there he moved on to conquer South America, finally pausing for just over a year in Buenos Aires. He'd loved Argentina; and the cost of living was so cheap, meaning he could work little and play hard. There were plenty of Europeans and Americans out there too, providing him with friends. He had a girlfriend there too: a lovely Argentinian who'd dazzled him with her Latin allure.

At some point, however, Geordie had realized that he was going to have to get on with life. So, to the relief of his parents and friends, he'd come back to England and almost immediately moved up to London, on the lookout for a 'proper' job. Jessica had been looking for a new place to live, so he'd moved in with her. And here he was, he thought to himself, his career under way, sitting in a traffic jam on the edge of London and rapidly ageing.

He felt faintly depressed. Having exorcised his wanderlust, his life now felt mundane. The lack of girlfriend was just beginning to really get to him. Christ, he hadn't even had sex for over a year. What was it? Was he becoming boring? He was certainly feeling bored. Or was it just that it was harder to meet people these days? How did you meet new girls? Walk into a bar and start chatting someone up? Hardly. He thought about all the girls he knew. Most were spoken for; of those that weren't, either he'd already been out with them, or didn't fancy them, no matter how desperate he felt. And others, like Jessica, were just friends and always would be. This competition was all very well, but just how was he going to achieve these goals? Rooting around in the glove compartment, he found his much loved *ELO Greatest Hits*. Best not to brood. In the safety of his car, he could listen to whatever he liked, and sing as badly as he liked without anyone complaining – *he* liked ELO even if no one else did. Singing along the wrong words to 'Mr Blue Sky', he felt his good humour slowly return.

Geordie had phoned Jessica to relay Flin's news, but she found it hard to feel too excited. She knew what Flin was like, knew that he always jumped in head first without pausing to think and that often his early enthusiasm came to nothing. And anyway, she could tell that Geordie was only phoning her because he was bored: he always repeated himself when he had nothing to say, and on this occasion told her for the second time that day that he and Flin would be out all evening. Still, she was quite pleased about that: it had been a bad day at the office and she felt in need of some quiet time to herself. Of course she adored Geordie and Flin, but they could be so noisy and exhausting sometimes.

13

Arriving back at the flat, she made a beeline for the sink, washed her hands, then applied a generous amount of hand-cream and morello cherry lip-balm, and poured herself a large glass of wine. Then she kicked off her shoes, switched on the television, and lay full-stretch on the sofa, checking through the post. Letter from the bank – boring; some mail for Geordie – boring, boring. But then an envelope that always cheered her up – her weekly edition of *Bunty*. Her friends found it extraordinary that someone who was normally so elegant and poised at all times should still subscribe to such juvenile drivel. But Jessica had read it ever since she was about ten, tenderly bought for her each week by her mother: it was comforting and she liked the assured regularity of this weekly package.

Leafing through pages of schoolgirl drama was as soothing as ever; after that she was looking forward to what she considered essential 'me-time' – time in which to unwind, have a bath, read a magazine or two and not talk to anyone. To her annoyance, though, she found she couldn't stop thinking about Richard Keeble. How dare he make a pass at her! Then to make matters worse, Rob was still trying to sit next to her, even though she'd told him nearly a month before that nothing further was going to happen between them. Despite looking as immaculate as the moment she had left the house that morning, she now felt soiled and unclean. Even the restorative powers of lip-balm and hand-cream had failed her on this occasion. It was too much.

Richard Keeble always flirted with the younger girls. Although forty-something and acne-scarred, he was convinced they loved being chatted up and that his particular line of amusing cuff-links and bright ties made him a consul of contemporary chic. Rumour had it that he had had his way with one of the receptionists at last year's Christmas Party, but Jessica could not have possibly cared less – she found him utterly repellent. That morning, however, she had been trapped by him between the third and ground floor as she was on her way to a meeting.

'That dress is invitingly short,' he had said to her, smirking and looking up and down her legs. Red with embarrassment and anger, Jessica had not been able to think of anything to say, so shot him a look of contempt instead. 'Although, of course, I'd much rather see you without any dress on at all.'

Then he had winked, the doors had opened and he'd waited for her to walk out before following after her. He'd not actually touched her or been aggressively abusive, but Jessica had felt degraded and foolish, and to her horror had not been able to help imagining him writhing around on top of her, dribbling lustfully. Too disgusting; so she tried to picture lying on a Bermudan beach to erase the image.

Working for an advertising firm with progressive ideals meant that no member of staff had their own desk; instead each employee at Farrow and Keene had a trolley and a locker, a lap-top and a mobile phone. Having been forced to arrive early as she was suddenly frantically busy, despite feeling in a bean-bag mood, Jessica had settled down on one of the most coveted spots in the building. Then there had been the contretemps with Richard Keeble, and she had only just arrived back at her work-station when Rob turned the corner and appeared beside her.

Older than her by four or five years, Rob was a senior account executive whom she had initially quite liked; she had certainly been flattered that he had so obviously developed a crush on her. He was also much taller than her – always an important consideration – and she thought him reasonably pleasing to the eye. Ever since splitting up with Ed eight months before she had remained more or less single. She'd had a few flings, but nothing serious, and so when six weeks before Rob had asked her out for a drink, she'd accepted. He'd hardly bowled her over, but he had made her laugh and she'd quite enjoyed herself. Emboldened, he had then asked her out to dinner. Knowing the implications, Jessica had accepted – after all, he was offering to take her to Sartoria.

They had drunk good wines, followed by liqueurs, before

15

going back to his flat in Notting Hill. By now quite drunk, she got into the cab with him, and he started to kiss her, gently at first and then hard and urgently. Vaguely aware that his style of snogging was a little aggressive for her tastes, she broke off. But by then they had reached his flat, and headed straight for his bedroom. Slightly cursing her drunken lack of self-control, she found herself looking up at his face, now etched with grim concentration, while he humped up and down on his black-sheeted bed.

That Saturday morning she made a quick escape. She hated mornings at the best of times, but on this occasion she had a persistently throbbing head and was disgusted with herself for letting things go so far the previous night. The last thing she wanted was any sort of conversation. So, making her excuses, she told him she had to drive down to her parents and that she'd see him next week.

Monday had been fine – not too awkward at work, and he had discreetly invited her back to his flat for supper. Although still a bit unsure about how she felt, she decided to go. From there the relationship moved forward, but not at all as Jessica had imagined. The first week found her liking him more and more, and she thought she might even want to go out with him properly – certainly his love-making seemed calmer. But then he became a bit . . . well, wet. He would say anything to please her and was no longer witty or interesting. When she began an argument – mainly to get a rise – he would simply acquiesce. She started avoiding him at work and finding excuses not to see him in the evening or at weekends. Eventually, she had realized that although he must have got the message, he had obviously chosen to ignore it, and so took him out for a drink and told him that any brief fling they might have had was over. He'd looked absolutely distraught, but then that wasn't her fault. He would get over it; and she'd make sure never to become involved with anyone at work again.

After that he'd been away for a couple of weeks, but since coming back had continually tried to sit next to her at work.

As a result, she'd taken to deliberately coming in later than him, which had meant having to put up with the worst work-stations. That morning, though, she'd had to arrive early and Rob had yet again made a move to sit close by, until she'd warned him in no uncertain terms not to. She hadn't seen him again until later after her meeting. He briskly sidled past her and dropped a note into her lap. She glared at him, but he was already walking off again with his back to her. She unfolded it and read:

Darling Jessica,
I know you think I was being a bit wet with you, but I swear I just wanted to make you happy. Now I know that's not the way, I will be much more how I was when we first started going out. I know we can be great together, if only you could know how happy you make me! Please don't ignore this – write back and let me take you out tonight and we'll start again all over, with the new improved me.

Rob

Pathetic! Passing notes was the sort of thing schoolkids did. She felt exasperated. Her instinct was to ignore it and simply tear it up. But then she thought that perhaps resorting to his level was the only way to get through to him.

Rob [she wrote],
Can't you see that by writing that ridiculous message you are being totally pathetic? I will never ever in a million years go out with you again – I'm sorry but it's the truth. But please just leave me alone, or else I might have to take this harassment to a senior level.

Jessica

Being firm was the only way to deal with him and her annoyance with Rob and men in general renewed her disgust

17

with Richard Keeble. Picking up her phone, she dialled his number.

'Richard? This is Jessica Turpin.'

'Oh, hi, Jessica, what can I do for you?' came the reply.

'I just want you to know that if you ever speak to me again like you did this morning, I will not be answerable for the consequences. I hope that's clear. Goodbye.'

She put the phone down and returned to her screen with a sense of satisfaction. Maybe she had over-reacted, but it was important to nip these things in the bud. She had been far too lax with Rob and look what had happened there.

Lying on the sofa that evening, Jessica looked at the long length of her legs extending from her tiny black skirt, which in that position was even more revealing than normal. They were pretty good legs, she had to admit; she was lucky, especially as her mother was so small. All the same, she wondered whether maybe she should buy a trouser suit or two. The day's events had upset her more than she'd imagined. And would she ever find someone she wanted to go out with for more than a few months? The longest relationship she'd ever had was with Ed and that had only been for a year. No one else had ever made it to the six-month mark. Why did all her boyfriends become so jealous and possessive? It was *so* tedious and *so* predictable, and made her feel that emotionally she hadn't progressed from her teenage years. Admittedly, Rob had never exactly set her heart on fire, but she hadn't expected him to crumble quite so quickly. She desperately hoped she would find someone to fall in love with, but sometimes seriously doubted it would ever happen. Perhaps she set her sights too high, expected too much. Perhaps she should ring Ed again. But then, even he had become a boring stay-at-home. And as soon as her ardour for him had started to cool, he'd turned into a drooling love-slave. Jessica sighed and turned back to her magazine. Really, it was too much, it really was.

chapter three

La Vita è Bella

Leaving Geordie drilling rawl-plugs into the wall, Flin vowed to do his 'bit' towards decorating the house in the evenings the following week, and headed off towards Victoria and the train that would take him to Sussex and his destiny. He'd not been sure what to wear, and so had taken Jessica's advice and decided on very dark brown jeans and a white cotton shirt. Simple and understated. And he was pleased that she had approved of his new haircut.

'I've never seen it so short – very George Clooney and rather sexy, actually,' she told him soothingly.

'I think you look a complete prat – trying to be trendy just isn't you,' was Geordie's contribution, although Flin ignored the remark. After all, Geordie had the worst dress sense of anyone he knew, whilst Jessica always appeared the epitome of style and elegance. He didn't think he was particularly vain, but when Jessica approved of something, he took note. He wondered what Poppy would be wearing, and what her house would be like. It was bound to be stunning. And was this the start of something big? He had a good feeling, he really did.

Standing on deep and sumptuous gravel, Flin was paying the taxi when the front door opened.

'Flin! You made it! It's so good to see you!' said Poppy, skipping over to welcome him with a delicate kiss on the cheek. With chestnut locks now loose and slightly dishevelled about her shoulders, and bits of grass on her bare feet, Poppy appeared a vision of simple loveliness. Leading Flin through the house to the garden, she eagerly told him who else was coming, who was here already, and what *fun* they were going to have. At this, Flin felt a wave of apprehension sweep over him. He had thought of nothing but seeing Poppy again, but now he was here, he felt suddenly shy. Just what was he doing here amongst all these strangers? Could he really expect to end up in the arms of someone like Poppy? He was beginning to think that he'd made a colossal mistake accepting the invitation. But it was too late for that: in the garden, a few people were milling about by the stream and Poppy gleefully led him over. A Pimm's was thrust into his hands and introductions made. Flin had never been very good with names. Someone had once taught him a fool-proof method of how to remember who was who, but he'd forgotten that as well. On this occasion he logged a Sally and a Duncan but forgot who everyone else was. But if he worried about being left to fend for himself, he needn't have done. Poppy suddenly looped her arm through his and asked him to tell her everything that was going on in his life, much to his delight. He started jabbering away enthusiastically, whilst she laughed and clung onto him as though he was quite the most important person in the whole world. Resisting the urge to continue talking about nothing but himself, he then asked her about her last sixteen years. They were now facing the back of the house.

'OK, but you must let me show you round Pepperfield. After all, we left Salisbury to come here,' she said, confirming his belief that large houses with one word for a name develop distinct personalities. And, of course, the house was stunning. It seemed to Flin, as Poppy led him from the flagstoned hall, through rooms and along creaking corridors, that every aspect of Pepperfield exemplified wonderful taste. Modern art vied for wall space along with contented-looking family portraits.

'It's wonderful, Poppy,' he told her as they paused to look at some murals, apparently painted by a famous artist who had been friends with her grandmother.

She rested an arm on his shoulder. 'I love it. I'm so glad we moved all those years ago. Can't imagine us not living here now.' She smiled at him, and Flin felt increasingly lustful for the girl who had years before made his life a misery. 'Come on,' she said, 'let's go back outside.'

At half past midnight, Poppy and Flin lay against the gazebo at the end of the garden. The brilliant almost-full moon was reflected in the stream; surrounding them were the chalk downs, dark, gently curving and ancient. Between long drags on their cigarettes and lingering sips of their wine, they gazed up at the stars trying to spot constellations that neither of them knew anything about. 'Doesn't the Plough look amazing tonight?' Flin said without really having the faintest idea what the Plough looked like.

'Wow, look at that shooting star!' Poppy said.

'Where?'

'Missed it.'

The setting was perfect and Flin watched his cigarette smoke drift up into the windless night air. Already seduced by the house and setting, Flin looked down at Poppy, her head in his lap. She looked lovely. It seemed to Flin as though they were held there in a glow of poetic beauty.

'It's a good job Mark can't see us now,' she suddenly said.

'Mark?' asked Flin, alarms ringing.

'My boyfriend,' she replied flatly, taking another drag on her cigarette. Flin's heart sank. By her behaviour towards him, Flin had assumed she was single. He should have known things were going too well.

'Oh,' he said, not knowing quite what to say.

'He's on a cricket tour,' she said by way of explanation, and then added, with barely concealed contempt, 'with all his mates.'

21

There was a pause and Flin, not wanting to lose the moment, daringly started stroking her hair.

'Hmm, that's really nice,' said Poppy, smiling contentedly, her eyes closed. 'Do you fancy a fuck?' she said suddenly.

Startled, Flin felt momentarily wrong-footed. 'Yes, actually, that would be just marvellous,' he replied, his heart quickening rapidly. What did he care if the ground was really pretty dewy and hard? Turning her over, he gently laid her on the grass and kissed her, carefully lifting her knee-length cotton dress to reveal legs of cool silk skin. This was turning into one of the best and most exciting nights of his life, and Flin felt his ego being massaged to new heights. The whole scenario seemed to him so unlikely – it was the sort of thing he used to read in the letters at the back of *Men Only* that did the rounds at school. He was also – and who could blame him? – truly struck by the beauty of the scene: the moon and stars above them, an owl calling in the trees nearby, the gentle gurgle of the babbling brook and the smell of damp, summer grass. Her face seemed magical. He loved looking at the pale outline of her neck and shoulders, creamy light against the dark blue of her skin in shadow, which was rising and falling with her quickening breath. He felt earthy and manly, Mellors with his Lady Chatterley, enveloped in the smell of the damp grass and soil. D. H. Lawrence would have approved.

Afterwards, it suddenly seemed cooler and they were soon back inside the house. A tender kiss and Poppy floated tantalizingly upstairs, the moment gone for ever. But as Flin settled down on the sofa, his mind was positively humming. Was that it? Tomorrow, would she act as though nothing had happened? Could her current relationship survive this? Or was his liaison at the gazebo nothing more than a one-night stand? Having gone over the same thoughts without progressing further for about the thirty-eighth time he finally drifted off to sleep.

At 6.03 a.m., he woke up on the sofa with itchy eyes, a pounding head and a mouth that felt as though it had been in the Sahara for a week with no water bottle. Sun poured through the open curtains in the drawing room. It was another beautiful English summer's day, and Flin, aware that thoughts of further sleep were useless, decided to walk up to the downs above the house. After a couple of pints of water and some Aquafresh had considerably improved his mouth situation, he was sure fresh morning air would clear the eyes and head. And so it proved.

Up on the downs, his feet sodden by the dew, he found the view everything he had imagined it would be. The sun broke through the morning haze of the valley below, a sylvan carpet encased by soft-curved hills of chalk. Droplets of dew covered the anthills and he marvelled at a prospect so fresh and succulent and green. He breathed in deeply, the pure, cooling air cleaning his nostrils and lungs. All his anxious thoughts had disappeared. Whatever the future held in store, nothing could take away his wonderful evening the night before. Smiling, he thought about the pleasure he would gain from reporting back so positively to Jessica and Geordie. Even at twenty-five, he still felt ridiculously competitive with Geordie and this pact had made him more so. He didn't know why; it wasn't as if relationships were a question of one-upmanship, but it had simply always been like that ever since they were young.

When he returned and went into the kitchen to make a much-needed cup of tea, Poppy was already there.

'Where have you been so bright and early?' she asked, kissing him casually on the lips.

'For a walk on the downs. It was fantastic, absolutely beautiful up there,' he told her as she poured him a mug.

'How brilliant of you,' she responded, then added, 'I adore it here, and I love it when other people love it too.' Then someone else came in and they were no longer alone. As more people woke, Poppy held court, organizing teas and coffees, and never tiring of putting in more toast, croissants and brewing more hot drinks. She was a perfect host, Flin thought, admiringly, so charming to everyone – including him but not especially so, as though nothing had ever happened at all.

She had affectionately kissed him goodbye, but he was pretty sure he wouldn't be hearing from her again, and admitted as much to Jessica and Geordie when he arrived home later. Geordie was still fiddling about with power drills and planks of wood, and Jessica was painting in a pair of old dungarees, yellow emulsion already covering her hands.

'So, I think we will still be a house of singletons for a bit longer,' he told them as Geordie passed him a paintbrush.

'Oh, well, never mind, darling, I'm sure it's for the best,' said Jessica. 'You certainly don't want to get caught up in some sordid love triangle. Much better you fall in love with someone who's unattached. Take it from me.'

'I agree,' said Geordie, 'and now you're playing catch-up with the painting, so get stuck in.' Flin reluctantly obliged, lamely slapping paint onto the sitting-room walls, but all the time his mind thinking furiously about Poppy and whether she might, after all, call again.

Tiffany wanted to know all about the party when Flin arrived back in the office the following Monday; she had lived Flin's eager anticipation of the week before and was dying to know the outcome.

'Sounds to me like you had a pretty successful time: a party at a great house and a night of hot passion,' she laughed after Flin had given a detailed account of his weekend's events.

'As one-night stands go, it was pretty good,' Flin admitted with an air of wistfulness not lost on Tiffany.

'Well, you never know.' She smiled consolingly at him from her perch on his desk. Flin wondered why he didn't see more of Tiffany out of office hours – they had lunches together and sometimes went for drinks after work, but so far that had been it – clearly a work friendship only. He supposed they had separate friends, but even so he felt he should ask her over to supper one night now he was in the new house. Or perhaps they would have a house-warming party and she could come to that. Conscious he'd done rather a lot of talking about himself recently, he asked about her weekend. She'd gone to a big party to say farewell to one of her friends who was going back to Australia, and then – and this had been the best bit, she laughed – she'd gone to the Tower of London on Sunday. 'It was fantastic,' she effused, 'and I loved seeing all the inscriptions in the cells. You just don't get that kind of history back home.'

Flin hadn't been there since he was a child. As a teenager, you didn't come up to London to go to museums – you came to hang out at Camden Lock and to see the Cult at the Brixton Academy. And since he'd been living here, sightseeing hadn't really occurred to him; there always seemed to be something else to do.

'Have you been to the Natural History Museum?' he asked her, suddenly remembering how he'd marvelled at the enormous dinosaurs when he was little.

'No. Is it good?'

'Brilliant, as far as I remember. I'd love to go again and see whether the dinosaurs really were that big.'

'There're dinosaurs?' said Tiffany, clapping her hands together excitedly. 'Well, let's definitely go one day. It'd be fun.'

'OK, you're on,' agreed Flin. But before they could discuss it further, Martina was yelling at them for the weekly department meeting, and they headed off without ever fixing a date.

By the middle of the week, Flin was convinced his weekend foray would be nothing more than a pleasant memory. But then, out of the blue, Poppy phoned. Tiffany took the call and put her through to him, saying in conspiratorial tones, 'I think it's her.' Firstly she apologized profusely for not ringing earlier and then asked him over to her flat. She'd cook him supper and they could watch a film or something. His spirits soared. She was coming back for more. Perhaps in those two days she had even cleared the way with Mark.

Jessica preached caution. 'Now don't go blindly rushing in like normal – you know what you're like.'

'Of course I won't,' Flin assured her. 'It's just a bit of a laugh.'

'Well, that's fine, but don't go falling madly in love with her until the boyfriend's out of the way, that's all I'm saying. Otherwise it'll only end in tears.'

'Clearly he's on the way out though,' Flin told her, 'otherwise she wouldn't be asking me over for a little one-to-one at her place.'

Jessica and Geordie both gave each other knowing looks, but Flin had little time for such cynicism. They were just jealous because he was making such good progress in the competition. This new romance with Poppy was fun and he was going to make the most of it. Spontaneity bred excitement and made life interesting.

Arriving at Poppy's mansion block on Prince of Wales Drive, Flin felt his pulse quicken with anticipation. Someone was leaving the main front entrance, so he walked straight in without calling on the intercom. At the top of the third flight of stairs he arrived at the door of her flat and knocked firmly, causing the unlocked door to open slightly.

'Hi, Flin?' came a voice from within. 'Sorry, I'm in the bath. Come in and talk to me.' Her hair was bunched up out of the way, but almost everything else was immersed in a mountain of bubbles. Her feet and ankles were resting on the taps and two nipples, very erect, were also making a point of their existence. 'Mark's working late tonight and won't be coming over, so you've got me all to yourself. Give me a kiss.' So that was clear: Mark was not out of her life yet. But seeing her reclining in the bath Flin thought it fairly apparent what her immediate intentions were.

Once out of the bath she put on nothing more than a silk dressing gown which periodically revealed tantalizing amounts of bare flesh – a breast emerging as she bent over, or a full stretch of thigh when she sat down – perhaps deliberately, but more than anything proving she was a woman at ease with her body and comfortable with having it admired. From the bathroom Flin followed her into the kitchen where she handed him a very chilled bottle of white wine to open. Producing two glasses, she then proceeded to knock up a bowl of pasta, chatting all the while.

There was so much to talk about, and every story seemed fresh and new. She made him laugh and, equally importantly, she laughed at all his jokes too. Having finished the pasta, they moved from table to sofa, and then seamlessly to the floor, where she was lying against him and he was at last doing interesting things with her breasts with one hand and stroking her head with the other. Flin was vaguely aware of a clock striking at least ten when the dressing gown finally slipped away and all the teasing glimpses merged into a whole. He was lying back against the sofa, still dressed, looking up at an incredibly beautiful, slender and totally naked body, her tousled hair hanging forward as her hands were tugging determinedly at his belt buckle. He wanted to savour the moment, so that when he was old and grizzled and had not been with a woman in years, he would be able to think back and remember this completely. Unlike under the gazebo, where their lovemaking had necessarily been urgent, they now had time to explore each other's bodies and make every stroke, lick and thrust long and meaningful. As Flin finally shuddered and stiffened, Poppy also tightened with pleasure and then, hugging him tighter in her arms, covered him in kisses. Bliss.

Later, Flin was to realize that the next couple of weeks were among the most exciting of his life. He saw few of his friends and spent as much time as he could with Poppy. At the house, his bed remained largely unslept in and at work Tiffany and Martina both commented on his sudden tardiness in the mornings. He knew Jessica would only ask him awkward questions about Mark and that Geordie would expect him to paint the house, so he tried to avoid them as much as possible. He was vaguely aware of a new-found selfishness, but then again, everyone was a bit one-track-minded at the beginning of a relationship and he felt sure his friends would understand.

Mark, he knew, was away on business, but Poppy never mentioned him, and so it seemed a pity to spoil things by bringing him into the equation. Anyway, after all the time they had spent together, it seemed impossible to believe Mark was a serious threat. They picnicked in the park, strolled arm in arm along the river, spent long nights of making love . . . and she always looked so lovely and sexy, her long slender limbs a healthy golden brown from days spent in the summer sun. It seemed as though they lived in a world where no one else could play a part and Flin honestly wondered if his time with this gorgeous woman could possibly be more romantic.

The bubble burst rather suddenly. One evening, Flin eagerly bounced up the stairs to Poppy's flat only to find Mark there. Impossibly good-looking, he had a chiselled chin squarer than a brick-end, making him seem healthy, confident and mature; self-confidence and success oozed out of every pore. Flin was taken aback. He had been convinced Mark must be out of her life. Still in his suit, Flin's rival extended an arm for a predictably firm handshake, his cuff-linked shirt retreating to reveal an impressively solid and genuine-looking Rolex.

'Good to meet you, Flin. What can I get you? Beer? Glass of wine?' Suddenly Flin's position as man of the house had been drastically reversed. It was more than disconcerting. Mark seemed so manly Flin felt he should opt for the beer. 'Good man,' Mark said, smiling, and disappeared into the kitchen.

'Hi, Flin,' said Poppy, coming out of the kitchen as Mark went in. She gave him a kiss on the cheek and said in a lowered tone, 'Sorry, darling, I wasn't expecting him tonight. But you don't mind too much, do you?'

Course he bloody did, he minded a lot. Mark had just ruined his evening, possibly even his life.

Returning with the beer, Mark said, 'So I gather you're coming to the concert too?'

What was this? What concert? It was the first Flin knew about it. Momentarily caught off-guard, he assured Mark he was; then immediately regretted his split-second decision. Why was he being so nice to them both? Why not snarl at Mark and stake his claim to Poppy right there and then? But he knew he'd missed his opportunity and anyway, acquiescence was easier than confrontation. But even more galling, there seemed to be no dampening Poppy's enthusiasm. If she had been worried about having her two lovers spending the evening together, she never showed it.

'Flin, you've been promming before, haven't you?' she asked.

'Um, no, I haven't actually,' he replied truthfully. He had only ever been to one classical concert and that was at school when he was going through his Brideshead phase.

'Well you'll love it. You just turn up, hand over your three quid and stand anywhere you want.' Flin was hugely relieved to discover this was not going to set him back a fortune, a fact that did not go unnoticed by Poppy.

'My poor darling, were you thinking it would cost twenty pounds?' she laughed, adding for the benefit of Mark, 'Poor Flin's been worrying that this would be horribly expensive!' Mark laughed too and assured Flin that he would never have come if it hadn't been for the fact that it was so cheap. Patronizing bastard, thought Flin, laughing too.

'It wasn't the money,' Flin lied, 'but don't we need flags to wave? I don't want to make a promming *faux pas*.'

'Flags are only for the last night,' Poppy laughed. 'Come on, it'll be fun.'

Afterwards, Flin left them to it. His self-esteem, which had been riding at an all-time high, had plummeted spectacularly. People like Mark made him sick, although he knew this was essentially envy. Standing briefly outside the Albert Hall, Mark gave Flin his leave, saying, 'Good to see you, mate,' as though saying 'mate' meant he was in touch with all rank of man. Poppy smiled charmingly, as if everything was perfectly as it should be. In a moment, they were hopping into a taxi. Flin despondently trundled off to the nearest underground at High Street Kensington wondering how Mark had been able to hail a taxi that quickly outside the Albert Hall on a concert night.

29

The situation had to change – and soon – but Flin was bleakly aware that he was leagues behind his rival in terms of wealth and stature.

Jessica and Geordie could not resist the 'told you so's'.

'I'm sorry, darling, but it's so obvious she's using you. This boyfriend of hers – whilst being good-looking, rich and successful, is clearly treating her like shit and so she's latched on to you to boost her self-esteem.'

'It's not like that at all,' Flin told Jessica weakly.

'All right, if you say so.' She kissed him affectionately. 'But just don't trust her an inch. Take on board my woman's instinct.'

'Yeah, give her a wide berth,' added Geordie. 'You know what you're like, you get all caught up in the romance and fling yourself headlong into completely unsuitable relationships. Anyway, what about your share of the decorating?'

A few days later, though, just as Flin was beginning to despair of ever seeing her again, Poppy suggested they go out for supper. He had very lamely offered to take her, but capitulated quickly on her insistence that it was 'her shout'. She had suggested it, she said, he could take her to dinner next time. Sitting at an outside table, Flin smiled at her as she popped an olive neatly into her mouth and smacked her lips. She took his hand and rubbed it and then looked down at the table slightly anxiously, before meeting his gaze again.

'I'm not being very fair to you, am I?' She had suddenly grown serious. 'I mean, you must wonder what's going on?'

Flin did not really want to respond to that, so smiled wistfully instead.

'Mark and I have been together a long time, and it's difficult to end it all. But I know I should. You're so much better than him in every way. And I've just adored the last couple of weeks. Mark's a complete shit to me, you know.' She took a large swig of her wine and accepted the cigarette that Flin offered her. 'Tonight, for example,' she said, exhaling her first drag, 'he's gone off for another of his boys' nights with his City chums. I'm not allowed to join in, of course. I'm strictly *persona non grata*, not able to drink enough pints and talk about rugby and stocks and shares.'

'But would you want to spend an evening doing that? It sounds pretty grim to me.'

'No, of course not, but that's not the point. It's just that he'd rather do that than be with me.'

'Surely not,' said Flin, gallantly.

'Flin, our relationship is totally on his terms: he still fancies me, and I'm sure he thinks I look nice on his arm at parties or what-have-you, but if I get in the way of him playing his sport, or seeing his stupid friends, then, well . . .' She trailed off. All that cash must be nice though, thought Flin to himself. He couldn't imagine she had to buy Mark dinner. Poppy had not finished, though. 'I know everyone thinks Mark is so wonderful. Under normal circumstances you'd probably like him too.' Flin doubted it, but kept quiet. She continued, 'Things haven't been great for a while, but then we'll have a great weekend or evening together and I think perhaps everything is OK after all.'

'But it's not?' said Flin.

'No.'

Although Flin had been enjoying listening to Poppy telling him how awful Mark was, he was keenly aware that Jessica's assessment of the situation had been uncomfortably accurate. But then again, now that Poppy was coming clean, this was clearly his opportunity to improve his own stakes. Delicate tact was what was required. 'Hm,' he said, feeling it was about time he said something decisive, but not quite managing it.

Poppy looked straight at Flin with large doleful eyes. 'I just don't feel I can trust him. Really, I'm a very insecure person. I need to feel wanted and . . . I don't know . . . a bit special.'

'Well, I'd look after you,' he told her emphatically. 'I wouldn't treat you like an attractive appendage to have around whenever it was useful.' Flin felt that was the sort of comment she was fishing for and a unique opportunity to prove that he

31

was sensitive to a girl's needs. She suddenly softened and smiled at him.

'Sweet Flin. I think you would look after me, wouldn't you? You're lovely, you know.'

The next morning, she invited him to Italy, and the roller-coaster that Flin's emotions had become soared again to the previous week's high. Her parents were hiring a farmhouse in Tuscany, she told him, in the vine-laden hills between Florence, Siena and San Gimignano, and it was enormous and needed filling up. Her sister was going too and had invited three of her friends. The prospect seemed impossibly romantic to Flin and he immediately filled his mind with images of Poppy swanning around Italian side streets in long, light summer dresses. She was offering ten days in a beautiful part of the world, wonderful food, delicious wine and, most importantly, time alone without Mark to get in the way of long nights of love-making.

He had already made plans to go on holiday with Jessica and a few others later on that summer, but still had enough days spare to fit in the time in Italy. He had a bit of spare money – living with his sister had saved him a lot of rent and although he knew he would need that later on, convinced himself that cash worries should not be a serious obstacle. After all, Poppy's parents were paying for the villa, he'd probably be spending just as much money if he stayed in London. And nowhere, but nowhere, was more expensive than London. So, all he was really looking at was the price of the airfare, and he could just about manage that. He accepted her invitation immediately.

Directly before Poppy was due to fly out with her parents, she had had to go on a long-arranged weekend with Mark. He had been invited by some clients to go fishing in Scotland and Poppy had agreed to accompany him. 'It'll be totally awful, but I promised and I have to go,' she had said. Flin was not at all happy about it, but the promise of great things to come convinced him not to make an issue of it. To add to the complications, Flin's late addition to the party meant that he could not get on the same flight as Poppy and the rest. He had to fly the next day, but Poppy assured him this was not a problem – she would simply meet him at the airport a day later.

Flin was careful not to tell Jessica or Geordie about Poppy's weekend with Mark.

'So the boyfriend's finally gone, then?' Jessica asked him.

'Yes, he's been shown the door,' Flin lied.

'Well, it seems I was wrong then. I hope you have a jolly time, darling.'

'You bet I will,' Flin told her eagerly. 'Ten days of love-making with a beautiful girl and Tuscan hills as company.'

'And her family,' added Jessica.

'Well, yes, but they'll be off doing their own thing, I'm sure. Poppy's hardly going to get me all the way over there just so I can join the family trips to the Uffizi.'

Jessica said nothing, but Flin was far too excited to worry about her scepticism. What did she know anyway? He was going to have a brilliant time, and at least Geordie was green with envy.

When he finally reached the arrivals door of the airport, there was no one there to greet him, no luscious Poppy in sight. There was an awful moment when Flin suddenly realized that he didn't even know the address of the farmhouse, let alone a telephone number. But no sooner had he started to panic, there was a honking of horns and up screeched a tiny Fiat Panda with arms waving madly from the windows. Poppy jumped out, ran up to him as he advanced grinning inanely, and gave him a huge hug.

'You've made it! How absolutely marvellous – you're going to love this, it's simply the most fantastic house in the most fabulous setting.' And with that, they skipped back to the car, which already contained four people including Poppy.

'Sorry it's a bit of a squeeze, but you sit in the front,' said Poppy. 'This is Dad, this is Alice and this is George.'

Flin shook hands with Poppy's father, a benign professorial-looking figure, and said, 'Hello, hello,' to the other two as the car lurched off into the city traffic. Her father may have a mild and gentle demeanour but Flin was quick to discover that his appearance was in strong contrast to his driving, which was fiendishly fast. Careering round corners, his expression never changed from one of quiet passivity – there was none of the deep-set determination or taut knuckles that are normally associated with motor-racing. Flin sat clutching his bag trying not to look at the road too much and feeling slightly conscious that he was the new boy and late arrival among what was really a bunch of strangers. Poppy and Alice chattered enthusiastically about the house and things that simply had to be seen, and Flin joined in whenever he could or should, all the time thinking that it would be good just to get there alive and talk to Poppy alone.

The journey lasted about forty minutes. Finally the tiny Fiat jolted along a track at a marginally slower pace with vines either side, then up a hill until they pulled into a courtyard. It was too dark to see whether the house lived up to Poppy's superlatives – but even so he could sense a certain aura of splendour about the place. The four of them walked straight in to the flagstoned kitchen and Poppy's mother strode over to greet the new arrival with a firm and formal handshake. Younger and taller than her husband, she cut an impressive figure in her three-quarter-length khaki trousers and white linen shirt.

'*Buon giorno*, Flin, welcome on board. Call me Liz.'

'Thank you so much for letting me come and join the holiday,' said Flin in his very best sincere and polite voice, 'it really is very generous of you indeed.' He dumped his bag on the floor and then met Alice's other two friends who had just appeared through the front door.

'This pair of love birds are Max and Charlie and I think they're marvellous,' said Poppy, tugging on Charlie's arm. Charlie was tiny – about five foot nothing and already bronzed, while Max looked relaxed and faintly disinterested in Flin's presence, leaning against the doorway and twiddling his goatee. He made Flin feel instantly unfashionable.

'How you doing?' said Max and then extended one arm for a handshake before spluttering something from the depths of his lungs into his other hand. 'Ugh, er, sorry,' he recovered.

Charlie smiled sweetly. 'You'll love it here, it's just so . . . um.' She waved her hand and gazed bashfully at the ceiling. The word or phrase she was searching for did not come. She shrugged. 'Yeah, it's so, well, perfect.'

'Come on, Flin, I'll show you your room.' Poppy took his hand and they walked through the kitchen and into a hallway and up some stairs. All the walls seemed to be white and the floor and stairs left bare stone. Flin's room had two single beds, but even at that stage Flin was deaf to any alarm bells ringing. In the corner was a tiny sink and in front of the beds were two huge windows with wooden shutters.

'Are you going to be OK in here?' she asked, kissing him lightly on the shoulder. 'I'm so glad you've come! Now, come down whenever you're ready but I've got to go and help Mummy with the supper,' and off she went.

Supper was quite lively, and it became clear to Flin that Liz liked good conversation with plenty of discussion and interesting debate. This was better than awkward silences, but Flin felt constrained by the fact that his conversation should be intelligent and pertinent at all times. Donald, Poppy's father, spoke very softly, but seemed to be so revered by everyone that as soon as he opened his mouth everybody else immediately shut up and listened keenly to what the old sage had to say. He appeared to be rather amused by his strident wife; in fact he seemed rather amused by everything, demonstrated by the faintest hint of a perma-smile and a frequently raised eyebrow. Whilst a heated discussion about the value of television took place, Flin decided to keep quiet and assess the gathering. Alice and George were an item and had a room in the main house, which Donald and Liz clearly had no objection to, while

Max and Charlie, who were also a twosome, had a room in one of the outhouses. Only then did it occur to Flin that he and Poppy were the only ones not sharing a room, and he began to feel just the tiniest bit irked. But then, he supposed, he was the last to arrive, and so put the matter out of his mind.

The meal seemed to last an aeon, and Flin began to feel increasingly frustrated. He was desperate to talk to Poppy on his own and to steal some kisses al fresco; Sussex revisited, but beneath an Italian moon. Eventually, after the coffee had been drunk and after helping to wash up, Flin excused himself and went outside for a cigarette. Poppy followed and at last the two of them were together and alone. He took her hand and kissed her soft cheek.

'I can't believe I'm here and that we've got over a week to go,' he told her as they strolled down the steps into the garden. There was a pause. Poppy suddenly seemed quite unaccustomedly embarrassed. All at once, Flin knew what was coming.

'Flin, I don't want you to be angry, but Mark and I patched things up in Scotland. We did a lot of talking and I think I've got to give it another chance.'

He absolutely couldn't believe what he was hearing.

'I mean, it's not as if we could have got up to much with my parents here anyway.'

Couldn't they? What was she on about? Of course they could! Why invite him otherwise? Did she honestly think he'd come all this way just to be told that she'd decided, after all, that she wanted to stay with someone, who was, by her own admission, a total shit? Flin reeled. What could she be thinking? Had she gone completely insane?

He took a long drag on his cigarette. Outwardly calm, his mind was racing in a panic. With eight full days to go, he desperately needed to be rational. If he said what he actually thought, life would become even more difficult. She was offering friendship. If he turned that down, he would be in even worse trouble. He took a deep breath.

'It's a long way to come to be told that,' he said with as

much dignity as he could muster. 'But this is a fantastic place and we are going to have fun, fun, fun with a capital F,' he said, smiling weakly. Thank God it was dark.

'We can still spend all our time together,' she said, hugging his arm and warming to the fact that her announcement had been so painless. 'I'm sorry though, and I do think you are gorgeous. You'll be better off with someone far nicer than me.'

He felt sick. This was a monumental disaster, and there was absolutely no escape.

chapter four

Geordie and Jessica have Dinner at Tommy Byng's

Jessica was just about to go and run her bath when Geordie finally walked through the door. As always (and it was no different now they had moved to the new house), he immediately asked Jessica whether there was any post or messages for him.

'Just some bills and a couple of messages for Flin from Josh,' she told him, without looking up from her magazine. And as always, he pressed the answerphone anyway.

'Yo, big man!' said Josh's voice. 'I've got your new number. Nice one. I need someone to get drunk with and you're the name I've pulled out of the hat. Call me immediately.'

The second message was even more concise: 'Of course you're not there – you're getting laid in Italy you little Julio. Forgot. Ignore that last message.'

Geordie sighed. 'No calls, no decent letters – not even a postcard from Flin.'

'Poor you, how trying,' replied Jessica, looking up at him. 'Get yourself a drink and then come here and calm down.'

A short while later, Jessica had made it into her bath and was testing a new body scrub when the phone rang.

'Hello,' said Geordie, picking up the receiver in an instant.

'Geordie, hi, how's things?'

'Flin! What are you doing calling? Where's our postcard?'

'I've only been gone four days. Give me a chance. Just thought I'd see how you guys are, you know . . . How's our house?'

'Great – I've painted the bathroom now and put up a new cabinet. What about you? How's the holiday of love?'

'Um, good, thanks. Really good. Great.'

Flin was being very odd, Geordie thought. Hardly very enthusiastic at all. 'Flin, are you OK?'

'Yeah, yeah, fine.' Flin paused. 'Listen, Geordie, is Jessica there?'

'In the bath,' Geordie told him, 'why?'

'Oh nothing – it doesn't matter. Look, I'm running out of money – I'll see you next week, OK? Have fun.'

Geordie immediately padded upstairs to tell Jessica.

'Something has definitely gone wrong, the poor lamb,' Jessica said through the bathroom door. 'I knew that girl was a cow.'

'He sounded very weird,' Geordie confirmed as he stood on the landing, leaning against the bathroom door. 'Not himself at all.'

'Well, let's hope he manages to resolve it, whatever it is,' said Jessica, splashing.

Geordie nodded. 'He's always fallen in love too easily.'

'I don't think he's ever been in love actually. I think it's more that he thinks he is.'

'Maybe.'

There was a short contemplative silence between them and then Jessica said, 'Oh, dear – and this body scrub is hopeless. I'll probably discover it's scarred me for life. Geordie, my love, what's to become of us?'

Geordie didn't bother to answer. Although he was loath to admit it to himself, he felt pretty low.

Still, at least that night he and Jessica were going over for supper at Tommy's. Tommy had been at school with Geordie and Flin and had then gone to the same university as Flin too.

Through them he'd got to know Jessica pretty well – everyone knew everyone, after all. He shared a flat in the Olympia side of Barons Court with an old friend of his called Jim Dawson. Both were hearty, fun-loving, beer-chugging sport fanatics.

As it was a pleasant evening, Geordie and Jessica decided to walk. Taking far less time than they had supposed, they ended up arriving a bit too promptly. Jim had not even arrived back home from work. Undaunted, Geordie took out a four-pack, Tommy poured Jessica some wine and they all sat down in front of the telly, which was murmuring and flashing images in the background. Although Jim and Tommy had made a slight effort to make the place respectable – throws over the sofa, a few plants and framed pictures – the ashtrays, empty tankards and various balls and other sporting accessories clearly indicated theirs was a bachelor pad and nothing more. Even the plants, that most elementary indicator of domesticity, were insipid little fronds, while pride of place above the fireplace was a print of the fifteenth hole at the Belfry. Dominating one corner of the sitting room was a complex music system and a massive television, with CDs and videos scattered haphazardly below. Long-dried shirts, socks and boxer shorts crammed the radiators.

It was quite apparent that Tommy hadn't even started preparing supper, and the arrival of his friends seemed to delay this further. He happily chatted away to them – how was work? What had they been up to? Where was Flin at the moment? He blew a multitude of smoke-rings from underneath the acutely curved peak of his Oakland Athletics baseball cap. Apparently Jim's new girlfriend – Katie Symons – was coming too.

'Lovely girl,' said Tommy, 'Jim's got himself a humdinger.' And then making up the party was a friend of his from work called Molly Duguid. 'So not a major bash,' Tommy continued, 'but it means we can all put in some serious chit-chat.' Then he got up and announced that he really should be applying his culinary talents and sorting out supper. Geordie's ears had twitched at the mention of Molly and he couldn't help wondering – as he did with any new girl he might meet – whether she was a) pretty, and b) single. Coming on her own was an encouraging sign, though.

No sooner had Tommy disappeared into the kitchen than Jim turned up. Looking slightly flustered, he went straight for the kitchen and the fridge and only then came in to say hello to Geordie and Jessica.

'Jessica, hi! You look gorgeous as ever.' He took hold of her shoulders and kissed her on both cheeks and then turned to Geordie. 'Good to see you,' he grinned, shaking his hand unbelievably firmly, 'how are you, mate?'

Slumping himself down on the sofa and pulling on the top of his can of beer, Jim asked them their news, and then ambled off to get changed. Both he and Tommy were just beginning to forge successful careers, albeit in different fields: Tommy worked for a pharmaceutical company as a brand manager, while Jim worked for a City bank. Geordie had always known Tommy would do well – he had the gift of the gab and bucketloads of self-assurance, ingredients that counted for a great deal. Both he and Jim were now earning pretty impressive salaries, even if the decor of the flat suggested otherwise; greater evidence of their material wealth could be found on the street below, where gleaming under the orange neon were Tommy's Beamer and Jim's MX5.

It was strange how quickly their lifestyles had changed, Geordie thought to himself. Only a few years ago, they had all looked so unkempt and slept and drank far more than they ever worked. Now pin-striped suits and cuff-linked shirts were the uniform, not worn-through jeans and ethnic jumpers. At first, he had found this change very disconcerting. When he'd set off to travel the world, no one had a proper job and they'd all still been students in attitude and circumstance, larking about with no responsibilities worth talking about. He'd been back in between, but only ever for Christmas when everyone else was on holiday and partying; so, on the surface, nothing much had seemed to have changed. But it had, irrevocably. The carefree days of early adulthood had gone for ever. Maybe that was why he had travelled so much: to perpetuate his youth, to delay growing up. All the same, it was a shock to discover that his friends no longer wanted to play every night.

Two years of travelling, however, had done little to clarify his career options, and he certainly had no better idea of how to achieve his entrepreneurial goal. But he'd vowed to himself that he would never sit another exam in his life, and determined never to join one of the professions like so many of his friends. He remembered having a huge argument with Eddie Fussle, who had been taken on by Freshfields. Geordie had told him that he'd only chosen law because it was expected of him: Eddie's background, class, his parents' expectations, guilt – all these factors ensured that he was bound to follow the safe path. Eddie had argued back that although perhaps that might in some ways be true, he knew he would always be comfortably off and able to work anywhere in the country, and that as far as he was concerned, Geordie was just a 'waster' and that he, Eddie, would have the last laugh. Whilst travelling, Geordie had often thought of such friends (as he settled down on the beach or contemplated skiing down another mountain), working harder than they ever had in their lives and probably ever would again. In the prime of their lives, in their early twenties, they were working flat-out. Such a shame; such a waste. All the same he'd felt left behind when he first came back. Most of his friends had done their hard graft at the bottom of the rung and were established in their various careers. Perhaps Eddie had been right. He'd been keenly aware he had a lot of catching up to do.

Initially, Geordie had sold advertising space. He quickly discovered he had a natural talent for selling things, but none the less hated it, loathing the tedium of being glued to a phone all day and repeating the same old patter over and over. But relief was at hand – within three months he was approached by a computer software company called FDU and offered a job selling computer monitors and managing various key accounts. Maybe not the greatest work in the world, and nothing he'd ever planned to do, but he got a company car and did a fair amount of travelling around the country seeing clients. In fact, he could often be out of London for the best part of the week clocking up enormous mileage and Argos Premier Points. It was an aspect of the job he quite liked, for he was always slightly relieved to escape London.

It was just before half past eight when Molly turned up. Jessica had gone to talk to Tommy in the kitchen and Jim was still changing, so Geordie went to open the door. As soon as he saw her, he felt a spontaneous attraction to her. It was her eyes, so perfectly light and shining and staring up at him, that caught him off guard, and although this took only a fraction of a second to register, it was she who spoke first.

'Am I at the right place? Only you don't look much like Tommy or Jim, unless either of them has radically altered.' She smiled at him again, and Geordie laughed.

'No, no, this is Tommy and Jim's flat all right. I'm just their new doorman. Actually, I'm Geordie. Hello.' He held out his hand, feeling a kiss to be too familiar on a first meeting. She took it, still smiling.

'I'm Molly. How do you do?'

As he ushered her inside they were hit by the powerful smell of simmering curry. Jim then appeared from his room and took over the hosting.

'Molly, darling, what can I get you to drink? We've got wine, or beer, or another colour wine.'

'A beer would be great. Where's Tommy?'

Geordie looked at her with even greater admiration. Quite tall, she wore her dark brown hair in a shoulder-length bob, which accentuated her eyes even more. Geordie thought she was beautiful, not in a classical way, but pretty, humorous and, he noticed appreciatively, she even had quite big breasts and liked beer.

Jessica could see Geordie blatantly staring at Molly as

Tommy came out to greet her, and wondered idly whether he might be in luck. She hoped so. Really, it was about time Geordie ended this lean stretch. His moaning about his lack of a girlfriend was beginning to become tiresome. She couldn't work out precisely where he was going wrong: Geordie was always entertaining, fairly good-looking in a blond, stringy-bean sort of way, and also moneyed: when added together, this made him quite a catch. Perhaps she should help him improve his dress sense and execrable taste in music. In the meantime, though, Jessica was conscious that Tommy was starting to flirt with her quite blatantly and so decided to stop worrying about Geordie and flirt back instead. Not that anything would come of it, she assured herself; it was just a bit of fun. Tommy might be good-looking but he was not her type at all.

Molly was sandwiched between Jim and Geordie. Much to Geordie's annoyance, Jim was totally monopolizing the conversation and she was responding by laughing at everything he was saying. Jim was gallantly serving her rice, filling up her glass and leaning in towards her as he regaled some other uproarious incident in his life.

Eventually, he pushed back his chair and disappeared out of the room, and Geordie quickly turned to Molly, a bottle in his hand. 'Wine?' he asked her.

'No thanks, Geordie, I think Jim is fetching me another beer.'

Smiling at her, he just said, 'Ah,' and slightly anxiously pushed his round metal-framed glasses back up his nose. By God he fancied her! 'I know you work with Tommy, but it would be very useful if you could tell me anything else I should know about you in, let's say, sixty seconds.'

She laughed. 'OK, you say "go" when I should start.'

Geordie primed his watch and then said, 'Go!'

'Born in India 1972, father worked for tea company, don't remember much about it but vaguely aware that it was always hot, sent to school here when seven, hated it to start with but gradually came to terms with being ordered about by oppressive lesbian teachers. Um, parents had by this stage moved to Sri Lanka, in fact only came back to England about five years ago when Father retired, he's quite a bit older you see and I have two brothers who are now both married and in their thirties, and whom I adore, so I must have been an afterthought or a mistake. Went to boys' school for sixth form, which I loved – all the attention was great, and I think I had about five boyfriends there. Um, um, what next? Oh, yes, read History at university, totally useless degree but great fun for three years – lots of drinking and parties, and then travelled for a year and a half to delay the inevitable. Went back to India and the Far East and then worked in Australia for a while. Now I live in Highbury in a flat with Lizzie, who was at university with me. I like food, drink, the countryside and old films and I dislike working, the London underground and having to queue or wait for anything. There, how did I do?'

'Bang on sixty seconds. Very impressive.' Her résumé had delighted him and he wondered whether, on that evidence alone, he could ever find a more perfect match. Jim had come back armed with cans of Stella, but his moment had passed and Molly's attention was firmly taken up by Geordie.

'Now it's your turn. Give me your watch so I can keep time.'

Geordie spewed forth. He was careful to mention anything that might appear alluring: that he was brought up in a village near Salisbury, that his house had a swimming pool and tennis court, that he had travelled extensively and that he hated London, and also hugely disliked 'good cause' ribbons. From then on it was plain sailing. They had so much to talk about – travelling exploits, working abroad, her childhood in the sub-continent, weekends in the country – jabber, jabber, jabber. They were in their own little compartment for the rest of the evening, to which no one else had right of entry. His attention totally held by this vision before him, what did Geordie care for Tommy's flirting with Jessica, or the discussion about computer technology being debated by the other four?

Jessica made the first move to order a cab. Although she had always liked Tommy, she did not want him to get the wrong idea. But on the other hand, he was pretty handsome and had been really quite entertaining ... whatever, it was time to go and she would just have to see how matters progressed. The ordering of cabs stopped all other conversation and Molly goshed, grabbed Geordie's wrist to look at the time and said she really ought to be getting back to Highbury.

'I've really enjoyed talking to you tonight,' Molly told Geordie, giving him a peck on the cheek goodbye. 'We must do it again sometime.'

'When?' replied Geordie, a little too quickly.

'Give me a ring.' She flashed him a smile and then said her thanks and farewells to Tommy and Jim and was gone.

In the cab back to Turneville Road, Geordie sighed contentedly. 'Jessica, I'm in love. I'm definitely in love.'

'Darling, I'm thrilled you're taking our pact so seriously. But it's a bit sudden, isn't it? I mean, I could tell, we could all tell, that you were keen on her, but you've only known her for a few hours. She might have a dangerous psychopathic side.'

'I've seen enough to know. I have to go out with her, I just have to, she is my perfect dream girl. And she said I could call her.'

'OK, darling, you do that. But hold back on the declarations of love. A girl doesn't like to be rushed.'

That night, Jessica fell asleep almost instantly, but in the adjoining room, Geordie lay awake for hours, thinking of Molly and hoping for a miracle.

chapter five

La Vita è Bella Part Two

Neither Jessica nor Geordie heard anything more from Flin until the following Sunday night. For Jessica, Sunday nights were sacrosanct and she always did her level best to make sure that nothing came between her and the television. She did not want to talk to anyone, go to a party, watch a film at the cinema or any other extramural activity; she just wanted to eat supper on her lap (preferably something that was easy to cook with minimum fuss from Marks & Spencer), watch telly and then go to bed, safe in the knowledge that she had passed a relaxing and undemanding evening in readiness for the week ahead. She had a television in her room, but it was good to be able to relax in front of the twenty-four-inch model Geordie had hired from Radio Rentals without his snide comments on her viewing choice.

When the phone started ringing, *Heartbeat* had only just begun with a group of teddy boys from Whitby arriving in Aidensfield to cause trouble at the annual fair. Generally speaking, Jessica tended to screen any phone calls whatever the time of day. If Flin or Geordie were there, they would pick up the phone but in their absence she just waited for the answer machine to click into action. There were several reasons for this, all perfectly valid from Jessica's point of view: firstly her mother had an annoying habit of phoning her at least once a day. 'Ah, Jessica, *chérie*, how are you, my darling?' she would start in her heavy French accent, and then barrage her with inquiries about what she was up to, how her day had gone, where was she going that night, who was seeing whom – questions, questions, questions. Jessica found it exhausting. Much easier not to pick up the phone and then she never had to feel awful about being rude to her mother and hurting her feelings. The second reason was that people like Rob would phone, or some other man she was trying to avoid, and she hated having to deal with awkward confrontational conversations, particularly during free evenings. Thirdly, quite often she couldn't be bothered to talk to anyone. If she were stuck on a desert island she supposed she might eventually bore herself, but on the whole she enjoyed her own company and was perfectly happy doing her own thing – reading books and magazines, watching telly and videos. So when the phone rang, she ignored it and carried on watching *Heartbeat*, where PC Mike Bradley had just arrived on the scene.

The answer machine switched on. 'Jessica, I know you're there. *Please* be there. It's me. Pick up the phone.' Sigh. Pause. 'Jessica, pick up the bloody phone, please. Jes—'

'Flin, do you realize what time it is? *Heartbeat* has just started,' she barked into the receiver. 'Stop being so selfish.'

'Listen, Jessica, darling, I'm really sorry, but I need a huge favour.'

'If you think I'm coming to pick you up from Heathrow, think again.' What was he on?

'Look, please, Jessica, I really need you to.' He always said her name a lot when he wanted something. 'I had my card swallowed in Florence, I've used all my traveller's cheques and I have no other way of getting home. You know I wouldn't ask you if there was an alternative. Please.' Flin continued through her silence: 'Can't you record *Heartbeat* and come back in half an hour and pretend I never interrupted your Sunday night at all? Please. I'll make it up to you.' Having

48

finished yelling down the phone at the open-air kiosk at Terminal One, Flin waited for her verdict.

'How?'

'How what?'

'How will you make it up to me?'

'I don't know. But I will and you'll be glad you came and picked me up, I promise. What about a subscription to *Jackie* or something?'

'Hm,' she said. She knew she would have to fetch him. 'Oh, all right – but this is the last time.'

'Thanks, Jessica, you are more than gorgeous. I'll be outside Terminal One. I can't tell you how good it is to hear a friendly voice once more.'

Jessica put the phone down and scrabbled around for a blank video and then headed off. Flin was so annoying. Typical of him to have had his card swallowed up, and even more typical of him to bank on either her or Geordie to come to his rescue. But what did he mean by that last bit? she thought to herself as she quickly put on some lipstick and tidied her hair.

Any irritation Jessica may have felt disappeared by the time she saw Flin standing helplessly by the pick-up point; somehow, for all his height, he looked like a lost little boy. Hopeless, but it was good to see him. For his part, Flin was elated to see Jessica. He'd forgotten just how beautiful she was. Elegance personified and a true friend indeed. An hour earlier, with enormous relief, he had said his farewells, and then, while waiting for Jessica, had wandered around happily looking at all the comforting signs of English life. Warmth stole over him as he recalled his life before Poppy.

'So?' said Jessica, as soon as they started off again.

'You don't want to know. It was awful. A total, unmitigated disaster.'

'I do, I want to hear the whole saga from start to finish.'

'Jessica, I just can't bear to – and please don't say "I told you so" in a superior way, or I'll probably go mad.'

'Well, I did, and I do think that in return for picking you up – on a Sunday night – the very least you can do is tell me what happened.'

Flin acquiesced. 'It was dreadful, J,' he told her, having explained about Poppy's bombshell. 'You were so right. She was just using me to bolster her confidence, but it was a bloody long way to go to find that out. I felt such an idiot although I completely realize it was as much my fault as hers. Should have known my image of being carefree and in love in Italy was too good to be true.'

'Not really – just with her,' Jessica said, hoping to sound sympathetic.

'The first morning I was there,' Flin told her, lighting one of her cigarettes, 'I remember waking up very early and sitting outside on the terrace and thinking, I would do anything to see Jessica and Geordie cheerily walk round the corner. Or any of my friends for that matter – just someone friendly I could talk to. I really wished I had a mobile I could call you on. Geordie would've had his internationally linked up and ready to use.'

'Of course he would,' Jessica laughed.

'The real tragedy was that it was such a beautiful place. The air was fantastically fresh and I was sitting there, drinking coffee and watching the early-morning sun beginning to lift the lingering mist from the slopes of vines. A bell even started tolling from the nearby village – I felt as though I was in some sort of advert or Merchant Ivory film.'

'Sounds heaven.'

'It should have been. Such a bloody waste.'

'My poor darling. So what did you do all week? Did you just pretend nothing was amiss?'

'Exactly. I mean, what else could I do? If I acted sulky and petulant, a) that would have made things worse, and b) it would have looked rude to her parents who quite clearly had no idea that Poppy and I had at any stage been romantically involved.'

50

'And what were they like?'

'Liz and Donald? Really sweet, but Christ, did Liz like sight-seeing. She *was* nice, but completely ran the show all week and we all trooped round museums and monasteries all day long while she gave us the guided tour. She was a bit like Eleanor Lavish from *A Room with a View*. Great if you're into history of art, not so brilliant if you're not.'

Jessica laughed once more.

'Well, I'm sure I'll laugh about it one day,' Flin continued, 'but there was one time when I very nearly lost it completely. We'd been looking round the church of San Marco and Liz had been giving us another lecture. "Just look at Fra Angelico's brushwork,"' he said, imitating Liz's precise speech. '"You can see every sweep of the brush as the paint was carefully applied to this figure's robes." That was the sort of stuff she'd come out with. What's more, I'd been there before with Josh when we went inter-railing and frankly, once you've seen one fresco, you've seen them all. Well, as you can imagine, by the end of it, I was pretty keen just to get back to the villa. But no, we then had to go round the bloody Duomo, with Liz starting yet another lecture. By the time we finally headed back to the cars, I was feeling decidedly tired and grumpy, but I was also determined not to get in Donald's car as he was just about the worse driver I've ever seen.'

'Worse than you, darling?' asked Jessica.

Flin ignored the jibe. 'Much, much worse. Believe me. Anyway, having engineered my way into Liz's car, I thought I was safe until Poppy and Alice, Poppy's sister, started singing rounds.'

'Rounds?'

'You know, singing the same tune but at different times.' Flin shuddered at the thought. He had never felt so awkward in his entire life, and doubted he would ever forget that particular car journey. With a renewed wave of gloom sweeping over him, he recalled his feeble attempts at joining in.

'Oh, Flin, haven't you ever sung rounds?' Poppy asked him.

'You know, I sing a line, then Mummy sings a line as I'm starting my second, then Alice joins in, then you join in and so on. You can sing, can't you?'

Yes, Flin thought to himself, but it always made him feel self-conscious, especially when he was the only male amongst three females. Liz started the ball rolling. 'London's burning, London's burning.'

Then Alice sung the same line as Liz moved onto 'Fetch the engines, fetch the engines.'

At the moment Flin was due to join in, Poppy and Alice, and Liz in the mirror, all nodded at him gleefully. But at that appointed moment, racked with horror and embarrassment, he remained mute.

'Come on, that's when you come in,' Alice said, at this stage still humouring him.

'I'm not very good at singing.' Flin knew he sounded lame.

'Nonsense, anyone can sing this,' Liz scoffed.

'Have a go, Flin, it's good fun, honestly.'

A dark cloud of self-consciousness lowered above his head before enveloping him completely. From its murky depths, he growled out his lines.

'There, that was easy enough.' Poppy smiled at him encouragingly.

'You'd find it a lot more comfortable to sing at the proper pitch, though, Flin.'

'Mummy, don't bully him. Flin can sing however he likes. Now what next?'

The next 'round' was considerably more complicated and, try as he might, Flin was not able to get to grips with it at all.

'Look, sorry, I'm spoiling your fun. You three sing without me. Let me just listen to you doing this properly,' he had told them.

Deciding that Flin was a lost cause and that any further attempts at coercion were useless, they finally ignored him and carried on singing increasingly complicated sequences. Flin chewed his fingers and abstractedly watched the Tuscan landscape drift past his window, conscious that his week from hell was descending into new depths of surreal horror.

'God, that sounds horrific,' said Jessica, laughing out loud yet again as Flin recounted the sorry tale. 'Why on earth didn't you just do your own thing?'

'I thought it would seem rude, but after the Day of the Rounds, I decided that I had to make a break for it, whether I offended them all or not.'

'And did you?'

'Not in the slightest, which made things even worse. I should have left them to their sightseeing much earlier.'

'So at what point did you lose your credit card?'

'The same day – my day of supposed freedom,' Flin told her.

This had been a further disaster. Liz had decided they should look round the church of Santa Croce in Florence and then spend the afternoon in the Uffizi. Flin had excused himself from both but had gone with them into Florence. After pottering about on his own he made for a café-bar in the middle of the Piazza della Signoria and had got chatting to two girls, fresh out of school and on their years off.

'That must have been quite fun,' suggested Jessica.

'It was really. They were quite impressed by my job and I enjoyed showing off a bit. But they also made me feel a bit maudlin. They were so excited about everything, with all that fun and freedom of college ahead of them. I really wished I was four years younger and sitting at the table with friends, with no responsibilities in the world. Being grown-up and constantly having to worry about work and money is so boring. I really liked idling about and being a student.'

'Yes, but when we were younger we couldn't wait to grow up. I remember that very clearly,' Jessica told him.

'Yes, I s'pose you're right.' Flin was silent for a moment. 'Anyway,' he continued, 'we all got quite drunk, especially one of the girls, who tipped her wine glass all over me. Her friend decided she should take her back to their hotel and I stayed

53

in the bar for a couple more drinks. I had wine all over my crotch and I didn't want to get up until it was dry.'

By that stage he felt quite drunk himself, but sleepy as well – the sun had been beating down all day – and so went for a nap under a tree. He was only supposed to sleep for an hour or so, but when he awoke realized that it was evening and that he'd missed his rendezvous with the others by several hours. Of course, he'd rushed off to the meeting place but there was no sign of them or the cars anywhere. What was he to do?

'What did you do?' asked Jessica.

'I panicked,' Flin confessed.

It was true, he had. He remembered that moment particularly clearly. His head was pounding furiously from the combination of hangover and exercise. It all seemed a bit bleak. He didn't have the telephone number of where he was staying – it had never occurred to him that once in Italy, he would need it. Nor could he quite remember the address, but was confident that he could find it – probably. Near Greve somewhere; Montefiore, or something like that. He would go to a cashpoint, take out some money and find a taxi to take him there, with a driver who hopefully spoke some English. It would cost him a fortune, but he could see no alternative. Wondering whether the others would have tried to look for him, or gone to the police, he tried to think what he would have done if he were them. He hadn't been able to think.

Finding a cashpoint easily enough, he put in his card and opted for 'inglese', but then realized with absolute horror that he could not quite remember his pin number. This was a new card he'd only had for a couple of weeks. He felt sure it was 4432, or 4423, or was it 2243? He tentatively tapped in 4432, but it was rejected, as was 4423. No, it was definitely not 2243. Holding his hands up to the sky, he circled round for a moment and then stood staring at the cash dispenser. This was too much. How could he have been so stupid? If Italian cashpoints were anything like British ones, it meant he had one chance left. What the fuck was the stupid number? There were definitely a couple of fours in it, and he was pretty sure there was a three and a two, or was it a three and a seven? He pressed 4473. And his card was retained.

'So then what?' Jessica asked him. By now they were approaching Hammersmith.

'I had to take a taxi ride and hope that I'd firstly be able to find the place and secondly the others would have enough cash to pay the driver.'

It was an experience he hoped he would never have to repeat. The taxi driver had clearly been confused by his nonsensical attempts at Italian. Flin eventually worked out where he needed to go by doing a lot of pointing and saying 'scusi' at regular intervals. First he directed his finger towards a dog-eared map in the taxi, and then pointed to where he knew the village was.

'Ah, Montefioralle!' the driver exclaimed with almost as much relief as Flin. By the time they reached the village it was dark and Flin realized that they were lost again. Eventually though, exhausted, thoroughly fed-up and nursing a splitting headache, he found the correct track down to the villa and made it back.

'Flin, that sounds just about the most horrific thing I've ever heard. I mean, what did they all *say*?'

'They weren't very amused. Especially as I'd racked up about fifty quid with the taxi driver. "Where on earth have you been? We've been worried sick," and all glaring at me accusingly. It was awful. And Poppy had a complete fit, at which point so did I.'

'What did you do?' Jessica was incredulous.

'I told her I was really ill, had sunstroke and had lost my card and that her yelling at me was the final straw. She swallowed it actually, and was really quite attentive for the remaining days. Still, if I never see her ever again, I can't say I'll be sorry.'

'You poor love. I don't know what to say,' Jessica told him as she pulled into Turneville Road.

'At least we're all in the same boat again. Unless, of course, there's something you haven't told me.'

'Well, something has happened, actually,' admitted Jessica.

'Oh, no, what?' Flin responded, unable to check himself.

'Geordie.'

'Geordie? No! What?'

'He thinks he's in love. Although nothing's happened yet,' Jessica added hastily. Then she told him all about their night at Tommy's and how Molly had asked Geordie to call her.

'Oh, great,' sighed Flin. 'So now not only will I have to put up with a love-sick housemate, but Geordie's also ahead in the competition. Don't tell me you've found someone too.'

'Don't be so mean-spirited. Anyway, I don't think I have, but Tommy was definitely acting keen.'

'Tommy? Not your type, surely.'

'I don't know. Maybe.' Jessica gave him a capricious smile.

'Oh, just brilliant. And I thought I was glad to be home.' Flin sighed once again and slowly stomped upstairs with his bags.

Sitting forlornly on his bed, Flin looked at his belongings. A few clip-framed posters and a couple of shelves of books, CDs, records he never played any more and a few other bits of bric-à-brac. And his tired-looking old Aiwa music deck. As far as his worldly goods went, that was about it. Twenty-five, he reflected sadly, and his most valued things were his cherished collection of Beatles vinyl originals and CDs. He had no trust fund like Geordie, no savings and brilliant pay package like Jessica and virtually all his other friends. Just a large overdraft not far from its limit once again after an extravagant and utterly miserable holiday.

Part of him was glad to be back, especially with the fun of living in the new house, but a larger portion still felt incredibly low that it was over with Poppy. He hated being single and the thought of having to start all over again depressed him. Three years down the line from graduating and he felt he'd hardly progressed. Eddie Fussle was getting married in three and a bit weeks' time. Perhaps that was the answer. Maybe they would be post-student workers one minute and then suddenly emerge from the chrysalis as fully fledged marrieds. Mind-boggling. It had never occurred to him that people of his age were even remotely ready to undertake something quite so . . . well, he supposed 'grown-up' was the only phrase.

Buying a house was probably the next big step. If he had his own house he would feel considerably more inclined to treat it with respect, but this seemed another impossibly futuristic scenario. How on earth was he ever going to be in a position to afford a house, let alone furniture to go in it? He thought about all the thousands of houses in London. How could *anyone* afford them? Even a tiny flat seemed ridiculously expensive, and despite his near-constant penury, he was aware he earned more than most Londoners. Life could be so demoralizing. Still, he should be glad for Geordie. Jessica was never going to have a problem finding a boyfriend, but Geordie – well, he had to admit his friend deserved a break, and if Molly did materialize into something good, then, competition or no, he should be glad for him.

Having unpacked, Flin was back downstairs being told by Jessica to stop feeling sorry for himself when Geordie walked in.

'Flin, you're back! How was it with the luscious Poppy?'

Jessica glanced at Flin to await his response.

Flin sighed. 'Not quite what it was cracked up to be, actually.'

'No?' Geordie grinned. 'The parents interrupting your nights of hot sex?'

'Something like that,' Flin replied, shifting on the sofa.

'You're going to have to tell him, darling,' put in Jessica.

Geordie was looking expectant. 'Tell me what?'

'Oh, nothing. Look, do you fancy catching last orders?' Flin asked him. Of course, Flin *was* going to have to tell Geordie about it, but he wanted it to be a highly edited version, out of earshot of Jessica. His car-ride confessional had been cathartic, but then again Jessica was a good listener. Admitting all to Geordie would take him down to a new level of humiliation

57

– Geordie may be his best friend, but there were some things that simply could not be discussed with blokes.

Over a pint in a quiet corner of the pub Flin explained how he and Poppy had had a bit of an argument and things had gone badly wrong from then on. He did tell the story of the taxi-ride, but skirted over the other details of the holiday.

'What a nightmare,' Geordie said, recognizing that tact and sympathy were required at the present. Making him suffer could be saved for later.

'Yeah,' said Flin sullenly.

'I mean, I really thought you had it sewn up.'

'Hm,' nodded Flin

'To be honest, I was jealous as hell! She was absolutely gorgeous! I had all these images of you shagging under the olive trees or vines or whatever. I bet she looked even better with a deep tan.'

Flin winced. 'Geordie, can you please stop going on about how gorgeous she must have been? It's very painful for me.'

'I'm commiserating,' said Geordie.

'Well let's just change the subject,' said Flin.

'Sure,' said Geordie, then added, 'but I must admit I wouldn't have wanted to be in your shoes. It does sound really embarrassing.'

'It was.'

They both sat in silence for a moment, looking at the brown, flat liquid in front of them.

'Anyway, on a brighter note, I think I'm about to fall in love.'

'Yeah, Jessica said. That's great.' Flin looked up wearily from his beer. 'Well done.'

'Well, aren't you going to ask me about it?'

'OK, sorry.' Flin took one of Geordie's cigarettes. 'Go on then, let's hear it.'

As Flin got into bed that night he decided he would just have to try and put the Poppy débâcle behind him. It was no good being permanently maudlin. And he may suddenly be behind with the romantic part of the competition, but there was still a long time to go and there was always work. Bruklin Sale was coming over – the talk of Sundance – and he knew that this presented a golden opportunity to make a big impression. He had the opportunity to help establish this bright, new and exciting director/star in the UK; and well aware that Bruklin was unspoilt by years riding the publicity bandwagon, Flin knew he would have more influence over what this new star would do to promote than the vast majority of campaigns he worked on. Internal promotion was difficult in his line of work; the way forward was to put together campaigns that people in the business noticed. Get noticed, and get head-hunted. It was as simple as that.

chapter six

Ponderings on Love

While Flin was lying in his bed and giving himself a talking to, Geordie was trying to relax in his nightly bath. This had become an important part of his day for several reasons. Firstly, he never slept well if he missed out on this ritual: he hated feeling soiled and grimy and especially loathed having to get under his duvet with dirty feet (if he ever had to forgo his bath, he at least made sure his feet were clean). Secondly, he loved lying in warm soothing water and reading. It enabled him to relax after the rigours of the day and he kept a stash of Tintins, Asterix and rugby magazines for this purpose. Recently he'd adopted the additional habit of taking a cup of tea in with him – Earl Grey with one lump of sugar and just a dash of milk was how he liked it. He'd discovered drinking caffeine never kept him awake; if anything it merely aided relaxation and so quickened sleep.

Surrounded by mountains of bubbles and sipping tea from a new mug bought for the new house, Geordie was trying to read *King Ottakar's Sceptre*, but found his mind wandering. He could not stop thinking about Molly. Jessica had told him to wait a few days before phoning and now he knew the moment was approaching. God, he so hoped it would all work out. The very thought of lifting the receiver and dialling filled him with nerves. He couldn't remember ever having felt like this before. No girl in the past had ever caused him such a sense of nervous anticipation. He thought about his past girlfriends. How he'd left Nadia in Argentina then tried to see Nell again once he'd come back from his travels. By that stage, she'd long got over him and was going out with a lawyer with red hair. Then he suddenly remembered his first girlfriend and smiled to himself at the thought. Geordie supposed he must have been about fifteen, just before O levels, and he and Flin had just started smoking and trying to look cool. The two of them had gone to a local girls' school social and had ended up snogging two girls called Vicky and Clarissa. He'd followed Vicky around all evening and in retrospect it was clear she'd been keen for him to make a move. But he had never snogged anyone before and his intense fear of rejection had made him hold back until, clearly despairing of ever making her conquest, she'd grabbed his collar and shoved her tongue in his mouth. He could remember it all so clearly. Flin, much to Geordie's irritation, had snogged several times before then, and had wrapped up the deal with Clarissa early on in the evening. At the end of the party they compared notes and Geordie had felt ecstatic, not so much because of the sexual pleasure, but more due to relief that he had crossed this teenage hurdle.

He'd gone out with Vicky for about three weeks. At one point, Flin and he had taken the girls to the fair and had swaggered about in trenchcoats bought from the flea market, smoking Marlboro reds. Whizzing around in the Waltzer he'd tried to remain unfazed, despite feeling nauseous, while the girls screamed and laughed, their hair across their faces and getting caught in their wide-open mouths. Between the strutting and prancing, though, there'd not been much sexual activity: a grope of a breast and more snogging, but definitely no activity below the waistline. Not that surprising really – there simply wasn't a lot of opportunity for clandestine meetings and one day he'd received a letter from Vicky, in handwriting considerably more mature than his, announcing that they were drifting apart and therefore she wanted to finish it. Geordie had never realized they'd been that close. Flin had a similar letter from Clarissa on the same day.

Thereafter the main opportunity for meeting girls had been at parties held during school holidays at the racecourse in Salisbury. Such functions provided three clear aims for Geordie, Flin and their mates: get very drunk, ask the DJ for obscure and thus very cool tracks, and pull a girl. It was on one of these occasions that Flin beat him to the next great hurdle of life. Up until then neither of them had talked about it. They discussed sex and girls all the time, but since neither of them had actually slept with anyone at that stage, they always skirted over the precise details of any sexual conquests. That night, however, while waiting for Flin's father to come and pick them up, Flin had been cock-a-hoop.

'What a great fucking party that was,' he said ecstatically and then turned to Geordie and added with great deliberation: 'literally.' Geordie clearly remembered Flin's smug expression.

'What do you mean by that?'

'Well, I, er, got my oats, didn't I?'

'No way!'

'Way, man, you better believe it. I shagged Sophie Stewart by the edge of the grandstand.' Geordie had felt intensely jealous, infuriated that his friend had one up on him. From then on it had seemed of paramount importance that he lose his own virginity as quickly as possible.

He went back to reading his Tintin wistfully. Those days had been fun. No careers to worry about and the future seemed all mapped out. How times had changed. Now he was developing lines on his face. And when he'd last had his hair cut, he'd discovered some grey amongst the otherwise blond locks. And what was even worse, he had a sneaking suspicion his hair was thinning a little. His golden youth was fading.

The following evening, he announced to Flin and Jessica that the time had come to phone Molly.

'Do you want us to make ourselves scarce? I'd hate to put you off,' offered Jessica helpfully.

Geordie thanked her – he could feel his heart beating loudly enough without having the other two there to distract and make him feel even more nervous.

'Do you think we should listen in?' Flin suggested to Jessica in the hall.

'Don't be so rotten, Flin. Come on, leave him to it.'

They pressed their ears to the door.

It was so embarrassing making the first call. Geordie knew that she knew that he fancied her, otherwise he wouldn't be calling. But at the same time, they both had to pretend that this was not so obviously the case. With a deep breath he rang the number. Come on, come on, he thought impatiently as the phone began to ring with no response. After about ten rings, there was an answer.

'Hi! Molly?' Geordie said, quick as a shot.

'No, sorry, this is Lizzie. Molly's not here.'

'Oh, um, sorry.'

'It's not your fault.' Smart-arse, thought Geordie, sending a false laugh down the line.

'Well, could I leave a message for her please?'

'Sure – just let me find a pen.' Geordie could hear the receiver being put down and some rattling about from the other end. 'Fire away.'

'Could you ask her to call Geordie.'

'Oh yes, Geordie. Sure thing. She met you the other night, didn't she? I was wondering when you'd call.'

Geordie had absolutely no idea how to respond to such brazen upfrontness. 'Were you? Well, if you could ask her to call me that would be great. I'm in all night. Thanks a lot.'

'Aren't you forgetting something?'

'Am I?' Geordie really was too taken aback.

'Your number.'

He told her and said goodbye and then slowly stomped through to the kitchen.

'Well?' asked Flin, in an innocent tone.

Geordie relayed his conversation with Lizzie. He thought it a good sign that Molly had obviously mentioned him to her, and felt encouraged.

'That's fantastic. She's clearly been waiting for you to call. She must be keen, darling, take it from me,' Jessica assured him.

'Are you sure? That's good, is it?'

'Definitely.'

An hour later they were all eating their way through a ready-to-cook Thai montage meal when the phone rang.

'That'll be it, old sport,' said Flin, patting Geordie on the back. It was. Geordie's mind raced. He felt quite heady with excitement.

'Hello, Geordie. It's Molly. Sorry I wasn't in when you called earlier.'

'It doesn't matter at all. Thanks for phoning back. How are you?'

'Fine, thank you. How are you?'

'Good, thanks, great. Molly?'

'Geordie.'

'I was wondering whether you might be around on Saturday afternoon.'

'No, I'm not. No, hang on a minute, that's Sunday. Yes, I am.'

'I thought it might be fun to do something.'

'OK, sure.'

So far, so good.

Geordie gingerly suggested that they meet in Richmond – he had thought it might be romantic to walk along the river, have lunch and maybe stop in at Ham House. Much to his delight, Molly agreed and arranged to meet him at Richmond station at midday.

After ringing off, Geordie clenched his fist in triumph. 'Yes, you little beauty!' he shouted. She must be keen. Well, quite keen. She must be, she must be. It was only Monday. Five days to contain his excitement. He prayed it would be sunny.

His Thai was almost cold and both Flin and Jessica had finished theirs.

'Just what I need,' said Flin ruefully, 'a delirious loved-up housemate.'

'This is very thrilling,' announced Jessica, then thought of her own situation. Despite her vows, she'd enjoyed Tommy's attentions. Perhaps she would go to the cricket match on Saturday and see him then. She could ask Lucie to come with her and then she'd have someone to talk to while the boys were fielding. Cricket matches could be quite fun if it was a warm and sunny day and there were plenty of people she knew. Add a bottle of wine or two and it made for quite a relaxing day out. She felt rather pleased with her plan, and smiled to herself at the prospect.

chapter seven

Money – Or the Lack of It

Despite the enormity of the events that had occurred to him since he'd last been in the office, Flin had arrived back at work to discover nothing much had changed; he felt as though he'd never been away. Thanks to Tiffany, both his e-mail and voicemail had been regularly checked and his in-tray neatly sorted. She was away his first day back, but on her return had made a beeline for his desk and flashed him one of her huge dimpled grins.

'Hi, you're back! How was it? I've been itching to know.'

'It was terrible. Worse than terrible,' he confessed, the humiliation returning once again.

'No way – why?' She was sitting on the edge of his desk, her out-sized shirtsleeves reaching her knuckles, and thick rubber-soled pumps dangling from the end of her legs.

'I don't know if I can tell you. I'm too embarrassed.' He was too, but somehow couldn't help smiling at her look of utter incredulity.

'Oh, Flin, you have to!'

He acquiesced, giving her the Geordie Heavily Edited Version. 'So as you can imagine, I'm almost glad to be back at work.'

'I'm so sorry. What a bitch – honestly.' She bit her bottom

lip for a moment, then added, 'Well, it's nice to have you back. It's been really boring without you.'

Her sincerity was genuine and spontaneous. Flin felt cheered – this was the nicest thing anyone had said to him in a long time. 'Thank you – and thanks for clearing the deck.'

'Oh, no problem,' she said, then trotted off to her own desk.

No one else really probed him too much about his holiday. Martina had said, 'Wow! You look really brown!' but didn't actually ask him whether he'd enjoyed himself or not and by lunchtime his being away was old news and quite forgotten.

He had also phoned his bank to order new cards and made an arrangement to take out thirty pounds from his nearest branch. It was a sum unlikely to last him a week, but Flin hoped it would at least encourage him to try and be a bit frugal. Noticing a day later that two-thirds had already gone, he phoned his bank again to check his balance. He wished he hadn't – just twenty-six pounds and eleven pence left until he was up to his overdraft limit. This revelation plunged him into renewed gloom. He knew he'd spent a lot of what he'd saved while being at his sister's on the holiday, but was sure he had at the very least in excess of a hundred pounds. How could he be so far out? It was depressing but, none the less, he was confident he could pull through until pay-day, so long as there was no extra drain on his resources.

'I'm broke too, if it's any consolation,' Tiffany told him later.

'Really?' Flin had never really given much thought to anyone else having cash crises. Obviously Tiffany earned less than him, being only an assistant publicist, but he just assumed everyone else was better than him at looking after their money. Hearing Tiffany's tales of financial strife rather cheered him up, he shamefully realized. A partner in debt, a fellow money-mismanager. He had always felt he was the abnormal one among his group of friends; they all seemed to live their lives with consummate ease on what they either earned or had inherited.

Geordie arrived back shortly after him that evening and quickly brought up the subject of outstanding bills.

'We've got to pay the gas, electricity and phone connection fee, I'm afraid. Here,' he said, handing Flin the letters. 'Sorry, but it always costs a bit to get everything set up in a new house.'

'So how much do I need to pay?'

'Your share is forty-eight pounds, I think. We really should send it off tomorrow. Sorry to be the bearer of bad news.'

Flin felt sick. 'The problem is, old man, I don't actually have forty-eight pounds. I've got thirty-six quid to last me nine days and ten of that is in cash. Can't we wait for a final notice before paying these?' Why did Geordie always have to be so organized about such things, and why did he always have to make him feel so bad about being poverty stricken?

Geordie gave Flin a rueful grin. 'Look, don't worry about it. I'll pay your share and you can pay me back next week when you get paid. But honestly, Flin, you are hopeless. I just don't understand how you never know the balance of your account.'

'I thought I did, and I thought it was a lot more,' he said feebly and added, 'But thanks – I'll pay you back next Wednesday.'

'You should keep a book and note down everything you spend, then you'd always know. Just get into the habit.'

'Yeah, yeah, I know.' His friend was right and Flin also knew that it was decent of Geordie to bail him out, but being patronized by his housemate made Flin feel resentful. It must be so wonderful, he thought, to have money like Geordie.

'Maybe I should change jobs altogether – perhaps that's the way to get ahead in the competition,' Flin told him resignedly.

'Don't be ridiculous – you love your job.'

'I know I do on the whole, but I clearly don't make enough to live on, do I? I'm sick of being perpetually broke and having to suck up to you to help me out.'

'You'd be mad to chuck it in. Where else are you going to

have the opportunity to meet all those film stars and so on? You may not get paid a fortune, but you don't do too badly considering you're being paid to watch films and visit sets. Can't you just put a bit aside once a month or something?'

'I do always do that, but then dig into it because I run out of the other. It's all very well for you to preach at me, but you're one of the main culprits in persuading me to do things.'

'You can always say "no".'

'And watch you and Jessica go off and have fun without me? I'd like to see you try it – honestly, Geordie, you have no idea what it's like always to be short of cash.'

'Look, I'm sorry, but I have little sympathy. You have loads of good mates, a fantastically interesting job, you still manage to go on holidays abroad and do nearly all the things you want to do. I know this Poppy thing's been a blow, but really, you have a pretty good life. You're just feeling sorry for yourself, that's all. And it's not my fault I'm not poor like you.'

Before Flin could respond, Jessica walked in. 'Hi, darlings, can you give me a hand? I decided to do a shop on my way back from work.'

The taxi outside was loaded with Tesco bags, a crate of beer, washing powder and an enormous bag of potatoes. Flin and Geordie dutifully obliged and took everything straight into the kitchen while Jessica paid the taxi. As they were filling up the fridge, she came in and gave them both a kiss and told them they owed her twenty-six pounds each.

'You can add it to the tab,' Geordie told a distraught-looking Flin.

'Thanks,' he mumbled quietly. Regardless of what Geordie had just said, he really hated life at the moment. How different things had been a few years before. At school and then university, no one had had a lot of money. They all seemed to be more or less in the same boat. Geordie may have had a trust fund, but they all had to do temping jobs in the holidays and during their years off; and somehow money was never much of an issue. And there were grants, parents and overdrafts to pay the bulk of life's costs. Now, they were all totally on their own, with no help from anyone. And there was an increasingly obvious divide between those who earned a lot (i.e. all his friends), and those who did not (i.e. him). He was wallowing in self-pity again. It was unlike him to feel down for long, but he really had to try and snap out of it, and fast.

chapter eight

A Sunny Afternoon in Richmond (and a Bit in Borehamwood)

Geordie had begun to think his boss had almost forgotten he existed when Burt uncharacteristically gave him the challenge of coming up with a new marketing package. He was to work on it with Mike, another sales manager who'd joined FDU just before him. The two had always got on well and Mike had even played in Geordie's rugby team on a couple of occasions. He was really the only person at FDU that Geordie saw for the odd beer outside work; Mike was bored too and was one person Geordie could whinge to about Burt and work who truly appreciated his grievances.

'It's time you two got your brains into gear,' their Taiwanese boss told them with typical frankness. 'You've both been cruising along for too long on your soft arses, so you better make it good.'

This had come as something of a shock to Geordie, who had become unaccustomed to applying his brain much at work. After all, he'd hardly had much need: he could sell monitors in his sleep. What was more, Burt had only given them a couple of days to get their plans together. All the same, he and Mike had worked hard and Geordie felt pretty pleased with their efforts. Furthermore, he'd quite enjoyed the whole exercise. His excitement about Molly had, he felt, if anything, given him a sharper edge that week.

Their plan was to link up with a graphics card company. This was something that was put into a PC to improve all the computer graphics and presentation. Geordie's premise was that if an individual wanted improved graphics it stood to reason that he would want a decent monitor too on which to use his improved presentation. Therefore he proposed to strike a deal with a graphics card company whereby FDU placed a voucher worth a small discount off any FDU monitor. This would give the graphics card company a competitive edge over other graphic card companies. He and Mike had worked out the finer points of how to implement this dazzling piece of marketing initiative and enthusiastically presented their plans to Burt.

'I am thinking this,' he said to them deliberately, 'it is like a flower in a piece of shit: you made it look very pretty and attractive, but underneath it, it is full of crap.'

'OK, fine,' said Mike, after a short pause, 'how about this: we create a link-save with a graphics card company whereby a buyer gets twenty-five per cent off both products when he or she buys them together.'

'Different flower, same piece of shit,' Burt said flatly. 'A whole lot of trouble for very small feedback. You come up with an idea that is simple to set up and makes us big money on big order, and then I might be interested. This idea of yours will never make us much money as we are only talking about individual sales. But keep trying. I want you two to keep thinking of a plan.'

'Well that was a bit of a waste of time,' Geordie grumbled to Mike after they left Burt's office.

'Yeah, it was a bit demoralizing,' Mike added, 'but he's right, you know.'

It was a comment Geordie had not expected from Mike, but it came like a sharp slap round the face. Mike was right: Burt was right. Geordie thought quickly. 'I can see that now,' he said after a pause. 'Well, we'll just have to come up with something really good instead and dazzle him with our sensational business acumen.' They chuckled, but Geordie realized he'd meant it; thinking up cunning marketing strategies was certainly more fun than not really having to think at all. And although he had little time for Burt as a man-manager, he greatly respected what he'd achieved. Burt was an entrepreneur, and had set up FDU from nothing, zipping between Taiwan and the UK. Although it was still a comparatively small company with only two dozen full-time employees in the Borehamwood office, it had a high annual turnover and Geordie reckoned Burt must be taking home at least a six-figure salary. What Burt had told him in so swiftly stamping on his idea was that it was no good wasting valuable time on small fry. You had to make the maximum use of time and expenditure and think big. If Geordie was ever going to make it alone, these were the sort of tenets he was going to need to follow.

Driving back home that night, Geordie realized he'd let complacency set in. He was a good salesman, but had been doing the job with his eyes shut. It was an attitude that would hinder his entrepreneurial dreams. He hadn't been challenging himself and it was no wonder he was bored. Bored and becoming boring. Hardly surprising he couldn't find a girlfriend. But now Burt had laid down the gauntlet: the challenge was there for the taking. He hadn't understood until it was spelt out for him that what Burt wanted was people with initiative and drive, two things that had been painfully lacking from his life in recent months. His boss had been ignoring him because he hadn't earned any attention. Successfully selling monitors was not enough.

It also became clear to him that the same principles applied to his quest for Molly's heart and that his time of reckoning was painfully close. It was Friday evening, the weekend had arrived once more. Geordie felt convinced that the next twenty-four hours had the potential to be one of the most important days in his life. He knew quite a few people would be going to the pub that evening, but was determined not to waste away an evening with idle debauchery. Jessica was going for dinner with Lucie, but he had persuaded Flin to stay in with him, reminding him that going out would only mean spending money he did not have.

'Well played,' Flin told him when he saw the pie, ice-cream and cans of beer Geordie had brought back with him. 'I'll go out and buy some more cigarettes while you fix up the fodder.'

'Look, I feel a bit guilty staying in on a summer's evening, don't you?' Geordie confessed.

'A couple of quick ones in the Rutland might not be a bad idea,' suggested Flin.

'Not a bad idea at all,' agreed Geordie quickly, 'although I'd sort of meant to stay in and prepare myself psychologically.'

'Don't be so pathetic. Honestly, Geordie, we'll only have a couple of pints and anyway, it'll relax you.'

'Oh, all right,' agreed Geordie. He'd always found it hard to say no to the lure of the pub.

'So tomorrow's the big date,' said Flin, as Geordie put two pints onto the wall outside the pub.

'Feeling a bit nervous about it, to tell the truth,' Geordie confessed. 'Honestly, old man, I took to her that night like I've never taken to anyone before.'

'You're making me very jealous. You're about to embark on the love of your life, while I've just finished with mine. One of life's strange little ironies, I suppose.'

'Look, I've only met her once. She might find me totally repellent by the end of tomorrow. And anyway, Poppy wasn't the love of your life, so don't be so melodramatic. Furthermore it would never have lasted.'

'How do you know?'

'It just wouldn't.'

'So are you suggesting that if a relationship isn't going to last it's not really worth getting excited about?'

'Suppose I am. I mean, what's the point at our age? I, for one, do not want to be spending my entire life going out with people for a month or two and then moving on to someone else. I think the idea of long-lasting companionship is quite appealing. It's different when you're younger anyway – you're surrounded by an enormous choice of women all after pretty much the same thing, so it's a hell of a lot easier to chop and change. Nowadays, it's a damn sight harder to meet new people, and, more specifically, new and single people. I don't want to have to embark, again and again on an increasingly difficult quest for girlfriends. Anyway, I thought we agreed this in our pact.'

'I didn't realize a proper girlfriend meant girlfriend for life. You're only saying all this because you're so loved up. We don't all have to follow Eddie Fussle's example, you know.'

'I never mentioned marriage, Flin. You say I'm loved up, but you're just bitter.'

Talking of which, Geordie and Flin managed four apiece before they finally made it back to the house. They still hadn't eaten and so were beginning to feel quite drunk. Geordie's choice of stodge helped soak up the alcohol, but they also drank the tins of beer bought earlier. At the end of the video they felt pissed enough to put on Flin's copy of *Withnail and I* for yet another viewing and sat sipping glasses of whisky, anticipating out loud their favourite lines.

When Geordie eventually made his way upstairs he determined to drink at least two pints of water before going to sleep. Overcome with a panic attack that he would be breathing alcoholic fumes all over Molly the next day, he stood in front of the bathroom mirror, forcing the water into his swelling stomach. How could he have been so weak-willed? Setting the clock for nine-thirty a.m., he finally lay back on top of his duvet and went to sleep, praying that the next morning his head would be clear and his breath more or less neutral.

When the following morning finally arrived, there was absolutely no way on earth Geordie was going to be late; so despite the rendezvous being only a few miles away, he left the house at ten o'clock. No heavy amount of Saturday morning traffic was going to catch him out. As a result, three-quarters of an hour later, he had not only made it to Richmond but had managed to park the car and make his way to the station. Feeling slightly at a loose end he decided to nip into McDonald's and get himself a sausage and egg McMuffin and a coffee and try and relax. He really hoped that Molly would be on time. Jessica was invariably late for things and he always let it annoy him.

Munching into his McMuffin, he read in the *Sun* that one of the Gladiators was having an affair with a married woman, who was – for the benefit of the nation's readers – openly confessing that this hulk of a man was a sensitive and passionate lover, unlike her husband. Geordie thought the Gladiator looked a complete animal and an unlikely candidate for the soft and gentle category. What was it that made someone particularly good or bad at sex? Geordie wondered whether he was sensitive and passionate. Just like any other teenager, he had read his fair share of porn and knew that he hadn't achieved half the things the people in such magazines seemed to get up to. Was he normal, he wondered? Should he by this stage be using sex aids? He was sure none of his friends did. At any rate, if he ever managed to seduce Molly he vowed he'd take things very slowly and not rip her clothes off in a sexual frenzy. He was pretty sure that women liked men who caressed more than uncaged beasts, men who put the emphasis on excessive foreplay rather than pummelling away like a forty-pounder in nanoseconds.

With still just under an hour to kill, he thought it would be a good idea to survey the scene a bit. Ambling down George Street, he felt that Habitat and Hobbs were not really what he'd had in mind as features on his proposed romantic Richmond walkabout, but as he continued to the end of the street he stopped at the Waterstone's bookshop. In a flash of inspiration he decided to buy a local guide with which he could obtain a few ideas. Not immediately finding anything devoted to Richmond alone, he browsed through the ample 'London' section until suddenly a book of guided walks stared out at him. Sure enough, there was a walk in Richmond.

'Perfect,' he said out loud and hurried off to buy it. Quickly flicking through, he realized that it was ideal. There had been a royal palace, he discovered, and hurried down towards the Green in search of the site. By the time he found himself on Richmond Hill, peering into the windows of the numerous antique and knick-knack shops, he felt really pleased that he had arrived in Richmond so early and had learnt so much. With H-hour finally drawing near, he made his way back towards the railway station, wondering again whether she would be on time.

She was early. He could see her waiting for him just outside the main entrance. Geordie felt nervous with excitement and yearning. 'OK, here goes,' he said to himself and at that moment she caught sight of him and her face broke into a large grin.

'Hello, did you get here OK?' Geordie asked, giving her a light kiss on the cheek. 'I hope it wasn't too much of a trek for you.'

'Hi! Actually it only took me half an hour on the train, and was incredibly easy. So where are we going?'

'Did you know there was a palace here?'

'No, I can't say I did.'

'Well, there is. I discovered this brilliant book in Waterstone's.' He had meant to keep the book hidden away in his small backpack and dazzle her with his local knowledge. What part of the brain was it that always overruled such important earlier decisions without warning? He showed her the guide. 'Look, there's a walk for Richmond: you follow the directions and it details points of note. I thought we could have a look at some of it.'

'Geordie, I don't know about you, but I think we should do the whole thing. It would be really fun.' So it was settled.

'Brilliant,' Geordie told her eagerly. 'Let's start and when we've worked up an appetite, we can stop for some lunch and then carry on.'

'Great, although I have to say I'm pretty hungry right now, so I think lunch should be sooner rather than later.'

Geordie was over the moon. Not only was she on time, she looked as stunning as he remembered and wanted to go on his guided tour. Somehow, he couldn't imagine Jessica doing anything other than 'popping into' every clothes shop along the street and trying on huge numbers of outfits.

'OK, which way do we start? Will you be in charge of the guide book?'

'This way,' he said, grinning at her and pointing in the direction of Richmond Green.

The All Bar One was heaving, the air filled with cigarette smoke, beer and salad dressing, but they managed to find one end of a table. Geordie found her incredibly blue eyes quite bewitching and could not stop staring into them. She had put her large Audrey Hepburn sunglasses on the top of her head, keeping her hair back. Taking his hand, she said, 'Geordie, this is great fun – thank you.'

'Totally my pleasure. It's good to have interesting things pointed out, isn't it? A bit like having a tour guide without lots of people and at your own pace. What do you fancy eating?'

'I could kill something like a burger, or a big sandwich with chips. I'm unaccountably hungry today.'

She looked so lovely, he thought. He just had to go out with her, he just had to. Please God make it so, he prayed, then remembered he was an atheist.

'I never do enough of this sort of thing,' Molly told him. 'I've been in London over three years now and I still don't really know where I am half the time. I suppose I always think of London as being areas of concentric rings around underground stations. A little bit round The Angel, a bit round Piccadilly Circus and Leicester Square. I haven't a clue how it all links up. That's what comes of using the underground all the time. In fact, that was one of the nice things about coming overland down here – I saw lots of London.'

'The secret is to walk or take the bus whenever possible,' Geordie told her sagely.

'You're probably right.'

'When I very first arrived here to live,' he continued, 'I worked for a dating agency doing street questionnaires. I very quickly got my bearings from doing that.'

'You did what?' Molly looked incredulous.

'I know.' Geordie laughed. 'It was a nightmare job. I had to stop people in the street and ask them whether they were single and if they'd ever thought about using a dating agency. The aim was to try and find out their phone number. It was awful. I only did it for about a week and a half.'

'That must have been very embarrassing.'

'It was. But I managed to get loads of numbers. It was bizarre. I'd never in a million years hand out my number to some idiot with a clipboard. Anyway, the point was that we were given an area and then you had to wander the patch preying on unsuspecting members of the public. It was great for sussing out how central London linked up, but definitely a job to get out of quickly. Then I sold advertising space. A pretty inauspicious start to my life in London.'

'Well, I had to work in Solihull first before I was moved down to London. It was really depressing, rushing around Boots'es in the West Midlands trying to flog face creams. And once I even worked in a motorway service station. I lasted two days.'

'That almost beats wandering the streets with a clipboard.'

They talked and talked. She told him about growing up in Sri Lanka, and about her family. She adored her older brothers and wished she saw more of them. One still lived in London while the other was near Bath and had a baby son as well. Her parents now lived in a village near Alderley Edge in Cheshire. She loved big family Christmases – it was the only time the family really got together, apart from weddings and christenings. Geordie agreed it was the same for him. He had an older brother in the army, who was in Bosnia. But Salisbury wasn't far away and he tried to get down there as often as he could; despite his life in London, he still considered Wiltshire home, and always felt a surge of relief every time he saw the spire of the cathedral on his way down from town.

'I love it there and I get on really well with my parents, and, most importantly, my mum always feeds me really well. Still, it's not the same. It used to be such a laugh when Flin and Jessica and loads of other people were all down there. We all had such a great time when we were growing up. I had a very happy childhood. Everyone still seems to get together at the pub on Christmas Eve and Boxing Day, but it's not the same.'

Molly's expression had changed, wistfulness appearing over her face. 'It's sad though, isn't it? I mean, for so long, your parents are the most important part of your life. They rear you, feed you, play agony aunt, put up with your sulking moods and adolescent phases and provide you with unconditional love. Then having supported you for so long, you just up stumps and bugger off. When I go home now, I never really feel like my old room is my old room. There are none of my things in it any more and in their place are sensible pictures, different furnishings and it always seems clean. If I need to use the phone, I ask – I used to just abuse it.'

Geordie could relate to this. He felt guilty because he no longer felt the urge to phone his parents at least twice a week as he always used to. Travelling had put a stop to that. And being away for such a long period of time had forced upon him a very clear and defined severance from his early life. Before he left for his world tour, he had very definitely still been living at, and dependent on, home and his parents. When he returned, it had been over. He had officially left home – flown the nest. All his friends in the area had gone too. Looking at Molly again, he realized he had never discussed such matters with anyone before. It was so easy to talk with her. When he was speaking, she seemed to be listening so intently, as though no one had ever said anything of more importance to her. Geordie was finding more and more to like about her. Or, rather, love.

They were ambling up Richmond Hill when Molly insisted they stop in an antique shop. Far from finding this boring, Geordie was delighted to be able to gain a bit more of an insight into Molly and her tastes. They compared notes on old dressers, antique wrought-iron beds and finely lacquered sideboards. Such matters had never really crossed Geordie's mind; his family home was strewn with good pieces of furniture, and paintings and other *objets d'art*, but to him they had always just been associations of home and nothing more. Looking at various pieces, he suddenly realized that he did have a taste for certain things and not others, conditioned almost entirely by the familiarity of the style of his parents' house.

'That may seem funky, but really it's horrid,' said Molly, eyeing a large elaborate cream dresser up and down.

'I think it's horrid full stop. It looks really scabby to me.' Geordie peered at it closely.

'It's distressed.'

'Sorry, but I think it's bloody stupid to pay that amount of money for a piece of wood which looks as though it's about to collapse.' Molly laughed and they moved on to stand in front of a massive gilt mirror with an ornately arched top. Molly was looking at it sideways when she caught Geordie's eye. They both paused for a moment and stared at each other.

Then Molly smiled and said, 'Shall we carry on?'

Geordie's second moment of significance came when they were in the gardens at Ham House. Wandering between the hedges of the gardens, the smells and sounds of summer all about them, she slipped her arm through his. 'I much prefer the garden to the house, don't you?' and, not waiting for a reply, went on, 'When I'm older I'd love to have a big garden.

81

I think gardens are wonderful. A big garden in the country would be just perfect.'

'With a tennis court and a pool, and a walled rose garden.'

'A rose garden too? I didn't really picture you as a sensitive flower-lover.'

'I just think they look nice and I like the smell. And somehow a rose garden is very English. It always makes me think of going to summer garden parties and village fêtes when I was younger.'

'It wasn't quite like that in Sri Lanka, I have to admit.' She squeezed his arm and added, 'Which is all the more reason for making up for it when I'm older.'

Geordie smiled at her, and jokingly asked, 'Do you think you'd like to tend to your garden or would you demand that someone did it for you?'

'No, I think I'd like to look after it – with a basket and some secateurs. I think I'd be quite good at it.'

They had arrived at a small white wooden hut and sat down on the bench.

'I went through a plant phase when I was about twelve,' Geordie mused, 'I absolutely can't think why. I used to make endless cuttings of various plants and grow avocado plants from the stones. I was a bit of a butcher actually. Anyway, the fad soon went, I got bored and they all died. There were loads of tiny plastic pots with crumbly earth and flaccid light brown remains. Isn't that sad?' He laughed, and then noticed that she was staring at him again, rather intently. Did her head move slightly towards him? He knew it did and he knew what it meant, but just what if for some reason he was wrong? Panicking lest he should make a colossal blunder when all seemed to be going so well, he quickly stood up.

'Tea and cake, I think,' he announced, substituting the potential sexual connection for matters of the stomach instead. In doing so, that brief, intense and almost palpable moment of intimacy was gone.

'Are you free tonight?' Geordie asked her as they climbed back up to Hill Rise.

'Geordie, I wish I was, I really do, but I have to go out for dinner. I'm sorry.'

'Not to worry,' replied Geordie, as jauntily as he could.

'But it's been a wonderful day. I haven't enjoyed myself so much in ages.'

'I had a fantastic time too. Well, can I at least drive you back home?'

'I couldn't let you. Honestly, it's so far out of your way. It's so quick by train.'

'Are you sure? It'd be no bother.'

'Honestly, I'm fine on the train.'

'Let me take you out to dinner next week then.' Geordie knew he was sounding a bit desperate. He hoped he was not pushing too far.

'I'd like that. I'll give you a ring, shall I?'

If Geordie had thought he was in love before that afternoon, by the time he arrived back at the house he knew it for certain. She was his dream girl, and she seemed to like him too – he felt sure of that. If he could just persuade her to go out with him, all would be well; they would never look back, he was certain. Never? Well, he could see them being together longer than his previous (and rather pathetic by comparison) relationships. As he sat down on the sofa and opened a beer, it dawned on him they were living in a house completely lacking in taste or style. The electric fire seemed particularly plastic and fake; the curtains an unattractive flowery pattern. The tables and chairs had a simple lack of sophistication which had never bothered him before. And it smelt ever so slightly of stale tobacco. He suddenly knew that he wanted more than just a glorified student house. That afternoon, Geordie realized he was ready to change a little.

chapter nine

Summer Games

Simon Stringer had organized the cricket fixture for five years on the trot, on the same weekend in July, at his family ground at Lasham. The ground, laid down thirty years before by his father, was idyllic. With the house at one end, iron fencing separated one side from open fields, while the other was lined with ilexes and horse chestnuts. Simon's side, the Laughing Cavaliers, had been loosely formed by Simon and Tommy when they had been at university and they had managed to keep it going ever since. Every summer they played a handful of games; since they no longer toured and the emphasis on drunkenness and trophy-stealing was no longer given the same importance, the annual Lasham fixture and the ensuing party was the only occasion when the Laughing Cavaliers returned to their hedonistic best. The game was also the most competitive of the season, as it was against Simon's cousin Guy and his team. It was always the most perfect weather for Simon's weekend. Never had there been anything like the vaguest hint of rain in the five years they had first played the annual fixture.

Flin had persuaded Josh to pick him up and give him a ride to Lasham. Flin was quite good at most sports, but cricket was his great love. He and Josh had both been a part of the Laughing Cavaliers since the beginning and neither had ever missed out on the Lasham fixture. At midday on the Saturday, Flin heard Josh's TVR Griffith purr to a halt outside the house, accentuating the volume of Jarvis Cocker emitted from the cockpit. Josh was waving a cigarette around in the air and singing in a strained high-pitched tone, 'Nah, nah, nah, the common people, got to nah with the common people . . .'

'Cheers, Josh,' said Flin, putting his bag in the boot and jumping into the passenger seat.

'No worries, always a pleasure,' replied Josh, moving off with the statutory screech of burning rubber.

However mercurial Josh may be, Flin had always counted him as one of his closest friends. They had shared a house in their last year at university, which had been an interesting experience for Flin. Josh was very, very wealthy, and his shiny British racing green TVR was just one indication of those riches. On the whole, Flin always equated money with happiness – if he had a million he would be the happiest man alive – but Josh was, to his mind, the exception to this rule. The youngest son of an ancient Scottish family, Josh was a man of extremes. One minute life was seemingly one big party, the next it was eternal purgatory. His father had left when Josh was fifteen, and his middle brother had drowned – with suicide suspected – six months later. Josh's mother, consumed by grief, had taken to the bottle. An ongoing theme in Josh's life was his attempt to keep away from this sad, lonely, alcoholic woman. She spent most of her time drunk and in this state blamed everyone but herself for her tragedy. Until Flin and Josh shared a house together, these dark secrets had been unknown to Flin; he had merely thought Josh was larger than life: always hearty, always the life and soul of the party. He would become drunker than anyone else and outdo them all with his outrageous exploits; Flin saw this as natural exuberance – it was part of his appeal. But living with him had made Flin aware that his friend's life had been ripped apart and irreparably damaged by the family tragedy. On occasions he would be as bouncy and funny as ever, but a phone call from his mother would change that in an instant. Flin would hear the phone slammed down and the front door crash and would not see him for the rest of the night.

However, he had seemed a lot happier in recent months. He had bought himself an extremely exclusive little mews house in Chelsea – and his TVR – and had been working from home as a headhunter for the last year, the longest he had ever held down a job. 'I can't exactly sack myself, though, can I?' he had said to Flin.

As they headed away from Barons Court, Josh turned to Flin. 'I'm going to score a bagful of runs today,' he announced. 'I'm in very sharp form. OK, the competition is to see who can hit the biggest six.'

'And what do you get if you win?'

'Eternal respect.' Josh clipped Flin round the head. 'Come on, Flin, a really big six. You know you can do it, Big Man.'

'OK – you're on,' said Flin.

Josh whooped and punched the air. 'I tell you, I just love this game. Lasham is my idea of cricketing heaven.'

It was amazing how fast a Saturday morning flew by, Jessica thought. By the time she had managed to wake up, have a bath, snatch a piece of toast, decide what to wear, drive to Lucie's, watch Lucie get ready, and stop off for some wine, cigarettes and newspapers, it was one o'clock. She supposed it was not really surprising that everyone else seemed to be leaving London as it was such a lovely day, but it struck her as unfair that all these people had decided to go at the same time as them. At least she had Lucie with her. Lucie had always lived in London and seemed to know every short cut available, which usually saved hours on their journey time.

'Light me a ciggie will you, Luce?' Jessica asked, clicking in a tape. They spent the first part of the journey with a companionable lack of conversation, instead stretching their vocal cords by singing along to Abba. As they twisted and turned and slowly travelled through London, Jessica thought about the vast number of advertising hoardings everywhere;

after all, it was her job to notice. Always some temptation or other bearing down on the gullible passer-by. A long, sylph-like girl, dressed only in silk underwear, paused to stare down coyly at them before turning into lines and then being replaced by the best four by four by far. Holidays, cars, clothes, make-up, music, all imploring the viewer to spend and extend that credit card limit.

Jessica decided she should tell Lucie about Tommy.

'I thought you were looking to fall madly in love with someone,' said Lucie flatly, 'and I can't see that Tommy's really the one.'

'Well, you may be right,' Jessica conceded, 'but I've decided I've taken a bit of shine to him.'

'But, Jess, you've known him ages and he's a bit of a rugger-bugger, isn't he? I can't see why after all this time you've suddenly decided you find him attractive.'

'Perhaps I've always found him attractive,' Jessica replied. Why did Lucie always sound as if she was chastising her?

Lucie was silent.

'What?' said Jessica.

'I didn't say anything, but I think you're mad.'

'He's very sweet, you know, and I have always thought him good-looking. And he's being very attentive and keen at the moment. And we have lots of mutual friends which makes everything very simple and neat.'

Lucie sighed. 'Jess, having mutual friends is no reason to go out with someone. I know exactly what will happen: you'll string him along for a bit, and then when he's completely fallen in love with you, you'll get bored and that'll be it.'

'Luce, don't be so harsh. Tommy's very sweet and, anyway, maybe with time I *will* fall in love with him. Maybe that's the way to approach it. Perhaps I'm just not the sort to fall instantly in love with people.'

'Rubbish.'

They sat in silence for a moment until Jessica added, 'Anyway, I haven't made up my mind about Tommy yet.'

Lucie smiled. 'I'll put a bet on it that you have a few drinks and snog him later.'

She was probably right – on all fronts. 'I couldn't possibly comment,' Jessica said, closing that particular discussion with a wry smirk. 'So what about you?' Might as well turn the conversation round.

'What about me?'

'Well, what's going on with you and Dave?'

'Nothing. The same as normal.'

'But I thought you said he was thinking of leaving the army so that he could come back and live with you.' Jessica knew she was stirring.

'Well, it looks like he's about to get a promotion, so I think he's now decided to stay on.'

'Lucie!'

'Well, what can I do? It's his career, not mine. I can't force him to leave, can I?'

'OK, maybe you can't, but just how long is he going to be staying in Germany? I mean, you hardly ever see him, do you, and when he does come over here, he always wants to see his mates as well. I just don't think you're being fair on yourself, that's all. And even if he does leave Germany, he'll probably be posted somewhere else instead, miles from you. At any rate, he's not going to be posted to London, is he?'

'Jesus, Jess, just give me a lecture, why don't you? I thought you liked Dave.'

'I do like Dave. I just don't think it's very healthy that you only get to see him once or twice a month and then with zillions of other people as well. For the amount of time you two have been going out, it should be heading somewhere by now.'

'What do you mean by that?'

'I mean that you are a gorgeous girl, darling, and it doesn't seem right that you have a boyfriend for two days a month. If he's got his career, then fine. But then he should be prepared for the fact that you might have to look elsewhere.'

88

'And the fact that I might just happen to love him is of no consequence?'

'Come on, Luce, you don't see him enough to love him. I think you just love what the two of you used to have, before he buggered off. And it's a false relationship that relies on memories of times past.' Jessica was quite pleased with her last line, and could see that it had hit a nerve with Lucie. 'It's a pity you never went out with Flin,' she added, trying to get a rise.

'Yeah, right, Jess,' said Lucie disparagingly.

'No, honestly – you're very similar in many ways.'

'Jessica, Flin and I are never, ever going to get together. Of that, I can assure you.'

'Why not? He's quite tall, nice-looking. You like him.'

'But, Jess, I don't fancy him,' Lucie countered then said, 'Why don't *you* go out with Flin?'

'Me?'

'Yes, you. As you've just said, he's quite tall, nice-looking. You like him.'

'But Flin's my friend, I couldn't possibly. Anyway, we went out when we were seventeen and it didn't work out then so I don't see why it should now.' Jessica looked at Lucie. 'And he couldn't afford to keep me.'

'Jessica, you are unbelievable sometimes,' Lucie told her, feigning outrage.

'Well, I love him being my friend – but I know I'd only get annoyed if I constantly had to pay for my own dinner. Anyway, this isn't about me, we're talking about you and I'm going to make it my mission to find you a replacement for Dave.'

In the little wooden pavilion at Lasham, the players were changing. Tommy and Jim were rummaging in their bags for various bits of kit. A Robbie was asking if anyone had a spare sock. There were more Johnnies, Eddies and Harrys – people that Flin hadn't met, but who all seemed to know each other. A shaft of sunlight poured through one of the windows, highlighting the millions of tiny suspended dust particles. The pavilion smelt of dried grass, dust and musty leather and the walls were lined with badly framed pictures of the village teams since the late sixties. Flin loved peering at the array of faces, particularly the teams from about 1972 through to 1980 with their squinting faces, big moustaches and huge hairdos. How could anyone have thought that was a good look?

Outside, the first shots of the day had been won by Guy in calling 'heads' correctly and announcing that the Cavaliers would bat first. Rugs were being laid out on the grass near the pavilion and Tommy was punting a rugby ball with some others. Some of Guy's side were practising catching while slowly moving out to the centre of the ground. Josh charged at Tommy and tried to tackle him while Flin went over to talk to Jim and Katie Symons, who had already spread out an array of newspapers in front of her. The setting was magnificent. There was a lone white cloud in the otherwise perfectly blue sky. A light warm breeze ruffled the edges of Katie's newspaper. At the far end of the ground, presiding over the very English scene unfolding before it, was the manor house.

'Afternoon to you all!' effused Stringer senior as he struggled into his umpire coat and corrected the tilt of his frayed panama. 'Beautiful day again.'

'Just perfect,' agreed Flin.

'Ha. Well. Good luck,' he said amiably and then wandered off to take up his position behind the stumps.

Tommy already had his pads on and was waiting to open the innings with a friend of Simon's called Charlie, whom Flin only vaguely knew.

'So is Jessica going to come down?' Tommy asked Flin.

'Think so. She was going to pick up Lucie on the way. I'm sure she'll be here soon to watch your performance.'

'Is Tommy trying to shark Jessica?' asked Josh. 'Nice one, Tommy!'

'Steady on, lads,' said Tommy, swinging his bat through an array of imaginary shots.

'Time for you two to go, I think,' said Simon and the two batsmen walked to the crease amid a ripple of light applause.

Tommy was still out in the middle when Jessica and Lucie finally made it and sauntered over to the group in front of the pavilion.

'Hi, darling,' she said to Flin, 'have you got lots of stumps or whatever?'

'Hi. No, darling, we're batting and we've only been playing half an hour or so. I haven't done anything yet apart from lie here enjoying the scene unfurling before me.'

'Well, it's a blissful day. I intend to drink my wine and make myself nicely tipsy with the sun shining down. Where's Tommy?'

There was a general raising of eyebrows and smirking.

'Have I said something funny?' she asked absent-mindedly, fishing about in her bag.

'Jess, I don't think it has escaped anyone's notice that Tommy has made his intentions pretty clear,' Lucie told her flatly.

'Yes, he's valiantly piling in the runs as we speak in an effort to impress,' added Josh.

'Well, I think it's boring of him. I'd much rather he was here talking to me, quite frankly. I'm not really interested in his on-field heroics.'

At that point Charlie was out and it was Josh's turn. He sprang up and jogged out to the crease with extravagant arm stretches.

It was clear after Josh had hit his first ball for six and had completely missed his second that he was unlikely to score the big innings he had boasted of. After every extravagant heave he would turn to his audience by the pavilion seeking approval; from the boundary the Rowdy Young People would shout words of encouragement back but then mutter words such as 'totally insane' and 'I give up' to each other. He managed to hit the ball to within about thirty yards of the house – had he not thwacked it quite so high in the air, he might have even reached it.

But in the end, he tried one premeditated shot too many and was comprehensively bowled. His twenty-run contribution had been short but entertaining. He sauntered back, swishing his bat, red in the face.

'I decided that Tommy is looking so set I wanted to make sure that everyone would have a chance to bat,' Josh said, tossing down his bat.

'Your generosity overwhelms me,' said Simon sarcastically.

The innings continued at a calmer pace. Batsmen came and went; Simon hung around for a while, playing with the responsible attitude befitting the captain of the side, before succumbing to a peach of a ball. Then Tommy reached his fifty. Everyone cheered and urged him to keep going, apart from Jessica who nonchalantly said, 'Fifty runs doesn't sound that many to me.'

Josh's dismissal brought Flin to the middle. He took guard, carefully glanced round at the opposition fielders and prepared to face his first ball. Flin could tell immediately that the bowler was the Aussie ringer Guy had brought in specially: healthier and more athletic than anyone else, he was the only player on the ground wearing a sponsored shirt. He wiped his sweat onto the ball and rubbed it hard on his thigh, and then began to rhythmically glide towards the crease. The first ball was the quickest delivery Flin had faced in quite a while and it took him by surprise. 'Come on, concentrate,' he muttered to himself. He wanted to make a big score – time was on his side, it was a beautiful day and the pitch perfect for batting.

But at the back of his mind was the bet with Josh, and for some reason his desire to hit the biggest six took control of the part of his brain urging caution and steadiness aforethought. As the Aussie delivered his second ball to him, Flin swung his bat and the ball catapulted back over the astonished bowler's head, landing some ten yards over the iron fence into the wheat field. Everyone was stunned into momentary silence, especially the disbelieving Aussie, and then Flin could hear Josh break into whoops of laughter along with the others watching by the pavilion. While a handful of fielders searched among the wheat, Flin leant on his bat with an air of casual indifference, and soaked up his minor triumph.

He was out next ball, however. The Aussie, his blood evidently up, fizzed a delivery past Flin's bat and uprooted his middle stump. He may have hit a six, but his innings had only lasted three balls. Three balls! And he'd been telling himself to bat for at least an hour. Disconsolately he trundled off. Now he'd have to wait a couple of weeks until he had another chance in the next match. As he undid his pads, he thought back to schooldays when he'd played twice every week and practised in between. If he'd failed then, he only had to wait a couple of days for the next chance. He really missed playing sport that regularly, another aspect of this adult life that depressed him.

The Cavaliers were all out just before tea for 159. Tommy had lasted nearly the whole innings and had scored an impressive eighty-four himself. Everyone had applauded heartily when he eventually walked back to the pavilion, although Jessica was glancing through the paper and clapped only briefly without really looking at him. She had been expecting a bit more attention than this and was not especially impressed by sporting heroics. When he had taken off his pads, he came and stood behind her, waiting for her to say something.

'You look very hot and sweaty,' Jessica pointed out.

'Well, it's hot work, you know.'

'Great knock, mate,' said someone, patting him on the shoulder.

'Yup, bloody well done,' added Simon.

'Tommy – you did *so* well,' put in Simon's girlfriend Sophie with tremendous earnestness.

'I think the score should be respectable enough now,' said Tommy with a nod towards the scoreboard. He sat down between Jessica and Lucie. 'Had a nice afternoon then?' he inquired.

'Lovely thanks. We've been tucking into our wine and chatting ever since we arrived,' Lucie told him.

'Hm,' murmured Jessica. 'So what happens now? I suppose you have to go and field for hours.'

'After tea, yes.'

'Couldn't someone field for you? I can't believe you spent all that time batting and now you're going to shoot off again. Why does cricket have to take such a long time?'

Tommy chuckled, although inside he was just a little alarmed that his epic innings had made so small an impression. He had concentrated extra hard in an effort to score his runs, yet if anything it seemed his sporting prowess had worked against him. Seriously annoying.

After tea, the Cavaliers made their way out to field. Jessica, Lucie, and a few other friends and girlfriends were left by the boundary and found themselves surrounded by hearty members of the opposition.

'I know we're having a relaxing time here, darling,' Jessica began to Lucie, 'but cricket is an unbelievably boring game. God, it doesn't half go on.'

'I might not approve of your intentions, but I thought you were a bit hard on poor Tommy,' Lucie told her.

'I was feeling a bit put out, that's all.'

'I know, but he thought you'd be impressed. Everyone else was – didn't you hear Mr Stringer congratulating him?'

'All right, I'll be a bit more friendly afterwards. Now I think the time has come for a quick kip.' And with that she lay back on the rug, feeling the brightness of the sun shine down on her face.

Out in the field, everything went quite well for the Cavaliers to start off with. The first two batsmen were out quite quickly; Flin was pleased that he had managed to bowl out the first batsman. Then the Australian came into bat. His equipment was top drawer and pristine. Flin knew this man was going to be a class act, merely by the way he took guard and then surveyed the field. He was chewing gum nonchalantly and had put white sun-block on his lips. Everyone knew that the game would be won or lost by this player. His first ball was effort-lessly hit to the boundary, and the Cavaliers groaned to them-selves.

The Aussie had scored a mere fifteen when the seemingly unthinkable happened. He mistimed a shot and the ball skied into the air. Flin was fielding out by the boundary and had been wondering whether Geordie had made a move on Molly yet, when he realized to his horror that the ball was heading straight for him. He ran forward too far, then desperately started to run backwards. The ball was heading straight for his head. Putting up his hands to catch the ball and to save his skull, he was unable to make a clean take. The ball bounced back into the air and Flin toppled over, flinging out a single hand. The ball hit his fingertips, inches from the ground, but it was a second attempt in vain. There was a momentary silence. The rest of the team tried very hard to be gracious to Flin – after all, everyone drops a catch once in a while – but it was obvious that Flin had been daydreaming and that the Aussie was unlikely to give any second chances.

'Sorry, everyone,' said Flin, angrily hurling the ball back to the bowler. He was burning with frustration, rage and humili-ation. That was it, he was never going to play the stupid game ever again. He could see the disappointment on the faces of his team-mates. Josh was staring at him, clapping ironically. It was an awful moment. 'What is fucking wrong with me?' Flin muttered to himself, kicking the ground.

Two members of the opposition were walking around the boundary, tapping a football while they walked. When they were a few yards from Flin, one of them picked up the ball and lobbed it to Flin. 'Here, catch this,' he said, and they both started laughing.

'Why don't you just fuck right off?' Flin riposted and hurled the ball as far as he could into the field.

'It's just a game. Don't be such a bad loser,' said the other, 'dickhead.'

Of course, that had been it really. The cool-headed Aussie went on to score ninety-four not out and won the game. In the pavilion afterwards, Josh slapped him on the back and said, 'You've got to sharpen up in the field, Flin,' and then added that in retrospect, watching him desperately flailing around for the ball had been a truly comic sight. Most of the other players agreed. 'You did look hilarious, actually, Flin,' added Tommy.

'Yeah, and when you threw that football away, I honestly thought I was going to die laughing,' put in Simon.

Outside, Mr Stringer was congratulating the Aussie.

'Well done, sir! Lovely little innings – a lucky escape though early on I thought?'

'Ah, yeah, I thought I was heading back to the pavilion on that one.' Flin heard it all and groaned once more. There was only one thing for it: he would have to get himself really drunk that night and forget all about it – not just his dropped catch, but his disastrous experience with Poppy, his cash-flow problems, his anxieties at work. All these recent blemishes in his life should be put to one side. It had been the perfect summer's day and was turning into an equally perfect evening. The Stringers had organized a barbecue and as everyone tucked into their first few drinks, wafts of charcoal and cooked meat mingled with the well-defined smell of dampening grass. Guy and Simon seemed to be taking turns to man the barbecue, while Mr Stringer wandered amongst the party guests offering beer or wine. A springer spaniel had also materialized and was darting in and out of people's legs. 'Bertie, here!' growled Mr Stringer occasionally, when he felt his dog was making a nuisance of himself. Some of the players were still in their whites, stained with green and red, whilst others had changed, but all were mingling by the barbecue.

Jessica had decided Lucie was right, she had been mean to Tommy. She knew she was semi-subconsciously testing him –

after all, it was all a bit of a game, wasn't it? Cat and mouse, give a bit, take a bit. That was what made the beginning of a relationship fun. But perhaps she should now show him a bit of attention, she thought to herself. And after all, it was quite sweet that he had been so obviously out to impress her. She sidled over to him and said, 'I finally get a chance to talk to you. Cricket does take a lot of time.'

Tommy grinned. 'I suppose it does.'

'Well, despite being deprived of your company, I think you were brilliant getting all those runs.'

'Not that it did much good.'

'Oh, of course, winning is all,' Jessica teased. 'Now, are you going to get me a drink?'

Later, long after the barbecue had died down and Mr and Mrs Stringer had retired, the party was still going at full throttle. The light was fading and an impromptu game of rugby was developing on the outfield. Jessica could see that Tommy was itching to join in and when Josh started yelling at him, he could resist no longer.

'He's just so unsporty!' said Lucie to Jessica ironically.

'Hm,' replied Jessica, lighting another cigarette, 'it all looks a bit too physical to me.'

Flin was by this time feeling the drink and, after being heavily tackled by a figure he could scarcely see, lay on the ground panting, staring up at the darkening sky until the threat of being trampled on became too great. He staggered back to where Jessica and Lucie were sitting. 'I've had enough of that for one night,' he confessed.

'Very sensible, darling,' said Jessica, 'it's only going to end in tears.'

She was right: the more the boys all drank the more aggressive they became. The tackles were harder, the grunts louder, until suddenly there was a loud crack that could be heard across the night and the game abruptly stopped. In an instant everyone was crowding round the two fallen braves. Tommy was lying prostrate, knocked out cold, while the other – the same man who had thrown the football at Flin – was rubbing his head.

'We need to pour a bucket of water over him or something,' said Josh, leaning over Tommy with a freshly lit cigarette in his mouth.

'Do you think we should call an ambulance?' asked Simon, breathing heavily.

Lucie was now squatting by him, lightly slapping his face. 'Tommy, Tommy, come on. Tommy,' she repeated.

'Ow, ow, fuck,' groaned Tommy after a lapse of about a minute and a half, raising a limp arm to his head.

Jessica was standing back from the crowd. 'What a ridiculous bloody stupid game,' she told Flin. 'I mean, honestly. And now everyone's crowding round him. Why don't they just give him a bit of space?'

Tommy was trying to sit up, still rubbing the side of his head. 'Ow. I have got a bastard behind the eyes,' he said, grimacing.

'I think it's probably best to call it quits for tonight, Tommy,' Simon was telling him.

'Yeah, I think you could be right.'

'Do you want a hand getting him back to the house?' Lucie asked Jim.

'Thanks, Lucie, but I think I can manage. I'll get Simon to give me a hand.'

The crowd dispersed mutely, and Simon and Jim grabbed an arm each and headed for the house.

'Is he going to be OK?' Jessica asked Lucie.

'I think he'll be fine, but he's going to have an almighty headache tomorrow morning.'

'No ambulance on the pitch then?' put in Flin.

'I think not,' Lucie replied. She smiled at him. 'Honestly, I think we're all getting just a little too old for this sort of thing.'

'You're probably right,' he slurred.

'Well, Tommy's blown a golden opportunity there,' said Jessica airily.

Lucie laughed, 'You're incorrigible.'

'I really fancied a bit of snogging tonight,' Jessica continued.

'What about your vow of chastity? I thought you were off all men,' said Flin.

'Oh, forget that,' said Jessica, emphatically.

Flin laughed. 'Don't worry, there'll be other opportunities, I'm sure,' he assured her.

'I might have found someone else by then,' Jessica retorted. She looked about her and then, gathering her things, said, 'I've had enough for one night. Time to find a bed. Night, night.' She kissed them both and headed towards the house.

The next day, Flin woke with a start.

'Oh, sorry, I didn't mean to wake you. Can I make you a cup of tea?' It was Mrs Stringer. Flin was squinting and realized that his old-fashioned feather sleeping bag had moulted all over him. Despite looking as though he had woken up in a chicken coop rather than a spacious drawing room, he managed to say: 'That would be very kind, thank you. Sorry I'm in such a state.'

'Not at all. It all sounded very jolly out there last night.'

'Er, yes, it was great – really good fun, as ever.' Please go, thought Flin, conscious that he was only wearing his boxer shorts and that he had an erection.

'I hear Tommy received a bit of a bash, poor chap.'

'Yes, he did, I expect he's got a bit of a headache this morning.' Flin felt awkward and rude lying down in the middle of her sitting room, especially as he hardly knew her. What was more, he was dying for a pee. Mrs Stringer chatted on. 'It's another glorious day out there. I do so love summer.' Just then, the two dogs, damp with the morning dew, charged in and jumped on top of Flin and Josh, who promptly awoke.

'Er, oh my God, fucking— Oh, sorry, Mrs Stringer. I am *really* sorry, that was so rude.' He looked dishevelled and alarmed, although, unlike Flin, had no qualms about revealing his torso to his host. Mrs Stringer laughed and called her dogs away out of the room. 'Tea for you too?' she inquired. Josh thanked her and apologized profusely once more and then she left them to it. As soon as she was gone, Flin grabbed his shirt and jeans and dressed himself under his sleeping bag. 'I can't believe I've just been woken up by a snogging spaniel,' Josh croaked, and added, 'You've loads of feathers in your hair.'

At the Little Chef they ordered fried breakfasts and mugs of tea. Josh and Flin had found Tommy, Lucie and Jessica and, declining the opportunity for polite conversation over toast and cereal with their hosts, had made a quick get-away. With bacon and eggs beckoning, Josh announced he was almost feeling human again.

'I wonder if this fixture will be as lively next year,' said Flin.

'Well, I can tell you now, I won't be playing late-night drunken rugby again in a hurry,' said Tommy.

'No, I don't suppose any of us will.'

Josh said, 'But a great party. Did you two enjoy it?' he asked Lucie and Jessica.

'I did,' Jessica told him, 'but I'm sick of waking up and feeling like shit. I'm not sure it's worth it.'

'I spent nearly every day of my first term at university drunk. How did I ever manage it?' said Tommy.

'Face it, we're getting old,' said Flin. 'We can't hack this kind of pace any more.'

'Next weekend will be another big one, though,' put in Josh, and then, looking at Flin and Tommy, added, 'at least for us anyway. I've never been to a stag party before, but I expect to feel worse this time next week. It's Bomber who's organized it, after all.'

chapter ten

In the Footsteps of Cary Grant and Ingrid Bergman

On Saturday afternoon, Geordie had felt ecstatically happy. By the evening he felt strangely disgruntled and for the next few days anxious and twitchy. He desperately hoped that he was merely inches away from securing his future with Molly, and yet there still seemed a massive gulf to cross. He had arranged to meet Molly in the centre of town – again he'd suggested they have dinner in her neck of the woods, but she'd demurred, saying it would be easier for them both to meet centrally. Was she deliberately trying to keep him away from Highbury? And another thing: their telephone conversation on Monday night had been just a fraction too short and abrupt. Could she be losing interest already? 'You're being over-sensitive, Geordie, my love,' Jessica had reassured him. 'Meeting in town is very sensible, and you should be grateful. You've got to stop reading so much into everything.'

'OK, OK, you're right, you're right.' But Jessica's soothing words did little to help. He was so love-struck that he could barely concentrate at work, and at the house was clumsy and distracted. When he dropped a glass, which then shattered into thousands of tiny pieces, he swore and cursed.

Finding him on his knees in the kitchen, searching for shards of glass and muttering, Flin pointed out that a broken glass was not really worth getting worked up about. 'Look, I'm the one who's supposed to be miserable and irritable,' Flin told him. 'You're in love and should be full of the joys of the universe, so stop acting so uptight.'

By Tuesday both Jessica and Flin agreed that the sooner he made it official with Molly the better for everyone.

'I've never in my life seen him like this,' Flin told her.

'He's just anxious about it, that's all. This is the girl of his dreams, don't forget.'

'Could I ever? He's becoming very tedious about it. You do think it will happen for him, don't you?'

'I should say the signs are very good, speaking from a female perspective, darling. We must will him the bestest luck for tomorrow.'

Geordie had asked Jessica for a good place to take Molly and Jessica suggested he try Café Fish in Panton Street. Girls like fish, she had explained, and added that Molly would not be expecting him to be so discerning. 'Perfect,' Geordie had told her, and duly booked a table for two.

Once again he was early for the date and, still feeling ridiculously on edge, found an amusement arcade and tried to expunge his pent-up frustration on various racing games. Normally he was quite good at such pastimes, but on this occasion had trouble making the second stages. Sod it, he thought, time to go anyway. As he dodged the crowds on Piccadilly, clutching his wallet tightly, he felt increasingly nervous. What was the matter with him? Why was he in such a state? His nerves kept making him fart. He needed to pull himself together.

She arrived only a minute or so after him and when he saw her he felt quite overcome. More than anything in his entire life he wanted her to be his. He had lusted over hundreds of women, from Alice Taylor at school to Ulrika Jonsson, but never had he had a viable chance of fulfilling those desires. Now, in the form of Molly, he was as close as he had ever been to realizing such a dream. But if he messed it up at the final furlong – well, it simply did not bear thinking about.

'Gosh, Geordie, you look smart.' She gave him a kiss – on

the lips this time, a fact not unnoticed by Geordie. He had never been at all interested in clothes and his usual attire was jeans, Timberlands and M&S jumpers. Not having had enough time to change, he was wearing his work suit.

'I do hate wearing suits though.' He knew he sounded ungracious, so hurriedly asked, 'Drink?'

'Er, yes, a G. and T. please.'

Geordie waited to be served but could not think of anything else to say. Come on, he thought to himself, get a grip. Taking their drinks, they moved up to the restaurant and were seated at their table. They chatted throughout the meal but there was none of the easy sparkle and banter of their previous two encounters. Geordie knew it was his fault, knew that he was letting his Venus slip away and this only made him increasingly miserable and monosyllabic. After the pudding menus had been put in front of them, Molly turned hers face down and said, 'Geordie, are you OK?'

'Fine, fine. Why?'

'You just seem rather distant and preoccupied, that's all.'

'Do I? Sorry.' He gulped at his beer. Molly was looking at him quizzically. He had to take a hold of himself, and fast. 'Look, sorry, I, um . . .' He took a deep breath. 'Molly, I . . .' He stopped again, and looked about him.

'What is it, Geordie? Have I said something wrong? What's happened?' She had knotted her brows together.

'Good God no, nothing like that, absolutely the opposite. Molly, I have never' – he paused, looked down, then up again – 'ever fancied someone more in my entire life – than you, that is, and I am feeling incredibly uptight and anxious in case you don't feel the same way about me. I loved our day out on Saturday; in fact, I don't think I've ever had a better day out, and I would like to do a lot more of that sort of thing, and much more besides. Tell me, put me out of my misery, am I sounding stupid and making a complete idiot of myself?'

'Yes, you are.' She was grinning at him. Could those teeth be any whiter? 'Why do you think I wanted to spend the day

103

with you on Saturday, or have dinner with you tonight? Come on,' she said, pushing back her chair, 'follow me.' She told the waiter she would be right back, and led Geordie outside. On the street she put her arms around his neck and kissed him. A long, deep, passionate kiss. It was the most erotic moment of Geordie's life.

'Wow,' he said. 'I could do that for ever.'

She gave him a mischievous look and went back inside. The relief, the triumph, the sheer joy at that utterly delicious moment conspired to make Geordie feel overcome with emotion. He wanted to punch the air and shout for joy, but instead followed her back in and ordered another bottle of wine and some pudding – to share.

Two months before, a Q & A session at the Ritzy had seemed to Flin a good idea. He'd even checked it with Martina. 'Yeah, great, Flin, that's perfect for him,' she'd agreed. It was hardly going to be the pinnacle of his promotional trip to the UK, but the Ritzy were keen and Bruklin loved the idea of sitting on stage in a south London 'hood talking to the people about *Gangsta Daze*. And until then, everything had gone as well as Flin had hoped: fame and the interview circuit was still new and exciting to Bruklin, and instead of trotting out oft-repeated phrases with the traditional weariness, he charmed his interviewers with his freshness and willingness to think of original answers to their questions. In return, he and his film were getting great press, and everyone at the office was patting Flin on the back as a result.

Bruklin was clearly enjoying himself, and chatted happily to Flin in between assignments, asking him about the British film scene, and about London and what he should know about the next interviewer. At the Ritzy, things still appeared to be running smoothly. It was a sell-out and, after the screening, the Q & A started well, with Bruklin continuing his charm offensive.

Then it all went wrong. A woman at the back of the auditorium suddenly said, 'Your film was shit, and what you're saying now is shit. What I'd like to know is this: would you be happy to give my money back?'

Bruklin froze, totally speechless. Then the two people with her also demanded their money back. A murmur spread across the cinema. Someone shouted back that they should shut up and leave. Two members of staff anxiously walked down the aisles until they were level with the disturbers' row, but by this stage one of the men was shouting, 'Well? Will you?' More people started defending the now mute Bruklin, whilst others joined the dissenters. The members of staff were asking people to leave.

'Don't worry, we're fucking going,' said one of the original rabblerousers in a loud voice, causing even more of a hiatus as they shoved past the other people in the row. Bruklin was still rooted to his seat, staring blankly out towards the rear of the auditorium. Flin, sitting in the front row, wanted to shrink into his chair and die. Should he intervene and get Bruklin off stage or let the Ritzy staff sort it out? He was weighing up his options when the *Guardian* film critic chairing the evening came to his rescue.

'OK, settle down, everyone,' he said as the noise quietened. 'Time for one more question, I think.'

Afterwards, Flin ushered the still stunned Bruklin out of the side entrance and into the waiting limousine. Not quite sure what he should say, Flin decided to try and play down the incident.

'That was great,' he said, as Bruklin, chin on hand, gazed out of the window. He continued, 'The shouting at the end was a bit unfortunate, but I wouldn't let it get to you.' Still Bruklin said nothing. Flin persevered. 'I mean, apart from that, it was clear that everyone loved your film and I thought you gave a brilliant Q & A.' At this, Bruklin slowly turned to Flin, felt inside his long black leather jacket and produced a pen and a piece of paper. He carefully wrote something, leaning on his knee, passed it to Flin, then continued staring silently out of the window.

Just stop talking to me. I'm too upset, man.

Flin folded the piece of paper. His heart sank further. He wanted to get home now, and not stay in this atmosphere of appalling awkwardness a moment longer. And there was still another day of publicity to do with Bruklin, although right now that did not bear thinking about. Everything had been going so well, and now the ego of this brilliant young director had been crushed in one small instance. Flin cursed the woman, cursed the Ritzy, cursed himself for ever agreeing to it in the first place. So now his work was finally becoming a nightmare too. After twenty minutes of silence, they reached the hotel; Flin felt he had to say something, so lamely said, 'See you in the morning, and please don't worry about it.' But without looking at him, Bruklin got out of the car and slammed the door.

It was almost dark by the time Geordie and Molly left the restaurant, but in no mood to end the evening, they walked across to Covent Garden, pausing to look at the street acts and in shop windows, then made their way down to the Embankment. Strolling arm in arm, ambling along the ancient river and past the ornate lampposts and benches, Geordie felt that he had discovered the meaning of romance.

'This is just like *Indiscreet*,' said Molly, looking out over the river.

'What do you mean?'

'The film *Indiscreet*. Cary Grant and Ingrid Bergman. She's an actress or opera singer or something, and he's an urbane businessman. They gradually fall in love and after a concert they walk along the Embankment just as we're doing now. It's a great film, really romantic. I haven't seen it for years though.'

Geordie had only ever seen one Cary Grant film and all he could remember was Grant being chased by a bi-plane; but he was going to make sure he watched *Indiscreet*.

They walked all the way back to Green Park. Outside the

underground Molly kissed him again and said, 'Not tonight. But I'll call you.' They held each other tightly for a moment and she added, 'Thank you for a wonderful evening,' and was gone. Geordie, on the biggest high of his life, decided to walk for a bit, not wishing to break the magic of the evening by returning straight to the house. He walked to Victoria, then decided to go on to Sloane Square. At Sloane Square he thought he might as well wander down the King's Road and then there seemed no point in not walking the whole way. On that night, as he passed the endless buildings, streets and squares of distinction and beauty, all the cafés, bars and restaurants – all the life of the city – he thought it an amazing place.

chapter eleven

Stag Party

They could hear Bomber's high-pitched laugh from the foyer
of the hotel. Neither Flin nor Geordie had been to a stag party
before and they were looking forward to it with a sense of
eager anticipation granted to all new experiences. It was just
such a shame that Bomber had to be involved, let alone organ-
ize the thing, Flin reflected. As they strode purposefully down
the corridor, straightening their bow-ties and dinner jackets,
Bomber's laugh rang out again. Flin winced. It was a sound
that had haunted him during the six months they'd shared a
house together with Eddie. Flin had quickly grown to resent
Bomber's aristocratic wealth (real name John, Viscount Barns-
ford), and moronic buffoonery. He could never understand
what Eddie saw in him.

'Bomber just takes a bit of getting used to,' Eddie had once
explained; they'd been friends from an early age which apparently counted for a great deal. Well, that didn't wash with Flin,
who found Bomber increasingly hard to tolerate. Flin was on
the verge of punching him if he heard him say 'as the actress
said to the bishop' one more time, when Eddie saved the day
by announcing he was bringing his wedding date forward. He
and Victoria were going to buy a place. As a result, they'd all
moved out six months earlier than planned. Hearing Bomber
once more brought back painful memories.

Flin and Geordie were among the first to arrive, although leaning against the bar with big cigars and studied swagger were Eddie, Bomber and Simon Stringer.

'Made it then,' said Eddie, a touch of apprehension apparent. They shook hands and patted Eddie reassuringly on the back.

'Bomber,' said Flin, nodding at his old nemesis.

'Flin-Flan!' said Bomber heartily. Another cause for dislike. 'Here, knock these back,' continued Bomber through the six-inch cigar wedged between his teeth and passed them each a glass of creamy liquid. Both swallowed their drinks and then broke out coughing. Flin shivered from the alcoholic after-shock. 'Ha, ha, good man!' laughed Bomber. 'Bit of a potent brew that one, but had to be done. Cigar?'

'Jesus, what was in that?' Geordie asked, helping himself from Bomber's cigar-box.

'Bomber's basher, I call it,' beamed Bomber, 'a secret concoction of my own invention. The barman's sworn to secrecy.'

'Christ,' muttered Flin to himself.

The party gradually assembled, and all seemed happy to take Bomber's drink and cigar. Predictably, Josh was the last to arrive. Knocking back the opening shot, he whooped and demanded another, then slapped Flin on the back with exaggerated *bonhomie*. 'Bad behaviour time!' he said, grinning.

Bomber tapped the edge of his glass. 'Quiet please, gentlemen,' he shouted, 'dinner is served.' They all followed him down some stairs into a wood-panelled room, where a large table was immaculately laid out. Each setting had a place name. Flin glanced down to see he was between two people he'd never met before: 'David Copplestone-Crow' and 'Tim Cummings'. After shaking hands and introducing themselves, Tim removed his dinner jacket and flung the brown bread roll on his side plate up the table, an act imitated by just about everybody else. Too much like the Drones Club, thought Flin to himself. Then a small projectile hit him square in the face and, looking up, he saw Josh punching the air in triumph and shouting in his direction.

The momentary excitement of the bun fight seemed to wear off quickly and everyone settled down again. Flin turned to Tim, who was sporting a set of black braces emblazoned with white skulls and crossbones.

'I like your braces,' Flin lied.

Tim gave him a sideways glance and smirked, 'Death and Glory Boys.'

'What?' said Flin.

'The old regiment.' Of course, thought Flin. Tim continued: 'Left last year before the fun stopped. Bloody good for a bit, but not something for life.' Warming to his theme, Tim went on to tell him how it was no good staying in the army – 'can't offer what it used to' – and how he was now an estate agent in central London – although no ordinary estate agent. He worked only on the most exclusive properties and as a result was 'making some serious wedge' through commission. He'd even found a house for Tom Cruise and Nicole Kidman. Flin knew for a fact he was lying, but decided not to mention it.

'Cruise seemed OK,' continued Tim between slugs of wine, 'bit of a short-arse though.' Having talked through his career, there was a pause in the conversation. Tim looked about distractedly and then turned back to Flin. 'So what do you do?' he asked uninterestedly.

'Film PR,' Flin replied.

'Oh, right,' said Tim and left it at that.

They slurped through the soup and then moved onto the second course. Periodically, Bomber would make everyone halt, stand up for a toast, and then order the party to down their drinks in one. Geordie found himself amongst far more convivial company; he and Tommy were having an earnest discussion with another of the stags about new technology and the future.

'The time has got to come when man will be able to teleport himself,' said Tommy, with great authority.

'What, like *Star Trek*?' Geordie had said incredulously.

Tommy took a deep drag on his cigarette and continued, 'I

got talking to this bloke recently and he was saying it was only a matter of time before we'd be able to fax ourselves.' Undaunted by Geordie's dubious expression, he continued. 'Think about it: what are we? Merely zillions of bits of DNA, and DNA that's been organized in a slightly different manner from the man next door, that's all. If you could find the formula for that pattern of organization, you could break it down and build it up again any time you liked. And then you could effectively fax one another.'

'I think that's absolute wibble,' Geordie told him.

'We shall have to see,' said Tommy sagely.

'You might be onto something with the DNA pattern, though. Very interesting,' said their companion, filling their glasses once more.

At the other end of the table, Flin was now talking with David, a rather thin man with a parting who looked older than his years. It turned out that David was an old family friend of Eddie's.

'Where d'you live?' asked Flin, giving in to small-talk.

'Mostly in London.' He had a curious patois, somehow rather dated and stiff.

'Mostly? So what about the rest of the time?'

'The family home's in Scotland and I try to get up there as often as possible,' David told him matter-of-factly.

'Quite a hike, isn't it?' put in Flin.

'I suppose so, but I've certain responsibilities and obligations up there. I inherited the place when I was nineteen and it's quite a handful.'

'So what exactly is this place you inherited?' Either David was being overly modest, or he was assuming too much of Flin.

'Oh, it's an estate – about fifteen thousand acres. Not the biggest up there by any means, but still quite a lot to manage. Apart from all the supervision of the land, there's all the tenants to look after, problems in the village to put straight. And of course they expect the laird to be there as much as possible.'

Could he be serious, Flin wondered? They were about to turn the corner of the next millennium and yet here was this person going on as though Archduke Franz Ferdinand was yet to be assassinated. 'So do you own a village or something?' he asked, slightly superciliously.

'Pretty much, yes,' David replied, not detecting the irony. 'It can be a bit of a bore sometimes, but there you go.'

Flin found it hard to feel much sympathy. 'And presumably this house of yours is no small country villa?'

David smiled. 'No, it's quite big. Takes a hell of a lot of maintenance too,' he explained. 'Obviously I'll move up there permanently at some point, but I'm in no great hurry. London's too much fun at the moment.'

Flin nodded his head, wondering how this relic of the Edwardian era could still be talking in such a way in the 1990s.

'Anyway,' David added, 'I've got to find a wife first.'

Flin stared at him in disbelief, but he did not betray even a hint of humour. Tenants, lairds, finding a wife? It was extraordinary. 'Well, you've certainly more choice down in London – I suppose the local Scottish lasses are a bit in-bred and thin on the ground,' Flin joked.

'Quite,' said David.

Flin wondered why it was he who was prompting all the conversation. Firstly Tim had talked about himself and nothing else, now David. Why was it that such people dared to presume so much and seemingly appreciate so little?

At about the same time, roughly four miles away as the crow flies, Jessica and Lucie were sitting in Lucie's kitchen preparing their supper. They'd spent the afternoon rollerblading in Hyde Park and although they'd toyed with the idea of going to see a play or going clubbing, had opted instead to go back to Lucie's and watch a film on the video. Having already finished one bottle of wine, Lucie was opening another while Jessica was concocting a particularly adventurous salad dressing.

'That looks very complicated, J,' said Lucie.

'Oh, it's one of Maman's, bless her. It's absolutely delicious though.'

'How are your parents, by the way?' Lucie asked her.

'Fine, I think. Maman still phones me twice a day if she can.'

'"Jessica, *chérie*, I am so concerned . . ."' said Lucie, imitating Jessica's mother in a bad French accent.

'Exactly,' Jessica laughed. 'I really should put some kind of restraining order on her. I'm sure my parents are slowly going mad. They've been rowing again this week; Maman is so upset with Pops she's refusing to talk to him or cook him any meals and is spending most of her time sulking in bed. And apparently Pops disappeared off in his car for the whole day, eventually storming back into the house just before midnight.'

'I can just imagine your mother playing the tragedy queen, all alone in her room, with no one caring a damn,' laughed Lucie.

'I know, she's ridiculous. Honestly, I give up on them. And now Pops has become best mates with a local mechanic called Carl and they spend their whole time in the garage with his old car. The Bentley's his latest fad and now he thinks he's an expert on anything to do with engines. He's driving Maman mad because they both come back to the house covered in oil and sit drinking and smoking for hours talking about cars.'

'That's hilarious. When are you going to invite me down again?'

'Very soon. I was thinking of getting people down for a long weekend at some point. I thought we could all take the Friday off and get the train down to Truro on the Thursday.'

'Count me in. I'd love to come,' Lucie told her emphatically.

Jessica adored her parents but why they had to be so odd, she could never understand. Geordie or Flin's mothers never seemed to ring up in hysterics, nor did their fathers call at one in the morning, 'for a chat,' or embark on crazy new fads, forgotten six months later. She worried sometimes that she might have inherited their genes, but so far felt she'd successfully reacted against their eccentricities by being generally stable and calm of temperament.

Lucie was idly flicking through *Harpers & Queen*. 'Jesus, just look at this woman.'

'What woman?' asked Jessica, not bothering to look up.

'Absolutely loaded, good-looking with pins for legs and a huge, stunning house in Norfolk, a husband who owns loads of horses and three cutesy little moppets. I don't ask for much, but I'd love to have that. What a bitch.'

'God, I agree. Who wants to work when there're horses to ride and little moppets to raise? There's only one thing for it: we must find some incredibly rich man with an estate in England, a chalet in Val-d'Isère and a huge gin-palace in the Med, and never work again. Then we'd be quite happy.' Jessica had never given much thought to her future, but held a vague notion that she should marry well and then regularly grace the diary pages of glossy magazines in elegant designer suits.

'Yes, I could just about handle that,' agreed Lucie. 'How is work, by the way?'

'Oh, fine. Actually I think there's a good chance I might be promoted – my boss has indicated as much at any rate. And it's just as well as we've made a pact in our house: all three of us have to have better jobs and be in a decent relationship by the time the lease is up in a year.'

'Sounds serious.'

'It is. Deadly. I'm already feeling a bit competitive. Anyway, Rob seems to have stopped hassling me, thank God. I swear, I am never ever going to get involved with a work colleague again. It's just so much hassle – and deeply traumatic.'

'What's happened to that creepy guy?'

'Oh, you mean Richard Keeble. Well I haven't seen much of him for the last couple of weeks. I'm pretty sure he got the message, but if he tries it on again, I think I might talk to my boss about it.'

'You definitely should, you know. That's quite simply sexual harassment.'

'Yeah, I know. Well, hopefully it won't come to that. Anyway, if I get promoted I'll be in an even better position to come down on him.'

'So that's the better-job bit wrapped up,' continued Lucie, 'but surely you can't still think Tommy's the decent relationship?'

'Oh, Lucie, I don't know,' Jessica told her dismissively. 'Maybe.' She licked her fingertips. 'Right, I think this is about done.'

Back at the hotel, the plates were being cleared away. David had continued to tell Flin about life as a Scottish laird, how lucky he was that he could fish and shoot up there and how, if you flew, it was not really that far to travel. Like Tim, David seemed indifferent to hearing about Flin's life and job. It was amazing, Flin thought, how David had just assumed that because they were both at Eddie's stag party, Flin must not only approve of, but also be interested in his tales of blood sports and feudal life. No wonder there were no Tories in Scotland.

As one of the waitresses leant in between him and Tim, Flin noticed her white blouse – previously buttoned up to the neck and tied with a black bow – was now half undone, revealing an impressive cleavage, neatly held in place by a lacy black bra. At about the same time, the penny seemed to drop for everyone else. Bomber was rubbing his hands together gleefully. 'This is where the serious fun begins,' he announced happily. Howls and cat-calls quickly followed; Josh stood up and downed his glass once more, then stepped onto his chair and started gyrating his hips.

The two waitresses returned with bowls of chocolate éclairs wearing only stockings and their underwear. They seemed totally unfazed by the continual yelling and shouts of 'Get your tits out'. Geordie was one of the few to remain quiet, he shifted noticeably in his seat. Now that he was in love, the mere thought of a stripper was making him feel disloyal. He desperately hoped nothing too shady would be expected of him. Someone else said, 'Chocolate éclairs – kinky!' and then one of the strippers, a blonde, young-looking girl, told everyone to take their shirts off. Flin, still not really drunk, was enjoying the different reactions this demand provoked. Josh ripped his off in an instant and started to rub his chest with mock provocation. Next to Flin, Tim also unbuttoned his immediately, revealing a fabulously lean and honed torso. Others were not so enthusiastic. He could see Geordie in agonies, slowly unbuttoning his dress shirt. Flin couldn't help smiling at his friend's discomfort, especially when Tommy pointed at Geordie and shouted accusingly, 'Come on, Geordie, take your bloody shirt off!'

'I've unbuttoned it, Tommy, and that will do,' Geordie had replied petulantly.

'No, you've got to bloody take it off,' reiterated Bomber angrily. At that point the dark-haired stripper, now wearing nothing but her knickers, came over to Geordie and sat on his lap with an arm round his shoulder. 'Shall I help you take it off?' she asked him coyly. The whole room erupted with laughter and jeering. Some started banging their spoons onto the table rhythmically and chanting, 'Off, off, off!' What could poor Geordie do? He arched his head like a tortured man. Insects could have been swarming over him rather than two smooth female hands. Finally bare-chested, she picked up his spoon and, scooping up a dripping piece of éclair, began to feed him. He tried to take the spoon, but its contents fell off, landing all over his chest. 'What a mucky pup!' the girl exclaimed and started to lick it off, her tongue working in long, wet, deliberate moves up and down the length of his upper body.

'I reckon you're in there!' shouted Tommy, followed by more hooting and cat-calls. But Geordie's embarrassment was soon forgotten as the two girls started to go round the table sitting on everyone's lap in turn. Having done the rounds they disappeared again, promising that they would be 'Back in a mo, boys' and everyone was left to calm down for a moment and to finish the meal.

'So, what do you reckon?' Tim asked Flin.

'Oh, charming,' replied Flin.

'No, I mean, are you going to boff one of them?' He was smirking smugly.

'But they're strippers. I'm not sure they want to be "boffed".'

'Course they bloody do. I'm going to, definitely. That's what totty like that are for.'

At the other end of the table Bomber was being bombarded with questions about what was to come. 'I'm afraid, you bunch of perverts,' he told them, 'you are just going to have to wait and see.'

Geordie, looking increasingly uncomfortable, was praying that whatever it was did not require further audience participation.

'That was such a lovely film,' sniffed Lucie as 'The End' showed up on the screen. Neither of them had ever seen *It's a Wonderful Life* before, and both had unashamedly enjoyed its romantic sentimentality.

'Maybe I'd just settle for a little cottage in the country with a loving, caring husband and a couple of bright-eyed young cherubs,' said Jessica.

'I feel we should go out onto the streets and do some good, don't you, J?' added Lucie.

'I know what you mean. It's the sort of film that restores your belief in basic family values. I feel quite emotional,' Jessica confessed, dabbing at her eyes.

The strippers were now performing a small show at one end of the room. Salivating, drunken males were clamouring for the best spots as the two girls gyrated and stretched and splayed. Josh started to dance between them until he was booed

117

from the little arena. Then they pulled out Tommy from the throng and started to undo his trousers. Tommy was far too drunk to feel any embarrassment and, feigning ecstasy, allowed them to caress his legs. The blonde girl then produced a small fronded whip and proceeded to spank him, accompanied by further baying and laughter. After Tommy was pushed back to the mob, others lined up to be spanked too. 'I want to be whipped!' shouted Simon Stringer, and then, as they removed his trousers too, he shouted in mock tones, 'Ouch, ouch, oh that really hurts!'

'I've never seen anything like this before,' Flin told Geordie as he joined him at the table, behind the baying crowd. 'I mean, watching nude ladies is one thing, but sitting here seeing people having their trousers removed and demanding to be flogged is quite another.'

'I have to admit, I'm feeling a little bit uneasy about it, old man,' Geordie replied. The room was now in chaos. The air was ripe with cigarette and cigar smoke and the tablecloth, once virgin white, was splattered and stained with spilt wine and the debris of haphazardly eaten food. There were a few broken glasses, and chairs had been pushed over in the rush to view the action.

'What would Simon's girlfriend think of this? Or, more to the point, what would Jessica think if she knew how Tommy was carrying on?' continued Geordie.

At that moment, Tommy was shouting, 'Whip him hard, you little beauty!'

'The bloke I was sitting next to was intending to shag one of them. He's got a girlfriend too.'

'I tell you, Flin, I tell you, I can't believe this is going on.' The drink was making Geordie full of righteous indignation. 'D'you know what?' He prodded the air with his cigarette. 'It's as though because we're all on a stag night that automatically gives us the right to behave exactly as we like. We may behave in a way that's totally unacceptable to our girlfriends, but it doesn't count because it's a stag party. Well, I tell you, Flin, this' – he nodded at the leering rabble – 'is bang out of order.'

'I'm not so bothered about the ethics,' Flin told him flatly, 'I just don't want to see a load of sweaty males being whipped with their trousers down. I'll never be able to look them straight in the eye again.'

The finale of the strippers' performance was approaching and Bomber pushed Eddie at the two girls who, like harpies, attacked him with their fingers, undoing every knot, button and zip until he was pinned to the ground, red of face and neckline, quite blanched everywhere else. Rubbing their bodies up and down him, they then pressed their crotches into his face.

'Go on, Eddie, get a stiffy!' yelled Bomber, a line that was repeated by various other members of the party. But Eddie, virtually comatose by this stage, was never going to oblige. As the girls efficiently covered him with shaving foam and wrapped him up in cellophane, he closed his eyes and meekly accepted his fate.

As soon as Eddie was trussed up as completely as a piece of Tesco's finest tenderloin, the two girls shed any pretence of enjoying the eroticism and snappily walked out of the room, their part in the evening's events over. Flin noticed Tim follow them as Bomber and Simon tried to get Eddie up onto his feet. Josh came over and sat by Flin.

'Great performance, I thought,' Flin told him. 'You really excelled yourself.'

'I'm coked up to the eyeballs,' said Josh flatly. 'What do you expect?'

'Nothing less,' Flin replied. 'So what now?'

'Well, I don't know about you, but I'm going to hit the casino.' He leant over and tried to pour himself some more wine, but most of the liquid missed the glass, adding another widening stain to the table-top carnage.

Eddie reappeared semi-dressed with lumps of shaving foam on his collar and in his hair and with Bomber steadying him. 'Time for a bit of dancing!' Bomber announced. 'Who's coming? Wimping out is not an option.' There were a few half-hearted moves to follow him, but it was clear that the party was a spent force.

Once outside in the cool and considerably cleaner air, Geordie turned to Flin and said, 'Bollocks to this, I want sleep.'

'Yeah, well, I've had enough of Bomber for one evening. We'll let them get cabs together and then we'll bugger off. After all, we won't be the only ones: Josh has already gone to the casino.'

Flin noticed Tim join the party outside and wondered whether he had been successful. The way he was still buttoning up his shirt suggested he had been. Finally someone managed to hail a cab and bundled Eddie in through the opened door. Bomber stood on the roadside as several others jumped in too. 'So you'll follow, yeah? I don't want any quiching out, OK? There's some serious dancing to be done.' And with that he was gone and Flin and Geordie's part in Eddie Fussle's stag party was over.

chapter twelve

Families

When Flin wandered downstairs the next morning to make himself a cup of tea, Geordie was already up. Sitting on the sofa in just his boxer shorts and a T-shirt, he was watching a farming programme and munching on his cereal with eyes glazed.

'What's this?' Flin grunted, as he, similarly attired, stood in the doorway scratching his head.

'Something about milking cows. Couldn't sleep very well.'

'Nor me. Christ, only half past nine,' he added, looking at the clock on the video. 'D'you want a cup of tea?' Trundling off to the kitchen, Flin returned a few minutes later with two mugs. 'So, last night,' he said.

'Funny old evening. Can't say it was the best night I ever had.'

'Got a bit out of hand, I thought. As though we were suddenly in some secret cult, where everything that went on between those four walls was fair game, and not to be judged by normal standards or principles. Honestly, I never thought the day would come when I would be sitting watching friends of mine with their trousers down lining up to be whipped. Really bizarre.'

Geordie nodded slowly in agreement. 'I think everyone'll be

feeling they made slight idiots of themselves when they wake up this morning.'

Jessica suddenly appeared, looking dazed and sleepy. She walked straight through the sitting room and into the kitchen, opened the fridge and drank half a pint of milk, and then said, 'God, you two make such a din in the morning.'

'Sorry,' said Geordie.

'So how was last night?' she said, coming back into the sitting room.

'Oh, fine thanks,' said Flin nonchalantly. 'Did you have fun?'

'Come on,' said Jessica, 'you've got to tell me a bit more than that.'

'OK,' Flin sighed. 'The dinner was fine and then everyone got very drunk.'

'So no scandalous behaviour or gossip?'

'None whatsoever,' confirmed Geordie.

Jessica doubted his integrity on the matter, but knew they would reveal nothing more. She said, 'Well, I think that sounds perfectly dreadful. I had a lovely evening with Lucie. Sounds to me as though you'd both have been better off with us.'

'Probably would,' Geordie agreed. Then, suddenly standing up and absent-mindedly scratching his crotch, he said, 'I've an idea: as we're all up so early and it's such a perfect day, why don't we head down to my house for lunch and a swim?'

'Brilliant, darling,' said Jessica.

'Yeah, sounds great,' agreed Flin. 'What about Molly?'

'Gone to her parents – so it's just us.'

Geordie's parents had lived in the same house in the same village near Salisbury for years and years; Geordie had never known any other family home. A Queen Anne manor house with outhouses and a barn resting on stone mushrooms, it had been a wonderful place to grow up. When they were younger, Flin had spent more time there than Geordie had at his home; both house and garden were bigger and there was more to do. As they'd got older its proximity to the Radnor

122

Arms had also been an important factor. In more recent times, it had become a favoured visiting place of many of Geordie's friends. Geordie had been brought up by two highly sociable parents, who never seemed to tire of waking up on weekends to find their house overrun by prostrate youths in sleeping bags. Indeed, Rosie Havers, Geordie's mother, was always telling her friends how much she liked having the 'young folk about the place', and what with Jerry, Geordie's older brother, being away so much with the Army, both parents encouraged their younger son to 'come down with some friends' whenever he felt like it. It was an offer they meant and one Geordie frequently held them to.

'Ah, Jessica, my dear, lovely to see you again,' said Geordie's father, John, clutching either shoulder and carefully kissing her on both cheeks. 'And Flin, how are you, sir? Good to see you. Come on in, come on in.' He was wearing shorts and a blue polo shirt covered his slightly bulging stomach.

'How's things, Dad?' Geordie asked him.

'Pretty good, I think. Your mother's had a great triumph in the village fête, but I'll let her tell you all about it.'

Geordie's mother, wearing a loose summer skirt and T-shirt, swooped into the hall. 'Hello, darling,' she said, kissing Geordie first and then turning to Flin and Jessica. 'It's super to see you. We thought we'd have a barbecue. A barbecue and Pimm's.'

While John and Geordie went off to light the barbecue, Rosie asked Jessica and Flin for gossip and the news from London.

'Well, the most exciting thing,' Flin began, 'is that Geordie appears to have fallen in love.'

'Goodness! How wonderful!' Rosie smiled, then added, 'Poor girl!'

'Big time,' added Jessica. 'She's called Molly. I've only met her once, but she seemed incredibly nice and more importantly appears to be very keen on your son.'

'Jessica's doing better than me, Rosie, as I haven't been allowed to meet her at all yet,' added Flin, 'but I can assure

123

you that he's become very soft all of a sudden and talks of little else.'

'How nauseating for you two! Well, I'm delighted,' said Rosie, 'it's about time he had a decent girlfriend. I'd almost given up hope. And what about you two?'

They both confessed they were fine and quite happy to be 'in between' relationships. 'What happened to that rather glamorous girl you were keen on, Flin?' Rosie asked.

'Irreconcilable differences, I'm afraid,' Flin told her. 'A great shame, but there you go.'

Rosie was determined to collar Geordie and grill him about Molly, but her son was bashfully reticent. 'Leave the poor man alone, Rosie,' John told her sternly.

'Thanks, Dad, I owe you.' Geordie grinned at him.

'Very well,' said Rosie, 'but I do think you're being a bit rotten. You must realize mothers like to know these things.'

Over lunch Rosie and John told them about the village fête, about Rosie's prize flower decorations, about meals on wheels and how the whole village was up in arms at the fact that the football pitch was due to have fifteen new houses built on it. It was ever the same: Rosie was always incredibly busy with local affairs while John quietly lent support; but as Flin listened with Jessica and Geordie, he felt comforted that some things never changed. Rosie's worries and anxieties were caused by whether she would have time to do the church brass as well as visit Mrs Riley – not girlfriend problems or whether some film director was going to make a particular interview. Flin didn't think his worries were more worthy or important, but rather found that Rosie's day-to-day affairs put his own trials and tribulations into perspective. And who was to judge what was or was not important to people anyway? After all, it was all relative, he thought to himself. Nothing had ever seemed to change at Martock House in all the time he had known Geordie, and he was glad of it. It was reassuring, as it was when he visited his own parents. They, like Rosie and John, seemed to have altered their way of life very little over the years. Whenever he walked through the door, he was greeted by the same pictures in the same hallway, the same over-excited dogs, as though they existed in their own microcosm untouched by the outside world. When just about everything in his own life seemed so unsure most of the time, it was good to be protected by what was absolutely certain and safe.

Now, outside in this most English of gardens with Geordie's parents, surrounded by an abundance of lightly scented flowers and cut lawns, Flin felt about as relaxed as it was possible to feel, and filled with an enormous sense of wellbeing. Maybe the Pimm's had helped too. Closing his eyes, he let the sun shine down on his eyelids. Calming sounds reached him: John talking, a few birds singing, a bee or two and then the splash as someone dived into the pool. The perfect English idyll. For that moment he was safely cocooned from the terrors of the outside world, and nothing could touch him.

When, later that evening, they returned to the house in London, there were four messages on the answer machine, one from Molly for Geordie, one from Jessica's mother, and two for Flin.

'Hi, baby broth. It's Sam,' said the first. 'I have some news for you, so can you give me a ring when you have a moment.'

The second message said: 'Hello, it's Mum stroke Helen – um, Flin's mother, er, here. Flin, can you call home when you have a moment? Bye. Parsnip! Will you get do—' Clunk.

Flin phoned his sister, wondering what on earth could be going on.

'Hi, is that Will?' he said as his sister's boyfriend picked up the phone.

'Yeah, hi, Flin! How are you? You got Sam's message then?'

'Sure did. So what's this piece of news which is keeping me on tenterhooks?'

'Well, I'd better let Sam tell you. Hold on a moment, and I'll get her.' Flin could hear him walk to the hall and yell 'SAM!' at the top of his voice.

There were hurried footsteps and then he heard his sister's

voice. 'Flin? Hi, my darling little bro,' Sam said in an excited voice. Sam had always treated him very much as the youngest in the family. There were seven years between them and to Sam, Flin was always the baby brother, the child her teenage friends had so consistently pampered and fussed over.

'My gorgeous big sis!' Flin responded playfully. 'So come on, what's the rumpus?'

'OK, but are you ready for this?'

'Yees! What is it?'

There was a pause, a voluble intake of breath, and then she said, 'I'm pregnant!'

Flin was stunned. Never in his entire life had he felt so lost for words.

'Alec? Are you still there? Say something.'

'Wow! I mean, bloody hell. Well, that's' – what could he say? – 'that's fantastic, that's brilliant, that's fucking incredible, Sam.'

His sister was laughing on the other end of the phone. 'So are you pleased? Tell me you are!' she pleaded, between nervous laughter.

'Course I am, I'm just – to be honest, Sam, I'm just caught a bit off guard. It's such a surprise.'

'Look, come over to supper tomorrow night, will you? That will give you a chance to get over the shock, poor darling.'

'Yeah, I'd like that. That would be great. Listen, Sam: I think it is great news, I really do. I just can't believe I'm going to become an uncle! I'm too young, for God's sake!'

'Alec, you're twenty-five. You could be married with three kids and you wouldn't be in any way dysfunctional, you know.'

'That's a horrible thing to say,' he said jokingly and then remembered to add, 'Send my congratulations to Will.'

He was still feeling stunned when he rang his parents. His mother, Helen, answered the phone and immediately asked him whether he had spoken to his sister.

'Mum, I can't believe it – I'm still in shock.'

'Well, I'm thrilled,' she said, 'I only hope that this will prompt them to get married at last.'

'Of course, what would the Mothers' Union think?' he teased.

'Alec, don't be horrid. You know what I mean. But I do realize that people don't seem to lay as much importance on such things these days, and that I should just try to be a bit more modern.'

'Well, don't ask me – I haven't the faintest idea what their plans are. I can't say I'd ever really thought about either eventuality. But how do you feel about becoming a grandmother?'

'I'm delighted, I really am and so's your father, although it does make me feel a bit old.'

'You feel old? How do you think I feel? I'm about to become an uncle and last night I went to Eddie's stag party – Eddie, who's a contemporary! Honestly, Mum, there's been a lot to take in recently.'

They talked on. Flin told her what had been going on his life and she told him how Parsnip had chased a sheep and how they thought they would never get him to come back. Then he spoke to his father, who also seemed a bit stunned and particularly taciturn, until Flin asked about the village cricket, a topic his dad felt far more comfortable discussing.

'They've been doing quite well, actually,' he told his son, 'and I scored a critical thirty-two yesterday,' he added proudly.

'So Sam's pregnant?' Jessica asked him, once he came off the phone. 'When's it due?'

'God, I don't know. I forgot to ask. I was too taken aback to ask any questions like that.'

'Are they going to get married?' Geordie put in.

'I don't know that either, I'm afraid. My mother's worried about that.'

'I think my parents would be too.'

'Come on,' said Jessica, 'in this day and age? I don't think it matters at all. The main thing is that they seem very happy.'

'Well, for all I know, they may well tie the knot,' said Flin dubiously. 'All this is making me feel very old. Anyway, I'm going over there tomorrow night, so I suppose I'll find out what the plans are then.'

Sam answered the door to her younger brother. Flin hadn't seen his sister for nearly a month and felt a bit bad about it. He'd lived in her house for free, then just buggered off. Really, he should make more effort. It would be tragic if they drifted apart, and then only saw each other at Christmas, on alternate years.

'Little broth, give me a big hug!' she cried. Obliging, he was careful not to hold her too tightly; after all, he didn't want to crush the baby to death. They held each other for a few moments and Flin could feel his sister's hair on his cheek and smell the distinctive scent that she always seemed to wear.

'I'm feeling very emotional at the moment, I'm just warning you,' Sam said into his collar.

Flin laughed, 'So it would seem. Am I ever going to have my shoulder back?' His sister started laughing, and Flin added, 'Sam, I'm unbelievably freaked out about this. It's amazing, but I just wasn't expecting it. When's it due?'

'Beginning of January.'

'That's not so very far away. And has it started kicking?'

'Not yet, but I'll be sure to let you know when it does. Now come and have a drink.' She led him through to the kitchen, a large room with two french windows at the end and a partially glass roof, which made it seem particularly light.

'Where's Will?' Flin asked.

'He's going to be a bit late, I'm afraid. There's some security thing he's got to work on, but, as ever, it's all a bit hush-hush.' Will worked at the Foreign Office and was, as Sam would say, 'doing pretty well'. This claim was certainly substantiated by the size and decor of their Wandsworth house, which Flin always looked upon as his ideal London home. He thought Will and Sam had done it up with impeccable taste. They had bought it nearly three years before, a shell of a place, covered from head to foot in very dated and by then completely tasteless wallpaper. Patterned moss green and very soiled carpet had covered every bit of flooring. The carpets had been pulled up immediately and either replaced with seagrass or the floorboards underneath sanded and varnished. The wallpaper, Flin recalled, had taken many weekends of hard toil to remove. He'd helped them occasionally and thought about how his sister had worn painted dungarees and always managed to get paint on her face and in her hair, as though she was taking part in some mortgage or coffee advert. Now the house was full of interesting things: books, CDs and small *objets d'art*, a few pieces of furniture abducted from their parents as well as key new pieces: a huge sofa and wrought-iron bed. They even had some original artwork on the walls. Whenever he went back home after visiting Sam and Will, Flin always felt a little bit dissatisfied with his rented accommodation.

'So, Sam, let's get this straight,' said Flin as they sat down in the sitting room. 'If the baby's due in January, then you must be about three months pregnant now. How've you managed to keep it a secret so long?'

Sam laughed. 'I honestly don't know – I've been bursting to tell you all. And I'm amazed you didn't twig: I haven't been drinking and I'm really fat now.'

'Absolute rubbish. You look pretty much the same to me.'

'That's very sweet of you, but I can assure you that I'm a whole load bigger. God knows what I'll look like at Christmas.'

'It's really very strange, you know,' said Flin, putting his arm round his sister. 'It doesn't seem very long ago that we were children, living at home, and now you're virtually married, living in your own house and about to have a baby. Then you'll have your own family.'

'It's a great feeling though, and I know you'll be just the most brilliant uncle,' she added, tears glistening in her eyes. She dabbed at them, half laughing, half crying. 'There, I told you I was feeling emotional.'

Flin looked a bit awkward – he never knew quite what to

say when people cried in front of him. So he asked her, 'Are you going to get hitched then?'

'What, and have a shotgun wedding?' Sam riposted, recovering quickly.

'Mum's dying to know,' put in Flin.

'I'm sure she is. What will the village think?' She laughed.

'That's pretty much what I said,' Flin told her.

'I honestly don't know in the long term. I suppose it might be difficult for a child by the time he or she goes to school. It also depends a bit on whether Will is posted abroad in the next few years. I'm sorry to disappoint, but I can't see it happening in the immediate future. Anyway, just imagine Mum fussing over a wedding while I'm waddling around looking fat and pregnant. It would be a total nightmare.'

'You're right. I can just picture it now,' agreed Flin, 'the whole experience would be the most colossal trauma.'

'Of course it would. Anyway, I'm perfectly happy as I am.'

Will arrived back not long after and the three of them sat down to supper. The talk was nearly all about the baby, imagining what it was going to be like, how their parents would cope and both Will and Sam correcting Flin whenever his preconceptions about pregnancies and babies were wrong. Flin liked Will a lot, which was a huge relief, as Sam'd gone out with a couple of people he'd strongly disapproved of in the past. But although Will was only seven years older, he seemed of a different age, and Flin could not imagine being anything like as adult and mature as Will when he reached his thirties. Maybe it was the responsibility of being in the Foreign Office that gave him such gravitas; maybe it was because his hair was so obviously greying at the sides. Sam did not seem as old. But then Sam was Sam; but things were bound to change once the baby was born.

A baby! Flin could not stop thinking about it throughout the following day. At work, Tiffany had been very excited on his behalf. It turned out she was an aunt several times over.

130

'Honestly, Flin, I was totally freaked out when my oldest brother had his first kid. I was, like, nineteen at the time and I just couldn't get my head round it at all.'

'It is weird – I don't feel grown-up enough to be an uncle.'

'I know, and I never had any interest in babies whatsoever before Greg came along. But when it's your own flesh and blood it makes all the difference. I've now got two nephews and three nieces and I just love them all to death.' She produced a dog-eared photo of all five of them from her wallet. 'But you know what? That's one of the big flip-sides about being here: I really do miss them.'

When he met up with Josh at the Blenheim the next night, he found himself still very much preoccupied with the topic.

'I don't know why I feel so odd about it, Josh; I know I'm being ridiculous.'

'It's because she's your sister and you can't imagine her being anything other than that. You can't picture her as a mother, creating a family with Will,' Josh told him sagely.

'Maybe, maybe. I must admit when we were in the middle of supper, I looked at Sam and Will and suddenly imagined them both having sex, completely naked, being really noisy and sweaty. It was horrible. I hadn't really thought of Sam like that before.'

'Like imagining your parents doing it.'

'Sort of. Maybe not that bad. Anyway, it's going to take a lot of getting used to.'

'It's difficult though,' Josh continued, 'when you realize you're suddenly at an age when it could be you. It's like the terrible moment when it dawns on you that there're people younger than you playing for Glasgow Rangers. That's it. You've missed your chance, and you know that whatever happens in life, you will never, ever be a professional footballer.'

'You know what? That's it! That's exactly how I feel. Babies, stag parties, weddings. We've entered a new era, our youth gone for ever.'

'It's sad, but true, my friend.'

131

There was a natural pause and then Josh disappeared to buy some more drinks. Flin and Josh had these quiet one-to-one sessions quite regularly. So often Flin would see his friends with a whole bunch of other people and he realized that, in fact, there were quite a few of his friends whom he never actually sat down and had long conversations with. In many ways, Josh and Flin led very different lives: Josh had a completely different set of friends as well as the old university crowd, was incredibly wealthy and spent a lot of his time gambling. Flin had never even managed to understand how a fruit machine worked and had never been skiing at Klosters. But despite these minor differences, they remained close, and Flin hoped Josh was one person he would never lose touch with.

'What did you think of Eddie's stag party?' Josh asked him as he returned with the pints.

'Bizarre.'

'I've a horrid feeling I went massively over the top and humiliated myself,' Josh admitted.

'You did seem to be particularly manic.'

'There's a lesson here.' Josh grinned at him. 'Don't do drugs, big man.'

'Well, I'm sure you had a much better time than me. I found it really hard to get drunk – I suppose I ate too much – and I had to sit next to two completely obnoxious people. And then having to watch people demanding to be whipped was too much. I mean, what was with all that kinky stuff?'

Josh shrugged. 'Dormant sexual frustrations?' he suggested. Flin smiled. They may be very different, but he always had a good time with Josh; and, Flin realized, sometimes that was all you needed from a good friend.

chapter thirteen

Playing Away

While Flin was visiting his sister, Geordie was finally making his way over to Molly's flat in Highbury. Her flatmate, Lizzie, was out for the evening and Molly was cooking him dinner. 'She'll probably be back at some point, but for the best part of the evening, we'll have the place to ourselves,' she had told him. This caused Geordie to feel a new wave of excitement and apprehension, as he knew that the time had come when he would finally share her bed.

The day after, Geordie was due to go to Manchester, so he was trying to find his way across London in his car. The journey took an eternity, but buoyed up by the prospect of the evening ahead, he managed to remain reasonably calm and only shouted once, at a cyclist who brushed into his wing-mirror. Finally reaching Highbury Fields, he quickly found the right house, parked and nimbly trotted up the steps and rang the bell on Flat 3. The door buzzer sounded without any interchange on the intercom and Geordie walked on in. From high above he heard Molly say, 'Right to the top,' and when he had climbed up three floors, she was waiting by the door in all her loveliness. She flung her arms round him and gave him a big, wet kiss on his lips.

'You made it! Did the traffic make you very cross? How does it feel to be so far north?'

He laughed. 'I was very calm all the way – well, almost all the way. I've never been to this part of London but that's a great park you've got out there.' Then he said, 'Here, I've brought you something,' and handed over a bunch of flowers. Having never bought flowers in person before, this romantic gesture had caused him deep embarrassment; he hoped that no one he knew had seen him. The flower-seller had asked him what he wanted and he had been completely stumped, expecting a bunch of ready made-up flowers to be instantly available. 'Just something that looks and smells nice,' he told the man, who then suggested a combination of various plants. 'Sounds perfect,' Geordie had told him, looking about shiftily. But the agonies were worth it though, for Molly's face lit up as he gave them to her. Jessica had told him a man could never go wrong with some flowers and she had been right.

'Oh, they're lovely! Thank you.' She sniffed at them deeply. 'And they smell gorgeous. Thank you, Geordie – I love getting flowers.' The florist had done well. 'And wine,' he said, producing a bottle from his bag, 'and I found this in downtown Borehamwood.' It was the video of *Indiscreet*.

'How brilliant of you! I haven't watched it for years – oh, thank you!' She then led him inside, put down the flowers and the video and put her arms around his neck, and kissed him again. 'It's lovely to see you,' she said, and Geordie gazed into her twinkling pale blue eyes, and felt his heart melt.

'What about a guided tour?' he asked her. On his arrival, he'd noticed how homely and tasteful the flat was and could not help thinking of the deficiencies of his own housing situation. In the sitting room, two sash windows were open and a cool evening breeze was slightly ruffling the heavy silk curtains. Everything looked perfectly in its place. The twin sofas were deep and large and comfortable with their array of accompanying cushions. There was a dining table – set for two, a delicate-looking sideboard at one end and a beautiful rug in front of the fireplace at the other. It oozed good taste and style.

'This is amazing,' said Geordie, conscious that Molly could only be disappointed by the house in Barons Court.

'It is nice. Lizzie's parents have owned it for years and they charge us pretty low rent as well. So all in all, I've been very lucky.'

The kitchen, too, was immaculate compared with the one he shared with Jessica and Flin, and Geordie again felt a sense of dissatisfaction at the way in which he was currently living. Molly's flat was lovely, conducive to spending time in, more than merely a rented property with mismatching 1970s furniture.

Molly grabbed two beers from the fridge and opened and closed the oven, and then led Geordie back to the sitting room.

'I don't think you'll like my house very much,' Geordie said to her as he stood by the window looking out over the park.

Molly smiled at him. She was wearing a summer dress and plimsolls and absent-mindedly playing with the label on her beer. The evening sun shone through the window, reaching across the floor and up over the sofa and onto her, highlighting a slight auburn colour in her brown hair, something Geordie hadn't noticed before.

'I'm spoilt living here, but at least you have the river close by. I'd love to be able to walk along the Thames whenever I liked, with all those great pubs along there . . .' She took a swig on her beer and Geordie came and sat down beside her. He suddenly realized he could hear birdsong from the trees outside. Being in love, he felt, was making him a far more sensitive soul. It thrilled him to feel and smell her hair on his chin and her arm on his shoulder, a signal to end the tense chastity between them. With his free hand he began to stroke her head.

'I really should start playing the lottery,' she said, smiling, 'and then if I won I could live in a house down there. Actually, I always forget to do it, but it's fun thinking about what you'd do if you won.'

Geordie laughed. 'I'd move straight out of London and try my best to buy this big house I've always fancied near Salisbury.

It's stunning and has a big farm with it. Then I'd probably want to take a big holiday, a year-long trip round the world.'

'You'd have to do that, but would you give up work?'

'Well, hopefully I'd have a farm to run, so presumably I'd need to go to agricultural college for a year or two first. But I'd chuck in computer terminal sales, that's for sure.'

'I'd give up work tomorrow, if I could. I could think of a million ways of spending my days. I'd have our chickens to feed for starters, and dogs to walk.' Our? Did she say 'our'? They were only joking, but she still said it, still spoke as though they had a future.

A bell suddenly started ringing in the kitchen. 'Supper time!' said Molly, breaking free from Geordie and disappearing out of the room. Geordie was delighted that Molly had obviously gone to so much effort. But he also felt strangely self-conscious. Suddenly there was a meal before him, and Molly was watching him eagerly. For a moment he yearned for the company provided by a restaurant, other diners to take away the spotlight from him. And then Molly was eating too, and chatting, pouring him wine. Relaxing as he tucked into his stew, his momentary awkwardness vanished.

The meat was succulent, the gravy rich, and Geordie eagerly relished each mouthful. Delicious, and he told her so.

'I remembered you saying traditional food was always best, so I'm glad it gets your vote of confidence. Just to really get in your good books, I've even made a pudding.'

Geordie beamed at her happily; could this girl really be faultless? On paper it was just the sort of meal he would have had at home with his parents, but somehow Molly had put something extra into the ingredients. The apple crumble was the finest he'd ever tasted, rich in raisins and cinnamon and eaten with thick cream rather than custard. Geordie felt a very lucky man. He felt so at ease with her, so perfectly happy. She was gorgeous. A little dribble of cream ran down her chin and she tried not to laugh. Geordie leant over and wiped it with a single stroke of a finger. 'Just delicious.'

They finished eating and moved back to the sofa. Geordie was conscious that The Time was approaching. Just the tiniest waft of apprehension floated over him, as though he were making the first move once more. He wished he didn't feel so incredibly full – but he never could resist second helpings.

'Let's watch the film,' suggested Molly. 'I want to see it with you.'

'Let's,' he agreed. Outside, it was getting dark at last and Geordie could see Molly was getting cold. 'Come here,' he said and she leant back against him, pulling his arms around her. The opening credits rolled and there was Ingrid Bergman, a little older than Geordie had imagined, but stunning all the same. He kissed Molly's head, and cupped his hands closer under her breasts. And then it was Cary Grant's turn to enter the fray.

'He really was very, very suave, wasn't he? You can't learn that kind of smoothness,' Geordie said to Molly, who murmured agreement. Geordie kissed her ear, and moved his hands just onto the underside of her breasts. They felt soft and firm beneath the cotton of her dress and the patterned material of her bra. On the screen Cary Grant and Ingrid Bergman were being introduced to each other for the first time – with an obvious frisson in those very first glances. Molly was rubbing Geordie's leg. He now had a full-scale erection and wondered whether Molly could feel it pressing through his trousers and into the small of her back. At the prospect of what was to come, he was feeling unbelievably aroused and excited. He could see the size of her breasts, her pale arms and neck emerging from her dress, but was desperate to feel and see her naked flesh in its entirety. Remembering the sensitive Gladiator he'd read about in the McDonald's in Richmond, he moved his hands over her breasts and started kissing her cheek, ear and neck repeatedly and with an increased sense of urgency. Molly closed her eyes, smiling contentedly, and slowly moved her legs abstractedly up and down, so Geordie lowered his hands and carefully, inch by inch, lifted her dress. He ran his fingers up and down her thighs, at first on the outside and then gently pushed her legs ever so slightly apart until he could feel the material of her knickers. Neither was listening to Cary or Ingrid any more and the conversation on the screen, interspersed with the searing musical score, became nothing more than a background burble.

Suddenly, Molly turned round and got up. 'Come with me,' she told him, her lips parted, and led him to the bedroom. She jumped on the bed backwards, laughing as she spread her arms out wide to welcome him. Geordie joined her and she leant forward to kiss him. He held her face in both hands and kissed her back, hungrily, no longer feeling quite so bloated, and felt her unbuttoning his shirt and running her small hands across his chest. He, in turn, took her skirt with both hands and started to pull it up. With her eyes closed once more and her mouth parted, she wriggled to help him lift it past her waist. He fumbled to undo the buttons at her back, while she repeatedly kissed him all over his face: on his eyes, on his nose, his cheeks and his lips, and ran her hands firmly through his hair. The buttons undone, he could feel the smoothness of her back, interrupted only by her bra which, like her dress, he unclipped without too much awkward fumbling. She sat up and, kneeling between her legs, he slowly raised the dress over her head and flung it across the room. She rounded her shoulders, and he pulled at her bra until she was completely naked except for her knickers. It was too much for him. Overcome by desire, he pulled off her remaining item of clothing while she was frantically pulling at his belt and trousers. Within seconds he was naked too and with urgency she was saying into his ear, 'Yes, Geordie, now.' Inside her, he was bucking like a mad beast. Was this sensitive? He had no time to consider, yet he knew that Molly had wanted him as much as he had wanted her. As both of them thrusted and panted and gasped, he knew it was not going to be long, but the harder he rammed into her, the more she moaned with pleasure and the more aroused he felt. The moment was beyond his control and he felt the wave of pleasure well up within and then, suddenly uncorked, thunder out of him and into her.

They stayed together for a while, then rolled side by side on the bed, their arms wrapped around one another. Both were flushed and sweaty and started laughing. At last Molly moved away and walked out of the room. Geordie lay back, feeling elated; it had been the best sex of his life, even if not the longest. Never had he wanted anyone so much; never had he felt such desire. From outside the room he could hear the bath running and after a few minutes Molly called him.

She was submerged in bubble bath, but there was room for two and he got in behind her. They lay there in silence for a while, Geordie running his hands over her soapy body and for the first time taking a proper look at her nakedness. How soft her breasts seemed, and how white and clear her skin was. So different from his.

'I've never had a bath with anyone before,' Molly said suddenly.

'I don't think I have either,' Geordie replied.

'Except maybe with my brother when I was little. I rather like it, don't you?'

'Definitely. We should do it more often.'

'When we've got our enormous country estate, I think it's of crucial importance that we have a very big bath.'

'With a jacuzzi.'

'With a jacuzzi.'

They moved back into the bedroom, and then Molly realized that the video was still on and rushed out to switch it off. Geordie was in bed when she walked back, naked still, into the room.

'Wow,' he said involuntarily. She smiled at him archly and came and lay next to him. 'You are beautiful.'

'You're not so bad yourself,' she said, and as he looked into those pale blue eyes of hers, strands of her hair fell across her face, and he wondered how he could ever have ended up being in this situation, with someone he loved so much, someone so perfect. What had he done to deserve such good fortune? And at that moment, he vowed to himself that he would never stop loving her and that he would never let her go.

Geordie played the sensitive gladiator to greater effect during the second half of the night and the next morning was delighted to find that Molly was still there and that the previous evening had not been an imaginary experience. But he needed to get up sharply and go, and so slid out of bed and found his boxer shorts and T-shirt and headed for the bathroom.

'How d'you do,' said a pyjamaed figure with a mass of long wavy blonde hair that covered most of her face. 'Geordie, I presume?'

'Hi – Lizzie?' Geordie had forgotten about Molly's flatmate. He'd heard her come in late the night before, but had not been expecting to see her first thing in the morning, moments after waking from a deep slumber.

'D'you want a cup of tea?' she asked as she walked past him into the kitchen.

'That would be great – thanks. Do you mind if I go in the bathroom?'

'Not at all, but clean the sink of shaving bristles and put the loo seat down after you've used it.'

A bit bullish, Geordie thought, but decided he should try and keep on the right side of her if at all possible, and so, after shaving, spent a few minutes examining the sink for any errant bits of stubble. He also missed the loo with his first squirt and so had to try and clean that up too with reams of loo paper.

'Your tea's outside the door,' shouted Lizzie from outside, as Geordie was on his knees cleaning the floor.

'Thanks a lot,' he yelled back.

After finally completing his ablutions, he returned to Molly's room to find Lizzie sitting on the bed chatting to her. 'Don't mind me,' Lizzie told him, but Geordie did. He felt self-conscious and awkward and wanted to talk to Molly on his own. In meek silence, he put on his suit and gathered his

140

things together, while Lizzie blithely carried on talking to Molly about her experiences in a Spanish bar the night before.

'Look, I've got to go,' he said at length.

'I'll leave you two love-birds to it, then,' said Lizzie and, winking at Geordie, disappeared out of the room.

'Sorry, Geordie, she takes a bit of getting used to, but she's lovely, honestly.'

'Thank you for last night,' he said to her. 'When will I next see you?'

'When are you back from this trip?'

'Thursday.'

'Well, come here on Thursday then. Will you ring me?'

Geordie promised he would. He kissed her, gave her a final smile, and left.

chapter fourteen

Jessica Eats Modern European

Compared with the excitements of Sam's pregnancy and Geordie's night with Molly, Jessica's week had been quite quiet. She was working on a major project at work and had been staying at the office quite late each night, and so hadn't had much of a chance for partying in the evenings. She hoped her boss was taking note. The promotion hadn't come yet, but she felt sure it was only a matter of time. She quite liked being frantically busy sometimes – not all the time, but once in a while; a project that she could really get stuck into made the days fly by and provided her with a welcome feeling of job satisfaction. On Thursday evening she had taken a bit of a set-back when Richard Keeble sauntered by her work-station. To her horror she realized that there was no one else about in the immediate vicinity, and horrible visions of this loathsome man forcing himself upon her and brutally raping her flashed across her mind.

'Why, hello there,' he had said to her. Jessica barely looked up to acknowledge his presence. 'That was quite an earful you gave me the other day. Why don't you let me buy you a drink and make up?'

'Surely you're joking,' said Jessica icily, still refusing to look at him.

'Joking? No, I mean it. To say I'm sorry,' he told her, now

perching himself on the stool next to her. Rage welled up inside Jessica.

'Richard?'

'Jessica.'

'Fuck off and don't ever talk to me again.' He looked stunned and Jessica could feel the heat rise to her face and her cheeks turn scarlet.

'Jesus,' he said and then added audibly, 'fucking uptight bitch.'

When Jessica left half an hour later, she felt in no mood to talk to anyone. And back at home, she went straight up to her room and to bed.

She had planned to go out on Friday however, and had passed the day without seeing Richard Keeble once. Kim had phoned her at work in the middle of the week and asked her to go to a new restaurant that a friend of hers had just opened. 'I haven't seen you properly for ages and it will be a scream. Paolo is great – you'll love him.' Jessica had been in the middle of doing something and had been concentrating more on her lap-top than the conversation, and so agreed. Kim was one of her closest friends, but she was someone whom Jessica always bitched about behind her back. There was plenty to like about Kim, but there was also a lot that she found irritating too. Still, it was good to have somebody to moan about – it would be too boring to like all one's friends. She'd got to know Kim after they'd left university and were both temping at Vogue House. Both liked clothes and shopping and there was an unofficial rivalry between them, although there was never any question that Kim pursued glamour with considerably more vigour than Jessica. While Jessica had moved into the world of advertising, Kim had stayed in glossy magazines and now organized fashion shoots around the world. She always seemed to be jetting off to Costa Rica or Tunisia or Paris or some other exotic location and she made quite sure that Jessica knew about it.

'Kim bugs me so much,' Jessica would complain, 'such a

name-dropper. She just had to tell me that she's been fixing up a shoot "for Naomi" in Spain.'

Flin and Geordie would tell her Kim was really nothing more than a skivvy who had to pander to the whims and mood swings of temperamental models, which was the sort of comment Jessica liked to hear; secretly of course, they thought Kim probably had one of the best jobs going.

On the Friday night they met in a bar in Soho, which was already heaving with all the end-of-week revellers. Kim had cut her normally long blonde hair short and was wearing a lightweight summer suit. She looked immaculate.

'Jessica, darling, how are you?' she said, giving her friend the lightest of brushes on each cheek.

'Good thanks, how are you? You smell nice.'

'It's a new one Dior are about to bring out. D'you like it?'

'Gorgeous.' There were a few minutes of mutual appreciation and then Jessica said, 'So what's the plan?'

'We have a drink or two in town, jump in a cab and head over to Notting Hill where we're meeting Paolo at his new restaurant and then have dinner there with him. But he doesn't want us until a bit later, so I hope you don't mind sticking around here for a bit.'

'Sounds fab. What's his place?'

'Barberino. It's modern European. Paolo's Italian, but he already has an Italian restaurant near Covent Garden.'

'What a guy,' said Jessica with just a hint of sarcasm. 'So how do you know him?'

'I used to go to his Italian place quite a lot with work and then through that just got to know him. He's very charming and brilliant at remembering names and faces. Knows loads of his regular clients, which I suppose is one of the reasons he's so successful. He used to be a property developer, but decided he wanted to own restaurants instead.'

'After this drink shall we go somewhere else?' Jessica suggested as an overweight suit barged past her. 'It's so packed here, and I can hardly hear myself think.'

'Sure. Let's go and drink cocktails in Quo Vadis.'

Jessica agreed – anything to get out of the bar they were currently squashed into. What the hell, thought Jessica, as she walked past a Damien Hirst cow's head. She'd just been paid, so a few extortionately priced cocktails wouldn't hurt.

'For you, madam, and for you.' An obsequious waiter handed them a cocktail list.

'Why is it that in central London, a waiter without a European accent is considered louche?' Jessica said to Kim. 'They're always thin, dark-haired and have silly accents.'

Kim laughed. 'I don't know. I suppose it gives a more cosmopolitan feeling to the place. And the English are not exactly known for their culinary sophistication, are they?'

'I don't know. You can eat pretty much anything you want in London from anywhere in the world these days. I think London's very sophisticated.'

'Yes, but that's international food, not homespun.'

'I suppose you're right. What are you going to have?'

'Has to be a Long Island Iced Tea.' Jessica followed suit and they embarked upon a conversation about how each of them were doing at work. Kim twittered away at Jessica, filling her in on all the latest fashion gossip and told her what she simply had to get for her wardrobe this winter. It was a slightly one-sided conversation as Kim was far more interested in talking to Jessica about her life in fashion than she was in hearing about Jessica's life in advertising, unless the two happened to cross over in any way. 'No, you're right, that was a great ad,' she said, as Jessica told her about the latest cosmetic advertising campaign Farrow and Keene had been working on. 'And quite a coup that Stella was prepared to do it. She doesn't come cheap.'

'Not our money, of course.' Jessica wondered if Kim was such a blatant name-dropper with all her friends, or whether it was just her that Kim was always trying to impress. It just annoyed Jessica rather than impressing her. She wondered if perhaps that was what Kim intended.

By the second cocktail they had moved on to discussing their love lives. It always came up at some point, and usually there was quite a lot to talk about. Kim had been going out with someone for quite a long time until about a year before, when she'd been seduced by a photographer in Hawaii. He had clearly been interested in nothing more than a brief affair while she was there, and she'd returned to find herself single for the first time in ages. There had been further flings, but no one had lasted the distance. The picture was not dissimilar to Jessica's own situation.

'D'you know what your problem is, Kim?' Jessica said to her after Kim had told her about her latest relationship with a musician called Jon, who she had just found out was two-timing her.

'What?' said Kim, between sucks on her brightly coloured straw.

'You have a very male attitude to sex.'

'What on earth do you mean? What a horrid thing to say.'

'No it's not – don't be so sensitive. What I mean is, you go after men just for the way they look, not for what they're really like. That's what lots of men do – that's why they all lust after Cameron Diaz and so on.'

'Well, I have to fancy them.'

'Of course you do. But most women fancy men primarily for what they are, not just whether they look like Ralph Fiennes.'

'Oh, I don't find him attractive at all. He's definitely not my type.'

'But he might be your type if you met him. Can't you find someone whom you like the look of, but who is not going to be a complete shit as well?'

'I wish I could. Introduce me to some of your friends.'

Jessica then told her about her dilemma with Tommy.

'I don't think you should, you know,' said Kim earnestly. 'From what you've said, I can't see it working out.' And as it was her way to do the opposite of what her friend suggested,

146

Jessica decided there and then that she would go to bed with Tommy at the next available opportunity.

Having drunk three cocktails, they made their way out of the bar. Jessica realized she was beginning to feel a bit tipsy, remembering that she hadn't eaten anything since lunchtime and even then hadn't had very much. No wonder she was feeling tight.

'I don't think I've ever been so hungry in my entire life,' she told Kim as they got into a taxi.

'I know. I'm starving. But don't forget this is Soho, and it's a Friday night.'

Her words of warning proved well founded. They managed to get onto Old Compton Street without too much of a palaver, but turning back up Wardour Street, the traffic seemed virtually gridlocked.

'God, I can't bear it!' exclaimed Jessica. She suddenly felt irritable with hunger. 'Bloody London stupid fucking traffic. It drives me nuts! No wonder there's so much road rage.'

Kim looked surprised and the cab driver glanced at her via his mirror. 'It's all the roadworks on Regent Street. That's what's messing everything up,' he told her.

'Sorry,' Jessica said to him. 'I didn't mean to swear in your cab.'

'Don't mind me. Know how you feel.'

'Look, Jessica, there's nothing we can do about it. It won't take that long anyway. Once we're out of Soho and clear of Oxford Street it will take no time. Anyway, this will just make you appreciate the food even more.'

Jessica lit a cigarette and looked out of the window. Soho was buzzing: people everywhere, walking in between the cars, spilling out of the bars, crammed into restaurants, shopping in perpetually open shops. It was the epitome of a throbbing, active city. There was nowhere like Soho, Jessica thought as she blew another waft of smoke out through the window. As the taxi trundled on, she occasionally caught snatches of conversations, or some laughter as a particularly good story

147

was told. Why did there have to be so many people? And why did there have to be so many cars? 'London is an amazing place and I love it,' she suddenly told Kim, 'but don't you wish it wasn't quite so over-crowded?'

'LA's worse,' replied Kim.

They didn't speak again until they were nearing Notting Hill.

It was about half past nine when they eventually walked through the door of Barberino. A waiter in a black Nehru jacket showed them to their seats in a small alcove away from the main floor of the restaurant. After they had ordered a bottle of wine, Paolo came over to them. Younger than Jessica had imagined, but with a heavy shaving line and dark hair and features, he was unmistakably Mediterranean.

'Hey, Kim. Good of you to come. I'd almost given up hope. Thought you had stood me up, you know?' He laughed infectiously.

'Yes, sorry, Paolo, but the traffic was a bitch. This is Jessica.' Paolo gave a look of mock amazement and took both her hands in his.

'It is very nice to make your acquaintance, Jessica,' he said slowly, eyeing her with a steady gaze. 'I have heard a lot about you. I hope you like my restaurant.'

Jessica giggled nervously and said it certainly looked stunning.

'But wait until you taste the food,' he replied and started laughing again. Jessica, the cocktails swimming inside her and the promise of food cheering her, started giggling too. This made Paolo laugh even more and soon Kim joined in too.

Eventually they managed to compose themselves and Paolo dashed off to fetch them some menus. 'This is particularly good,' he said, pointing out a dish of calves' liver with creamed savoy cabbage and sage risotto cakes. 'You tell me what you fancy eating and then we will bring you the perfect meal. Jessica, what sort of mood are you in?'

'I'm just very, very, hungry, Paolo, and need food asap.' Paolo collapsed into laughter once more, as though he'd never heard anything funnier.

'OK,' he said, his mirth suddenly making way to an expression of concentrated seriousness, 'you must have the lamb.' He leant towards her, stressing his words with a delicate roll of his thumb and fingers. 'It is very tender, and beautifully cooked with a herb crust and courgette and aubergine salad. I really think you will love this dish.' He gazed at her, rubbing his chin thoughtfully and awaiting her response.

'I think I will go for that. But I need a starter too. Definitely the asparagus.'

'I'm going fishy tonight,' said Kim after perusing the menu at length. 'Crab chowder and then the monkfish.'

'Your wish is my command,' Paolo told them, bowing graciously and bursting into laughter again. 'I'll tell the chef your orders and then I'll be right back. OK?'

'Does he always laugh this much?' Jessica asked Kim.

'Afraid so. He's rather sweet though, don't you think?'

'Why don't you go out with him, Kim? He's good-looking and seems nice. Perfect for you I'd have thought.'

'I couldn't possibly. He's too short.'

'Not particularly.'

'He is! He can't be more than half an inch taller than me. What if I wear a hat?'

'Oh, for God's sake don't be so ridiculous. I give up on you, I really do.'

By the time her lamb arrived, Jessica was feeling even more giggly. She couldn't help herself. Every time Paolo opened his mouth – to tell them some story or yarn about Italy or a building he had worked on – he finished by breaking into more laughter, and then Jessica would join in too. She was vaguely aware that Kim was not enjoying the hilarity quite as much. Jessica could also sense that Paolo was leaning closer and closer in towards her with every tale told. Occasionally he would lean back and refill their glasses, or signal to a waiter to come over. Then he would say something under his breath and the waiter would nod and disappear.

When the main courses had been taken away, Paolo handed them the menus again. 'For dessert, what will you have?'

'I'm going to pass, Paolo, if you don't mind,' said Kim.

'What?' he exclaimed, horrified. 'Come on, Kim, how could you do this to me? You must try something, just a taste.'

'Well, I'd like a pudding,' said Jessica.

'Ha, ha, good girl. I like a woman with a healthy appetite. I like anyone with a healthy appetite! Ha, ha, ha, ha!' he laughed, sweeping his arms around the emptying restaurant. And so they ordered exotic rich desserts: a chocolate dish and a tart of many fruits, and the three of them shared the puddings between them. Jessica had never felt so bloated and wondered whether she might be sick.

The restaurant was now empty, save for their little corner and for the waiters, hovering patiently in the gloaming light at the back. But it was not time to go just yet, Paolo told them. First they had to have some coffee and a shot of the finest liqueur he knew. Nothing could round off a meal better, he told them with his brows furrowed together in earnest insistence. So they drank the coffee and knocked back the shots; then Jessica noticed that the room was spinning round and round to the dissonance of Paolo's laugh.

chapter fifteen

Eddie Fussle Gets Married

Geordie was having a trying morning. He'd stayed over at Molly's, but knowing he had to get back to the house sharpish because of the wedding, had got up as though it were a normal weekday. Molly had mumbled slightly when the alarm clock went off, but otherwise had carried on sleeping. Tiptoeing out, he'd locked himself in the bathroom and had just turned on the shower when he heard a knocking on the door.

'Yeah?' he said loudly above the noise of the shower.

'Can you keep the fucking noise down? Jesus, anyone'd think there was a herd of bloody elephants in here the way you're banging about.'

'Oh, shit, sorry,' Geordie replied. He thought he'd been pretty quiet.

'And do you always have to bloody sing in the shower? Honestly, you drive me up the bloody wall. Jesus, Geordie, it's the weekend, for Christ's sake.'

Geordie had always sung in the shower and had no idea Lizzie could hear him. He'd assumed it was something private between him and the bathroom. 'Sorry,' he said again. He felt bad about this. Flin and Jessica occasionally complained he was too noisy as well, although he certainly didn't mean to be. He'd have to try a bit harder from now on to be even quieter. The Lizzie Problem was getting worse though: no matter what he did, she always seemed to be pissed off with him. He supposed the bottom line was she simply didn't like him, but it was making life at the flat awkward.

Then, having got up early and ruined Lizzie's lie-in, he'd made it back to the house only to discover that Jessica was missing and that they were consequently running late.

'Where the hell is she?' Geordie said to Flin, helplessly looking down the empty street.

'How're we doing for time?' Flin asked.

Geordie glanced at his watch. Good timing was something of an obsession with him. 'It's getting pretty tight,' he said. 'If we don't leave in the next twenty minutes or so, we'll be in danger of turning up late. I can't see that we'll ever have time to go to the B & B before the wedding now.' It was nearly half-past twelve and Eddie was due to be saying his vows in two and a half hours' time, in a church in a little village halfway between Henley and Reading.

'We're still all right. Don't worry – she'll get here.'

As they were worrying over such logistics, Jessica was sitting in a Porsche, flying through the narrow back streets of Kensington. She felt terrible, and the sudden braking and acceleration of the Porsche was making her feel extremely queasy. She'd woken up half an hour before, and as soon as she'd opened her eyes, she'd realized something was amiss. She was in a bed in a split-level mezzanine apartment, with very, very shiny floorboards and minimal furniture. Turning over, she was confronted with a dark-skinned male back. Then she realized she was naked. What had she done? What was she doing there in bed with this alien male? The last thing she remembered was knocking back a very sweet liqueur and Paolo laughing his head off. Had she slept with him? Groaning to herself, she vowed that that was the last time she was ever going to let herself get drunk. Ever. Or, at least, that drunk. She cursed herself. It seemed she had been doing little else recently. So much for her promises to herself. Slipping out of the bed, she started hunting around for her clothes. Where were they? Wandering naked around a virtual stranger's flat made her feel conspicuous, vulnerable and embarrassed, all rolled into one.

'You are a very beautiful lady.' Jessica nearly jumped out of her skin and clasped her hand to her chest in shock. Paolo was lying in his bed with his head on one side, eyeing her in all her glory.

'Where are my clothes?' she snapped.

'What do you want them for? Come back to bed.'

'Paolo, where are my fucking clothes? This is not funny.'

'OK, OK. They're over there, in the cupboard. Hey, what did I do wrong? Or are you always this grumpy in the morning?'

She hurried over to the cupboard and found her things. 'Where's the bathroom?'

'You mean you can't remember?' Paolo looked incredulous.

'Paolo, please!'

'End of the room, turn right.'

Jessica hurried out, clutching her clothes. It was just too appalling. In no position to have it out with him at that point, she would put things straight as soon as she was washed and dressed. It was horrible putting on dirty clothes, especially when they reeked of stale tobacco. Drinking too much and waking up in strange beds was beginning to become a habit, sordid and unpleasant, she thought to herself; a habit that had to be quashed with immediate effect. 'And I do not like myself for it,' she said out loud to the mirror. Her eyes looked like bleary narrow slits, and to make matters worse, she had left her eye-gel behind. *Quel* disaster! Then a horrible thought struck her – the wedding! What time was it? Darting back into the main room, she said solemnly: 'Paolo, I'm really sorry to have to ask this, but where am I? I need to get back to Barons Court immediately.'

Paolo scratched his stubbly chin. 'Look, don't worry, I'll

take you. We're in Notting Hill, it's not so very far. Give me two minutes and I'll drive you home.'

Jessica found the kitchen and drank as much water as she could without feeling like a water tank. She had a dull, persistently throbbing headache, and thought she might be sick. Why, oh why did she do this to herself? 'You're an absolute fool,' she said out loud.

'Are you OK?' Paolo put an arm on her shoulder as she leant over the sink, and made her start for the second time that morning.

'Yes, sorry, I'm fine. It's just that I'm supposed to be going to a wedding today, and I should already be home. Are you sure you don't mind driving me back?'

'Course not. It would be my pleasure. But on one condition,' he said, pausing and looking her straight in her bleary eye. 'You let me take you out for another meal very soon. Capiche?'

Jessica knew she was in no position to argue. 'Done.' She smiled at him weakly. He was being quite sweet, she supposed, all things considered, and he had made her laugh – a lot – the night before.

'Paolo, do you mind me asking . . .' she said as he locked the front door. 'Last night. Um, did, you know, anything happen between us?'

'My God, you were a crazy thing last night. All that pent-up passion just came flooding out. Wow, it was something, I can tell you.' He grinned at her, but Jessica had grown even more ashen. She was appalled.

'Oh my God,' she said, burying her face in her hands.

'Hey, only kidding! In my dreams, in my dreams, ha, ha, ha!'

Jessica felt a tide of relief break over her. 'It's not funny!' she said, hitting him on the arm.

'Ow, ow!' he yelled, 'now this crazy woman is attacking me!' He flashed her another smile. He really was a bit of an idiot, Jessica thought to herself, but laughed all the same.

Once in his bright red Porsche, he turned to her and said,

'I know I like to joke, but seriously, nothing happened, I promise. You fell asleep in my restaurant, so good was your impression of my hospitality, ha, ha, and then I took you home and put you to bed. Kim was going to take you to her place but she was not in so good shape either, and my apartment, it is not very far away. That's all.'

'So who undressed me?'

'I did, but what was I supposed to do? I could hardly let you go to sleep in your dirty clothes, could I?'

Jessica thought he probably could have, but acquiesced. Perhaps it was his Italian upbringing. 'Well then, thank you for looking after me. And I'm sorry I fell asleep and was such a bore.'

'Look, we had a great night, didn't we? You had fun, yes?'

Jessica nodded.

'So there's no problem. Hey, tell me where you want me to go, will you?' he asked her as they roared past the advertising hoardings by Whiteley's Depository.

'This car delivers power smoothly without any annoying interruptions,' said one billboard with a picture of a pantheresque machine underneath. Not in London, Jessica grimly thought to herself.

Geordie had wandered out of the front door and was gazing down the street for the third time when the red Porsche appeared. It paused outside their house and out stepped Jessica, still in her work clothes of the night before. With a revving of the engine and a few toots on the horn, the car disappeared as quickly as it had arrived. Jessica swept past the open-mouthed Geordie, saying, 'Don't ask,' and hurried inside. By the time he had walked back into the house, he could hear her upstairs, bedroom and bathroom doors opening and shutting. Flin shrugged unhelpfully from the sofa. 'From the bangings and rushing around going on, I think we can assume she knows she is running late.'

When Jessica reappeared, a mere fifteen minutes later, the transformation was complete. Looking serene and composed in a very elegant cream jacket and mini-skirt and wearing an enormous wide-brimmed hat, she radiated sophistication and sleekness.

'OK, shall we go?' she said to Geordie and Flin.

'Wow, you look fantastic, darling,' said Flin.

'Stunning,' added Geordie.

'Ahh! You know how to say the right things. Haven't I got you well trained? And you both look very smart yourselves.' Both were dressed up in their morning suits, their makeovers as radical as Jessica's. Everything about Eddie Fussle's wedding was a novelty, including the dress code.

'These outfits may look smart,' Flin complained, 'but they're too hot on a day like this. I've got a shirt on, then a waistcoat, and then this morning coat, which is made of thick wool.'

'Well, just keep it on when you have to, darling, and leave it off when you don't,' Jessica told him. She was feeling much better. The water and aspirin had done the trick.

'So, Jessica,' Geordie began as they drove off, 'what happened last night? You know it's essential we find out.'

'Honestly, it's a long story, and you really don't want to know.'

'I think you'll find we do,' put in Flin. 'Come on, spit it out.'

'Well, if you absolutely insist.' Jessica sighed deeply, lit her first cigarette of the day, and told them about her night with Paolo.

It was a beautiful day once more. Eddie was going to be lucky, especially as the forecast had predicted rain. Geordie needn't have worried as they made the village in good time and decided they would go to their B & B before the wedding began. Having parked the car, they gingerly crossed over the yard of the farmhouse where they were staying. A heifer was mooing from the captivity of the small metal-framed pen and an old tractor caked in dried mud sat opposite. Geordie pulled the bell on the front door and an enormous woman with flushed cheeks answered soon after. Inside, it was a ramshackle place. 'Excuse the clobber,' she said as they edged their way around boxes of fruit and jam jars in the corridor and followed her up a narrow staircase.

'Who's in the twin and who's got the double? Only you never can tell these days,' she chuckled, her body shimmering.

'We're in the twin,' proffered Flin, pointing to Geordie.

'Well, here you are then,' she said, opening a door to a room plastered with bright flowery wallpaper, 'and the double is just down the landing. The bathroom is in between. Have you got everything you need?'

'I think so, thank you,' said Geordie.

She gave them a front-door key. 'Just come in whenever you're ready. Breakfast is between eight and ten tomorrow. Full English all right?'

'Absolutely,' Geordie nodded.

'Right then, I'll leave you to it,' she said and disappeared down the stairs.

'What a sweet woman, all rosy and rural,' said Jessica as they all stood aimlessly on the landing.

'Shall we go for a quick drink then?' suggested Flin.

'No, darling, don't be silly,' said Jessica firmly. 'We must go to the church now, and get a good seat.'

Seeing the church tower from the farm, they agreed to walk. The village was so peaceful compared with the hubbub and constant throng of London, and so Geordie and Flin, with their morning coats folded over their arms, and Jessica with her enormous hat casting an impressive shadow on the road in front of her, set off down the sunlit road.

'D'you know, I don't think I've ever stayed in a B & B before, and I know I've never been to a wedding. So that's two firsts already today,' said Flin.

'I haven't been to a B & B, but I did go to a wedding once. Years ago though,' said Jessica.

'Well, I can't remember the last time I was even in a church,' said Geordie. 'I feel really excited. The novelty factor really adds something.'

'I wonder who'll be next,' said Flin. 'There's no obvious candidate. I can't really see anyone else about to pop the question, can you?' Jessica and Geordie shrugged, and Flin continued, 'I've decided that Eddie must be a bit of a freak doing it this early. I mean, look at us. I feel the same as I did the day I left university, and I still find the same things funny and prat about like I always did. I'm not mature enough to get married. Actually, I think we're probably all a bit juvenile.'

'Darling, you don't have to suddenly change into an old man to get married, you know. Do you think Eddie seems any older and more mature than us?' Jessica asked.

Flin pointed out that Eddie had always seemed a bit of an old man, but conceded that Jessica had a point. 'Maybe you're right,' he sighed.

They passed the pub. People attired as smartly as the three of them were parking cars and loitering outside. Women of all ages were straightening hats and chatting eagerly, their outfits – in yellows, reds, greens, pales, darks – a riot of colour.

'Look at everyone,' said Flin, waving at Jim, Katie and Tommy, who had just walked out of the pub.

'So, Jessica, what about Tommy?' Geordie teased.

'Never you mind,' Jessica replied, wandering over to the others.

'The sense of anticipation is almost palpable, is it not?' said Katie, who also looked the image of petite elegance.

'It's going to be seriously weird hearing Eddie spurt out his "I do's",' said Jim, hitching up his pinstripes.

'It's going to be bloody hilarious,' added Tommy. 'I can't wait.'

Jessica was talking to Katie. 'D'you have any idea what she's wearing?'

'Not about the actual cut of it,' Katie told her animatedly, 'but Sophie Champness, who knows Victoria from way back, told me she was buying it from Phillipa Lepley.'

'Very smart,' said Jessica approvingly. 'Column dresses are the way forward for weddings this year – or so I read somewhere.'

'Well, one thing's for sure – it won't be a meringue. *Four Weddings and a Funeral* has been the death of puffy sleeves and big clusters.'

At the church door, Simon Stringer and Eddie's brother, Chris, were handing out service sheets and ushering people to their seats. The photographer, curiously out of place with his high-cut suit and bright green shirt, was busily snapping everyone as they entered. In the front pew, Eddie was looking nervous and rubbing his fingers, while Bomber, immaculately groomed, sat by his side, occasionally looking round to witness the various arrivals. The little group of six that Flin and company had now become took a whole pew on the right-hand side, two-thirds of the way back. Plenty of familiar faces were already there, including some Flin had not seen since university. He made a mental note to try and avoid them if possible.

'I knew I shouldn't have had those drinks, I'm desperate for a pee,' Tommy whispered loudly to him.

'There's probably still time to nip out if you're that bad,' Flin told him.

'I don't know,' said Tommy, looking about him. 'I don't think I'd make it to the pub and back before three.'

'Well go round the back of the church.'

'I can't. I'll be all right,' he winced.

At three o'clock on the dot, Josh rushed in looking slightly flushed and sheepish.

'Trust him to be late,' Jessica said to Flin.

'You should know by now that he's incapable of making anything in good time,' he replied, just as the organist broke into the 'Arrival of the Queen of Sheba'. 'Here goes,' whispered Flin to Jessica, rising with the congregation. Victoria *was* wearing a column dress, Jessica was pleased to note. They couldn't really see her face hidden by her veil, but her father, Mr Beagle, seemed relaxed and contented, beaming at the passing pews. Eddie visibly exhaled with nervous tension as he stood up to greet his bride-to-be. The tension was broken by the opening hymn. Flin, Tommy and Jim all bellowed as loudly as possible and nudged and cajoled one another, while Geordie, without a musical strain in his brain, mumbled into his service sheet. 'Stop showing off!' hissed Jessica, elbowing Flin sharply in the ribs.

They all waited with bated breath while Eddie and Victoria said their vows and then in a flash the service seemed to be over. They had roared out 'Jerusalem' even more loudly than the first hymn, and before they knew it, Mr and Mrs Edward Fussle were beaming their way down the aisle and out into the summer sun.

The guests had to walk through the front half of the garden and round the side of the ageing Beagle pile to reach the towering white marquee, where the reception was being held. Flin and Jessica were standing with Josh, Tommy and an anorexic girl called Melissa Todd, waiting for their turn in the receiving line, as a waiter offered them a glass of champagne.

'Hell of a lot of standing about at weddings, isn't there?' said Flin, looking about him.

'The photographs took so long, didn't they?' Melissa added, putting on her sunglasses.

'Yeah, but once we're inside that tent, it's a free-for-all party and all that standing about will have been worth it,' Josh grinned.

'I really hope I've got a good table with people I know,' said Flin. 'It's such an effort talking to complete strangers.'

'But you might be put next to some gorgeous single bird who's gagging for someone like you to sort her out,' Tommy suggested encouragingly.

As it turned out, Flin was on a table with Simon Stringer and Sophie, but the other five were strangers. He sighed. Typical. On his right was a rather bored-looking cousin of Victoria's called Anna, but to his right was a girl called Zoe who seemed a bit more hopeful. He thought she had a cool demeanour about her that matched her almost striking good looks. Something prevented her from being absolutely stunning, but Flin couldn't quite put his finger on what it was. Offering round the wine, he launched in with the unavoidable small-talk.

'I'm Flin,' he said. 'How d'you do?'

'A nickname then?' she responded, barely turning to look at him.

'Yes, exactly. But I so rarely get called Alec, I sometimes forget that's my real name.' He smiled at her, but she did not respond in kind.

Then she said, 'Well, I'm Zoe, not short for anything.'

'So presumably you're from Victoria's side of things?' Flin continued.

'Yes. I was at university with her.'

'I've got to admit, I don't know her all that well,' Flin continued eagerly. 'I mean, I've met her quite a few times with Eddie, but I haven't had the opportunity to really get to know her properly. But hopefully that will change now they've done the big deed.'

'Well you should – she's great,' was Zoe's curt response.

Flin was beginning to feel a little disheartened by the lack of feedback, and it was only when he pushed her about what work she did that she became fractionally more forthcoming. It turned out she was an assistant producer for a small film company.

'Really?' said Flin with relief. 'I work in film PR.'

They soon became embroiled in a deep discussion about all the new films that were upcoming, recent classics and who was doing what. Flin thought her film preference was typical of a young style-conscious person in the film world, as she eulogized about various cult directors, their dark social dramas and works of menacing, gritty violence. He, on the other hand, liked to suspend reality when he went to see films, and hated

161

emerging from a cinema feeling depressed. When he told her so, she looked at him with utter contempt, and made disparaging remarks to him about wanting more from a film than just vacuous romantic fluff. She was really beginning to annoy him. Why did he always get seated next to such arrogant people? Or was it something about him that provoked such conversations?

At that point the waiters delivered the first courses and the man to Zoe's left took the opportunity to start talking to her instead. Feeling quite relieved, Flin turned to talk to Anna. Just then there was a pause in the conversation and Simon said to the couple next to him, 'Well if you think that's bad, you should hear Flin's horror story! He had a major shocker.'

'What horror story?' Flin asked. Alarm bells were ringing.

'That bird you went to Italy with.'

The bastard, thought Flin. He chuckled nonchalantly, 'Oh yes, that was a bit unfortunate,' and tried to carry on eating in an attempt to avoid the issue.

'Why, what happened?' asked the girl next to Simon, refusing to let him off the hook.

'What? Oh, nothing really. Simon exaggerates.' He sighed and sat back in his seat, but everyone was looking at him expectantly. 'OK, well, basically what happened was . . .' he said and gave them a watered-down outline of the story. 'So the moral is,' he told them cheerily, 'don't go on holiday with a girl you've only just started going out with.' He grinned at them all and hoped he had got away with it.

'Didn't her old boyfriend turn up or something?' Simon pressed on. Flin wished he could kick him under the table, but was not sure which legs were Simon's.

'Now that would have made things interesting!' he laughed, aware that his humour was hardly convincing. 'No, Simon, it wasn't quite that bad. If he had, I probably wouldn't be here now to tell the tale.' He was going to kill Simon. How dare he humiliate him like that.

Between courses, Flin excused himself and passed by Geordie and Jessica on the way to the portaloo. Not only were they on a table together, but with Tommy, Josh and a girl Flin had always vaguely fancied called Sally Summerson.

'How's it going over on your table?' Geordie asked him as Flin stopped by.

'Horrific. I'm sitting next to a really snotty cow and Simon has been telling everyone about my trip to Italy.'

'Bastard,' offered Geordie sympathetically. 'Well, we're all having a great time over here – couldn't have asked for a better table.' Geordie suddenly realized that Flin probably hadn't wanted to hear that and so hastily added, 'But at least you're in a good position for the speeches.'

'Oh, great. Why do you always get to sit next to decent people? It was the same with the stag party.'

'I dunno. Just luck of the draw, I suppose.'

'Yeah, that'd be right,' Flin retorted and slunk off.

Flin survived the rest of the meal by talking across at Simon and Sophie and by chatting to Anna, who was affable even though they had little in common. And after coffee it was time for the speeches. Victoria's father beamed heartily, told everyone how lucky he was to be gaining a son, not losing a daughter, and that he was the proudest man in the world to see his Victoria looking so beautiful on her wedding day. There were murmurs of 'hear, hear'; and Victoria smiled prettily and a little bashfully.

When Eddie stood up, he was visibly shaking the list in his hands with nerves. He starchly thanked everyone, made a feeble joke, and flattered his 'wife'. And then it was Bomber's turn.

'This is the one I want to hear,' said Simon across the table to Flin.

'I hate to think what he's going to say,' Flin responded.

'Well, he's a bit of a prat really, isn't he?'

He was, Flin agreed, but even so, he did pity him a little. It was tough trying to make two hundred people of different ages laugh, especially if you were a novice at public speaking.

Bomber tapped the microphone and breathed into it, 'Check, one, two.' He looked up and grinned. There was a small ripple of laughter, and Bomber cleared his throat. 'Ladies and gentlemen,' he began, 'when Eddie first asked me to be his best man, little did I realize that it was going to be a bit like going to bed with the Queen Mother.' He stood back from the microphone for a brief moment before slamming home his opening punchline: 'The honour far outweighs the pleasure.' There were whoops of laughter from a few of the younger male members of his audience, but his opening gambit bombed. While more elderly guests were looking appalled, Flin put his hand to his mouth cringing with embarrassment. It made for painful listening, although Bomber seemed oblivious to the muted reaction to his first joke, and continued unabashed with stories of Eddie stealing from the school tuck shop and getting the cane, being caught 'with his tongue down the throat' of some girl by his Geography master, and later forming the 'Diced Carrot Club' and puking all over the college principal's front lawn. Eddie's changing expression throughout Bomber's monologue suggested that he, too, was regretting having asked him to deliver the speech. Rounding off with a joke about the size of Eddie's penis, and hoping Victoria would be able to find it later on that night, he finally called a toast and sat down. Smiling happily as he put away his notes, Bomber appeared delighted with the obligatory, yet blatantly unenthusiastic applause, his perpetually flushed cheeks even pinker than normal.

'If I ever, ever get married, old man,' Geordie said to him afterwards, 'don't you dare do a speech like that.'

'Vice versa, old sport,' Flin replied, then added, 'but at least we now know where he got his nickname from.'

Later on the tables were pushed back and a disco was set up. Everyone seemed to be at hand to watch Eddie embarrass himself with the first dance, but soon after the oldest guests discreetly disappeared, and then the dance floor quickly filled up. Tommy and Jessica were soon gyrating into each other and Flin, jiggling nearby, thought to himself that Tommy was probably at last going to reap the rewards of his patience.

Outside the marquee, the light was fading. Geordie, who hated dancing and was always overcome with self-consciousness at the mere suggestion, had run into Victoria's father in the garden. After thanking him for putting on such a splendid occasion, they started talking.

'D'you fancy a cigar?' Mr Beagle asked him, offering him six inches of finely rolled tobacco.

'Er, thanks, thanks a lot. Beautiful evening again.'

'Yes, couldn't have been luckier. Due to rain, you know.' He looked up at the sky and then at Geordie and said, 'Sorry, I didn't catch your name.'

'Geordie. Geordie Havers. I'm a friend of Eddie's.'

'Nice to meet you, Geordie. Call me Tony. Now, have you had enough to eat and drink? Where's your glass?'

Geordie confessed that he had put it down somewhere. 'Well, let's get another one, shall we? I'm parched.' And so Geordie followed him back into the marquee; after Tony had snatched a bottle of wine the two of them sat down at one of the tables at the back.

'You must be very proud of your daughter,' Geordie suggested.

'You're right, I am. Didn't she look stunning?' Geordie agreed that she certainly did. 'It's the most peculiar feeling, y'know,' Tony continued, 'and you'll discover this later on in life. One minute she's this tiny little thing with a ponytail, who looks up to you and worships the bloody ground you walk on, and then suddenly some young buck comes along and whoosh!' – he gave an exaggerated swish of his arm – 'she's swept off her feet and buggered off, all grown-up all of a sudden. William's a bit younger, but he's pretty much left home too. So now it's just me and the wife again, just like it was in the beginning. Except, of course, we're that much older, not quite so active, if you get my drift.'

Geordie smiled. 'So how old were you when you got married?' he asked as Tony sucked on his Havana.

'Twenty-five, and Margaret twenty-one. People tended to do it a bit younger then. How old are you?'

'Twenty-five, actually. I have to admit, Eddie and Victoria are the first people of our age to get married. It's a novel experience.'

'I'll tell you something else,' Tony slurred, 'by the time Margaret was Victoria's age she already had two children.'

'I can't imagine what it must be like having children,' Geordie confessed. 'I don't feel grown-up enough to take on that sort of responsibility.'

'Nonsense. You just bloody well do it. Look here, I don't feel any older in myself than the day I was eighteen. Tell me, what d'you do for a job?'

Geordie told him.

'Well, what happens when you get a promotion?'

'How do you mean?' Geordie asked, noticing he had made only the tiniest inroad into his own cigar.

'When you get promoted you take on more responsibilities, right?'

'Right.'

'And how does that make you feel?'

'I don't know. You just sort of get on with things, I suppose.'

'Exactly my point, Geordie, exactly my point. You get on with it at work, but when you come home at the end of the day, you still feel the same. You may work longer hours, and you may have more to think about, but you're still you, aren't you? That's what having kids is like. Can't understand why younger people today are so keen to put it off. It's the best thing in the world.'

Just then one of Tony's friends came by and, losing track of his argument, Geordie's host turned to this new companion instead. Geordie wandered back outside again and ambled over to the portaloo. Mulling over what Mr Beagle had said, he realized for the first time in his life that responsibility did not have to mean change; if he married he wouldn't automatically

166

become a different person, or suddenly stop having fun. This, Geordie understood with sudden clarity, was Flin's problem: he saw such progression as an end to any fun in life. But for how much longer would there be fun in living in a grimy rented house with tasteless carpets? Surely that was being staid and boring, the two things Flin dreaded becoming?

Standing at the urinal, his cigar between his teeth, he was still thinking about this revelation when one of the older guests puffed up the steps and stood beside him, smacking his lips together. Geordie was just about to leave when the man grabbed his backside and gave it a tight squeeze. 'That's what all you young men really want,' he chuckled.

'Bloody hell!' exclaimed Geordie, and fled down the steps and back into the marquee. He looked about for Flin and found him animatedly talking to a girl he'd never seen before – blonde and very pretty too.

'Hello,' said Geordie, walking over to them.

'Oh, hi,' said Flin, 'this is Claire. Claire, Geordie.'

Geordie sat down, poured them all more wine and then related his experience to much disbelieving laughter. 'I wonder who he was. What a very strange thing to do,' said Flin.

'I've never seen him before. D'you think I should do anything?'

'Like what?'

'I don't know. But I can't believe the Beagles would be too chuffed to know there's a groper in our midst.'

'What a fantastic story,' said Claire, a look of shocked disbelief still etched across her face.

Suddenly there was a clamour from the other side of the tent, and Flin said, 'They've obviously caught him,' but in fact the commotion was due to Eddie and Victoria reappearing in their going-away outfits. Victoria was animatedly hugging everyone in sight while Eddie looked sheepish, and then the crowd followed them outside where their car, decorated with the traditional paraphernalia, was ready to go. A cheer went up as Victoria turned her back and threw her bouquet over

167

her shoulder. Then, with much waving and tooting of the horn, they were gone.

Tommy and Jessica, who had paused from their exertions on the dance floor to see the happy couple off, ambled round the edge of the marquee and sat down on one of the garden benches. They said nothing, but as Tommy dared to lean towards Jessica, she lifted her face to his and kissed him. 'Come on,' she said after coming up for air, 'it's very chilly out here. Let's have one last dance and then find the B & B.'

'That's a great call,' Tommy replied, elated, and they headed off back into the marquee.

The party started to thin quite quickly once the music stopped. Jessica had disappeared into the night with Tommy, and Claire was now gazing up at Flin, with one arm draped round his shoulders, hanging on his every word, when there was suddenly a loud slap and everyone looked up to see Josh holding his face and Zoe marching out of the marquee. There was a hushed murmur from the girls and some cheering from the boys; Josh stood up and bowed and walked over to where Flin and Claire were sitting.

'Bollocks, that hurt,' said Josh, pouring himself another drink.

'What was it all about?' Claire asked him.

'Oh, nothing. We were having a perfectly decent discussion to start off with. But she was so bloody up her own arse and self-opinionated that she got huffy when I disagreed with her. So I told her what I thought and she slapped me. Can't say that's ever happened before. What a day of firsts this is.'

'So what did you say?' Flin asked him.

'That she was up her own arse and too self-opinionated. I wouldn't have done if I'd known she was going to belt me round the face.'

'I wouldn't worry about it,' said Flin. 'I sat next to her and she was pretty snooty then.'

'Yeah, but she didn't hit you. Anyway, time to go, I reckon. Where are you staying?'

'At the farm down the road. What about you?'

'In the pub, I think. I must find the others,' and off he went.

'Isn't he hilarious?' Flin said to Claire.

'Fantastic,' she told him, and put her other hand on his leg.

Geordie had been observing Claire drape herself all over Flin and assumed that his friend was well and truly in for a good night. Flin had done well; after all, Claire was pretty damned attractive. And far be it from him to cramp Flin's style – he would simply head off back to the B & B on his own. He was just looking for his jacket when Flin ambled over.

'Shall we hit it?' Flin asked him.

'Sure. What about Claire?'

'What about her?'

'Anyone could see she was all over you like a rash.'

'Really?' said Flin casually.

'Yeah, and what's more she was fit as hell.'

'I suppose she was, quite. Still, there was no way I was going to get off with her.'

'Why on earth not?'

'Because she kept saying "fantastic" all the time. Every other word. I can't tell you how annoying it was. Just imagine waking up tomorrow morning: "How was it for you?" "Fantastic!" You'd be lying there, just waiting for her to say it. Sweet girl, but I'm afraid absolutely no.'

'I think you're mad,' Geordie told him emphatically. 'I'd have thought you could put up with it for one night.'

'That's a bit rich coming from you – the serious relationship man. Anyway, I can't see the point of one-night stands any more.'

'Well, I never thought I'd hear you say that, but at least you know you could still do it if you wanted.'

Flin grinned. 'Of course.'

They walked on in silence and then Flin said, 'So what d'you make of it?'

'Excellent fun. Just think, though – all that planning and all that preparation and now it's all over. And Eddie and Victoria – they're married. That's it, for ever.'

'Yeah, it must be a bit of an anticlimax to begin with. Everything's thrown into getting ready for the big day, all your attention and focus building up to those few hours and then suddenly you're on your own, life goes on as normal, only there's the two of you now.'

'Makes you think,' Geordie said.

'Sure does. Although I suppose they've got their honeymoon, and then moving into their house together and setting up a home. But all the same . . .' Flin trailed off.

'Anyway, at least Jessica got lucky. I suppose we'll be seeing Tommy for breakfast.' They chuckled, and then fell silent once more. The air seemed incredibly still, their footsteps very clear and pronounced, and Flin looked up to see the sky full of stars, shining with the same intensity as they had on that night with Poppy when they had lain by the gazebo. The moon was also nearly full, casting a curious glow over the sleeping village, so that the two friends could easily see their way back.

'Geordie?' Flin suddenly asked.

'What?'

'Do you think you'll marry Molly?'

'Bloody hell, Flin, are you serious?'

'I don't know. Are you?'

'It's a bit late in the day for this sort of conversation you know, old man. If you must know, I suppose I can see myself being with her for a long time, but marriage . . . well, that's something else.'

'We're getting older. It makes me depressed. Ah well, at least we've got a big cooked breakfast tomorrow.'

'You're right, you know. We mustn't lose sight of what's really important.'

Flin put an arm around his oldest and most trusted friend

170

and gave him a reassuring pat on the back as they continued towards the farm at the end of the village, their steps ringing out in cool night air.

autumn

chapter sixteen

Long Weekend in Cornwall

Summer was over and autumn had definitely arrived. As a child Jessica had always marked the changing seasons by when holidays ended and terms began; summer was over the day she went back for the Christmas term. But as an adult, she felt the seasons still came and went overnight. One day it was still warm and balmy, then all of a sudden there was a sharpness in the air, the leaves on the trees looked worn out, and it was October and distinctly autumnal. She hated the onset of winter, so every year, in an effort to cheer herself up, she made sure she took a few days off or a long weekend; a small act of defiance just as it seemed appropriate that the holiday season should be over.

Very often though, the weather was fine. Cooler, noticeably darker in the evenings, but still sunny and clear during the day. Then Cornwall was a great place to be – not so crowded and much calmer, and Jessica was glad her parents had moved there. With this in mind, it had seemed a good idea to invite her friends to spend her onset-of-autumn break with her at her parents' house, and she had been greatly looking forward to it.

Standing in the corridor as the train pulled into Truro, she watched the rain lash down outside. Just so long as it improved by the morning, she told herself, refusing to let the bad weather dampen her spirits.

'Where's Pops?' she said, cupping her hands around either cheek and straining to see through the thick glass, the others standing anxiously behind her. She couldn't see him. A minute or so later the little party was gathered on the station, with still no sign of her father.

'Oh, bloody hell, where is he? Trust him to be late when it's cold and pissing down with rain.'

'Look, I'm sure he'll turn up in a minute,' said Lucie. No one else could think of anything to say.

'Well, I'm going to phone them,' Jessica stated firmly, producing her mobile from her handbag. The others watched patiently while she waited to connect. 'Pops! What are you doing at home?' Lucie and Geordie smiled at each other. They'd known Ted and Celeste Turpin for many years now, and were well aware of their eccentricities and unpredictability.

'Well, that's just bloody fantastic,' Jessica said, shoving the phone back in her bag. 'Pops is "one over the eight" and so can't come and pick us up. We've got to take taxis and he'll pay them when we get there. I'm really sorry. God, I haven't even got home and already they are behaving completely madly.'

'Why didn't they phone us?' Lucie asked her.

'Apparently they couldn't get through,' she replied, 'although they probably just forgot. They really are hopeless sometimes and such an embarrassment to me. I don't know how I put up with them.'

Jessica had warned Tommy and Molly about her parents on the way down. 'They're barking, I'm afraid, honestly quite mad. One minute they're rowing and raging, and then Maman will fly into a huge sulk and disappear to her room for days and Pops heads off on his boat, or in his car, or whatever's his latest fad. Then all of a sudden all is sweetness and light once more. It never lasts long and they're really very sweet most of the time; and the house is lovely even if it is a bit chaotic.' Seeing Tommy and Molly looking slightly dubious she added by way of reassurance, 'Anyway, we'll be doing our own thing most of the time, so'll hardly see that much of them. I just thought it fair to warn you that they can be a bit embarrassing sometimes. Oh, and they have six dogs, who shed hairs over everything,' she had added casually. In truth, Jessica rarely seemed to be either fazed or embarrassed by her parents' antics; while Flin and Geordie would have been mortified beyond belief if their mother or father ever behaved in the way Jessica's did, Jessica seemed to take it in her stride. And family eccentricities never seemed to stop her inviting friends down to stay.

It was well after midnight when they clambered out of the two steamed-up taxis at the end of the drive. Hurrying to gather their bags, they were greeted firstly by a barrage of dogs of varying sizes and barking pitch, and then by Ted Turpin who stood in the doorway singing 'Raindrops keep falling on my head', before finally collapsing into fits of laughter and proclaiming that everyone was most welcome and how glad he was that they had finally arrived. 'And, Jessica my darling, how truly lovely to see my gorgeous daughter once again,' he continued, holding his arms wide to embrace her.

'Pops, I can't believe you left us to fend for ourselves in the torrential rain. I've never felt so wet in my entire life!' Jessica scolded him as she gave him a begrudging hug.

'Blame your mother, she wouldn't let me drive,' Ted countered.

'Well, of course she didn't – you've drunk too much. D'you want to kill us as well as let us all catch pneumonia? Anyway, get out of the way so we can get into the house.' Ted shrugged and started shaking hands with everyone as they stumbled into the house, tripping over dogs and wellington boots left by the door.

In the hallway, looking as elegant and poised as ever, was Celeste, who in a quiet voice said, 'It's so lovely to see you, my darling,' to Jessica, and then in turn welcomed the others. 'Jessica, I'm going to show everyone their rooms and then I'm going to bed. I've left you some supper in the kitchen. It's too late for me.'

'Don't be such a bloody puritan,' bellowed Ted as she turned towards the stairs. 'Surely you can stay up for five whole minutes and have a quick drink with us? Surely it would be more welcoming to our guests, rather than buggering off the moment they arrive?'

Celeste stiffened momentarily before scrunching her face up and uttering in a highly strained voice, 'Oh, for goodness' sake, Ted, you are driving me insane.' While everyone else shuffled awkwardly, Celeste looked to the ceiling and quietly said, 'Give me strength.' Then in a calmer and deliberately more composed voice she continued, 'Ted, I am not prepared to have a scene in front of Jessica and her friends. They can bear to do without me until the morning, as can you. Now, everyone follow me, and I'll show you to your rooms.'

No one knew quite who to side with, or where to look, or what to say. Even the dogs, now sitting alert in the centre of the hall with their tongues hanging out, were shifting their gaze uncertainly between master and mistress.

'Pops,' said Jessica, rubbing her father's tummy affectionately, 'why don't you and I get some drinks for everyone while Maman shows them their rooms?'

'All right, but I don't know what's got into your bloody mother. We've been rowing all ruddy night.'

As Ted trundled out of the hall, Jessica encouraged the others to follow Celeste. 'Honestly, you'd have thought they were the kids and I the parent sometimes,' she said in a low voice. A rather mute little troupe followed her mother up the stairs.

'They're completely mad!' said Molly to Geordie once they had been shown their room.

'Yeah, aren't they?' grinned Geordie back. 'But entertaining.'

A moment later Tommy and Flin, who were sharing a twin in the next-door room, bounded in, equally amazed by the scene which had greeted them.

'I can't believe they shouted like that in front of us!' said Tommy.

'Old Ted's well gone,' put in Flin, 'that singing was hilarious. Jessica did warn you.'

'I promise you,' Geordie told them, 'we're going to have a fantastic weekend. These people are such good value.'

'Well, I'm feeling a bit nervous about it,' Molly told them, 'despite what Jessica said, it makes me feel a bit funny.'

'Don't worry, we'll hardly see them and anyway by tomorrow they'll probably be fine,' Geordie assured her.

'OK,' said Molly, and then added, 'but what an amazing place.'

Despite the pervading smell of musty, damp dog, the house was impressive: a huge, solid Lutyens pile, set on the hill overlooking the Helford river.

Pausing by the window to look out at the estuary and lights dotted about on the water, Molly asked, 'What is that accent of Ted's? I can't quite work it out.'

'I think it's slightly West Country,' Geordie told her. 'Funny, isn't it? She's so French and he's got this slightly wurzel streak. And Jessica sounds so normal. He was born around here, but they only moved back a few years ago. They've lived all over, and he's done loads of different things. A local boy done good.'

'Shall we go down?' suggested Flin.

'Definitely. I'm unbelievably hungry,' said Geordie, making for the door.

'You always are,' smiled Molly.

'Well I'm especially so now,' Geordie countered. In the corridor they met Lucie, who had stayed before on numerous occasions and who had immediately gone to her normal room.

'As I see it,' announced Tommy in hushed tones, 'we're either on for a humdinger of a weekend, or it will very quickly turn seriously pear-shaped.'

As they walked into the sitting room, Ted was peering into the drinks cabinet in the corner and humming to himself. Looking up, he said, 'Right then – what are you all going to have to drink? Wine? Beer? Martinis? What d'you all fancy? Have anything you like!' But before anyone could answer he suddenly said, 'Hold on a minute – we should celebrate your arrival. Where's the ruddy champagne? Hey? Does that sound good?'

Geordie and Flin grinned at each other and there was a general murmur of enthusiasm from the assembled party. The room was littered with objects both tasteful and curiously out of kilter: a beautiful antique sideboard stood alongside a stainless steel drinks trolley on wheels; the dogs lay stretched out on a matted and clearly soiled fluffy rug in front of the marble fireplace. Dog hair covered the sofas and chairs. And centre-piece on the long wall was a large painting of what was clearly Celeste, twenty or so years before, spreadeagled on a large bed, totally naked.

As Ted was disappearing to find the champagne, Jessica wandered back in. 'Bloody hell, Jessica,' said Tommy, pointing to the reclining nude, 'that's a pretty punchy picture.'

'Wasn't she stunning? I'm so proud of Maman, even if she has gone a bit loopy,' Jessica airily said to him, then added to all of them, 'Now you don't have to drink all night with Pops. Be firm with him and go to bed if you want to.'

'Nonsense, they all want a drink and some grub,' roared Ted as he bustled back into the room with the champagne, a triumphant look on his face and a cobweb clinging to his mass of greying swept-back hair. *Phlomb* went the cork as it flew off the bottle and shot across the room. 'Whoa!' cried Ted. 'A glass quick!' as the sparkling liquid spilt out from the bottle.

They moved into the kitchen to eat, a room crammed with foodstuffs, boxes, magazines, letters and other accumulated jumble. There was hardly a single clear space on the work surfaces beneath the cupboards; and on the table and the window seat along one length of it there were huge piles of newspapers, and letters, opened and unopened. Ted swept away a space on the table by creating a bigger pile elsewhere.

Flin noticed he was sitting next to a stash of opened bank statements and credit card bills. He tried not to look, but found himself glancing at them all the same. He balked at the amounts, and the vision of the future.

Flin suddenly felt exhausted. It had been a long journey down at the end of a particularly taxing week at work. He looked at the others, who were also looking pretty beat as they toyed with their quiche and salads. The exception was Tommy, who was talking animatedly with Ted about cars.

'Jessica,' he said, turning to her eventually, 'I can't believe you never told me your Dad had a Bentley Blower.'

'Well, that's women for you,' Ted guffawed, pouring out more wine into the gargantuan glasses provided.

'Didn't I?' said Jessica, ennui coursing through her. 'Well, that's probably because it's not something I find particularly interesting. Have a look at it tomorrow if you want. It's quite smart, but very noisy and if you go out in it you'll freeze.'

Flin smiled at Geordie, knowing they were both thinking the same thing: Jessica and Tommy was simply never going to work out.

'So what model is it exactly, Ted?' Tommy was saying.

'A 1928 four and a half litre.'

'What a beauty!' said Tommy. 'They're just fantastic. Presumably British racing green?'

'Most certainly is,' Ted replied, giving him a broad grin, 'with a Union Jack on each door. I'll show you in a moment.'

A few minutes later, Ted and Tommy got up to go out to the garage and the dogs all started barking and hopping about believing it to be walk time; the cacophony of yelping, Ted shouting and slamming doors was deafening.

'Now you know why we live away from the rest of the village,' said Jessica.

'Your poor mother,' added Lucie. 'Not much chance of sleep with that going on.'

'I can't bear Tommy being so male and boysey,' said Jessica.

'It's so boring. Why can't he be soft and fluffy and whispering me sweet nothings instead?'

'So why're you going out with him then?' asked Geordie reasonably.

'Oh, I don't know. When he's not playing sport or being laddish he's great. Honestly, Molly, you don't know how lucky you are.'

'Yes I do,' she answered, prompting Geordie to glow happily.

'That's lovely,' said Flin flatly and then he stood up. 'Time for bed, I think.'

'I think I'm on for sleep too, if that's OK,' said Geordie, after catching Molly's eye.

'Me too – I feel absolutely shattered all of a sudden,' added Lucie, yawning involuntarily.

'Well, I'm certainly not waiting for Tommy and Pops,' put in Jessica, and as if voicing what everyone else was feeling added, 'let's clear up and go to bed.'

Jessica felt irritable: furious with her parents for making such a ridiculous scene and slightly cross with Tommy for appearing to be more interested in a car than her. Oh, well, at least she had warned everyone that her parents were mad; and regardless of whether Pops and Maman were being peculiar or not, they would all still have a great time – there was plenty of drink in the house, there was the sea, the yacht club disco and lots else besides. What she really needed was a good night's sleep, although she realized that Tommy would probably come into her room at some point. Well, if that was the case, she would just tell him that she was tired, not interested in drunken fumblings and that he should go to sleep too.

Just after four in the morning, Flin woke up, feeling thirsty. Sensing that Tommy's bed was still empty, he switched on the light. There seemed to be no glass in his room and so he decided to go downstairs and find one. The house was still quite dark, and he struggled to find the light switches. He was fumbling about in the hall when a noise made him stop dead. As the moon appeared through a gap in the clouds, he could see Celeste walking down the stairs in a pale nightdress.

'Oh, Celeste, you made me jump,' he said, 'I was just coming down for some water.'

Celeste stopped, looked around her and then glided past him into the kitchen, without saying a word.

'Celeste?' he called again, but there was no reply. Flin shook his head and headed up the stairs. Sleep, that was what he needed.

By morning the rain had stopped and although there were still a few clouds about, it looked as though it was going to be a fine day. In the kitchen, Celeste, wearing a long silk dressing gown, was busying herself.

'Morning, *chéri*,' said Celeste brightly, the drama of the previous night seemingly forgotten, 'did you sleep well?'

'Like a log,' Flin lied, stretching. 'Look, I'm sorry if I startled you last night.'

'Startled me?' Celeste looked at him quizzically. 'What do you mean?'

'On the stairs.' Celeste looked at him blankly. 'In the early hours this morning,' Flin continued, 'on the stairs in the hall.'

Celeste laughed gaily. 'Dear Flin, you've been dreaming. Probably all that cheese.'

What on earth did that mean? Flin wondered. He hadn't eaten any cheese. It dawned on him that she must have been sleep-walking. Feeling himself pinking with embarrassment, he decided to drop the matter.

'I'm afraid you and I are the only two up, but please help yourself to anything you like. I've decided to go on strike for most of today since I still have a terrible migraine.'

'Oh, I'm sorry about that,' Flin offered.

'Yes, I'm sorry too – it's terribly boring, but lying quietly in bed's the only solution. I must say, though, that matters are not helped by my husband shouting and banging about in that ridiculous manner, but that's not your problem.'

Flin smiled ruefully. The conversation was beginning to feel a little awkward. 'Well, I'll just make a cup of tea, if that's OK,' he continued.

'Oh, yes, do – kettle's on the stove,' she told him as she opened and shut cupboard doors. Flin made for the Aga and nearly tripped over a tiny mangy dachshund standing obdurately in the doorway of the kitchen.

'Eugene, come out of the way, darling,' cooed Celeste, pausing to scoop up the scrawny-looking hound.

'Sorry,' said Flin, 'I didn't see him.'

'Poor darling – always being tripped over,' she continued, kissing him tenderly on the top of his head, and then turning to Flin said, 'It's time for his early morning snack.' Gingerly putting him down again, she took a huge *saucisson* from the fridge and started slicing it. 'There you go, sweetie,' she said in a baby voice, as Eugene snap-jawed his luxury meal. 'He does love it so,' she explained, 'and an old dog needs a few small luxuries in life, don't you, Eugene? Yees!' Eugene looked up at Flin and smugly smacked his chops.

'I hope you feel better soon,' said Flin as, armed with his tea, he retreated out of the room.

'Yes,' said Celeste airily, still joyfully feeding her hound.

By midday Jessica was holding court in the kitchen. 'I think we should go to the beach,' she announced as she cleared away toast-crumbed plates. 'We'll go to Perranporth. It's a little way, but has the best beach in the whole of Cornwall. Tommy and Pops, you're about to go out for a quick spin in the Bentley, aren't you? Well, we should head off. Everyone happy?'

Yes, they all agreed.

'D'you think I could come with you?' Flin asked Ted.

'Course you can,' boomed Ted, 'let's go.'

As the remote-controlled garage door gently hummed open, two enormous round headlights revealed themselves, peering arrogantly out from the darkness of the Bentley's lair. Tommy was standing back, his baseball-capped head on one side, admiring the beast. 'That's a beauty,' he said with obvious awe. Ted went inside and within a moment the engine sparked into life with a resonant roar, and slowly inched into the open air.

'Jump in,' called Ted, having put on his baggy flat cap and goggles. Sitting in the back, Flin stretched his arms along the back of the smooth leather seat, while Tommy hopped in beside Ted. 'OK, let's take her out!' shouted Ted, and off they lurched. Imperiously perched at the helm of the magnificent motorcar, Ted reminded Flin of Toad of Toad Hall, roaring round the winding Cornish roads, blaring his horn as every new corner approached, and waving madly at startled passers-by.

Flin leant back and let the wind race through his hair and buffet his face. He might be broke, he might be a failure with girls, but, he thought to himself, he had some great friends and, all things considered, he managed to have a lot of fun in life really. After all, it was not everyone who had the chance to whizz around tiny country lanes in a 1928 open-top Bentley. Large cotton-wool clouds reflected in the mirror-shine of the long, sleek bonnet. It really was a wonderful machine: the deep-throated purr of the engine, the luscious curves, the dazzling chrome. Flin could see why Ted had become so hooked; and as they finally turned back towards Porth Navas, he thought about how much he would one day like a car with as much style, class and charisma.

At Perranporth, the tide was out and the beach almost empty, but a few families still wandered the sands and in the car park Jessica nearly ran over a small child who was running with a single-mindedness that excluded watching out for dangerous obstacles in her path.

'I do wish people would keep their children under control when I'm trying to drive,' she muttered crossly.

'Why are English coastal resorts so fantastically naff?' asked Flin.

'I don't know,' laughed Lucie, 'but you're right: you can't really imagine the French setting up Mr Whippy vans on the Riviera, can you?'

'I think it's sweet,' put in Jessica, 'a part of our cultural heritage.'

They walked past a surfing hut, where bleached goateed surfers in wetsuits loitered with studied menace.

'Now that's something I really want to do,' Tommy told them.

'Riding the waves?' asked Geordie.

'Absolutely. It looks seriously awesome.'

It was a long way to the sea, but they could hear the thundering breakers long before they reached them. 'I've got to have a swim,' Tommy told them.

'Me too,' said Geordie, already unbuckling his belt.

'But it's freezing,' exclaimed Jessica.

'Nonsense,' grinned Tommy, 'all in the mind. Anyway, a few minutes in the sea will soon warm us up.'

'What're you going to swim in though?' Molly asked Geordie.

'My boxers,' he told her matter-of-factly.

'Oh God, such rugger buggers,' said Jessica, as Geordie and Tommy pulled off their shirts to reveal dazzling white torsos, offset by a neat brown 'v' around their necklines. 'When you've finished splashing around like children, we'll be over by that rock,' she added with a smile, pointing to a large megalith jutting out of the sand.

'Anyone else coming in?' Tommy asked eagerly as he peeled off his jeans.

'It's a little tricky for us women,' said Lucie, 'so I'm going to pass, if you don't mind.'

'Oh, all right, I might as well join you,' said Flin, as Tommy and Geordie were about to make a dash for the sea. 'I'll catch you up in a minute.'

'They're such fools – just big children,' Jessica said as she, Lucie and Molly watched Flin running out to the waves, whooping and calling out to Geordie and Tommy. Then, as they sat down by the rock, she asked Molly, 'So how's it going with Geordie?'

'I think he's just gorgeous,' Molly told her, looking out towards the three of them crashing about in the sea. 'I think we're going to have a lot of fun. We seem to have quite similar tastes. I'm pretty keen, I have to confess.'

'Ahh.' Jessica smiled back at her. 'I love it when things work out. And I can assure you, Geordie has talked of little else the last few weeks. You were incredibly popular with me when you finally got it together – I don't think I could have coped with him moping about for much longer.'

'Well, I do hope he hasn't been boring you all too much,' Molly laughed.

'Not at all – I've been enjoying all the excitement. Poor old Flin's a bit depressed, although he's trying hard not to take it personally.'

'Yes, poor Flin,' Lucie said, joining in the conversation, 'he's going through a bit of a bad patch at the moment, isn't he?'

'I suppose if you've just been given the shove and then you come home and find your best friend is just starting a relationship, it might be a bit trying,' Molly said.

'You've heard about Flin's Italian saga then?' Jessica asked her.

'Oh, yes – Geordie filled me in. And I suppose most of London knows now as well.'

'I should think at least,' laughed Jessica, 'poor lamb.'

'She sounds like a complete bitch,' said Lucie. 'It must've been awful for him.'

'What he needs, darling, is you to show him a bit of loving sympathy, and then he'll feel much better.' Jessica could never understand why Flin and Lucie had never got together: as her two best friends, weren't they made for each other? Sheer stubbornness on both their parts, and she sincerely hoped that this weekend they could be encouraged finally to make it together; in fact, Jessica felt the yacht club disco might be just the perfect time and place, especially if they drank enough and felt suddenly lonely enough. Lucie put a swift halt to her schemes.

'Now stop that, J,' she said sternly.

'Honestly, you two would be so good together, it's such a shame,' Jessica continued.

'Jessica, I'm going out with Dave, so just forget it!'

Molly was looking slightly confused, and Lucie, noticing her expression, said to her, 'Dave is in the army and based in Germany, so I hardly ever see him.'

'And when she does, he always wants to see all his other stupid friends so Lucie never has any time with him on her own,' Jessica cut in.

Lucie sighed. 'It's not as bad as she makes out. Jessica has this ridiculous idea that I should bin Dave and go out with Flin.'

'You should,' said Jessica truculently.

'Does Flin fancy you then?' Molly asked.

'I don't think so, just another minor flaw in Jessica's scheme.'

'Course he does, anyone can tell.'

'Jessica?' Lucie prodded her friend.

'Yes, darling?'

'Can we change the subject please?'

After the boys had dried themselves off and hopped about trying to put their clothes back on, they wandered off along the wide beach. Molly was talking to Tommy, so Jessica caught up with Geordie and said, 'She's lovely, you're very lucky.'

'I know. I'm so glad you like her. I just hope Flin's not too pissed off.'

'I think he and Lucie should get together.'

'Flin and Lucie?' he said incredulously. 'But they've been friends for years, why would anything happen now?'

'Because they're both lonely souls looking for love, and because they haven't realized how suited they are,' Jessica told him.

Geordie shrugged. 'Maybe, but what about that ice-cream? I can't come to Cornwall and not have a Mr Whippy.'

*　　*　　*

Inside the club house, the annual yacht club disco was getting under way. Fading photographs of yachts and yachtsmen and mounted boards with lists of presidents and honorary secretaries vied for wall space with clusters of balloons and streamers. At one end of the hall, an ageing rocker was setting up the disco and shuffling through boxes of records, while sitting at the tables around the edge were small groups of apprehensive-looking teenagers and village youths.

'Fantastic,' proclaimed Tommy. 'Let's get some beers in pronto.'

'Just look at the DJ,' Flin whispered to Jessica, 'he looks so early eighties!'

'Ssh – you mustn't be rude,' Jessica told him with mock seriousness, and commandeered a table while Tommy and Geordie went to the bar to buy the drinks.

'So when does the music start?' Lucie asked.

'Any second now, I think,' said Jessica.

'I think I might just get a bit drunk tonight, darling,' Flin told Jessica matter-of-factly.

'*Quelle* change. I think I might too.' Soon after the room shook into life as the two enormous amplifiers started to belt out Hot Chocolate.

'"I believe in miracles – yeah!"' the DJ breathed into his microphone. 'So let's have you all up on the dance floor and really boogying!'

'All right!' yelled Tommy, rapping his fingers on imaginary drums.

'Come on then,' Jessica shouted to him and together they sprang into action in the centre of the room. Geordie was looking slightly uncomfortable and explaining to Molly that he would dance with her, but that he needed to drink a bit more first to give him the courage.

'Lucie, would you care to dance?' Flin asked her, standing up and holding out his hand.

'Why thank you – I'd be honoured,' she replied, breaking into a big grin.

Three hours later, just about every disco classic had been played and the group of friends were all sitting back down at their table, hot and exhausted and not a little drunk. Even Geordie had clumsily shaken his arms about.

'This is so much better than SW1!' exclaimed Lucie.

'Isn't it just! Who needs drum and bass when there's China Crisis?' Flin laughed. He had spent a large part of the evening with Lucie but as the DJ announced 'Dancing Queen', he looked at Molly and offered her his hand. Giggling, Molly glanced quickly at Geordie and then stood up. 'Come on then,' she said, 'let's go.' Flin hurled himself into a sequence of swirls and arm flailing, then took Molly by the waist and spun her round. He could hear Tommy clapping and whistling, Molly was laughing and shrieking, so he spun her round again, before pulling her suddenly towards him.

'Geordie'll get jealous!' yelled Tommy, and Flin just grinned, looking towards Geordie and pretending to waggle his tongue in Molly's ear. Then the two of them were giving each other seductive glances and pretending to run their hands up the sides of each other's bodies. Flin could see Geordie scowling from their table and so whispered in Molly's ear, 'Your boyfriend's jealous.'

As Flin gyrated his hips with hers, she looked round towards Geordie then turned back to Flin, laughing. 'Bless him, what an idiot.'

As they sat down again, Geordie picked up his pint and threw it at Flin.

'Geordie!' yelled Molly.

'Calm yourself, mate,' said Tommy.

'What the fuck was that for?' shouted Flin, the beer running down his face and chest.

'What d'you think?' said Geordie, his face flushed with anger.

'Fuck you,' said Flin in a calmer voice and then flung his beer at Geordie.

'Right, that's it, you fucking twat,' Geordie said, scraping back his chair. Before Flin had time to react, Geordie pushed him over onto the floor and stormed out of the room.

'You'd better go after him,' Jessica suggested to Molly, who, nodding anxiously, hurried out.

'OK lads, break it up,' said the DJ, a little too late. By now most of the people in the hall were staring in the direction of the commotion. Flin looked up at Jessica, but the room was starting to spin. She was talking to him, but he couldn't really hear her. 'Urgh,' he groaned.

Tommy tried to lift him up. 'Are you all right, mate?' he asked, barely able to control his laughter.

'I think so,' said Flin groggily, rubbing the back of his head.

'You bloody fools, honestly,' said Jessica.

What could he say? His shock and anger gone as quickly as it had arrived; he felt ashamed and contrite. 'What have I done?' he wailed drunkenly. 'I've ruined everything for Geordie. He'll never talk to me again.'

'Don't be so ridiculous,' Lucie told him, 'tomorrow you'll have forgotten all about it.'

'Who's up for a bit more dancin'?' slurred Tommy, swaying slightly. 'We've got to dance now the Spice Girls are on.'

'I'll have a dance with you, Tommy,' said Lucie, pushing back her chair.

'*Excelente!*' he grinned.

'I'm going to take Flin back, I think,' Jessica told him, but Tommy was gone, already shimmying along with the rest of the throng.

'Thanks, Jessica, you're a real mate,' Flin told her as they staggered into his room.

'That's OK, darling, but you've got to get that shirt off – it's covered in beer.'

'I know – it's horrible.' But as he tried to undo the buttons, he felt Jessica's hands reach down to his waist and start pulling it up his chest. Despite his drunkenness, or perhaps because of it, Flin felt a tingle run down the back of his spine and instinctively took Jessica's hands in his. She looked at him for a moment, but did not let go. She suddenly looked fantastically sexy and alluring. Flin leant forward and kissed her, just on the lips at first, but then he could feel the warmth of her tongue on his.

'Come with me,' Jessica told him softly and led him out of the room and down a corridor to a large bathroom. She kissed him again, then very deliberately turned on the shower and started taking off her clothes.

'Come on,' she said, as Flin struggled with his belt. It felt wonderful holding her naked body once more, the warm water pounding down on them. Kissing and soaping each other was something the seventeen-year-old Jessica would never have done, and Flin felt an enormous wave of excitement and exultation course through him. Covering her with kisses he could feel and hear her urging him on until he was inside her, her legs wrapped tightly round his, her back against the wall of the shower, and with the water still running over them. Afterwards, as they towelled each other down, she hardly said a word, just twinkled at him mischievously. Then a door banged downstairs. 'Shit,' said Flin, 'they're back.'

Jessica smiled, hugged him tightly, said, 'Time to go – sweet dreams, darling,' and disappeared.

Flin could hear a wood pigeon sounding its familiar morning cooing and realized that he was awake. It was early and, turning over, he was ready to go back to sleep when with alarming clarity he remembered his fight with Geordie. 'Damn!' he cursed out loud. 'Shit!' And then Jessica. That was even worse. What had he been playing at? He had potentially ruined his two greatest friendships in the space of one drunken hour. And just what had Jessica been thinking of? Why had she had sex with him? More to the point, would she want more? Flin lay in his bed staring up at the ceiling. Perhaps that was the answer to both their relationship crises; perhaps they should go out with each other again. He certainly found Jessica attractive – who didn't – and their drunken session had been great.

What's more it was perfectly obvious that she and Tommy were never going to go the distance. Flin knew he was one of Jessica's best friends, but was Jessica looking for something beyond just friendship? Had the night before been her way of telling him she wanted a deeper, more intimate relationship? His head was swimming. What *was* he to think?

Upstairs Jessica was awake as well. Beside her, blissfully unaware of her infidelity and snoring loudly, was Tommy. Why, oh why had she had sex with Flin? How could she have been so stupid? She knew what was bound to happen: Flin would decide he was in love with her, that they were clearly made for each other and then when she rebuffed him in favour of Tommy, he would become jealous and prickly. She could see it all. It was all too traumatic for words. It had been fun though. Illicit, exciting. And he had looked rather gorgeous, his big sad eyes and scruffy hair quite irresistible. She knew deep down that Tommy was hardly the answer to her dreams, but she did like him a lot. He made her laugh, was good-looking and fun to be with, and she didn't want Flin to ruin things between them. Jessica bit at her bottom lip. She would have to talk to Flin, and just hope, really hope, that all would be well. Of course, she loved him dearly, but as her friend, nothing more. She prayed they could pretend it never happened. Carefully, she slipped out of her bed and went downstairs.

'Jessica, hi,' Flin said, his heart leaping as Jessica quietly slipped into his room.

'Ssh,' she said, tiptoeing over to his bed. Sitting down, she smiled at him, trying to form the right words. 'Last night,' she said slowly, 'was a one-off.' She could see Flin's expression change, clearly crestfallen. He was so transparent. 'It was a lot of fun,' she added, 'but we were both slaughtered and it should never have happened. I love you far too much to risk our friendship over a silly one-night stand.' She felt quite pleased with the last line.

'You're right,' Flin told her, nodding exaggeratedly, 'absolutely right. Great fun, but definitely not to be repeated.' He smiled weakly.

'Good. So we're still best mates then?'

'You bet.'

'And we won't ever mention it to anyone?'

'Not a soul.'

Jessica bent over and kissed him lightly on his head. 'Great. I'm glad that's sorted. See you at breakfast in a bit. I'm desperate for a long bath with my new *Hello!*'

Of course, he knew she was right really. Still, just for a moment or two, it had been nice thinking about making love to Jessica every night. And of course, whichever way you looked at it, it was another rejection. He was left feeling a bit depressed – another blow to his ego. On his way to the loo, he met Geordie. 'Geordie! Glad I've bumped into you, old man,' he said as heartily as he could.

'I was coming to find you,' Geordie replied and kicked him lightly on the shin.

'Sorry, old man,' said Flin sheepishly.

'No, I'm sorry – I was bang out of order,' admitted Geordie.

'So was I. Bloody stupid, weren't we?'

'Ridiculous. Did you see everyone's faces?'

'Yeah,' laughed Flin, 'quite a scene.'

'Well, sorry anyway,' said Geordie again.

'Ah, forget it. It's quite funny really.' There was a slight pause. 'Molly OK?' said Flin.

'Yeah, I think she's forgiven me.'

'Good. Well, say I'm sorry too.'

'Sure,' said Geordie, turning back towards his room, 'see you in a bit.'

Unable to go back to sleep, but glad he had at least made his peace with Geordie, Flin dressed and went downstairs. In the kitchen he found Celeste and Ted cheerfully breakfasting. He hadn't seen Celeste since the previous morning, but on this occasion she was fully dressed and had apparently shaken off her migraine. It seemed she and Ted had patched up their

194

differences too; together, over their coffee and papers, they appeared the very epitome of married bliss.

'Morning! Come and sit down and tell us all about last night,' beamed Ted heartily.

'It was a lot of fun, very jolly,' he told them, not wanting to elaborate, 'although I've a slightly sore head this morning.'

'Splendid, always a good sign!' bellowed Ted. Both he and his wife were in good humour – and Celeste for once seemed almost as verbose as her husband, peppering Flin with questions about London life, his job, about Molly and Geordie, Jessica and Tommy; and Flin, for his part, was happy to talk back.

'You see, I know Jessica only ever tells me half the story,' Celeste told him. 'It's so difficult being a mother – I worry all the time about what she's getting up to. After all, London, like any big city, is such a dangerous place. But she wearies of me phoning her all the time, I know.' Flin smiled sympathetically. 'And these times, when you all come down and see us – they are so precious – and such fun!' she continued, clasping her hands together, her frosty reception and almost two-day absence conveniently brushed over.

'And it's always brilliant to be here – you're fantastic hosts,' he said to them, knowing that flattery is rarely misplaced.

'Very good of you to say so,' said Ted, leaning back and stretching. 'On days like this, you can't beat Cornwall and the English countryside. I'm so glad we don't live in those ridiculous tin-pot places like Kuwait any more, sweetheart.' He blew Celeste a kiss through his large hand.

'Me too, *chéri*,' she smiled, lovingly taking her husband's hand. 'You know, Flin, Ted used to have to deal with some bad people.' Flin felt slightly uncomfortable. Should he be hearing this?

'Some real what I call megalomaniacs,' continued Ted. 'And then I suddenly thought to myself: I'm fifty-two years old, I've got a bit of cash in the bank, what on earth's the point in muckin' about trying to do business with these ruddy unreliable people? And I had this yearning – didn't I, sweetheart? – to be back in England, or rather, I should say, Cornwall, so back we came. To be perfectly honest, I can still do quite a lot of work from here, so it's worked out rather well.'

'Well, from a selfish point of view, I'm very glad you did too,' confessed Flin.

'Ha, ha, you're a good fellow, Flin,' laughed Ted as Celeste got up to make more coffee. 'I'll tell you something though,' he continued, 'to my mind there's no point in slogging your guts out all your life if you can't then have a bit of time to enjoy it.' And as if to emphasize the point, he swept his arms around the kitchen and glanced out of the window and across the estuary.

Flin nodded earnestly. How right Ted was: life was for living, surely? 'I often worry about the future,' he admitted after a pause. 'I can't see where any of us are heading. Computers becoming ever more sophisticated, more cars on the roads than ever. When's it going to stop? It's frightening really. As though we're spiralling out of control somehow.'

'Honestly, we've never had it so good, I can assure you,' put in Celeste. 'When we were your age we never had half the things you have, or went out partying anything like as much as you lot do.'

'Speak for yourself, sweetheart,' chuckled Ted, and gave Flin a wink.

'I'm right, Ted, sweetie, and you know it. And Flin, you've never had to live through a war. My father fought in the Resistance. Many of his friends were killed; it was a terrible, terrible time. He was in his twenties then, just as you are now. The best years of his life were taken away from him.'

Flin thought about what she said. She was right: he might be feeling a bit unimpressed with life at the moment, but thank God he'd never had to fight in a world war, or see his country ruled by insane dictators.

'Enough of such matters,' said Celeste at length, 'will you take the boat out today?'

'I'd love to – are you sure that's OK?' Flin replied. His spirits were slightly returning.

'But of course!' said Ted, slamming his hands decisively on the table, 'you could hardly come down here and not take the boat out, not when we're virtually living on the water!'

And so it was settled. Gradually, one by one, everyone ambled down to the kitchen and by lunchtime everyone was up and ready to go. There was no tension at all between Flin and Geordie; both were so relieved that each bore no grudge against the other that, if anything, they felt firmer friends for the experience. They naturally suffered a barrage of jokes about their brawl, but they had been quickly forgiven. Jessica, however, was avoiding Flin's eye and she seemed to him to be overly attentive to Tommy. She laughed with the others at their antics at the disco, but Flin suddenly became aware that she wasn't talking directly to him. At one point she even offered tea and coffee to everyone but him. Why was she trying so deliberately to hurt his feelings? He desperately didn't want to feel overly sensitive and upset but he couldn't help it. If only they could turn back the clock.

Outside, tied to a little wooden jetty, was the *Jolly Buccaneer*. Unaware of Flin's anguish, Geordie and Tommy were listening intently as Ted told them about how to use the simple outboard motor and pointed out its foibles.

'She's only a small little thing, and there's quite a lot of you, so mind you go steadily,' he warned them. 'How far are you intending to go?'

'We thought we'd go across to Helford and have lunch in the pub there, Pops,' Jessica told him.

'Well, have fun,' he told them as Tommy pulled the cord and the little engine whirred into life.

They reached the pub, tied up the boat and found an empty table inside. It was still sunny, but decidedly cooler and no one fancied sitting outside.

'Naughty boy,' said Lucie to Flin as they stood at the bar ordering the drinks.

'She told you,' said Flin, not looking at her. 'Stupid cow was supposed to keep *stumm*.'

'You know what she's like, though.'

'Yeah, but I haven't even told Geordie and I tell him everything. I'm sorry, Lucie, but that really pisses me off. Especially as she's being so bloody tactile with Tommy. Why's she being so horrible?'

'She feels guilty, that's why, so she's over-compensating by being all over him. Come on, you're as much to blame as she is.'

Flin scowled across the bar.

'Flin, don't get upset by this. Please.'

'Sorry, Lucie, but I am a bit,' he said, picking up the drinks and turning to face her, 'not that she could give a damn.'

Flin wanted to talk to Jessica but there was never the opportunity. Everyone else seemed to be laughing and chatting with increasing animation as Geordie and Tommy recounted tales of university debauchery and men behaving badly. He wanted to join in, but knew there was little conviction in his forced smiles.

'I could sit here all afternoon,' Geordie announced happily, putting down his empty pint.

'Me too,' put in Tommy, 'I'm feeling seriously chilled out.'

'Why don't we have another drink then?' suggested Jessica. 'Flin, give me a hand, will you?' She had noticed him scowling. Really, he was so unsubtle. She cursed herself; what a complete idiot she'd been.

'Why did you tell Lucie?' Flin hissed as they reached the bar.

'Oh, Flin, come on! I had to tell Lucie,' Jessica told him incredulously.

'But you said not to tell a soul! I haven't told Geordie.'

'Lucie doesn't count. And I wasn't to know you wouldn't tell Geordie. Now just calm down, darling, and stop looking so angry. We both agreed it was a mistake, so stop feeling so hard done by.' She tried to tickle his side, and could see him trying not to smile. 'Please, Flin. Don't be all hurt and grumpy. I can't cope with it.'

'Well, stop ignoring me and overdoing it with Tommy,' said Flin petulantly. 'It's getting on my nerves.'

'All right, all right,' she agreed, 'but what about a little smile in return?'

He felt slightly – only slightly – placated, and was relieved when Jessica began to pay him a bit more attention. The others still appeared totally unaware of any contretemps and gaily continued drinking, so that by the time they wobbled back to the *Jolly Buccaneer* they were feeling a little tipsy. Not drunk, or incapacitated in any way, but just laughing a little bit too much, and acting rather foolishly. Geordie took the tiller and soon started swerving the boat from side to side, so that everyone clutched onto the gunwales and shrieked. It was all just a bit of a lark. Then Tommy took over and, not wanting to be outdone, insisted on heading straight for a boat moored in front of them, swerving just at the last minute. Jessica yelled at him to stop, but he just laughed and did it again as Flin and Geordie egged him on. Entering the Porth Navas creek, Tommy was swerving to and fro increasingly sharply until the boat suddenly lurched off balance and Lucie was flung over the side. Immediately the others leant over to see if she was OK, and a great wave of water burst over the boat and flooded it.

'Tommy, you stupid idiot!' yelled Jessica.

'OK, sorry, everyone,' Tommy cried, slowly circling back to where Lucie was flailing about in the water. 'Just keep calm and still for a second.' As they drew alongside her, Flin jumped into the water too. He'd thought Lucie might be in trouble and it seemed the noble thing to do.

'Oh, brilliant,' sighed Jessica, 'now we've got to get two people out. Flin, why did you have to do that?'

'I was trying to save Lucie,' spluttered Flin from the water, 'not that you'd give a shit.' The water was freezing, and with the tightening of his chest, Flin felt a new wave of anger spread over him.

'Look, don't panic, anyone,' said Tommy as he and Geordie carefully leant over and grabbed Lucie's arms. They pulled her gradually over the side and back into the boat where she collapsed into the murky brown water swilling about the bottom boards.

'Flin, can you swim to that boathouse over there?' Geordie said, barely able to stop laughing and pointing to a ramshackle structure fifty yards away. 'I really think we could do without your extra weight.'

'But it's freezing!' he spluttered.

'Start swimming and you'll be all right. It's only thirty yards or so,' Geordie insisted, giving in to the laughter.

This was the icing on the cake of a truly appalling day, Flin thought to himself as he sadly half crawled, half doggy paddled towards the boathouse, desperate to keep his head above the water. It was far colder than the sea at Perranporth; muddy too, and his clothes clung heavily to him, making his progress slow. He'd been foolish to jump in after her, he realized, but it had been a purely instinctive move. Now he would probably contract pneumonia and die. Still, he thought as the boathouse seemed to be getting no closer, it would solve some of his problems.

Tommy had managed to get the outboard going and, humbled, sedately took the boat back to the jetty, while Molly and Geordie tried to keep the sodden and shivering Lucie warm.

'I told you to stop being such a prat,' Jessica glowered at him, 'someone could have drowned.'

What could Tommy say? Nothing at all. He'd been playing the fool, showing off, and his stunt had backfired.

'Is Flin OK?' Lucie stammered.

'What was he playing at?' muttered Jessica.

'I can see him climbing out at the boathouse now,' Geordie told her. 'Poor old Flin. He's not having much luck at the moment.'

'Well, you haven't helped,' put in Molly. Geordie looked sheepish. He deeply regretted overreacting the previous night, and he winced just thinking about it. It was a huge relief that Flin hadn't held it against him and he determined the episode should now be a closed book. The best way to deal with it was pretend it never happened.

After edging round the boathouse, Flin found a path and squelched back towards the village. He felt cold, tired and foolish. His face and hands were caked in briny grime, and no doubt his shoes were ruined. That meant more wasted money needlessly thrown down the drain. And the previous night he'd nearly managed to ruin two friendships. 'I'm sure I never used to be this sad,' he said miserably to himself as he walked into the drive, a line of drips following in his wake.

Ted had laughed off the incident as soon as he heard his boat was safe and that no one had been hurt, but Celeste had flown into a rage. 'For God's sake, look at you all, you are twenty-five! Twenty-five and supposedly grown up now! And yet still you muck about and drink too much and risk drowning everyone in this juvenile manner. It distresses me so much. When are you ever going to grow up and act your age? And Flin – look at you! You could have died! What would I have said to your mother? Honestly, you lot are pathetic!' She dabbed at her eyes. 'I feel so disappointed, so let down. This is too much for me – I'm going to go upstairs and lie down.'

Jessica had said nothing but there were thunder clouds forming above her, and as soon as Celeste had gone, she too disappeared to her room without a word. This on top of the Flin débâcle had proved too much. The others felt belittled, humbled, awful – it was a terrible moment. No one knew what to say or how to react, until thankfully Ted interjected, 'Listen, chaps, all of you have hot baths, relax, then come downstairs and have a drink. They'll both be fine later. You've all been bloody fools, but don't worry, these things happen in life.'

None the less, the weekend never really recovered and for the next week Flin and Jessica more or less ignored each other.

She spent more evenings than normal at Tommy's house and worked late, and since Geordie was away at Molly's flat, Flin found he had the house largely to himself. Which he found increasingly disheartening.

chapter seventeen

Jessica's Turn to Feel Disgruntled

Jessica was conscious that despite making their pact nearly six months before, her career and relationship situation had not improved exactly as she'd hoped, and found herself becoming increasingly disgruntled. She and Tommy were getting along fine, and he spoilt her with dinners and theatre tickets; but, yet again, she was going out with someone who didn't exactly set her heart racing. Admitting as much to Lucie one evening, her friend told her flatly that if that was how she felt, she should finish it immediately.

'But I don't have a bad time with him or anything,' Jessica told her, 'and he's very sweet really.'

'That's all very well,' Lucie responded, 'but where's it heading? If you're not going anywhere what's the point?'

Jessica disagreed completely. 'There's every point. I'll stick with Tommy until my dream man turns up and if he doesn't, well, I'll see. Anyway,' she added, 'I think that's a bit rich coming from you.'

Lucie sighed irritably, and said, 'I'm not even going to begin to rise to that sort of comment, but don't forget you've also been unfaithful to him. I just don't think you're being very fair.'

'Well, I freely admit that was a huge mistake, but Tommy

doesn't know about it. And what he doesn't know, won't hurt. Anyway, I'm not going to do it again.'

'That's very big of you.' Lucie raised her eyebrows and Jessica looked just the slightest bit sheepish.

Work was another problem. Damien, her boss, had been intimating for a while that a promotion was imminent, and then sure enough, a few weeks before, a better position had come up. Senior Account Manager handling a major car company account. She knew very little about cars, but started swotting up. She felt sure she could more than handle the job.

The first blow was Damien opening up the position to outside competition. Consequently, instead of having the job handed to her on a plate, she found she had to face an interview for it. The second blow was that Richard Keeble was on the interview panel. As soon as she saw him, her heart sank. Initially, he said nothing, not even making a passing reference to incidents in the past. He just sat at one end of the table, fiddling with a pen, a slightly amused expression on his face. Jessica was feeling quite flustered with him just being there – he was like a cat idly toying with his prey until the moment came to strike, and she felt it keenly, shifting unnecessarily in her seat and aware of her palms sweating profusely.

'OK, let's start with something very simple,' he interjected suddenly, fixing her with a hard stare. 'What is the difference between, say, a VW Golf GTi and a one point four litre model?'

'One's got more power?'

'Yes, exactly,' he continued, smiling now, 'but can you be a bit more specific?'

Jessica hadn't a clue. All she knew was that boys liked the GTi's and girls preferred the other. 'No, I'm sorry, I can't.'

Richard Keeble turned to Damien and the other member of the interview panel with a look of disbelief. 'It's quite important,' he said in a slow and patronizing voice, 'that someone looking after one of the most important car accounts in London knows a little bit about their subject.'

Jessica said nothing. The bastard, she thought. She knew he was deliberately spiking her.

'OK,' he continued, 'precisely what is your interest in cars?'

Jessica was thrown completely. She'd learnt names and various models, studied previous car advertising, even asked her father a bit more about his Bentley, but she couldn't admit to having a passionate interest. So, after taking a deep breath, she talked about aesthetics, and design of both the exterior and exterior and the challenge of making greener, safer machines. Now that was interesting, she explained, that and the challenge of persuading the punter that one particular model was more worthy of his or her money than the other. That was where she felt excited by cars, rather than getting her kicks from whether Michael Schumacher was winning the World Championship or not.

She knew as soon as she left the room that she would not get the job, and she was right. Damien had taken her into the central glass-walled meeting area and told her the job had gone to an outside candidate. 'I'm sorry, Jessica,' he told her, 'I know you're itching to move up a notch, but you don't know enough about cars – to work on these accounts you need to be obsessed with machinery.'

'I can become obsessed,' she told him.

'Look, you're doing really well. When the right position comes you will be promoted. It's a question of when not if.' Small consolation – well, she might just have to start looking elsewhere. Couldn't he tell she was desperate for greater stimulation and something more challenging? It was so frustrating. She knew, and knew that Damien knew, that she was perfectly capable of doing the job. The only reason she'd been overlooked was because of Richard Keeble and his pathetic male ego.

Lucie suggested she lodge a complaint.

'I can't,' Jessica told her, 'I'd be marked for ever if I did that. It's a company run by men who, when push comes to shove, stick together.'

'But they'd have to take notice and do something.'

'Sure, but I'd never get the promotion and I'd probably never get a job anywhere else. They'd think I was a devious, untrustworthy squealer.'

'So what? Would you want to work for such people anyway?'

The simple answer was yes, she did. She liked her work, was good at it and wanted to succeed. The way forward was to grit her teeth and either look to other companies or dazzle Damien so much that he simply had to promote her. Still, it was far from an ideal situation, and also meant she was behind in the house competition – which was galling.

In fact, the house was another issue. Living there simply wasn't as much fun as it should have been. Geordie was away a lot of the time with Molly – perfectly understandable – but the house seemed emptier without him, especially since Flin had been so out of sorts in recent months. Things had never been quite the same between them since their night in Cornwall. They were still openly affable with each other, and spoke to each other on the phone from work, but he didn't come and chat to her late at night any more, or hug and kiss her as he used to. If she sat next to him on the sofa, he would edge to one end and no longer tickle her arm in an abstract manner. Flin had always been so tactile – but since Cornwall that had changed. Part of her suspected that as soon as he snapped out of his general state of gloom, he'd be fine again, back to normal. But it wasn't her fault things weren't going his way. And he could have ignored her advances after the disco. She had started staying at Tommy's more frequently, but that was even more unsatisfactory: she liked her own space and her own things about her and had never liked his flat anyway.

So when Paolo rang out of the blue it was just the breath of fresh air she needed.

'Hey, Jessica, guess who this is, baby!' he said when Flin passed over the phone.

'Paolo! Hi! How are you? How lovely to hear from you! Where are you?' she gushed. He was unmistakably calling on a mobile and she could hear chatter and clamour in the background.

'Guess what? I'm in my new restaurant! You must come over and let me give you dinner. It's even better than Barberino's.'

'Even better? OK, when?'

'Come this Friday, and we'll have a perfect evening, just you and I. I'll tell you everything.'

'Sounds wonderful!' she replied cheerfully.

'And this time, I promise not to take off your clothes without your permission.' He burst out laughing.

Jessica giggled back, 'OK, that's a deal.'

'Tommy'll be chuffed,' Flin said sarcastically when she told him her plans.

'Tommy's not going to know,' she replied tersely, reasoning that since he was planning to be out drinking anyway, what he didn't know wouldn't harm him. 'Anyway,' she added, 'it's not as though we're married, you know. He's going out with his mates and I'm going out with one of mine. It's not a big deal.'

'OK, OK,' Flin riposted defensively, 'but Paolo's not exactly a mate, is he? You've met him once and you ended up in his bed. You're going on a date, whichever way you look at it.'

'Well, so what? Someone's got to have a bit of fun around here,' she snapped.

Managing to make it home quite early on the Friday, she found she had the house to herself. She'd been looking forward to her night out all day, and took extra long with her 'me-time' that evening. With new magazines for the bath and a different moisturizer to try out she spent a relaxing hour pampering herself, then took a deliberately long time to get ready, going through her wardrobe carefully, choosing then discarding an assortment of combinations.

She even ordered a black cab to Berlini's, Paolo's new restaurant on Kensington Church Street, rather than a minicab or the tube, in order to heighten the sense of occasion. Seduction by Paolo was not really a part of her plans – or was it? – but she did fancy flirting with him a bit and was looking forward to a good dose of flattery throughout dinner. It was just what she needed to restore her good spirits.

As soon as she walked through the door, the maître d' was swept aside, and Paolo, with arms outstretched, rushed forward to greet her. 'You look beautiful,' he told her, kissing her lightly on both cheeks, 'thank you so much for coming.'

'Sweet Paolo, thank you for inviting me,' she replied. He was looking very dapper in his black suit and open-collared white shirt, revealing an impressive pelt of chest hair. The restaurant, softly lit from an array of contorted wrought-iron lamps, was a mezzanine affair, each level painted a slightly different shade of Mediterranean earthen hues. This was going to be fun, she thought to herself.

'Come with me,' he insisted, taking her hand. 'Before we eat, I want to introduce you to a few of my people,' and then took her into the kitchen to meet the chef and all the various waiters, who as with his other restaurant, were all kitted out in neat black Nehru jackets.

'This is a very special friend of mine,' he told them, while Jessica stood there and giggled like a bashful schoolgirl. 'OK, I'll take you to our table now – it's discreet, you know, and I think you'll like it. We're going to have a good time.'

Initially Paolo's promise held true. Suggesting dishes, as was his way ('You simply must have the char-grilled sardines wrapped in vine leaves with aubergine raita'), he chattered and laughed merrily. The waiters were especially courteous and attentive, giving her and their boss the very best treatment. Jessica was enjoying feeling spoilt. But after talking about the setting up of the restaurant, and Kim and various other inconsequential topics, Paolo tentatively asked her whether there was a man in her life.

'Oh, he's good fun, Paolo. You'd like him – he's called Tommy,' Jessica told him.

'I do if he lets you come out with me,' he responded.

'Well, actually I didn't tell him,' she confessed. 'He's out drinking with some of his mates. I mean, we're not at all dependent on each other and we do our own thing.' She smiled at him. 'What about you, surely you have a girlfriend Paolo, to take out in that flash car of yours?' It was an innocent remark, and she was just making conversation really; but suddenly Paolo's whole demeanour changed. He looked down at the table and then back at her, all joviality gone.

'Sadly, no more. She left me last week. You know, we had been dating three months and she made me the happiest man alive. Jessica, I tell you now, I thought she was the one.' He looked at her plaintively, tragedy etched across his face. 'I thought we were going to get married.'

'Oh, Paolo, I'm really sorry,' she told him earnestly. He looked so miserable; it scarcely seemed possible. 'So what happened?' she asked, immediately knowing it was exactly what he had wanted her to say and recognizing her mistake: over an hour later, he was still talking about his ex, pouring his heart out, asking her advice 'from a woman's viewpoint', glad to have found someone to whom he could talk about his personal tragedy. 'It's so hard,' he told her, 'I have to carry on working as though nothing has happened, carry on being the happy, laughing Paolo that everyone expects, but sometimes . . .' His eyes glistened over.

Jessica 'yesed' and 'uh-huhed' and tried to look sympathetic, but it was starting to become a bit much. Listening to a distraught Paolo going on about his lost love was not how she'd imagined the evening would pan out, and although Flin had been moping slightly less of late, she rather felt she'd had a bellyful of heartbroken men.

'I'm sorry to have gone on like this, Jessica,' Paolo said eventually, 'honestly I am. You don't know how much it has helped being able to talk to you.' When he looked at her with his deep brown, maudlin eyes she did feel sorry for him; but then when he tried to jolly himself up and talked of going off to a club 'for some dancing, you and me', she firmly declined the offer. She'd had quite enough, thank you.

In the cab on the way home, she felt a little foolish. In retrospect, she realized she'd overhyped the evening to herself beforehand, and so disappointment was inevitable. She also felt a little bit used. It was obvious to her now that he'd only phoned her up because he was feeling lonely and wanted some female company. In fact, now that she thought about it, his invitation had been pretty last minute, and she wondered how many people Paolo had asked to dinner before she'd gaily accepted his invitation. And to think she probably would have gone to bed with him had the evening gone as she'd hoped. She scolded herself for being so cheap. No, despite a delicious meal, the evening had not gone at all to plan, and she felt empty and petulant.

She couldn't remember the last time she'd spent a Friday night either sober or on her own, and was not sure how she felt about entering the cold and empty house. What she needed, she decided, was something comforting, so, undressing quickly, she put on her dressing gown and made herself some cocoa. Then, tucked up in bed, she read her latest *Bunty* from cover to cover.

Jessica had cheered up somewhat by the next morning, and by relating her evening with Paolo to Flin, found it seemed considerably more comic than it had the night before. But her mood of equable calm was unfortunately shattered when she caught up with Tommy for lunch later that day. Still looking hungover when they met up at the Atlas, he had pulled the peak of his baseball cap even lower over his face than usual.

'You look well,' Jessica told him cheerily. Tommy just grunted and gave her a terse peck on the cheek in response. 'What's the matter with you?' she persisted.

'Nothing,' he answered sulkily.

'OK,' she said slowly, and tried another tack. 'Well, how was last night then?'

'Great,' Tommy said flatly.

'And are you going to flesh it out for me a bit?' Jessica asked him, exasperation creeping into her voice.

'OK,' he said moodily. 'We all drank lots of beer and got drunk and then we all went home.'

'Tommy, what's got into you? Have I done something wrong?'

Suddenly Tommy grew more animated and retorted, 'I don't know, Jessica, you tell me.'

'And just what exactly is that supposed to mean?'

'I'll spell it out. Where were you last night?'

'Oh, for God's sake,' Jessica said dismissively.

'Well?' said Tommy. 'Where were you?'

Jessica thought about lying, but quickly realized that firstly, he probably knew anyway, and secondly, that in actual fact she had nothing to hide. 'Jesus, Tommy, what's got into you? I'm allowed to go out if I want to. You did.'

'Jessica,' he said slowly and deliberately, trying to control his anger, 'just tell me where you were.'

'All right, if you must know, I was invited out to dinner by an old friend who owns a restaurant. He'd just broken up with his girlfriend and wanted to talk about it. So you see, nothing untoward at all. Honestly, Tommy, I really do not like being given the tenth degree like this.' This little interchange was putting her back into a very bad mood.

'Oh, don't you? Well I think I have every reason to be pissed off,' he said, his voice rising. 'Firstly, you never told me you were going out with this creep, which tells me you have something to hide about it, and secondly you're supposed to be going out with me, and that means not going around on dates with other people, which is exactly what you did.'

Jessica sat in silence for a few moments, fuming. How dare he talk to her like that? But Tommy had not finished. 'I mean, it's not as if you were even subtle about it. Katie Symons saw you getting out of a black cab, all dressed up on Kensington Church Street. Worth making such an effort for, was he?'

This was taking the cross-examination too far. 'Tommy,' she said as calmly as she could muster, 'Paolo is a restaurateur. He's just opened a new place. It's smart, and therefore requires looking smart.' She glared at him. 'Honestly, I cannot believe you are talking to me like this. I am perfectly entitled to go out with whoever I want whenever I want, without feeling spied upon by Big Brother Tommy. You don't own me and when you're off boozing and playing the lad, I'm damned if I'm going to meekly stay at home waiting for my macho man to finish his fun and turn his attentions to me.' Tommy tried to interject, but Jessica was not finished. 'No, listen, Tommy. I think I should warn you that if there is one thing I hate in life, it's jealous men, and I never, ever want to be spoken to like that again. Now, I think it's best if I leave.'

'Jessica –' said Tommy a bit weakly as she gathered her bag and coat together.

'No, Tommy, I'm not interested at the moment. Call me when you've calmed down a bit. But I mean it: I'm not going to play the meek little girlfriend, so it's up to you. You take me as I am or not at all. When you've decided what you want, give me a call.' Not even pausing to give him a kiss on the cheek, she swept out of the room in a flurry of righteous indignation.

'Poor Tommy,' said Flin the next day as they drove over for Sunday lunch at Lucie's flat, 'I bet he didn't know what hit him.' He seemed quite cheered up.

'I know, poor lamb. He just sat there looking absolutely shell-shocked. He was trying to be all manly and assertive but was shouted down. But honestly, I was so cross. I don't think I've ever felt so angry in my whole life.'

'Brilliant – I take my hat off to your unique ability to turn the argument round. Tommy starts off being the aggrieved party and ends up being culpable.'

Jessica looked slightly sheepish. 'Well, I can't be doing with him getting all jealous and possessive on me. It's just too boring for words.'

'Jessica, I think I'd have been a bit pissed off about it if I'd been Tommy. I mean, why didn't you just tell him in the first place?'

212

'Because I don't have to tell him everything. He doesn't own me.'

'Nonsense, you just knew he wouldn't like it.'

Jessica grinned at him. 'Well, maybe that had a bit to do with it.'

He smiled back. 'You're incorrigible.'

Lucie was on her own again that weekend, although she had been out to Germany to see Dave the week before. Jessica loved seeing Lucie, but she really did wish her friend could have a more practical relationship. She still hadn't given up hope of getting her together with Flin; she was convinced it was only a matter of time. After all, it made so much sense. Just before they arrived at her flat Jessica said to Flin, 'I wish you and Lucie would get together. It's so obvious you should.'

'Jessica, not this again please,' Flin told her firmly. 'It's never going to happen.' Maybe he did fancy Lucie – kind of – but not enough to ever go out with her. More crucially, he knew she didn't fancy him. They could only ever be friends and nothing else. He also knew that this was as it should be.

Lucie was predictably firm with Jessica. 'It seems to me there's even less reason for you to be going out with Tommy now,' she told her. 'If you were at all keen on him you wouldn't be flirting with people like Paolo. Tommy's only going to end up getting upset – you should put him out of his misery and end it now.'

'I do like him though,' Jessica countered lamely, 'and on the whole he's fun to go out with. Come on, Luce, you know I hate it when people start becoming possessive. But I've told him that now.'

'He won't change, though, which is precisely why you should end it.'

'Look, I admit things could be better between us, but now I've told Tommy how I feel, hopefully all will be well from now on.'

'Come on, J, you know it's not as simple as that,' Lucie persevered.

'Isn't it? To be honest, I don't think I've ever been out with anyone where everything's been fantastic. I've certainly never been in love with anyone.'

'Not anyone?' asked Flin. 'Not even when you were eighteen? I thought everyone fell in love then. I did, all the time.'

'Don't think so,' said Jessica.

'Weren't you ever in love with me?' Flin persisted. 'I adored you.'

'Nope,' she said, staring blankly down at the table.

'I'm sure you will eventually,' Lucie reassured her, 'you obviously haven't met the right person yet. At least that explains why you've been such a tart recently.'

Jessica had been a bit hurt by that comment, but really, Lucie was right, she had been playing about too much. Even mucked about with Flin and look what had happened there. She wondered sadly if Lucie was also right about falling in love; a part of her worried that she simply wasn't capable of it. Sometimes she thought the answer was to do as she and Lucie had so often discussed: try and marry a fabulously rich landowner with houses in London and Tuscany, give up work and swan about shopping and meeting friends for lunch. That would make her happy. Or would it? Because at other times she thought that what she really wanted was to rise to the peaks of her profession. She did think that she wanted to be rich though, but then didn't everyone? The truth was she didn't know what she wanted in life, and that recently the only certainty seemed to be her dissatisfaction with the status quo.

Flin and Lucie were right about Tommy too. It was no good; she simply couldn't move on while still going out with him. She'd originally hoped he would provide the spark she was looking for, but it had soon become clear that this was never going to happen. Tommy wouldn't change. And it dawned on her that by shouting at him, she'd probably only undermined his confidence in her even more. She wasn't proud of herself – she'd treated him badly, but for the first time in her life, she realized that if she was going to have a successful relationship

214

it had to be on equal terms. Going out with someone because she liked them, and they adored her, was simply not enough any more.

Tommy was gutted. Completely thrown. Jessica had gone round that night to see him and told him it was over between them.

'Why?' Tommy had asked her incredulously.

'I just don't feel we're going anywhere, Tommy,' Jessica told him.

'I don't know what you mean,' he said, 'I thought we were really good together.'

Jessica looked down at her feet. She did not want to see his wounded face. 'I want more from a relationship, Tommy. I think you're great, and good-looking and a lot of fun, but . . . I'm not in love with you, and just having fun and a bit of sex is not enough. I'm sorry.'

'I can't believe this,' he told her. 'I'm sorry, but this is a bolt out of the blue.' He sighed. He had never been dumped by a girl before and this was a new experience. 'Of course if that's how you feel . . .'

'I do, I'm sorry. Look, we were friends before and we should be friends again. You'll be upset for a bit, but soon enough you'll see it was the right thing.'

Tommy looked devastated as she left him. She felt terrible about it and upsetting someone as essentially decent and sweet as Tommy was something she hated doing. Giving him a final kiss on the lips, she could not avoid his utterly forlorn face. It was a Tommy she had not seen before; he who was normally so confident and extrovert. But walking back to Barons Court, she felt a wave of relief coming over her; she'd done the right thing and a weight had been lifted from her mind.

chapter eighteen

Flin's Annus Grows More Horribilis

Flin literally walked straight into Poppy. He'd done his bit at
Mr Young's screening room: welcomed everybody in, handed
out film notes and made sure everyone had a drink. But he
didn't fancy seeing the film yet again and with the time coming
up to five o'clock, had discreetly walked out as soon as the
lights dimmed. Out onto D'Arblay Street and straight into
Poppy.

'Sorry, clumsy me,' he said apologetically and then looked
up to see – coincidence of coincidences – just who it was.

'Flin darling, my God! How are you?' said Poppy, flinging
her arms around his neck enthusiastically.

'Poppy, wow! What are you doing here?' he replied, completely wrong-footed, and hugging her with matching
vigour.

'I've just had a meeting in Soho,' she told him in an oh-my-
god-I-don't-believe-it voice; then immediately resorting to
mock-injured tones said, 'Why haven't you called me?
Where've you been?' If she had wanted an answer, she certainly
didn't wait for one – before Flin could even begin to gather
his composure she'd taken his hand and was saying, 'Come
on, I'm going to take you for a drink. You're not doing any
more work now. If they give you a hard time, just say you
were entertaining a client or something.'

Flin felt he should have made his excuses and skedaddled, but something deep within him was glad to see her again, and a few minutes later he found himself in a bar in Greek Street buying the drinks. Why was it that in a city of thirteen million, Flin managed to bump into Poppy of all people? If he'd walked out of Mr Young's a couple of seconds later, had gone for a pee *en route* to leaving the building, they might never ever have seen each other again. Was fate deliberately flinging these challenges at Flin, safe in the knowledge that he was bound to fail?

Standing at the bar, Flin knew he was being weak. If anything, he should have been positively curt with her. He'd not rung or contacted her or even desired once to see her since parting company at Heathrow back in July. As Jessica had told him, he was better off without her. And yet it was good to see her again – she was always entertaining and she did look stunning, all dolled up in seasonal winter chic. Flin also had a cowardly dislike of unnecessary awkward confrontation – it seemed much easier in the short term to be chummy, as though nothing had ever happened.

'I can't believe I haven't seen you since July,' Poppy gushed at him as they sat down. 'That's four months in which you haven't rung me once, you rotter.' She lightly smacked his thigh.

'Well, I haven't deliberately ignored you, you know,' he lied, 'I don't know where all the time has gone. You know how it is. Anyway, I don't remember you phoning me ever, so you can't be too cross.'

'I did actually, several times,' she retorted, 'I left a message at least twice and on other occasions the line was busy.'

Flin didn't believe her for a minute. There had certainly never been any messages: Jessica and Geordie would never have forgotten to tell him that. 'Well, it's very nice to see you now,' he told her.

'And it's lovely to see you. Especially looking so dapper in your suit,' she cooed.

Flin laughed. 'I can look smart when necessary, you know,' he told her.

'And you have forgiven me about Italy, haven't you?' she continued. 'Poor Flin, it must have been a bit nightmarish for you. And I'm sorry my mother was so strident. She was being particularly over-the-top that week.'

It was hardly Liz who had been the problem, Flin thought to himself. If he'd been having the most romantic time of his life, Liz could have waxed lyrical about Giotto and co. as much as she wanted and he'd not have cared a jot. No, the problem had been totally Poppy rejecting him; it was her fault, and her fault alone that his holiday had been ruined.

'Look, it really doesn't matter,' he assured her, 'anyway, we still had some funny times.' She visibly brightened. God, why was he such a sucker? he chastised himself. She'd reappeared, looking amazing, seemed delighted to see him, thrown in a compliment or two and semi-apologized, and he'd fallen for it, letting her off the hook entirely for ruining his holiday and, for a short while, his life. What was worse, he knew she'd only been trying to make herself feel better – and still he toed the line. Falling for her transparent guile was pathetic.

Chatting on, they skimmed vaguely over each other's job situations and what they'd been up to recently. Light and inconsequential.

'So who's the lucky girl who's snapped you up then?' Poppy asked eventually. Flin looked for the hint of facetiousness, but there was none.

'No one at the moment actually, Poppy. Barren times, I'm afraid,' he confessed.

'Well, we're in the same boat then,' she told him, casually lighting a cigarette in the way he remembered she always did. 'Mark and I have split up.'

'When?' was all Flin could think of to say.

'Last week. But to be honest, things haven't been going well for months now. So you see, I should never have spurned you after all.' She looked at him quizzically for a second and then turned to take a sip of her wine. Flin's heart started to race. Was this a come-on? No, he was being stupid. She was just flattering him a bit, that was all.

'So what happened?' he asked, trying not to let ideas slip into his head.

'Oh, you know, he continued to act as if I was hardly there and as though I was of zero importance in his life. I got so fed up of being made to feel worthless. In the end we had a big argument about it and I accused him of having an affair and then he stormed out.'

'Had he?'

'I don't know. Don't think so. Unless you count pubs and sport.' She shrugged.

'So you haven't actually finished it then?' Flin said, suddenly feeling less optimistic.

'Oh no, we definitely have. I haven't seen or heard from him for over a week now, and if he thinks he can come back and expect to be forgiven, he's hugely wrong. I'm not making that mistake again, I can tell you.' She suddenly placed her hand on his. 'You're lovely, you know. I'm sorry things never worked out between us. I'm sure I'd have been far better off with you.'

She was being quite blatant with him now, and he couldn't help mad thoughts zipping across his brain: might he end up with her after all, Italy nothing more than an ill-judged blip? Was this her way of trying to tell him it had all been one huge mistake? And she seemed so particularly alluring, he felt he could forgive her anything. He tried to give one of his most winsome smiles and, feeling his confidence growing, he suggested, 'Should we get some supper?' He hoped he sounded casual, as though this was the most obvious thing in the whole world to do. Really, he should have been heading home: he was due to meet Geordie and Tommy for a drink. Well, he was sure they wouldn't hold it against him – and if they did, that was too bad.

'I think we should.' Poppy smiled back at him. 'I certainly don't have any plans tonight.'

Having found a snug little place off Broadwick Street, Poppy had spent the first part of the meal talking about Mark; the compliments to Flin seemed to have dried up. It was just beginning to become tiresome.

'Look, Poppy,' he said, filling her glass once more, 'you're a stunning girl in every respect – you can do better than Mark.' He felt by now he was licenced to return compliments and hoped he sounded conclusive.

'Yes, you're right. I can do better than him,' she said, punching the air to emphasize her resolve.

'That's the spirit,' Flin told her and they both laughed.

Then she said, 'I'm sorry to go on about it. You don't want to hear all about me and Mark, do you?' She was dead right, thought Flin; taking his lack of response as an affirmative, she resolutely added, 'Right – subject closed. Let's talk about something else.'

Throughout the rest of the meal she was true to her word. Witty and amusing as ever, she made Flin laugh out loud, so that for whole minutes at a time he quite forgot about what had gone before and remembered why he'd liked her so much. She was fun to be with and he was enjoying himself.

As they left the restaurant, the initiative was there for the taking, but Flin lost his nerve and could only mumble, 'Right then. Well . . .' When it boiled down to it, the fear of rejection was greater than his carnal desires; that was how much his confidence had shrunk of late.

He needn't have worried, though, as Poppy matter-of-factly said in the tones of one confident of landing her catch, 'You are coming back to my flat, aren't you?' Flin hardly dared to believe what he'd heard. This was more like it.

'Sure,' he replied eagerly, as she raised her hand and began scouting for taxis. They picked one up in a trice, and in the back seat, Poppy took his hand once more.

'It's been so lovely to see you again,' she purred, 'I've had a really fun evening. And so unexpected!'

Flin was feeling buoyant, and the depression that had been

hovering over him for the last few months was disappearing like the mist from a steamed-up mirror by an open window. Now that Mark was off the scene, perhaps he did have a chance for a future with Poppy. After all, why not? She'd clearly taken to him before, and it appeared was doing so again. All these thoughts were suggestively furrowing into his mind when Poppy, interrupting his jangled musings, said, 'I probably shouldn't do this, but I'm finding you simply impossible to resist.' She twinkled at him mischievously and then, displaying a notable amount of concupiscence, she was kissing him, her tongue doing interesting things with his. How fickle fate could be, Flin thought as his jaw muscles started to ache.

The cabbie brought them round by announcing they had reached Prince of Wales Drive.

'Oh, God, how embarrassing,' laughed Poppy, 'caught out snogging in the back of a cab!'

Flin was laughing too, almost recklessly, then they were dashing up the stairs and outside her door, Poppy fumbling for her keys. Once inside, they could barely get their clothes off quickly enough. Poppy slammed the door shut, leant against it, giggling and kissing Flin at the same time, her hands frantically tugging at his coat, jacket and tie. Flin felt supremely aroused and responded by pulling desperately at her sleeves. Somehow, between the gropes, fumbling and laughter, they stumbled into her sitting room, the debris of their discarded clothing left in their wake.

'You are bloody gorgeous!' he told her as he kissed her naked body. He meant it. Never had he felt more turned on in his life. This was more exciting than their *al fresco* dallying in Sussex. More urgent, more carnal. Within moments, Poppy was tightly holding onto his hair and moaning – fantastic! thought Flin – quite volubly, while he put into practice some tips he'd picked up from one of Jessica's copies of *Cosmo*. From his vantage point, he could see the perfect curves of her breasts rising and falling in quickening movements, her bud-like nipples prominent; he could see the slightly concave

221

pale skin of her belly and felt his head juddered by the involuntary movements of her pubis. Then he felt her tense, arch her back and she pulled even more tightly onto his hair. It hurt, but in the best possible way. She grinned a Cheshire cat smile and pulled him upwards, guiding him into her. Knowing he wasn't going to last long, he thrust into her as hard and furiously as he could. 'Oh yes!' she cried, and then again, her fingernails digging into his back. Flin couldn't help gasping too. It was without doubt the best sex he'd ever had, and frankly, he wanted more. Right then, he felt like making love to Poppy for ever.

Afterwards they remained for a while clinging onto each other.

'I'm exhausted!' said Poppy, still panting.

'Me too,' agreed Flin, feeling his face flush after his exertions. Extricating herself, Poppy stood up, and walked sprightly out to the bathroom, leaving Flin feeling curiously conspicuous. Various bits of his clothing lay by the doorway, while he sat in the middle of the room, white of body and limply swollen of penis. But waiting there for something to happen, he felt well pleased: the whole evening had been fantastic, not just his triumphant return to sexual activity.

'D'you want a shower, or are you going to sit there all night baring your wares?' Poppy asked him a short while later, reappearing with wet hair and a towel wrapped around her. She stooped to pick up various items of clothing. 'Goodness, we were in a hurry. You can tell we haven't had much of it recently.' She smiled at him and blew him a kiss. Then he got up and ambled into the bathroom himself, vaguely hoping she might follow.

But she didn't, and when he'd finished, found her lying in bed, virtually hidden under her enormous thirteen-tog duvet. They chatted for a short while, stroked hair and limbs, but there was to be no sexathon that night. She said lightly, 'So are you going to look after me?' and Flin assured her he would. Soon after, she fell asleep. If he was slightly conscious of her ardour cooling a smidgen, he didn't let it bother him: it was late, they'd both drunk quite a lot, had very energetic sex and it was mid-week. Instead he just happily watched her sleep. The orange neon from the streetlights outside glowed through her thin cotton curtains, so he could see her quite clearly. Her mouth was slightly ajar and occasionally her eyelids slightly flickered. She seemed younger, quite vulnerable, and he watched her fondly, with hope in his heart.

Waking early the next morning and aware that he had to make his way to Barons Court before going into work, he rose as stealthily as he could, kissed her lightly on the cheek and let himself out. It was a cold morning, and still dark. Even so, the city seemed to have long since awoken and, not feeling fully awake, narrowly avoided being knocked down crossing over to Battersea Park. Feeling slightly indecisive as to the best home, and distrusting buses, he decided to walk to Sloane Square. The dim light of the still-lit lamps in the park betrayed the frost that covered the ground; and the tiny crystals stretching over the tarmac made for slippery walking, so he scrunched across the grass instead, leaving wayward tracks behind him. The park was quiet, unaccustomed to the frost. There were the all-weather dog walkers, but the chill air and slippery roads seemed to have deterre the joggers. Flin buried his hands deep into his overcoat and felt the cold bite the edge of his ears. He could see his breath. It was the sort of winter's day he really liked – crisp and clear, with the promise of bright sunshine lighting up the heart of it. He was feeling pleased with himself, convinced that this time all would be well. It may have been pure chance that they had bumped into each other, but surely that was some kind of providence. Their conversation had flowed so easily, and both so clearly enjoyed the other's company. They'd laughed a lot. And then afterwards: the taxi ride, making love on the sitting-room floor. Why, it had been great! Surely she felt the same. Surely? Hadn't she said as much? Hadn't she asked him to look after her? She could not spurn him again. It defied logic. Ambling out of the park and across Chelsea Bridge, he continued to feel elated.

Back at Barons Court, he'd missed Jessica, but Geordie was just about to leave as he wandered in.

'What happened to our drink?' he grunted.

'Yeah, sorry about that, but I knew you wouldn't mind,' Flin replied cheerfully, slapping his friend on the back.

'Yeah well, you missed out. I went out with Tommy and Josh and had a huge night of it. Tommy was still drowning his sorrows, but he seemed to perk up by the end.'

'Great – so you didn't need me there, did you?'

Geordie ignored that comment, then, putting on his coat, asked, 'So, come on, who was it?' There could be no other reason for being out all night.

'Poppy,' Flin told him triumphantly, and then, seeing Geordie's aghast expression, continued, 'I know what you're thinking, but things have changed. She's single at the moment, and from how things went last night, I think you can expect to see a bit more of her from now on. Honestly, Geordie, it was great. She was just gagging for it.'

'Well, that's amazing – congratulations. I've got to go now, but make sure you tell me everything later.'

'So am I forgiven?' Flin asked him.

'Just about,' Geordie replied, shutting the front door.

At the time, Geordie had been a bit annoyed by Flin's no-show, but it had been good to see Tommy and Josh. He'd realized that he'd been so pre-occupied with Molly that apart from rugby training and matches, he'd not seen much of his friends recently; a night in the pub with just the boys had been really fun. By the time he'd left, Tommy was very drunk, announcing loudly to Geordie and Josh – and everyone else in the vicinity – that he was not going to take Jessica's rejection lying down; instead he was really going to let his hair down, get back to his old pulling ways and play even more rugby than usual.

'To be frank,' he told Geordie, showering him in spittle, 'it will be good to have my life back. No more pandering to Jessica and doing what she wants to do all the time. *Carpe diem*, as they say. Sheeze the day.'

Geordie too had drunk more than he'd intended. Part of his policy of trying harder at work meant cutting down on mid-week drinking. Furthermore, Molly had pointed out that beer throughout the week was not good for him. He would get fat, she told him. This was patently ridiculous, as Geordie had always been thin as a rake, but none the less he felt going to work without a hangover was probably a good thing. Certainly he'd been feeling more alert, and over the last few months had made it his quest to learn as much about the company and industry as he possibly could. Looking back, he realized just how blinkered he used to be: doing his own job and nothing more, not wishing to know or understand how he fitted into the bigger picture. The most important thing he'd learnt was Burt's overwhelming desire to find a way to cut out the middle man. As their business stood, the route from manufacturer to market was achieved through resellers and distributors and was known in business parlance as 'the Channel'. Burt wanted to cut out this channel and go what he called the 'Robin Hood' route. 'We take from the rich and give to the poor,' he told him. Thinking about it, Geordie could see what he meant; instead of selling in mass to big, rich distributors, he wanted to sell direct to the individual buyer. But how? This was the key question, as setting up as distributor as well as manufacturer would obviously cost a great deal of money and was high in risk. It sounded simple enough on paper, but in reality – well, that was a different ball game altogether. Nevertheless, as Geordie continued meeting and making presentations to his distributors, it was a dilemma that he spent a considerable amount of time thinking about. And that day, Geordie drove to work with a feeling of eager anticipation. He had the seeds of an idea which he was anxious to put to Burt.

* * *

Flin had to be out of the office for the middle part of the day, but when he got back later that afternoon, there were two messages for him to call Jessica.

'Darling, what's all this I hear?' she said to him when he finally got through. Flin told her: told her about the drinks, then the dinner, told her how well they'd got on, and how now Mark was out of the way he felt all would be well. 'After all, she's not going to demand mad, passionate sex and then sling me out onto the street, is she?'

'Well, I think you're mad,' Jessica told him flatly. 'I hope I'm proved wrong, but I'd have thought that there's every chance she'll do just that. After all, she has before. And there is such a thing as a comfort shag, you know.'

'But she virtually said she wanted us to be together. Come on, J, can't you be a bit pleased for me? Do you need to be quite so catty?' he retorted.

'I'm not being catty – I'm just giving you a bit of female insight. Just don't get too carried away yet.'

Their conversation left him feeling niggled – he was conscious that his lame defence had sounded just that, but still he remained undaunted. He'd thought she'd be delighted that he'd found someone else once more, especially after what had happened between them. Anyway, what did Jessica know? She hadn't been there, had she? Jessica had never approved of Poppy, she'd admitted as much.

This was true, but really only because she felt protective towards Flin, and so disliked Poppy on principle for treating her friend badly. Her heart had sunk as soon as Geordie told her what had happened and she felt concerned at just how delighted Flin was. For all his cynicism in some areas, he had a remarkably trusting nature when it came to people. The strain on their friendship seemed to have been slowly easing over the last couple of weeks and she felt a wave of affection and concern for him. It was so typical of Flin to assume that all would be well, largely on the basis that Poppy would not ditch him twice.

But that was exactly what Poppy did when she rang him later that evening.

'Hi, Poppy,' he said excitedly as soon as he heard her voice. And then his heart started to beat rapidly and he felt himself frozen to the spot. He could feel himself reddening and an enormous sinking feeling overpowering him.

'Flin, about last night . . .' she began, a harder, less ebullient tone in her voice giving off exactly the desired message. He could say nothing, just wait for the next line. 'I've been thinking about our evening all day, but it was a mistake to sleep with you. I'm not over Mark yet, and it wouldn't be fair to you to . . .'

'I see,' said Flin. This was awful.

'I don't want to hurt you, and I do think you're lovely. I want us to be tremendous friends – but not lovers.'

Flin did not say anything. What was there to say?

'Flin? Don't be too upset, I'm not worth it, honestly,' she said in softer tones.

'No, no, I'm fine, Poppy. That's fine. I mean, I guessed it was just a one-night stand.' He felt choked. He'd been hit where it really hurts.

'Oh, good, then we can be friends then?' She sounded relieved, eager almost.

'Of course we can. You bet. Ring me whenever,' he told her and put the receiver down. That was quite enough bravery for one night. For a few moments he stood rooted to the spot. God, he felt so humiliated, his pride battered to a pulp, and the thought of never sleeping with that gorgeous-looking woman again was too awful. What had he done to deserve it? He felt so sickened, so disappointed. What a gullible, idiotic fool he'd been – and to have fallen for it twice, sucked in by her flattering his stupid vanity. He deserved everything he got, he thought to himself, trusting in someone as capricious as Poppy. Slowly he walked upstairs to Jessica's room. His expression told her everything.

'Oh, Flin, my poor baby – I'm sorry.'

227

'Bitch,' mumbled Flin.

'I know it's horrible, darling, but it's for the best. You're just so trusting, Flin, and that's lovely, but people like her will always take advantage of people like you.' She put her arms around him and hugged him closely, realizing it was a time when actions spoke louder than words, and that 'told you so' comments would be misplaced. And what could she say to someone whose confidence and ego had taken such a pummelling?

Flin was watching but not watching television when Geordie bounded in with Molly.

'So here's the Love God!' he grinned. 'Come on, spit it out, let's hear the details.'

'Fuck off,' said Flin, getting up and stomping up to his room.

He apologized before Geordie disappeared to Molly's flat, but as he sat again alone in the sitting room not watching the telly, continued to feel wretched. Throughout his short life, Flin had noticed that when things went wrong, invariably more of life's trials would be thrown at him, and so it was the case now. That afternoon, having not checked his statements and having not kept any form of personal accounting as Geordie was always advocating, he'd discovered he had much less money in his account than he'd supposed. Then he remembered that this latest balance figure did not include the cost of his evening with Poppy, and he recalled painfully that in trying to impress, he'd paid for the vast majority of it. This left him with a pathetically small sum of money for the next ten days until he was paid. None of his other friends ever seemed to face similar situations. He really had to take stock, get a firm grip of his life, and look for a job with more money.

At least he'd been headhunted recently. It was a better position and slightly more money, but the company was much smaller and the sort of films he would have been working on were less prestigious, low-budget affairs. As careers moves

228

went, it would not have been a great one. He went along to the interview – more out of curiosity than anything – and then turned them down. Flattering, but not quite the thing. Actually, not really even flattering. The world of film PR was quite a small one, and at his level, poaching other publicists was the only way people were hired. Job adverts in the *Guardian* simply never happened. He knew he should be doing better, but the company he worked for was one of the biggest in London and so for any move to be worth his while it would have to be a major step-up.

The trouble was that to date no film or independent film PR company had asked him to make such a move. He needed a few more really good campaigns under his belt; the sort of campaigns that got noticed. Bruklin Sale should have gained him lots of good press, but unfortunately news of the Ritzy débâcle had spread and a golden opportunity had been missed. Bad luck, that was all. He did have some good projects coming up, but felt little enthusiasm at the prospect. It was all such an effort.

So perhaps he should embark on another career. If he wasn't even especially enjoying his job, he might just as well do something he disliked but which paid him a lot. But then again, what was he qualified for? He knew little about computers and had nothing to his name but his English degree. And he was terrible at maths, so that was accountancy out. The reality was, he probably couldn't get a better-paid job even he really wanted to. It was a depressing thought. Best not to think too much about it. Anyway, maybe something would come up. Maybe he would be headhunted by someone who really counted. Surely his luck had to change at some point.

He was still mulling over such thoughts when the phone started ringing. The answer machine switched itself on before he had a chance to pick up the receiver. Their message really was too long, he thought to himself, as Geordie's voice went through a lengthy list of mobile phone and alternative numbers on which the three of them could be contacted. The machine then emitted a series of short bleeps and, adopting Jessica's screening process, Flin waited to hear who it was.

Someone called Geoffrey Bailey announced himself; he was trying to get in touch with Jessica Turpin.

'Hello?' said Flin, 'it's Alec Flinders here. I live with Jessica.'

'Ah yes,' said the voice. The tones were worldly, pukka, Flin thought. 'I'm Tommy Byng's godfather. I believe you're a good friend of his.'

'Absolutely, known each other for a while now,' Flin replied, then, feeling he ought to substantiate the claim, added, 'We shared a house at university a few years back.'

'Well, I'm afraid I have some terrible news for you,' Tommy's godfather continued in strained tones. 'There's no easy way of saying this, but Tommy was knocked down by a van late last night and died on the way to the hospital.'

chapter nineteen

Nadir

For a moment Flin thought it was Tommy he was listening to, playing a particularly sick practical joke. The only problem was that it so evidently wasn't Tommy. Flin reeled. People of his age didn't die – this was too much to take in, too unexpected.

'No,' Flin replied, 'that can't be true. What do you mean, dead?'

'I know it's difficult to comprehend. None of us can believe it. It's a terrible, tragic accident.' Bailey paused, then added by way of explanation, 'It's been left to me to try and let his friends know. His mother wanted me to call you.'

'God, no, I simply can't believe it,' Flin spluttered again, 'I mean, how? What on earth happened?'

Tommy's godfather sighed wearily. 'We're not completely sure, but apparently he was crossing the road on the way back from the pub. It was an icy night and the van braked too late and skidded into him.'

'Jesus, I'm sorry, I'm just so stunned. I just, I mean, it's incomprehensible.' Flin's mind was spinning.

The older man cleared his throat. 'I hate to mention distasteful practicalities, but I ought to tell you that the funeral has been set for next Wednesday at two o'clock, at the family church in Croft.'

'Funeral?' Flin felt confused. 'Oh my God, Jesus, of course. Sorry, it's just so . . . of course I'll be there.'

Tommy's godfather, who was no longer a godfather, rang off. Afterwards, Flin just felt numb. He did not cry. He didn't do anything. He sat on the sofa and gazed at the wall.

Flin was still sitting in the same catatonic state when Jessica came downstairs.

'Cheer up,' she said to him, and then Flin told her. She dropped her bag and turned ashen.

'No,' she said, 'no, I don't believe it,' and then her bottom lip started to quiver and she put her face in her hands, crying deep, convulsive sobs. 'No, no,' she wailed, 'it's all my fault. If I hadn't told him it was over, he'd probably still be here.'

Flin thought about Tommy getting drunk with Geordie, clearly cut-up about Jessica. It was the same night he died.

'No, Jessica,' Flin pleaded, 'it was an accident. An accident.'

'No.' She looked at him, mascara streaming down her face. 'This is my punishment for being such a bitch, such a selfish, horrible bitch.'

At that point Flin cracked too and together, they wept uncontrollably on each other's shoulders.

Later, he managed to regain enough composure to phone Molly and Geordie; Geordie and Tommy were very close mates – after Flin, Tommy was probably his best friend. He too was stunned. He'd been with him only an hour or so before he'd died.

'I knew he was drunk – I should have stayed with him, and then none of this would have happened,' Geordie told Flin.

'No, Geordie, you can't think like that. We've all been drunk before and made our way home. Tommy was just unlucky. It wasn't anyone's fault.'

Geordie too sounded inconsolable. Thank God he had Molly with him, Flin managed to think. Jessica was in a terrible way and quickly retreated to her room and locked the door. Later, Flin could hear her sobbing on the phone to her parents. Flin tried to speak to his own mother, but found that announcing the death of a friend for the third time in one evening was just too much; he was reduced to a drivelling wreck, while his mother tried in vain to calm him down.

When the sobbing had at last exhausted itself, Flin ventured up to Jessica's room. 'Jessica? Let me in.'

Slowly Jessica opened her door, her face still streaked with make-up, her eyes red and puffy, her expression one of blank shock. 'We should try and watch a film or something,' she said eventually.

'OK,' Flin agreed and they settled down on her bed to watch *City Slickers*, which happened to be showing on television that night.

At one point, Jessica could not help laughing, and then looked at Flin, horrified. 'I forgot,' she said to him, 'for a moment then, I just forgot. That's dreadful.'

Flin looked at her miserably; he didn't know what to say.

'Don't leave me tonight, Flin. I couldn't bear it.' And so he stayed, fully clothed, lying sleeplessly while Jessica held onto him.

Flin was surprised that he still felt depressed about Poppy. He felt ashamed about this, as he felt such matters should dissolve into insignificance when compared with the news of Tommy's death. But he couldn't help his feelings, and was sure that he must now have approached his nadir. All three of them went to work as usual – what else could they do? But they found themselves occasionally forgetting all about the death. Concentrating on something else, suddenly a deep despair would fall upon them – despair for the event and shame for having been momentarily distracted. Somehow it seemed sacreligious to feel anything other than sorrow and depression for twenty-four hours of the day; anything less was an insult to Tommy's memory. Jessica also seemed to be suffering from a sense of guilt. No matter what anyone said, she couldn't help feeling in some way responsible. If only she hadn't finished it, he might have been staying with her and then would never have

233

crossed the road. If only she hadn't been so mean to him, he wouldn't have been drinking himself into a state of oblivion and then would have seen the van. If only, if only, if only . . . Geordie came home to the house for the next few days. He too felt a certain responsibility for what had happened. But the pub was only round the corner from Tommy's house. It hadn't occurred to him for a minute that Tommy was so drunk he wouldn't be able to make it home safely. They'd all walked home drunk before – as Flin had pointed out – countless times; being killed as a result was something which had seemed so impossible, he'd never, ever given it a moment's thought. Quite simply, it was something that didn't happen to people they knew.

Flin could not help thinking about his walk through Battersea Park. At the time he'd been day-dreaming about the now accursed Poppy and happily crunching through frosted grass, Tommy was dead. The very frost that was cheering Flin had been the death of Tommy. And at what precise point had it happened, Flin wondered? It must have been about the same time as he and Poppy were giggling naked on the floor of her sitting room. Had he felt anything different at that precise moment? He did not think so, as much as he wanted to have done. The moments between life and death were hard to contemplate. When he and Poppy had arrived at her flat – and he'd missed out on a drink with Tommy in order to be there – Tommy had been alive, but by the time he'd had sex, his friend had been dead. Only a week before, a mere seven days, they'd been in the pub together. Tommy had seemed so particularly alive and was on such good form. Jessica hadn't finished it then. Had Flin kept his appointment would things have been different? He would never know. And there was an irony. If Tommy was going to die young, Flin would have thought he'd have crashed a car, driving too fast in his BMW, convinced he was Damon Hill as he careered round winding country lanes, or in a rugby accident. But instead he was just run over by a van; it was so banal.

Jessica announced she couldn't possibly go to the funeral. All Tommy's family must hate her. It would be wrong to go. But both Flin and Geordie told her they needed her support, and Flin, in his gravest tone, said he would really, really appreciate it if she would come.

'But they won't want me,' she protested, 'I'll just blub hysterically and make a fool of myself.'

'That's absolute rubbish. They'll be offended if you don't go, and anyway, it's not as though no one else will be upset, is it?' Flin argued back.

Geordie was even more emphatic, talking about doing one's duty and saying one's last respects to a friend, however awful; much to Flin's relief, she eventually agreed.

Further complications arose for Flin when he realized that he didn't have enough money for his train fare to Darlington. The ticket sales girl on the end of the 0345 number assured him that had he booked as late as four weeks before his departure date then she could have given him the lowest fare. However, she scolded him, since he'd left it until only five days before he was due to go, then he'd have to pay the maximum ticket price, and that was a neat seventy-five pounds. Having ranted and raved to himself and cursed the privatization of the railways and railway company fat cats, he phoned his mother for help. It was a cheap stunt, he knew, and effectively emotional blackmail, but he felt he simply had no choice. It wasn't something he felt proud of.

'Just calm down, Alec,' his mother told him, after he had successfully worked himself up into another lather down the phone. She agreed to help him out, of course, but Flin felt mean for asking.

'I'll pay you back in ten days' time,' he promised her, as much to make himself feel better as anything else.

'Have it on me on this occasion,' she told him soothingly, 'and I hope it's not too awful for you all.' Thanking her profusely, he told her she was the best mother in the world; it did nothing for his self-esteem.

Many of Tommy's friends came up to Darlington on the same train – old university and school friends who were all now based in London. Geordie and Molly and Jessica and Flin sat together in virtual silence on the way up, and even at the station as everyone milled about waiting for taxis, no one said much. There didn't seem a lot to say. In fact, the four of them hadn't really talked about it at all, seemingly unable to articulate their thoughts. Half an hour later, they skulked into the church, a discreet two-thirds of the way back. No one seemed to know where to look, or how to hold themselves. To smile or look in any way cheerful would have been thought-less, an act of betrayal. The church filled rapidly, and then Tommy's family came in, his mother helped down the aisle by his elder brother. And there, in front of the altar, sat Tommy's coffin. It seemed impossible to Flin that Tommy was lying in there, all stiff and white. He'd never seen a real dead body before, but knew what dead bodies looked like and couldn't help remembering an article he'd read once in a Sunday magazine about a person who prepared bodies for burial – it had been horrible. Trying desperately to put it out of his mind, he was appalled to discover he couldn't erase images of this man preparing Tommy. For a moment he thought he would be sick. When Tommy's father stood to say a few words, Jessica, who had sat demurely elegant in black for most of the time, pulled out her handkerchief, while Geordie looked seri-ous and dignified next to her. But Flin could feel nothing. That sense of numbness had returned. He was not hearing the priest or Tommy's father. He was not really hearing anything.

Tommy's mother wailed as she watched her youngest son being lowered into the ground, a terrible sound, full of unde-served grief. It was impossible not to be moved by this pitiful sight, and everyone seemed affected. Even the men were dis-creetly wiping tears from the edges of eyes. Later, Flin recalled his father telling him of a funeral where everyone had been laughing and smiling as they thought of the deceased. But there were no light moments at Tommy's funeral.

The three of them went to the wake, miserably slurping cups of tea until Tommy's mother came over to Jessica.

'Thank you so much for coming,' she said kindly. She looked terrible. 'Tommy thought the world of you – you made him very happy. I just wanted you to know.'

Flin was standing right by her and could see what was happening. Tommy had never told his mother. She thought her son had died happy and in love. Jessica blanched and stared at her in horror. Then her face crumpled and her legs buckled. 'Oh, God, I'm so sorry,' she suddenly blurted out before Flin caught her as she dissolved into hysterical sobs.

'Quick, Geordie, give me a hand,' Flin called and the two of them, with Molly close behind, led her outside and away from Tommy's mother and the shocked onlookers.

'Oh, God,' she cried again, trying to break away from her friends and kick the wall, 'it's so fucking bloody fucking awful. Just get me out of here.'

'It's OK,' said Flin, holding her tightly as Jessica heaved tearful gulps.

'I'll call a cab,' said Geordie, whipping out his mobile. Molly was crying too. None of them said anything else while they waited.

Jessica did not speak again until they'd gone well past York. 'Sorry,' she said quietly then, 'I didn't mean to make a scene. It was just Tommy's mother. The last straw, I suppose.'

'I know,' Flin said, taking her hand. He felt a deep pity for his friend and looked at her fondly. How ridiculous he'd been, getting so upset over the Cornish fling. Tommy's death had put that into perspective. Life was too precious to waste on wounded pride and self-centred conceit. Since Tommy had died, their old, close relationship had returned. How ironic that their feuding had, to some extent, started as a result of Tommy in the first place. Relieved to be back on track with Jessica, but feeling guilty about Tommy's part in that, he felt a peculiar mix of emotions sweep through him.

Jessica put her head against him. 'It's just so sad, so awful.'

'I don't know,' said Flin, 'I just find it so incomprehensible that we'll never ever see him again.'

'It's totally incomprehensible,' Geordie agreed. 'We'll never see him acting the fool, or wearing his baseball cap, or screeching around in that Beamer of his.'

'It's horrible at work,' added Molly, 'they've already cleared his desk. I really, really miss him.'

'It's just so final,' sniffed Jessica. 'What's got to me is the realization that we aren't immortal. As far as I'm concerned, death is for old people, people like my grandparents who've been around a long time and have had a good life. I know young people are dying all around the world, but not people we know, not people like us. It just doesn't happen.'

They sat in silence for a while, pondering their simple philosophies on death, and then Flin said, 'Another thing that really gets to me is that one minute Tommy was a living, thinking, active person and then next minute he was nothing. I find it a difficult thing to accept.'

'I wish I was a proper Christian or Muslim or whatever,' put in Jessica. 'At least then I could feel happy in the knowledge he was in heaven. But I don't, and I don't think there's anything out there once you're dead.' Jessica didn't know anyone her age who was religious at all; no one she knew went to church beyond Christmas – and now weddings and funerals. Her parents had never gone to church, although her mother was supposed to be a Catholic, and Jessica had always hated being forced to go at school, finding the whole process a ridiculous waste of time.

'I'd like to think he's somewhere,' said Flin, at length. 'In fact, I'm sure he is. I don't know where, but I don't think Tommy ever did anything too awful, so I expect he's doing fine. Probably playing rugby with the angels.' He smiled ruefully.

Days later, they all agreed that however awful Tommy's funeral had been, they were glad they'd gone. Seeing him buried and then talking about him on the way back to London, after days of shocked introspection, had helped them slowly come to terms with what had happened. Gradually, as the days and then weeks passed, they all found life was slowly returning to something resembling normality. There was a gaping hole where Tommy had once been, and he was never far from his friends' minds – but they were still there, and even Jessica began to discover just how resilient the human spirit can be.

PART THREE

chapter twenty

Ring in the New

It was only half past three, but already virtually dark. And it was raining. According to the electronic temperature gauge on Geordie's dashboard it was also only three degrees centigrade. Cold. Cold and dark and wet. Geordie was driving back from Bristol, one afternoon not long before Christmas. He generally hated the short days of winter. Dry, bright, crisp and frosty days were all right; good for walking in with cosy evenings by the pub fire to follow. But these conditions were just miserable. It was the sort of day that made summer seem an impossibly long way off.

As he cursed the rain and mounting traffic, he suddenly felt pangs of guilt about Flin. Flin was his oldest friend in the world and he hadn't seen him properly for ages. He'd been so busy being in love with Molly that he'd hardly been to the house in weeks. Flin was having a rough time of it and he hadn't really been there for him. Determined to do something about it as soon as he possibly could, he switched the car mobile onto hands free and rang Molly.

'Well, we have been a bit antisocial recently,' Molly agreed with him, 'but you'll see him over Christmas. Why don't you go down to Salisbury a day early or something?'

'We could, I suppose,' Geordie replied, 'and he could come and stay with me for a night before he goes to his parents.'

'Exactly. You can go for a long walk and bond.'

'And you don't mind me going a day earlier?' he asked her.

'Of course not. You should spend some time with Flin.'

Satisfied that the all-clear had been given, Geordie called Flin. The usual 'I'm either on the phone or away from my desk . . .' crackled out of the car-phone speaker and so Geordie left a message stressing the importance of his call and the urgency with which Flin needed to phone him back.

Miraculously, he did so after a few minutes. 'This had better be important,' he told Geordie with mock seriousness, 'I'm extremely busy and don't need my time wasted by bored motorway drivers.'

'It is. When do you break up for Christmas?' Geordie asked him straight away.

'On the twenty-third. Why?'

'I was hoping you might be able to finish on the twenty-second and then come down to my house. I thought we could go for a hike and have a night in the pub before you have to go and see your parents. Could you finish a day earlier?'

'Well, I just might actually – I am owed some time in lieu. It'd be fun to have a few beers in the Radnor.'

'Exactly,' said Geordie. 'It'd be just like old times, and I've hardly seen you recently.'

'That's true enough, you turncoat. Too in love to remember your oldest friend.'

'Yeah, yeah, but what d'you think?'

Flin thought about it for a few seconds. 'OK, I'm sold on the idea. Leave it with me and I'll call you back later.' Which he did almost immediately, having easily negotiated the extra day's holiday.

So that was all sorted out, Geordie thought to himself with satisfaction. It was amazing to think that ten minutes before he'd been worried about Flin, and that by pressing a few buttons, he could resolve the problem and still be driving at ninety miles per hour past Membury services.

As planned, they made it down in time for supper with

Geordie's parents. Geordie was already missing Molly, but knew he'd be seeing her in four days' time – and, aware that absence makes the heart grow fonder, was determined not to pine and spoil his time with Flin. And they'd said their farewells to Jessica, who was spending the entire Christmas break with her French family near Lyons.

Over a long supper, they filled in Rosie and John with their latest news from town. Rosie, as ever, wanted to know everything that was going on, lapping up Flin's assessment of his lovesick friend and commiserating about Tommy. With John, on the other hand, they talked about work and jobs and their short-term prospects.

'I'm really feeling almost ready to leave town actually, Dad,' Geordie told him. 'After all, most of my work is out of London. Even Borehamwood is out of Central London.'

'So what would you think of doing?' John asked his son.

'Well, Burt is thinking of moving the company to the M4 corridor, and if he did, I think I'd seriously consider moving out of town. It would seem pointless fighting London traffic twice a day. It's bad enough getting to Borehamwood.'

'Fair enough,' said John.

'You didn't tell me any of this,' put in Flin.

'That's because it's only just come up. And anyway, nothing has been decided. But you know I want to get out of London.'

'And what does Molly make of this?' asked Rosie.

Geordie looked a little bit sheepish. 'We'll cross that bridge when we come to it,' he told her as he poured out more wine.

Later, as Flin was helping Rosie clear away, she said to him in conspiratorial tones, 'So come on, Flin, what do you think? Is he going to ask her?'

'Sorry?' Flin replied, genuinely baffled.

'Do you think Geordie will propose to Molly?'

'Seriously?'

'Absolutely. They're perfect together, aren't they? We think she's wonderful – she's tremendously helpful, you know, nothing too much trouble. And so charming. I think Geordie's jolly lucky and the sooner he marries her the better.'

'But they haven't exactly been going out very long. I don't think Geordie is a man to rush into anything.' Flin paused and then added, 'I have to admit, I hadn't ever thought about it.'

'Why don't you try and find out?' she said, clutching his arm.

'All right,' Flin told her, 'I will, and if he does say anything to me about it, I promise I'll report back.'

The next day, there was barely a cloud in sight. It was a perfect cold clear winter's day, just right for walking. Both Flin and Geordie had woken reasonably early and after a cooked breakfast, headed off with the dogs. Flin had been thinking a little about what Rosie had said and decided to ask Geordie straight away.

'Your mother thinks you should get married to Molly,' he told him, looking at his friend for his reaction.

'Yeah, well, Molly seems to have been a bit of a hit with her,' Geordie replied, then added, 'which is great, obviously.'

'You're telling me: "so helpful, so charming, absolutely delightful". Made me feel rather sick.'

'Yes, Molly's very good at doing the polite and helpful bit.' Geordie smiled proudly.

'So are you going to get married?' Flin persisted. They had just arrived at a fence and Geordie stopped by it and pulled out a cigarette.

'Look, Flin, I don't know. It seems a bit soon. But – and this is strictly between you and me—'

'Yeah, yeah, of course,' interrupted Flin.

'I do think Molly is the one. We have such a good time, she makes me laugh, I find her bloody sexy, she gets on with all my friends – you two get on really well – and my parents think she's wonderful. To be honest, old man, I'm not sure that you can do better than that.'

'No, I suppose not,' said Flin thoughtfully, 'but there's no need to rush into anything just yet.' Selfish thoughts had been crossing his mind. If Geordie and Molly were married, he would no longer be able to share a house with his friend. Part of him worried he would be left behind. And wouldn't their friendship be irrevocably changed?

'Of course there isn't,' Geordie assured him, 'and I don't think Molly's going to run away.'

They were walking an old and favoured route, through the fields and up the hill behind the Haverses' house. When they were younger they'd both had a summer holiday job working for the local farmer roguing the wheat and barley fields, pulling out unwanted wild oats. At the time they'd complained about the paltry pay and the boredom of the work, but now, in restrospect, they viewed those times through Laurie Lee-tinted spectacles. For Geordie in particular, those times were held in his mind as long, carefree summer days that seamlessly blended into one another. How simple their worries had been then, they agreed. How their responsibilities had changed.

At length, they reached the now wooded Iron Age fortifications of Clearbury Rings, and here they paused once more. To the south they could see the Gallops stretching away from them. To the east lay the Avon valley, with its villages and Trafalgar House, nestled amongst the trees above the valley. And to the north, they could clearly see the famous spire of Salisbury cathedral, silver Chilmark stone shining in the winter sunshine. How many times had they paused up here and reflected upon their lives? Countless times. The beauty of the place never ceased to instil a feeling of longing in Geordie, so that for all the travelling he had done in his life, he knew that this was his favourite place on earth.

'It's fatal coming up here on a day like this, isn't it?' said Flin, pulling on a cigarette thoughtfully. 'It seems too perfect. Makes me want to move to the country instantly and lead the simple, rural life.'

'I know what you mean,' Geordie replied, wistfully.

247

'Geordie?' Flin asked. 'This moving out of town. Are you serious about it?'

'I think so. The move's not definite yet. But there is something else which is potentially quite exciting.'

'Oh, yeah? What's that?'

'Well, I've had a bit of an idea for an off-shoot company and I think it might actually happen.'

'Really?' Flin was impressed.

'Well, just maybe.' Geordie had an idea that FDU could manufacture mouse mats and mice, keyboards and other small components as well as monitors. They already paid for bulk packaging in the process of delivering the monitors, so the cost of adding smaller parts as part of the same package would be minimal. The manufacture of mice was virtually nothing and was easy to do. It made sense to offer these other components. Firstly, he had told Mike his idea and after talking it through together for a couple of days, Geordie had mentioned it to Burt. Much to his surprise, Burt quite liked the plan, but pointed out the big stumbling block was the cost of setting up. Geordie had assumed that was that; Burt certainly never mentioned it again. Then, just before Geordie was leaving for the Christmas break, Burt had called him into his office and told him there might be a way to implement his plan: they could make a deal with one of the big computer manufacturers and get financial assistance in starting the off-shoot company. In return, FDU would make the parts exclusively for the computer manufacturer and they would also have a small stake in that part of the business. He'd had secret discussions with a leading manufacturer and they were, Burt said, 'more than interested'. Geordie was thrilled about it, especially as Burt had given him a generous Christmas bonus in recognition of his good work.

'Wow,' said Flin, 'I never realized you were being so dynamic.'

'I didn't want to say anything in case nothing came of it, but I've been itching to tell you. It still might come to nothing, but I'll tell you one thing: it's made work a damned sight more interesting.'

Flin looked across to the cathedral spire, just peeking out above the curve of the hill. 'Well, it seems to me you've pretty much fulfilled the pact: madly in love and full of business zeal. I've got a lot of catching up to do.'

'You'll be all right. You'll see. Everything'll work out in the end.'

Flin nodded wistfully. 'And just say you do marry Molly – hypothetically, of course – would she want to live out?'

'I think so; at least she said she wouldn't mind. She likes her home in Cheshire, but has no great desire to live there. I don't know, Flin, I'll just have to wait and see.'

That evening, after an afternoon of drinking tea and watching films on television, they headed off to the Radnor. Flin was glad that despite the way their lives were evolving, they both still seemed to take delight in the same activities that they had enjoyed so much firstly as schoolboys and then students. It was also comforting to see that several of the old regulars were still sitting at the bar whenever they made such visits, and this particular evening was no exception. Greeting them with his normal taciturn grunt, the landlord automatically started pulling two pints for them, in handle glasses, of course: these made them feel more local and regular for some reason they would not have been able to explain.

Once seated, Geordie brought up a subject that had been bothering him for a while. This was his relationship with Lizzie, Molly's flatmate and one of her oldest friends.

'I don't think she likes me very much,' he told Flin, 'and she's always making sarky comments in front of me, which I can never think of an answer to.'

'It's sort of understandable though,' Flin suggested.

'Thanks a lot.'

'No, what I mean is, they were living together quite happily and then you turn up out of the blue and virtually move in. She probably feels a bit jealous of you for taking up so much of Molly's time, and she quite likely resents having to have an extra person in the flat.'

'I hadn't really thought of that,' Geordie admitted.

'It's not as though you've contributed to the rent or bills either. But when you're there you're presumably using your share of electricity and hot water and so on.'

'I suppose I am,' Geordie agreed.

'How often do you think you stay there? You haven't spent more than a couple of nights a week at our place in ages,' Flin continued.

'Maybe I should try and get Molly down to Barons Court a bit more,' Geordie suggested, then added, 'it's just that their flat is about a hundred times nicer than our grotty house.'

Both freely accepted their house was a bit shabby. 'It seemed fantastic when we first moved in,' Flin said sadly. 'Perhaps we've outgrown it. And I can see that Molly's flat is great. It's like living in a proper grown-up home rather than student digs.'

'I must try and make more effort with Lizzie though,' said Geordie thoughtfully. 'What do you suggest I do?'

'Offer some money towards the rent? You can afford it. I don't know. What about trying to talk to her and showing her that you're sensitive to her grievances?'

Geordie nodded uncertainly.

'One thing's for sure though,' Flin continued, 'you've got to sort it out.'

'You're right. Molly and I had our first major argument about this a couple of weeks ago.'

'Well, that's a relief. I was beginning to feel quite nauseated by your mutual even-temperedness. Look, it's quite simple, Geordie: talk to Lizzie. Have it out.'

As they walked back to the house, Geordie told Flin, 'I love going to the pub like that, you know. Just a few pints and a damned good chat.'

'Especially at the Radnor,' agreed Flin.

'Wouldn't it be great if we both ended up living here for

good? Then we could do this all the time: walks round about, quiet drinks in the pub. It'd be fantastic.'

'It would, although God knows what I'd do down here. But it's something good to think about,' Flin admitted. He had enjoyed their day together, and had put out of mind his recent worries. Stretching ahead of him was Christmas and then Scotland to stay at Josh's place. Then there would be a new year, a year in which Flin was determined to improve his situation, come what may.

Twenty-four hours later, Flin was standing by his family in the village church singing 'Hark the Herald Angels Sing' as loudly as he could. Sam, heavily pregnant and buttoned up to her chin in a long dark coat, was on one side of him, while his mother, Helen, equally wrapped up, was on the other.

Geordie had dropped him at his parents' house early that morning. He'd arrived before Sam and Will, and had spent an entirely enjoyable day helping his mother put up decorations around the house and generally get ready for Christmas. Charles, his father, arrived home at lunchtime and the two of them had taken the dogs out for a walk. When they got back they found Sam and Will there. Sam was not due for another week, but Flin, who hadn't seen her for several weeks, gawped at the size of her bump. Waddling around, she looked in deep discomfort.

'It must be a nightmare at night, isn't it?' he asked her sympathetically.

'Don't talk to me about it,' she answered him ruefully, 'the sooner it comes the better.'

During verse two, Flin suddenly became aware of his sister becoming quite agitated and Will looking down helplessly at her feet.

'What's the matter?' he whispered to her.

Sam just had her hand over her mouth and then, utterly appalled, she looked down.

'Jesus,' he said, noticing the fluid appearing on the wooden

251

floorboards beneath the pew. Will had his arm around her, while Flin nudged his mother, until then obliviously singing on.

'Sam's waters!' exclaimed his mother, a bit too loudly, and suddenly people were looking around.

'Ohmygod, ohmygod,' blurted Sam, beginning to look quite hysterical. 'Will, get me out of here quick!'

The volume of singing became noticeably muted as all eyes in the congregation turned to see Sam and her helpless family hurry out of the church. Flin recognized many of the faces, people in the village he – and Sam for that matter – had known all their lives. He smiled bashfully, and followed the little entourage down the aisle and out through the church door.

'OK, OK,' said Will frantically as Sam sat down on the bench in the porch, 'I'll run and get the car.'

'No,' said Flin assertively, 'I'll get the car; you and Mum stay with Sam.'

'Right,' agreed the ashen-faced Will.

'Bring back a cloth and some disinfectant, will you?' said his mother after him. 'It's going to have to be cleared up afterwards.'

'Mum, do you mind?' said Sam, and then, running her hands through her hair, said, 'This is so embarrassing. I'm never going to be able to look at any of these people again.'

'It's certainly going to be a Christmas Eve with a difference,' said her mother, trying to give her a reassuring smile.

Quarter of an hour later, they were back at the house, and just before they phoned the hospital, Sam had her first contraction.

'Oh,' she said, her face contorted, 'oh shit, this is it.'

'It's OK, darling,' said Will, clearly terrified.

'Try and keep calm,' said Helen, 'and I'll go and phone the hospital.'

Sam was sitting on the sofa with Will on one side; Flin and Charles stood in front of her looking helpless.

'I'm very grateful for your concern,' Sam said, looking at them, 'but could you try not to ogle quite so much? You're making me feel like a museum piece.'

Charles looked embarrassed and said to Flin, 'Come on out of the way. Your sister needs a bit of space.'

The hospital told her to come in straight away as her waters had gone.

'Good, well, that's that then,' said Charles after Will had driven off with Sam and Helen to the hospital. Charles, who hardly ever drank a thing, looked at his son and suggested a whisky to calm themselves down. So Flin stood with his father wondering how long Sam's baby would take to arrive, until they decided they might just as well go to bed.

Sam's baby was born just after seven a.m. on Christmas morning. Helen phoned from the hospital and spoke to Charles who was already up and awake. It was a baby girl, and there had been no complications – Sam was fine and the baby was a healthy seven pounds and six ounces, even though she was a week early.

'So what happens next?' Flin asked his father as he stood shivering in the hallway in his boxer shorts and T-shirt.

'Um, I'm not quite sure really,' his father muttered, 'I suppose we await instructions.'

It was the most peculiar Christmas Flin had ever known. Christmas always followed a strict routine: Midnight mass, Christmas breakfast, present giving, lunch, Queen's speech and so on, but at breakfast Flin and his father felt at a loss as to what they should do.

'Do you think I ought to be cooking or something?' Charles asked his son. 'There's a turkey in the larder. Oughtn't it to be stuffed, or whatever it is that your mother does?'

'Dunno,' Flin answered unhelpfully, then, trying to be more constructive, said, 'Well, when do you think they'll come back from hospital?'

'I'd have thought your mother would be back before too long, and presumably Will will leave the hospital at some stage today, but I shouldn't imagine Sam would be out for a couple of days or so.'

'Hm,' said Flin thoughtfully, 'I wonder when we can go and see Sam and the baby?'

'Your mother said she would ring back, so I think for the moment we should just sit tight.'

Helen did ring and told them that they should all come over to the hospital in an hour. Then, she said, she would come back too and try and get some rest. To Charles and Flin's surprise she said Sam and the baby would probably be home that afternoon. As for the meal, she suggested they should go ahead with it, but have it in the evening instead. They could now celebrate a double birth.

'Ah, yes, quite so,' said Charles who, unlike his wife, was not a religious man.

At the hospital, they saw Will first, who looked exhausted but hugely relieved. He seemed so happy that he uncharacteristically started hugging everyone, even Charles, who, unused to such open displays of affection, nervously patted his back. Flin couldn't believe how tiny and pink the baby looked, protectively held in Sam's arms. And Sam, Flin thought with admiration, looked serene and content, her ordeal over.

'That's unbelievable,' Flin told her, looking down at the tiny bundle, 'to think that was made by my big sis.'

Sam beamed. 'We're going to call her Emily,' she said proudly and then, looking down at her daughter, said in a tone of voice that Flin had never heard her use before, 'That's Uncle Alec, yeees, and he's going to be the best uncle in the world, oh yes he is.'

Flin met up again with Geordie two days later. Christmas Day had rushed by. Helen had been exhausted, but they'd all helped with the Christmas dinner. Charles had even managed to prepare some Brussels sprouts after lengthy instructions from his patient wife. Will's parents turned up on Boxing Day and pandemonium reigned. Helen, still over-tired, had started to become irritable at the responsibility of having to entertain Will's parents unexpectedly. Charles tried to be helpful, but only managed to get in his wife's way, while Will still seemed completely fazed by the whole experience.

'It sounds a lot more exciting than my Christmas,' Geordie said as they started the long trip up to Scotland. His brother was still out in Bosnia, and apart from the Haverses' annual drinks party, it had been just Geordie, his parents and one uncle on this occasion.

'It was complete mayhem,' Flin told him, 'and I was glad to leave when I did. Everyone was on a huge high to start off with but by the time I left the mood had changed noticeably to one of high tension.'

'So what's the baby like?' Geordie asked.

'Small, pink, you know,' said Flin unhelpfully. 'Sam kept on calling me "Uncle Alec". It's a very odd sensation, having your sister give birth. And then there's all that breast-feeding. Honestly, Sam would whip it out at any time – I didn't know where to look.'

It was a long day's drive, especially since they picked up Molly *en route*, but by evening they were turning up the rough track that led to Josh's house.

'Guys, you made it,' exclaimed Josh, hugging everyone extravagantly.

'Are we the last?' asked Flin.

'Yeah, Mr and Mrs Fussle got here at lunchtime and Jim and Katie a couple of hours ago. Come on in and have a drink,' he told them, gallantly grabbing Molly's bags. Flin loved this place – it had been left to Josh by one of his wayward uncles and was the perfect retreat. Overlooking the Tay, and perched on a plateau halfway up a small mountain, it was isolated in the extreme, but ideal for a week of drinking, eating and long walks. There were only three bedrooms, and a smaller room in the little tower protruding from one end of the house – which meant Flin pulled the short straw for the camp bed in the sitting room.

'Sorry, big man, but I felt I had to give couples priority, and I get the tower as it's my house,' Josh told him.

'That's discrimination,' Flin said, although he refused to let himself get annoyed by it.

'Just make sure you have a girlfriend next time, and I promise you the master bedroom – a bit of an incentive for you.'

The next day it rained solidly, with dark clouds shrouding the valley. It was a winter's day that never really seemed to get light, but in the afternoon Josh, Eddie and Flin had made a run into Pitlochry to stock up on drink and provisions, and they had then spent the rest of the day playing endless games of Perudo and Trivial Pursuit on the large round kitchen table in front of the bay window.

But then the rain had given way to a band of high pressure and the ensuing days had been bright and sunny, the air clear and fresh, and the little party had been able to leave the cosy surroundings of the cottage and go for walks in the mountains and along the river. The boys had even trooped off for some golf on the quiet nine-hole course at nearby Strathtay.

One morning they all decided to walk to a mountain loch, not too far from the cottage. Geordie found himself walking ahead with Eddie and before long they had moved onto the subject of marriage.

'Honestly, Geordie,' Eddie told him, 'I can't recommend it highly enough. I just love being married.'

'I'm glad to hear it. What's so great about it then?' Geordie asked him.

'Well, Victoria's my best friend apart from anything else, and it's great to live with your best mate. Also, it's such a relief to know that you've always got someone to talk to and share things with. It's the little things really. It's fantastic sleeping with her every single night. Obviously I saw a lot of Victoria before we were married, but now that I look back on it, constantly shifting between flats was a complete bore. Life is so much easier now.'

'I can see all that. But it's just that it's for ever. Doesn't that worry you – just a bit?'

'Not at all,' Eddie told him equably. 'I find it a huge relief. I know I'll never have to go through that process of trying to pull someone ever again. I slept with quite a few people before I met Victoria, and frankly now that I'm married, I'm not at all bothered that she's the only person I'll be sleeping with from now on. After all, I think she's bloody gorgeous and what's more –' he grinned at Geordie – 'she's seriously good in bed.'

Geordie thought about what Eddie had said.

'Do you think you'll marry Molly then?' Eddie asked him.

'I don't know. One day I suppose. It's a big step.'

'Of course. Personally, I just knew it was the right thing to do. I'm sure you'll feel the same when the time's right. It's a sort of instinct thing.'

'I guess so,' said Geordie, 'but it seems such a mature thing to do. I know we're at a marrying age now but . . .' Geordie paused, then said, 'Do you feel very different now that you're hitched?'

'Not in the slightest. Tell the truth, it feels pretty much the same as when we were just going out, except now we live together. Honestly, Geordie, there's nothing to be frightened about: you should come on in, the water's warm.'

To make the New Year's Eve dinner a bit different from the previous evenings, Josh had told everyone to bring their black-tie kit. This idea had been received enthusiastically, and it certainly added a kind of ersatz formality to the evening. They all made greater effort to make a sumptuous dinner, bought port and cheeses and even some champagne for the toasts. There was an air of convivial harmony; even Flin laughed harder than he had done for ages. At midnight they counted down the seconds then embraced one another and drunkenly sang the first line of 'Auld Lang Syne', before realizing that no one knew any more words. Then they toasted Tommy – who should have been there.

257

Everyone felt emotional, not least Geordie. He missed Tommy, but at the same time felt overwhelmed by his love for Molly. He had never seen her in such an elegant and formal dress and thought she looked more lovely than ever. Half an hour into the new year, he took her outside and, sitting against the stone wall, they looked up at the sky full of stars. He put his jacket around her shoulders and held her tightly. He knew he could no longer imagine life without her, but marriage – that was such a big step. He didn't feel old enough or grown up enough for that. Not yet.

From the doorway, Flin watched them: holding each other, laughing and kissing. He pulled out a cigarette, and wandered round the back of the house to the little stream without being seen. Sheep were bleating in the field next to the house. The air was wonderfully fresh and the mountain brook was burbling on its route down from the mountain. It was a new year and Flin had just five months remaining in which to fulfil his part of the pact. When the three of them had sat outside the Atlas and made their pact all those months ago, he'd had no idea they would all take it so seriously. But it had come to take on enormous importance; partly because of the competitive nature between them, but also because they all recognized that their lives needed to change. They all felt the need to move onto the next stage in life and finally leave their youth behind. Geordie had achieved this: he'd found a new kind of enthusiasm for his work and true love with Molly. Well, now, Flin determined, it was his turn.

chapter twenty-one

Jessica Starts to Realize her Plan

Jessica was in a bit of a predicament: she and Tommy had been due to go skiing with Jim and Katie at the end of January. It had been booked and paid for ages before, but Jessica felt it somehow wrong still to go. Hadn't she done enough to poor Tommy without this final insult? Wouldn't it be laughing in his face to go on a holiday he loved above all others without him? She wondered what she'd have done if he'd still been alive. Probably sold her package to someone else. Or maybe he'd have forgiven her by then and they could have gone together as friends. Whatever – it was pointless speculating, because Tommy was dead. She remembered his excitement when they'd agreed to go, but now the prospect gave her an uncomfortable sensation that did not sit well. The problem was firstly, Jim and Katie still really wanted to go, and secondly, everyone told her it would be an insult to Tommy not to go. And it was hard enough trying to persuade someone to take Tommy's place let alone hers as well. Even Lucie thought she would be foolish to drop out.

'You don't need to do penance, you know. I know you feel bad about Tommy, but honestly, J, you have nothing, absolutely nothing at all, to feel guilty about. Go skiing – you'll have fun with Jim and Katie.'

Jessica looked at her sceptically.

'Anyway,' Lucie continued, 'I can't bear the thought of a good holiday going down the drain. And, you never know, you might meet someone.'

'Not interested. I couldn't possibly even think about another relationship for a long time yet. I'm a menace to men, so I think it's probably best for everyone if I remain celibate for a while.'

But she did go. Her friends patiently worked on her, gradually wearing down her resistance; and since the chances of finding someone to take her place grew less and less as the departure date drew closer, she finally acquiesced. It would be ghastly, of course, but maybe going could be her penance, rather than staying and opting out. It had been Flin who'd put it like this, and Jessica had decided (with a sense of relief) that he was right. And once Josh had agreed to take Tommy's place, her anxiety about going on her own with a couple was resolved.

By the fourth day there, though, Jessica was feeling exhausted and finding the trip a bit of a strain. They had driven out to Val d'Isère in Katie's Golf, which had seemingly taken for ever, even with Jim driving at over a hundred miles an hour virtually all the way. Feeling cramped in the back seat and driving through much of the night had not been Jessica's idea of fun. Once there, they had all skied as much as possible for the first few days as well as going out every night drinking and dancing until the early hours. One night they had all got a bit drunk and tearful about Tommy, but otherwise no one talked about him at all. Still, it was no wonder she felt tired. Reaching the top of the mountain for the second time that morning, Jessica decided to pause, telling the others to go on without her.

'Are you sure you'll be OK?' said Jim, trying to be gallant, but itching to ski some more.

'I'll be fine. I just want to stop for a bit and have a drink,' she told him, waving him on his way.

The bar had yet to fill up, and Jessica found a seat out on the wooden terrace overlooking the mountains and the whitened valleys. Below her swished the skiers, a flash of turquoise, a zip of red, as they started their descent into the valley.

She stretched and lit a cigarette, watching a group of ski-boarders trying to out-cool each other as they shouted and swirled down the mountain before finally disappearing off-piste. Her feeling of exhaustion had come upon her quite suddenly and she felt relieved to be sitting still for a while. Nor did she feel in the slightest bit cold: there was no wind and the sun was shining brightly, warming her face. She thought about what she would do for the rest of the day and decided to do a couple more runs and then probably take a very long lunch. It would be good – and sensible too – she thought to herself, to have a quiet day, alone with her thoughts. And anyway, there was no point going back to work the next week feeling absolutely shattered.

Whilst sipping her glühwein and pondering these idle musings, a small group of skiers sat down at the next table. Not long after, another man walked over to them and then turned to Jessica and asked her if he might use the empty chair opposite her.

'Please do,' Jessica smiled at him, thinking how nice-looking he seemed, then instantly cursing such impure thoughts. He smiled back at her, and Jessica noticed the laughter lines appear around the edge of his humorous eyes. Once he had sat down, Jessica realized she could still see his face. She wondered how old he was – probably early thirties, she thought. It would have been interesting to listen in on their conversation, but they were just a little bit too far away. He did seem to be making everyone laugh, though. Jessica was still staring at him, wondering what he did for a living, when he turned and looked at her, catching her gaze. Immediately averting her eyes, she felt embarrassed at having been caught out; but out of the corner of her eye she was conscious that he kept glancing back at her.

Feeling suddenly conspicuous and with her idle reverie disturbed, she decided to head down the slopes straight away and try and catch up with the others at the bottom a bit later. Coming round the side of the building a few moments later, she glanced up and saw the same man leaning over the edge pointing something out. Noticing her, he waved. Jessica felt quite flustered, and it affected her concentration. It was a difficult run, and a short way down she took a bad turn and lost balance, tumbling down the mountain. When she came to a halt she realized with annoyance that one of her skis was quite a distance above her.

'Damn,' she cursed out loud, dusting herself down, and then struggling to remove her other ski. 'Come on, you stupid thing,' she said as she tried to press down on the clip.

Right behind her, someone pulled up and a voice said, 'Leave it on if you like. Here, I think this must be your ski.'

'Oh! Thanks a lot,' Jessica said as she turned to see the man who had been on the terrace.

'My pleasure,' he beamed and then, offering his hand for support, said, 'Here. Very annoying, falling over when you're on your own.'

'Yes, and so embarrassing having to clamber back up the slope with everyone watching,' Jessica said, smiling back.

The man laughed, 'I know, I've done it countless times myself. Are you all right, by the way?'

'Oh, thanks, yes I'm fine.' Quite tall too, she realized, his even tan giving him a healthy, attractive glow.

'Look, why don't you let me escort you down?' he said, as Jessica slotted on her errant ski. Taken with his gallantry, she felt it would be rude to refuse his kind offer.

'That would be lovely, thank you.'

Despite being an extremely accomplished skier, the man patiently swooped down the slopes at Jessica's less assured pace. At the bottom, 'Made it,' he said to her. 'My name's Titus by the way.'

'Well, thank you, Titus. I'm Jessica.' They stood together for a moment, neither of them quite sure what to say or do next. Jessica did a quick scan but could not see the others anywhere in sight.

'Are you with friends?' Titus asked, following her gaze.

'Yes, I was really supposed to meet them up at the top, but I thought they might just be down here.'

'Well, shall we go back up then?' he said. Jessica really liked his voice. It was gentle and assured. She had thought she would stay put but Titus seemed so polite and charming that to rebuff his offer of company would, she felt sure, seem churlish. Anyway, where was the harm in just chatting?

'OK then,' she said to him. 'Great.'

As they stood in the queue and were then slowly winched up the mountain, Titus took the trouble to ask her all about herself. Talking quite freely, Jessica found herself telling him all about her life in London, and how she and friends had driven down that week and why she had been sitting on her own, although she was careful not to mention Tommy – after all, what was the point? She didn't want to depress him as well. As she chatted, quite freely now, Titus listened attentively, looking thoughtful about and interested in all she said.

'Gosh, I haven't even asked you what you do,' she said as they approached the top.

'I suppose I'm a farmer, really,' he told her, 'I've got some land in Norfolk, but I also run a racing circuit as well.'

'Wow!' said Jessica, impressed. 'What sort of racing?'

'Cars. It only really runs during the summer, but we have a lot of fun with it and it's a good sideline to the farming.'

'What a very nice life you must lead,' Jessica told him.

'I think so,' he grinned at her, 'I'm very lucky. Very lucky indeed.'

'I can see Jim and Josh,' said Jessica involuntarily.

'Well, it's been very nice talking to you,' said Titus. 'Perhaps if you decide to take it easy again tomorrow, I could give you lunch?'

Jessica felt the hairs on the back of her neck stand up at the prospect; he really was very gorgeous. 'That's a deal,' she smiled, 'and I can assure you I will be taking it easy.'

'Who was that?' Jim asked her as she went over to join them.

'Don't know,' she lied. 'Just someone on the lift.'

'You seemed to be having a nice chat,' he said with just the faintest hint of suspicion.

'Yes, he was quite friendly,' she said indifferently. 'How's the skiing been?'

Was she being terrible? New waves of guilt swept over her. He had seemed so nice, so gentlemanly and ... mature and self-assured. But she'd been chatting to him, nothing more, and the next day they were only meeting for a bit of lunch. It wasn't as though she was having passionate sex with him or anything. And after the holiday she'd very probably never see him again. No one could possibly think ill of her. But she did feel ashamed, ashamed that she was suddenly thinking less about Tommy and more about this suave landowner from Norfolk. Well, the others must never know. She might feel a hypocrite and an appalling cow but not enough of one to make her miss her date.

The next day, Jessica ingeniously managed to extricate herself from the others, telling them she wanted another quiet morning, but would meet them for lunch in a bar at the bottom of the runs at around two-ish. And she had arranged with Titus, before she slid off the lift, that they'd meet in a different bar at midday. The others were all quite happy anyway – they were better skiers than her; she only held them up and prevented them doing all the off-piste skiing that Josh, in particular, loved. And at least Lucie would approve – hadn't she suggested she should try and meet someone new?

Throughout their little lunch date, Titus was utterly charming. So gentlemanly, Jessica thought, carefully filling up her glass and asking her whether there was anything she needed at regular intervals. And he seemed so interested in her, and what she had to say. All the same, she did manage to find out a bit more about him too. He was thirty-two, and had worked in the City straight after university, but then his father had become ill. This made him decide to leave London and go to Cirencester for a year so he could take over the running of the farm. He loved it, he said, and could not imagine going back to work in London.

'But I do still come down quite a lot. A lot of my friends, including the people I'm with out here, live and work there. To be honest, Jessica,' he said, holding her gaze perfectly, 'I find that's the best way with London: I make fairly regular visits and gain all the benefits without the hassle.'

What about his father? Jessica asked him.

'He died, sadly. It was a hard blow, but by the end it was the best thing for him. My mother has remarried though, which is great for her. They don't live in the house any more, but they're fairly close. So it's just me who rattles around the place at the moment.'

Jessica felt as though she could have carried on talking to him all afternoon, but the time was approaching for her to meet up with the others.

'I've had a lovely time, Titus, and thank you so much for lunch,' she said after he'd insisted on paying.

'I've had a great time too,' he replied.

'Well then,' said Jessica, 'goodbye – and thank you for keeping me company.' She gave him a light kiss on the cheek.

'Maybe I can call you when I'm next in London,' he said, hopefully.

'I'd love that, please do,' she smiled back, although she doubted he would. Perhaps that was for the best. Nothing had happened; honour had been maintained. All the same, she couldn't remember ever liking someone so much so instantly, and maybe a few months down the line, if she met him again . . . it was a tantalizing thought.

Yet as the days passed and she returned to London, she thought of him less and less. Moreover, a few days after her return, she was distracted by some good news. She had gone into work as normal and, feeling in a bar-stool mood, had taken her position against the long curved counter by the tropical fish tanks. Not long after, her boss had ambled over.

'Would you mind swapping places?' he said to the person sitting next to her.

'Not at all,' said the junior account executive who'd been harbouring a secret crush on Jessica ever since he'd joined.

'Hi, Damien,' said Jessica apprehensively. What was all this about?

'Hi. How are you getting on with that?' Jessica was developing an advertising strategy for a new shampoo.

'Fine, I think,' she nodded. 'I'm quite pleased actually.'

'Good, excellent.' Damien rubbed his chin thoughtfully, looked at Jessica sternly and then broke into a smile. 'Promotion time!' he whispered at last, beaming at her.

'Really?' said Jessica eagerly.

'Yeah, really. Come on, let's go out. I'll get you breakfast.'

It was such a relief. At last. And what's more, it was a better post than the one she'd been overlooked for a few months before. Damien told her how she was now definitely ready to take on more responsibility. He'd liked the fact that she was hungry for more challenging work and he'd been really impressed with the work she'd turned in recently. Over coffee and cigarettes Jessica discovered that she was being offered considerably more money and would be a higher grade than Rob and at the same level as Richard Keeble.

'You're going to be a key-player here, Jessica – so congratulations.'

After the most depressing winter she could remember, at last things were looking up. She'd fulfilled half her part of the pact and as she attacked her work with renewed vigour, visions of life as a farmer's wife gradually appeared less and less attractive. Fresh from the skiing holiday, she'd thought of life on the farm as clucking chickens, sunshine and newborn lambs, but now saw only muck and slurry. And who wanted to look filthy all day when she could be looking glamorous in her array of close-fitting suits, and coming up with fantastic ideas for various international brand leaders? Kim had also scoffed when, meeting up one evening, Jessica had told her all about Titus and how much she'd been attracted to him.

'I can't really see you as enjoying the country bumpkin life, to be honest,' Kim had sneered. 'You'll probably be expected to pluck chickens and have hundreds of babies. Sounds hell to me.'

'Couldn't I be a fashion-conscious farmer?' Jessica asked her.

Kim laughed long and hard. 'He sounds completely unsuitable,' she insisted bluntly, and Jessica had gone home that night thinking her friend was, just this once, probably right.

So really, Titus had been almost erased from her mind when he suddenly phoned her one morning at work.

'Titus, how brilliant of you to call!' she exclaimed, absolutely delighted to hear his voice.

He laughed, and said, 'So how have you been?'

'Fine thanks, but when are you next going to be in London?'

'Well,' replied Titus, 'it just so happens I'm here today. I've had to come down for a few meetings. You're not by any chance going to be around tonight, are you?' It just so happened she was; she was working so hard her social life had taken a back seat in recent weeks. In that case, he told her, he'd very much like to take her out to dinner. Jessica was thrilled, especially when he asked her not to go home first but to meet him straight from work. 'That way, we'll have longer,' he told her.

She had never told anyone about Titus, apart from Kim, and she now wondered whether that had been a mistake. Not even Lucie knew, and she generally told her everything. Before, there'd simply been no point, but even now, she decided – for the moment at any rate – she would keep him as her secret. There was no reason to complicate matters by having to feel guilty about Tommy, which she would if she told her friends,

267

especially if nothing ever came of her clandestine rendezvous.

They agreed to meet at a little bar off Leicester Square and then move on to dinner at the Criterion; it was with a certain amount of apprehension that she walked the small distance from Berkeley Square up to Leicester Square. Would they still have lots to talk about? And would he be as charming and attractive as he had been in France? It was a worry, but, she admitted to herself, an exciting worry all the same.

He was waiting for her and, dressed in a double-breasted navy pinstripe suit and Charvet tie, appeared far better looking than she had ever remembered. She'd been expecting him to be wearing tweed or corduroy trousers and a brushed-cotton checked shirt. Beaming at her, he kissed her lightly; and after just the very slightest of awkward pauses, they were chatting happily. Jessica's apprehension dissolved into the air. He was delighted to hear about her promotion, and then told her a bit more about his life in Norfolk and the race circuit. Jessica became aware that before he had been considerably playing down both the size and success of both parts of his job. And as he paid for dinner, she couldn't help noticing the gold card which he discreetly placed under the bill. She loved this modesty of his; and his self-assurance seemed to be without any hint of arrogance whatsoever. It was an attractive maturity which, she realized with jarring awareness, made her previous boyfriends seem impossibly boorish – and well, juvenile really – by comparison.

It was a magical evening and she told him so, thanking him repeatedly. 'I really must get home,' she said as they left the warm air of the restaurant for the cold outside. 'Where are you staying?'

'Oh, just down the road,' he told her, pointing in the direction of St James but without elaborating. 'Let me call a cab for you.'

One with its 'For Hire' light on appeared almost immediately and Jessica hopped in. She had pecked him on the cheek goodbye and he had not tried for more. Instead he stood still, waving as her taxi moved away, smiling after her. Was she in love? She was not sure about that, but she was certain she'd never felt more attracted to anyone in her life: his slightly old-fashioned suavity; the courteousness with which he looked after her; and his lack of ostentatiousness. But what about Tommy? she thought to herself, biting her bottom lip as the taxi, slowly but surely, made its way towards Barons Court. Wasn't it terrible of her to want to be with Titus so soon after Tommy's death? It was a dilemma. Perhaps Titus would call again and make the decision for her. He had no girlfriend, that much she knew, but was she the sort of person someone like him would want? And if she did end up going out with him, would it work with him in Norfolk and her with her new promotion in London? She thought of Kim's words on the matter and found she now resented her dismissive scorn. Oh, it was all too much to think about – events would take their own course.

Titus called again two days later and invited her to come and stay with him in Norfolk the following weekend.

'I'd absolutely love to!' she told him without hesitation. Then, to her dismay, she remembered Flin's birthday party. 'But I can't make next weekend.'

'OK – well, the weekend after.'

'Perfect! Will anyone else be coming too?' she asked.

'I wasn't going to invite anyone. Is that all right with you?'

'Yes,' she told him firmly, 'yes, that's perfect. I can't wait.'

As Jessica put the phone down, a wave of nervous excitement rippled through her. That was it then: just as she'd hoped. His invitation was clearly a euphemism for actually asking her out, and she realized with sudden clarity that no feelings of misplaced guilt were going to stop her. But she had to wait nearly two weeks! It would seem an eternity, but there was no way she could let Flin down. Immediately calling Lucie, she confessed all.

'How exciting!' Lucie told her. 'So now you've got your rich man with the huge pile in the country!'

'I don't think it's a huge pile,' Jessica said to her.

'Well, I bet you it's not small, put it that way,' Lucie riposted. 'A six-thousand acre estate is not a little family farm, and you say he runs a motor-racing circuit and has gold cards.'

'So you think six thousand is quite a major estate, do you? I don't think I looked very impressed – I just assumed it was normal. I haven't got the faintest idea how big an acre is.'

'Well, take my word for it, that's a big, big farm. Honestly, J, I bet you he's absolutely loaded.'

'How wonderful,' giggled Jessica, then added, 'but don't forget I was attracted to him before I knew that, so you can't accuse me of gold-digging in any way.'

'Of course not,' Lucie laughed.

'Although I'm not complaining if he does turn out to be fantastically rich,' she added.

They laughed again, but then Lucie said, 'I think you're doing the right thing. It's time for you to move on.'

'I know it is, Lucie. And I'm not going to feel bad about it.'

chapter twenty-two

Birthday Surprise

That evening over supper Jessica told Flin, Geordie and Molly all about it, from their encounter in France to his invitation to the country.

'Sounds a bit mature to me,' Flin told her.

'No, it's great,' said Molly, 'I think he seems perfect.'

'Let me get this straight,' said Flin, waving his fork at her, 'you fancied him before you knew he was a wealthy country squire.'

'Yes, although I don't know that he's wealthy now. He might be an impoverished country squire,' Jessica told him.

'Yeah, right,' said Flin, 'so what if he was poor? Would you still fancy him as much?'

'Of course, although I have to admit it'd be nice if he's loaded and then he can take me on holidays and out to dinner a lot.'

'Well, clearly this is my problem then,' said Flin. 'QED. Girls like rich boyfriends. I'm just going to have to become a merchant banker.'

'Oh, Flin, stop talking nonsense,' said Jessica crossly, 'I was joking. Honestly, this constant feeling-sorry-for-yourself is becoming boring.' She got up and went into the kitchen.

'She's right, Flin,' said Geordie, 'come on, show a bit of fire.'

'Well, it's all very well for you three to say that, isn't it?' Flin retorted angrily. 'You lot are all so fucking sorted. But when's my luck going to change? You've pretty much fulfilled your part of the pact. It looks like Jessica completely has. But I haven't got anywhere. Frankly I think I have every right to feel sorry for myself. After all, one of my best mates dies, I get shafted by some stupid girl and all around me I see happy smiley people in love.'

'It'll be all right. Things'll pick up,' Geordie told him lamely.

'Yeah, yeah, I know,' said Flin, his anger waning. 'Look, I'm sorry, I didn't mean to say any of that. And I'm really pleased everything's working out for you guys, honestly I am. It's just . . . you know, my life is crap at the moment.'

'Flin darling, you need a break,' Jessica told him as she walked back into the room. 'Why don't you go off somewhere and do nothing for a week. It'll be restorative and you can come back feeling bright and breezy and raring to go.'

'Maybe,' said Flin gloomily, conscious that he'd hoped Scotland would have been the revitalizing break he needed.

'Well, I think it's a brilliant plan. You've been gloomy for far too long now. It's really most unlike the old Flin I used to know.'

Jessica and Geordie had another, smaller plan for cheering him up. They'd decided to hold a big party for his birthday, which that year fell conveniently on a Saturday. They felt they had to do something to raise his spirits and had so far managed to keep it all a secret. And anyway, as Jessica had pointed out, they never did have that house-warming they'd talked about and it was about time they made up for it. The two of them had discussed it endlessly: should it be themed? How would they get Flin out of the house the afternoon before? How many people should they invite? In the end they decided to make it a James Bond party – Flin loved the Bond films and they could serve martinis, and it would make it a very easy fancy dress. Jessica got a friend at work to design the invites with a picture of Flin's head superimposed on top of Roger Moore's, and then the two of them sent them out to as many people as they could think of.

'I want this to be really big,' said Geordie excitedly.

'And we're giving them plenty of warning,' Jessica pointed out, 'so no one will have any excuse not to come.' Flin's birthday was, at that stage, six weeks away. Geordie also managed to get his hands on two tickets for the England rugby international at Twickenham, which gave him the perfect excuse to keep Flin out of the way all afternoon and was sufficiently exciting to stop his friend from arranging anything else in celebration.

The plan worked perfectly. Flin was delighted with his present from Geordie. 'I've got to tell you now in case you booked anything else,' Geordie told him, 'but the match is on your birthday, so you won't get your ticket till then.'

'As if I'm going to have anything else to do,' Flin said sarcastically. 'Spend a wild birthday weekend with my parents?' Flin had been amazed Geordie had remembered. Usually they just bought each other a pint or two, and he immediately hoped Geordie wasn't going to expect such a generous gift in return.

'To be honest, I got them through work,' Geordie lied, reading Flin's thoughts and not wanting to arouse suspicion (they hadn't been best of friends for nearly twenty years for nothing), 'and anyway, Molly's no great rugby fan and I thought we'd have a laugh.' Also, he didn't want his gift to appear an act of pity; which, of course, it was.

'It'll be great. Thanks, old man, I can't wait,' Flin told him sincerely.

While Geordie and Flin were at the match, Molly and Jessica got the house ready. James Bond posters and a large self-standing cut-out of Sean Connery from the movie shop in Soho were stuck to the walls and positioned in the hallway and balloons hung to the corners of the ceiling. Jessica had bought Bond music and together they had prepared food and a huge urn of vodka martini punch, singing along to 'The Man with the Golden Gun'.

Jessica and Geordie had realized that most of their friends would not turn up until much later, but had made sure that certain people arrived on time, so that having had a couple of pints after the match Flin walked into the house to find Josh, Molly, Eddie and Victoria, Simon and Sophie, Jim and Katie, Lucie and Sam and Will – and James Bond in his various incarnations staring at him from every angle.

'Happy birthday, darling!' beamed Jessica and ran over to him with arms outstretched.

'Oh my God,' said Flin, 'I can't believe I never found out!'

'It's been extremely hard, as you can imagine,' Geordie told him, thrusting a large martini into his hand. 'I've been itching to tell you for ages.'

Flin was so touched he felt quite emotional. What good friends he had; how lucky he was. They'd obviously gone to so much effort. First the rugby and then this, all in an effort to cheer him up. He'd been such a miserable sod the past few months and he felt quite ashamed: the way he'd been carrying on he didn't deserve to have such good mates.

Sam had even made him a cake, and they all sang 'Happy Birthday', swiftly slicing it up and eating it before too many other people arrived.

'I think this has gone down well, don't you?' Geordie said to Jessica.

'Definitely, I feel very pleased with myself. Flin!' she shouted across the room and signalled him over.

'Darling,' said Flin happily.

'Flin, my love, you've got to get changed into your dinner jacket. This is a fancy-dress party and you're supposed to be Bond.' And leading him into the kitchen, she gave him his present. 'The perfect accessory for the evening,' she told him. It was a model Walther PPK.

By midnight, the house was heaving, and the James Bond theme music had long been forgotten. Josh had appointed himself DJ and around Geordie's music system were scattered an array of CDs and CD cases, as he rummaged through the collection finding songs for everyone to dance to. Flin was at the very centre of the main room, dancing manically with Jessica and Lucie, but Geordie was sitting on the staircase talking to Jim.

'It's good to see Flin back to his old self,' Jim told him, as Flin laughed and danced in the centre of the room.

'I know – I hope it lasts. He's been really out of sorts for quite a while now.'

'Yeah, I've got to admit I'd never really seen him off-form before. He always seemed one of those eternally optomistic types. Nothing gets them down.'

'Well, he's had a few knocks I suppose. And Tommy going off like that.' He trailed off. It was a difficult subject. This was the first big party any of them had had since Tommy's death and it seemed odd that he wasn't there too. Jim gulped at his drink.

'I always feel as though he's just gone travelling, or been posted abroad or something,' Geordie told him.

'Yeah, except that he's never coming back and we don't get any postcards,' Jim replied. 'It's still impossible to take on board. Made me change my outlook on life though.'

'How do you mean?'

'Well, I've realized that you've really got to live life to the full, make the most of every opportunity – all that sort of thing. I know it's a cliché, but you never know what's round the corner, do you?' With that he got up and went to find another drink. Geordie strained to see Molly. Flin was dancing with her now, but unlike before, Geordie felt no jealousy; he realized he was just lucky they had become such good friends. Molly caught him staring at her, beamed and made her way towards him.

'Come with me,' Geordie told her, leading her upstairs and into his room. Sitting her down on the bed, he looked at her again.

'Geordie, what is it?' she laughed. 'You're being very mysterious.'

'Marry me.' The words came out surprisingly easily.

'What did you say?'

'Marry me,' Geordie said again. 'Molly, will you marry me?'

Molly looked up at him and kissed him happily. 'Yes, Geordie, I will.'

Geordie had not exactly known he was going to ask her until a few moments before he did, and even then, he'd wondered whether he might bottle out. He'd certainly been giving the matter a great deal of thought in recent weeks. His conversation with Eddie in Scotland had done something to stiffen his resolve, but he'd still had a feeling in the back of his mind that it would be a short while before he could muster the courage actually to say those magical words. Then all of a sudden, sitting on the stairs talking to Jim, it seemed the right thing to do. Jim's simple philosophizing had made him think. He adored Molly, thought she was stunningly beautiful and knew he never wanted to be with anyone else. So what was stopping him? Nothing. And so with those two simple words he made the great leap forward. Hugging and kissing one another again, they started giggling with nervous excitement.

'What are we going to do now?' Molly asked.

'I don't know. We're going to have to tell everyone here, aren't we? I don't think I'll be able to keep it a secret.'

Molly laughed once more. 'I can't believe it. I'm so happy, so, so happy! Let's tell them now,' she said, hopping up and down, 'but then we must go straight up to my parents tomorrow.'

'Are you sure you mean it?' Geordie asked, his arms around her.

'Oh yes!'

Back downstairs, Geordie found he was unable to stop himself grinning. Tightly holding on to Molly's hand, he led her up to Flin and tapped him on the shoulder. 'Flin,' he said, barely able to contain himself, 'Molly and I are going to get married.'

The colour drained from Flin's face and he just stared at them as though he'd seen a ghost. Quickly composing himself, he smiled weakly. 'You old dog,' and then added, 'congratulations.' Molly came over to him and threw her arms around him.

'Are you pleased?' she asked him nervously.

'I'm delighted, really I am,' Flin told her. He felt peculiarly emotional and worried that he might cry. 'You're the best thing that's ever happened to Geordie – he's very lucky.'

'Thank you, Flin, that's a lovely thing to say,' she told him, kissing him fondly on the cheek, tears welling up in her eyes. In an instant, the whole party seemed to know and while everyone clamoured to congratulate Geordie and Molly, Flin took himself up to his room. He wanted just a few moments alone to take in the consequences of what Geordie had just told him. Geordie was winning the pact hands-down. But more significantly, his engagement to Molly meant the house would definitely have to split up. His childhood friend was finally breaking off their early life together and making another life on his own. He desperately wanted to feel happy for Geordie, and he knew his friend was doing the right thing, but he couldn't help feeling deserted, left behind. Life was changing far too quickly and it scared him.

Geordie poked his head round the door. 'Are you OK?'

'Of course,' Flin smiled, 'just a bit drunk and a bit freaked out.' Geordie sat beside him and Flin continued, 'But I know you've done the right thing. I think Molly's absolutely fantastic.'

'You'll be my best man, won't you?' Geordie asked.

'Be delighted to, old sport.'

'Thanks, Flin. It won't change things much, you know,' Geordie said, 'and I promise,' he added, with a display of sentimentality that clearly cost him a great deal, 'you'll always be my best mate.'

'I know,' said Flin. But things could never be the same again.

The following day Geordie and Molly, still scarcely able to believe they were engaged, headed towards Cheshire and the Duguid family home.

'You've got to be the one to break the news, darling,' said Molly firmly.

'OK,' agreed Geordie, 'but do you think I should ask your father on his own first, or do you think it should be when both of them are present?'

'God, I don't know,' said Molly, suddenly looking worried. 'I suppose you should ask my dad first – he's quite into doing things the proper way.' She looked nervously at her fiancé and bit her lip.

'Fine,' said Geordie emphatically, 'as soon as I have a moment with him on my own, I'll ask him, straight up.'

The closer they got to Cheshire, the more nervous they both felt.

'I feel sick,' said Geordie as they drove within ten miles of the Duguids' village. 'Do you think your father will beat me out of the house?'

'I don't know, darling,' said Molly anxiously, 'I'm really not sure how he'll react.'

It was with a good deal of trepidation that they eventually pulled into the drive and walked through the front door. They had phoned beforehand, saying they would call in for lunch, so that at least Molly's parents were expecting them.

Molly's mother came out to greet them. 'What a lovely surprise you coming up.'

'Yes, well, I just felt I hadn't seen you in ages,' said Molly unconvincingly, and embraced her mother.

'Where's Dad?' asked Molly.

'Out playing golf, but he shouldn't be too long,' she told her as they walked through to the kitchen.

'Oh,' said Molly, crestfallen. Geordie felt the acid in his

stomach churn with a new wave of nerves. The next hour was one of the longest in Geordie's life, as they sat waiting for Molly's father to return and filling in time by trying to sound interested about the Duguids' New Year.

'You seem a bit quiet, Geordie,' said Mrs Duguid at one point.

'Sorry,' he said. 'Still feeling a bit tired after last night.'

'And it's a long drive you know, Mum,' added Molly.

At last the front door opened and they heard Mr Duguid put down his golf bag.

'Hi, Dad!' said Molly chirpily, rushing out to greet him.

'Hello,' he said gruffly and then added, 'Just shot my worse round for as long as I can remember.'

'Oh, bad luck,' put in Geordie, instantly regretting the comment.

Mr Duguid eyed him suspiciously, and then said, 'I'm just going up to change. I'll be down again in a minute.' Geordie was finding the tension unbearable. He kept firing himself up for his little speech, then was forced to calm down again as his moment was delayed once more. And just to add to the unfolding drama, Mr Duguid was clearly in a less than brilliant mood.

When Molly's father joined them a short while later, he fixed himself a drink, asked if anyone else wanted one and then sat down. There was a slightly awkward pause, and Geordie looked at Molly anxiously.

'Well, if you'll excuse me,' said Molly's mother, 'I must just check the joint.'

'I'll come and give you a hand,' said Molly, glancing at Geordie.

'There's no need,' replied Mrs Duguid.

'No, I insist,' said Molly, following her mother out of the room. Geordie felt his heart pounding.

Mr Duguid looked about him and then said, 'Well, young man, good time in Scotland?'

'Excellent,' said Geordie, 'really, a very good time. Um, Mr

Duguid, there's, er, something I've been wanting to say.' He straightened his glasses and sat up in his seat.

'Hm?' said Mr Duguid, absent-mindedly picking up a newspaper.

'It's about Molly and me,' he continued.

'Ye-es,' said Mr Duguid, putting the paper down and looking him square in the eye.

'The thing is, we'd like to get married.' Mr Duguid looked at him for a moment, then scratched the back of his head.

'Mr Duguid?' said Geordie.

'I see,' he said eventually, then yelled, 'Molly! Susan!' Molly and her mother scurried back in.

'What, darling?' Mrs Duguid asked her husband.

'Molly and Geordie are proposing to get married,' he said matter-of-factly. Mrs Duguid let out a little cry and held her hands to her mouth, aghast.

'Is this what you really want, darling?' she said, turning to Molly.

'Yes, it is, Mum,' said Molly, her eyes glistening over.

'It's just so unexpected,' Mrs Duguid said, moving to embrace her only daughter.

Geordie wanted to die. Never in all his life had he felt so awkward. He did not know what to say or where to look, but was conscious he was involuntarily grinning inanely. He couldn't stop himself.

'It's all right by me,' said Mr Duguid eventually, and then turning to Geordie added, 'but, by God, you'd better look after her, or you'll have me to answer to.'

'I promise I will,' gulped Geordie. He wanted to call him 'Sir' and shake hands, but instead just stood there looking foolish.

'Oh, Dad, please be pleased!' begged Molly, 'Geordie's made me the happiest person alive, and I promise we haven't rushed into it. This is something we both really, really want, but we need your blessing.'

'You've got it,' replied Mr Duguid, 'but you can't be surprised we're shocked. After all, one minute you're introducing this new chap in your life and then next time we see him you're engaged. See it from our point of view, Molly.'

'Oh, we are delighted, darling,' said Mrs Duguid, hugging her daughter again, 'but it will take a bit of getting used to. Surely you can see that too, Geordie?'

'Absolutely,' agreed Geordie, still grinning, 'I see that clear as crystal.'

'Well, er, welcome to the family anyway, Geordie,' said Molly's mother awkwardly, and then went over to embrace her prospective son-in-law.

'Thanks, Mrs D.,' said Geordie, aware that Molly's father had just left the room.

Lunch was fairly torturous, but although Mr Duguid barely uttered a word, as time went on Molly's mother started to become a bit more excited. By the time they were on the pudding, she was eagerly discussing dates and churches and how they should place an announcement in the *Telegraph*. Relieved that her enthusiasm was growing, Molly and Geordie happily agreed with everything she said, until at last it was time for them to go.

'Thank God that's over,' said Geordie as they drove off.

'It was horrendous,' admitted Molly, 'but think of it as a test of your love for me.'

'Which I passed with flying colours,' added Geordie.

'This is turning into a big year for us, darling,' Molly said to him.

'I know, but do you think your parents will come round?'

'Mum already has,' Molly assured him, 'and you mustn't take any notice of Dad. He'll be fine.'

Well, so what anyway? thought Geordie. They were going to have a wonderful life together, and the Duguids had given their blessing, hadn't they, albeit with some reservation? And his mother would be delighted, Geordie thought with satisfaction as they headed back down the M6.

PART FOUR

spring

chapter twenty-three

A Life Beyond London

That Friday, Jessica stepped onto the train at Liverpool Street and began her voyage into a new world. Outside, it was still just about light. Spring was in the air and the days were lengthening once more. And then up ahead, summer. Geordie's announcement had been a shock for Jessica too, and gave their date of May 24 even more importance. Not only would they all have to have fulfilled the pact, but now they would definitely all have to move out of the house as well. At least she had fulfilled half of her part of the competition. Maybe by the end of the weekend she would have achieved the second half as well. A shiver of excitement and nerves made her jerk. What she would behold at the end of her journey, she did not know, for in truth, however attracted to Titus she may have been, they had, until this point, seen each other only on neutral ground. Had he merely been enticing her to his lair, or was he really as decent and kind as he appeared? She tried to imagine his farm, her mind producing images of flagstones and barns with straw and the constant smell of animals. But really she had no idea and she could not visualize what the house would be like. A surge of panic swept over her. What was she doing? She hardly knew him, and she'd accepted an invitation to spend a whole weekend with him in a house that she'd never been to before. They'd not even kissed! The train thundered on, the book on her lap remaining unread, Bishop's Stortford, Audley End and Cambridge coming and going, taking her closer towards her destiny.

Titus was standing on the platform at King's Lynn eagerly waiting for her with a large bunch of flowers. As soon as she saw this from the train, her anxiety largely disappeared, and her nervous panic made way for excited anticipation of a simply blissful weekend in the country.

'Ah, you made it,' he said, rushing towards her to help her with her bag and giving her a warm kiss – on the lips this time. 'I thought you might have changed your mind at the last minute and decided that a weekend with someone you'd only met a couple of times might be too risky a proposition.'

'Never in a million years,' Jessica beamed at him.

He led her to his Range Rover which seemed to her positively palatial compared to her Golf.

'This is rather smart,' she told him as they drove off.

'Oh, they're great these cars, although they do rather guzzle petrol,' he told her, then added, 'I thought we'd have supper at home if that's OK with you. I only hope it isn't over-cooking.'

'Sounds perfect. How far away are we?'

'Not far – twenty minutes or so.'

Jessica looked at some of the tapes spread around the car, aware that she had no idea what his musical tastes were. Blur, Bowie, Mahler, Finley Quaye – pretty eclectic, she was pleased to note. 'I can't wait to see your house, Titus,' she told him, 'I've been trying to picture it, but I'm sure I'm completely wrong.'

Titus laughed. 'Tell me how you imagine it then,' he asked her. She told him and he laughed once more.

'Well?' Jessica said. 'Am I warm? Or completely freezing?'

'I'd say cold. But I do hope you like it. Tomorrow I'll show you round the whole place.'

Before long, Titus turned off the main road and they headed down a drive lined with trees and old wrought-iron fencing. Jessica couldn't see much beyond the lights of the car, but then quickly the drive opened out onto an expanse of gravel and there was the house. White, with a huge front door and portico and large elegant windows, it was far bigger than Jessica had ever imagined. To the side of the house were a plethora of outbuildings and stables and a stable yard. Jessica could hear dogs barking excitedly.

'You live here?' Jessica exclaimed.

'Yes,' Titus replied humbly.

'But, Titus, it's so big for just one person!' she exclaimed as they went in. She was thinking of her house in Turneville Road and how tiny it was by comparison.

Leaving her bag in the hall, he then led her through to the kitchen. As he opened the door, two Dalmatians leapt out, wagging their tails and wriggling with pleasure at the reappearance of friendly persons.

'They're beautiful,' Jessica told him, 'but which one's which?'

'The one with the black eye is Nelson and the other is Hardy,' he told her, patting each of them in turn.

'Aha,' she said as she stepped down into the flagstoned kitchen, 'so this is why I was cold and not freezing.'

Titus grinned at her and went over to the Aga to check on his cooking. 'Looking good,' he pronounced. 'Fancy a quick tour?'

Jessica loved it – a beautiful house filled with beautiful things: wonderful pieces of furniture and paintings of luxurious landscapes and Fairbairns past. The drawing room was large and light and comfortable with french windows leading to the garden, while the dining room was more formal. There was also a billiard room, lined with framed photos of Titus and his father in various school and college rugby, football and cricket teams.

'You haven't changed a bit,' she said, looking at one of the pictures.

'I know. I still feel like I'm about fifteen most of the time.'

He hovered uncertainly by the main staircase and Jessica said, 'I think upstairs can wait for the moment.'

'OK, well, let me show you the cellar,' he said eagerly.

Cool and musty, it was perfect for housing the huge bins of wine.

'My God, look at this!' Jessica exclaimed.

'My father laid down most of it and, to be honest, I don't drink that much of it when I'm on my own,' Titus admitted.

'I've never seen so much wine,' Jessica told him, open-mouthed. None of this had played a part in the mental picture of the place she'd been musing about on the train; it seemed simply fantastical.

'Let's take some bottles up with us,' he said, pulling three dusty samples from one of the bins.

Over supper, Jessica bombarded him with questions, while Nelson and Hardy lay patiently in front of the stove. Conscious that up until now, she had told Titus far more about herself than he had told her, she suddenly felt hungry to know everything. She asked about his father, about the history of the house and about growing up in such a place. Eating with relish whilst he talked, she listened attentively as he told her how the house had been built in the eighteenth century on the foundations of a much older dwelling; that beyond the stables were still the faintest remains of a Norman keep; he mentioned the story of how when his father had been a boy during the war a German bomber had crashed in the field behind the house. Then he spoke about being brought up with his two sisters and how wonderful it had been to have the freedom to run about the garden and the outbuildings and the stables.

'Such a happy family and now just you living here all on your own,' said Jessica sadly.

'But hopefully I'll have a family of my own one day, you know,' he told her. His sisters, Sarah older and Cordelia younger, were both married, although Sarah still lived close by.

'I see her and my mother a lot. You know, it's funny, because when I left university I was determined never to come back here. I wanted my complete independence and so that's why

I went for the City. But now,' he said, looking about him, 'now I wouldn't change anything for the world. I love it here. It's become my life, I suppose.'

Jessica thought that was wonderful, so romantic, and sitting there in that large and beautiful kitchen, surrounded by the empty house, she was aware she felt closer to him; their relationship had moved up to another level, the change imperceptible to anyone but themselves.

Much later, they slowly climbed the staircase, Titus carrying her bag. On the landing, he paused and said, 'Jessica, thank you for coming,' and then she knew the moment had arrived. Smiling, she kissed him. Titus dropped the bag and folded his arms around her. Oh heaven! thought Jessica, hoping their weekend would last for ever.

That night they did not make love. Titus could not stop kissing her though, which she loved, but eventually they had fallen asleep (in each other's arms, naturally). When Jessica awoke, Titus was not there, and for the first time she had a chance to take a proper look at the room. She had never imagined having so much space in a bedroom; at one end was a wide bay window and window-seat. Naked, she got out of bed and pulled back the curtains to reveal the garden stretching out in front of her. And then past a few fields was the sea, shimmering in the winter morning light. She had no idea they were so close to it. Titus had talked about trips to the coast as a child, but hadn't mentioned that it was virtually in his back yard. It was a breathtaking view, and Jessica stood for a while in the warmth of the room looking at the winter scene spread before her.

It was a terrible wrench to leave on the Sunday evening and as Titus waved her off from the platform at King's Lynn it suddenly seemed an eternity until she would see him again. She felt she could have stayed on at Manor Farm for ever. London, with its dirt and overcrowding, seemed suddenly a hellish place to be after the wide-open spaces and fresh air of Norfolk, and the prospect of getting on the smelly old underground for three-quarters of an hour at the other end depressed her no end. She decided to think more pleasurable thoughts to while away the time.

They *had* made love that weekend, soon after she'd woken on Saturday; coming back into the room, fresh from his morning rounds, Titus had undressed quickly and taken her in his arms. In his enormous bed, in that enormous room, Jessica had been a very willing partner. The long and sensuous foreplay had made her tingle and writhe gleefully in a way she had never known possible. By the time they finally lay still once more, she felt she had just had the most luxurious sex she had ever been fortunate enough to experience. Later he had shown her around the rest of the house and the farm. There had been no one to bother them. It felt so liberating having the whole of the house and the surrounding estate in which to indulge the beginning of a relationship. Even walking along the beach she'd not really been aware of noticing anybody else.

But what a different way of life! Their two jobs seemed poles apart, and she would never be able to bring him home to London – she would feel too embarrassed, the contrast was too great. Would he like her friends? Lucie definitely, but Flin and Geordie and everyone else? She did hope so. And was she finally in love? Well, she smiled to herself triumphantly, she thought she just about might be after all.

chapter twenty-four

It's Always Good to Pause and Reflect

Of course Flin was delighted that Geordie and Jessica were so incredibly, ecstatically happy and successful from whichever way you looked, but after spending the fourth Sunday evening in a row on his own in their frankly now rather unpleasant house, he couldn't help feeling extremely narked off. It was not that his social life fell apart without them (he still went out a lot and saw plenty of Josh and Jim and co.) and it was true that outside the summer months there was less going on (no cricket weekends, summer parties, no weddings even), but that was not really the issue. No, it was more the fact that within the space of six months everything possible seemed to have gone wrong in his life, contrasting starkly with his two best friends, whose lives seemed to be coming close to perfection. He thought about the last time he'd lost his temper with them and how Jessica had suggested he go off on his own for a few days. Perhaps she was right. In the middle of the week he was due to go to the west coast of Ireland for a couple of days' location work. After that, he'd be less busy at work and could probably take a few days off. Go home, be fed by his mother, take a few walks. Get away from everything – and everyone – for a short while. Tiffany would cover for him, he was sure.

Tiffany thought it a great idea. 'It's just what you need,' she told him. 'You're looking tired. A bit of TLC from your mother will sort you out.'

Flin looked at her: tiny in her hipsters and T-shirt, a hint of midriff between the two, and her blonde hair loose for a change. He smiled. 'Don't you ever feel down?' he asked her.

She smiled back. 'Not really – sometimes, a bit, but you know, life's pretty good really. A man would be nice, but otherwise can't complain.' After she'd gone, Flin stared out of the window, thinking that Tiffany was the most normal, uncomplicated person he knew.

'I've got just the thing for you,' Geordie told him over a drink one night. 'It's one of the best books I've ever read.' Geordie was no great reader but none the less this short tome called *Alchemy of the Gods* seemed to have left a great impression. The author was Paulus Campostello, and Flin, aware of Geordie's penchant for all things South American, suspected that this was a major reason why his friend had been giving the book such good press. Geordie was quite insistent. This book, he assured him, would definitely pull him out of the doldrums: blending ancient wisdom with a modern fable, it was all about following your heart, feeling positive and pursuing your dreams. But, Geordie told him, it was also big on being thoughtful and contemplative; perfect reading for his week off.

'Honestly, Flin, I found it really inspirational. It's just a small book,' he told him, as though this made it more attractive, 'and I strongly recommend you buy it immediately.'

Flin found a copy at the airport. *Drawing heavily on the Hermetica and the knowledge of the lost ancients, this is a book that teaches us, as only few books can, about the essential wisdom of listening to our hearts, learning to read the omens strewn along life's path and, above all, following our dreams*, he read on the back of the jacket. Perfect, he thought, happy to try anything that might lift the mist of his general gloom.

Much to his surprise, he found it utterly charming. He

thought it made sense of the kind of spiritualism he'd always found lacking in religion. As Geordie had promised, Flin did find himself rather inspired and determined to make a renewed effort to put aside any sense of lethargy and pour all his energies into the next few days' work. And once in Ireland, things did go well. He was lucky – the actors and crew were an easy-going bunch on this occasion, which made his life easier. None the less, by exhibiting a bit more enthusiasm and vigour than he'd been able to of late, he generated far greater co-operation from everyone involved. He couldn't remember a location trip that had been so enjoyable or had gone so smoothly and perfectly according to schedule. And at the end of the three days, Flin felt the satisfaction of a job well done, a feeling that he'd almost forgotten, safe in the knowledge he had a week's holiday ahead of him.

As the train trundled on past Basingstoke and Andover, Flin gazed out at the familiar countryside. Spring was very definitely in the air; in no time it would be summer. Initially cheered as he thought of this, he then remembered with startling clarity that the summer meant the end of his old life. Jessica and Geordie had succeeded in their part of the pact, but he had failed – completely. Time was running out. So what was he doing, halfway through his twenties and still running home to his parents?

Although his mother no longer worked, Flin had had little idea how much she was out of the house. WI meetings, meals on wheels, art classes and lunches with friends meant Flin hardly saw her at all during the day. To begin with he quite enjoyed sitting around the house reading and watching the afternoon film on TV, but by his third day there, he felt bored and frustrated. There was absolutely nothing for him to do, and he realized that isolated contemplation got to be a bit lonely after a while. Inspiration finally came when he was rooting around his father's shed. At one end, covered in dust and cobwebs and with a heavily rusted chain, was his old bicycle. How he'd loved that bike – he and Geordie had cycled everywhere when they'd been younger; it had been their primary occupation during their early teens. Flin remembered the Christmas he'd been given it: the disappointment at the size of the wrapped matchbox under the tree which had housed the first clue; then his mounting excitement as he'd been led from place to place finding each little message which led him to the ultimate goal – the brand-new, gleaming ten-speed racer carefully resting against the wall of the garage, a big bow tied round the handlebars.

He felt a sudden wistfulness for those days and decided there and then to clean it up and rediscover the rides of his youth. The rust was not as bad as it had first appeared and with a bit of polish the chrome shone once more. It was not the bike it had once been and he needed to raise the saddle substantially, but riding carefully through the village he found it still seemed to work perfectly well.

He rode for miles. Eventually his route took him to a point where the whole valley opened out beneath him, the long, rippled bank of the chalk downs stretching protectively away to one side. Setting the bike down on the edge of the road, he ambled over to a solitary beech and paused, admiring the view before him. That book of Geordie's had made him think. He'd been pretty sceptical when Geordie had first mentioned it – sounded like New-Age twaddle. But its basic tenet of being true to oneself and striving to fulfil one's potential, however simple and obvious, sat well with Flin. Suddenly his work was more fun again – one simple trip to Ireland had completely renewed his enthusiasm for the job. Of course, that wasn't just the book, but it proved that feeling depressed did little to help your work life. And then he realized something else for the first time: being without a girlfriend for six months or so was hardly critical. It just seemed like a big blip because everyone else seemed to be going out with someone. But so what? he thought to himself. They were older now, and relationships were not so facile any longer. He realized that a major reason for not finding anyone was because he'd become more discerning; he wanted to be going out with someone whom he could be with for a considerable length of time. Not just three weeks or two months – he was ready for a proper, serious relationship. The revelation came as something of a shock, but cheered him too. And he wasn't so bad looking really; he might not be as skinny as he used to be, but he was tall and dark-haired. What's more, when he wasn't wallowing in self-pity, he felt he was quite a fun person to be around. He had lots of good friends, which proved that.

And money. He should simply cut back a bit. Learn to say 'no' if he could not afford something, and make a renewed effort to try and save a little bit each month. Do his damnedest to try and take a bit more personal responsibility. At least without Geordie around so much there was less to tempt him. Honestly, it was ridiculous still having to ask his parents to bail him out, and he determined it must stop. He knew he earned far more than most people – and that constantly comparing himself and his salary with those of his friends was both ridiculous and utterly pointless. OK, so he lived in a city and an age of extreme consumerism, but he should learn to stand up to it. He'd given himself such lectures before – every time he ran out of money or exceeded his overdraft limit, in actual fact – but this time he felt he meant it. Something had suddenly clicked, as though he'd crossed a terrible barrier which had been obstructing him from developing his life. Was it *Alchemy of the Gods*? Or was it the realization that all this time he'd been saying he wanted to progress but secretly fighting it, terrified of letting go of his youth and the lack of responsibility that went with it? Flin smiled to himself and felt the wind buffet his face, making his eyes water. He thought of Tommy. The book had taught him that the whole purpose of existence was the afterlife; it was a nice idea, and he hoped his friend was OK. Aware that he had unexpectedly reached a pivotal moment in his life, Flin paused for a while longer to take in his surroundings. In years to come, he wanted to remember it, to be able to recall the lie of the land and the colour of the hills and the wind making his eyes stream. He wanted to be able to remember that he had given himself a talking to and that he had listened.

chapter twenty-five

Renaissance

Geordie had to admit being engaged was not exactly how he'd imagined. He had thought that, happily hand in hand, he and Molly would skip around jewellers looking for a beautiful ring, that he would be drinking endless amounts of champagne and then a bit nearer the time they would discuss a few details for the actual day. How wrong he was. He had skipped around jewellers happily holding Molly's hand for one day, but they could find nothing that was, well, just right. So they had another crack at it one late-night shopping evening, and then again on the next Saturday. The skipping had turned to trudging and Geordie had thought that frankly, if he never went in to a jeweller's again he wouldn't be sorry. Losing enthusiasm for the hunt, Molly had become cross with him. 'It's important you love it too,' she said, 'so please try and look interested.' Eventually the matter was resolved, Molly deciding that a solitaire was the best design for an engagement ring. It didn't go unnoticed by Geordie that it was very similar to a ring they'd looked at in the first five minutes of their search.

They *had* drunk lots of champagne to start off with, but the toasts quickly dried up. Instead they discovered that they were being asked over to supper by people who had never asked them to anything before, and suddenly realized that these people were just trying to secure an invitation to the big day.

And then, whom to invite? The wedding – set for June – was still some way off, but the guest list became an early priority. Molly's parents insisted on inviting every member of the family and family friend they had ever known, which left Molly and Geordie with fewer numbers for their friends than they'd hoped. And that was before all the hundreds of Geordie's relatives were taken into account. But how were they going to say to so-and-so, whom they saw all the time, that he couldn't come? It was an impossible impasse, and it made Geordie's blood boil. Not wanting to seem rude or to lose his temper in front of his prospective in-laws, he instead took his frustration out on Molly. Caught between the two sides, Molly pleaded with her parents to cut a few names off the list. 'I haven't seen them for years, and neither have you,' she told them.

'But they were very good to you when you were a little girl and they'd be terribly offended if they weren't invited,' Molly's mother said.

'And just remember who's paying,' her father added.

Geordie sighed and bit his tongue. 'I'd much rather have paid for it myself and done it our way,' he told Molly later.

'Come on, darling, don't get stressed about it. Please?' said Molly anxiously.

Organizing the wedding list also proved quite trying. When Geordie had asked Molly to marry him, he had never thought of any of these matters. Rather like the ring hunting, spending one Saturday morning looking round Peter Jones was quite fun, but two or three Saturdays, specially when there was a big rugby international on, made the excitement wear a bit thin.

'I'm really very happy to let you choose everything,' Geordie told Molly generously.

'No, darling, we have to choose everything together. These things are supposed to last our married life. I don't want to decide on something that you then hate.' She was quite adamant. Half the problem was that they had not resolved where they were going to live, so were anxious not to plump for anything that might not match the house they eventually lived in. So that meant everyday items or fairly neutral tones. But then that was boring, wasn't it? It was all so difficult to know what to do and when Geordie did try and take a more pro-active role, Molly simply scolded him wearily. 'We don't need a forty-two-inch wide television, darling.'

However, it did look more and more likely that Burt would be setting up a new separate office in Southampton. Geordie and Molly had talked about it and had decided they would move there if he was offered the chance. Her skills were fairly transferrable and they had enough money to enable her to be between jobs for a while. Furthermore, they were both eager to move out of London and embark upon the rural idyll as soon as possible. Working in Southampton would mean they would even be able to find somewhere near Geordie's beloved Salisbury. The only problem was that Burt seemed in no hurry at all to make any decisions – it was just one other thing to worry about, another matter unresolved.

But what Geordie found most disturbing was the amount of times they were expected to trek all the way up to Cheshire in order to go to church. They had to meet the vicar, then go to a couple of services to look keen and then nearer the time they were due to go up even more to listen to banns being read. Geordie loathed going to church and had it not been for the insistence of Molly's and his own parents that they have a proper church wedding he would have been perfectly happy with a register office. In fact, he was beginning to think a beach wedding in St Kitts would not have been a bad idea.

At least he'd made up with Lizzie. Doing as Flin suggested, he'd offered to contribute to rent and bills. She'd declined his offer, but it was clear she was glad he had suggested it. Then, when Molly was going to be late one night, he had brought back a really good bottle of wine and they'd drunk it together. At last, frankly and openly, she had lain her grievances out on the table. She'd not been expecting to share the flat with two people, nor had she realized her friendship with Molly would change as a result of Geordie being on the scene. 'I'm sorry,' she said to him, 'but it drives me up the wall that you're in the bathroom when I want to be. It's silly, but it just bugs me, especially since you haven't been contributing to the cost of it.' Geordie, for his part, took it all on board, insisted on putting something towards the bills, even if she would not accept any rent money, and said that they should all spend more time together.

Geordie acted immediately by arranging for Lizzie and Flin to meet one another: as best man and chief bridesmaid, it seemed like a good idea. Molly invited Flin over to the flat and the four of them had supper together. Flin and Lizzie seemed to get on well and all of them were laughing as Molly recounted wedding preparation horror stories.

'I had no idea getting married was so traumatic,' said Flin. 'And there I was feeling jealous of Geordie getting engaged.'

'Yeah, you're far better off as you are, I can tell you,' added Geordie.

'Geordie!' said Molly, looking slightly hurt.

'Only joking, darling,' said Geordie, 'but you have to confess dealing with your parents is a bit of a nightmare.'

'They just have different ideas to us. They're a different generation. It's difficult for them too, you know.'

'I know that, but all I'm saying is I'll be glad when it's all over.'

There was a slight pause, and Flin looked at Lizzie uncomfortably.

'What do you mean by that?' Molly was now looking decidedly hurt.

'Nothing,' replied Geordie irritably, 'just that trekking up to Cheshire virtually every weekend and having to listen to your dad droning on and sitting bored shitless in the church is not my idea of fun. Hence, I'll be glad when it's all over.'

'What a horrible thing to say,' said Molly, her voice just beginning to tremble. 'This is our wedding you're talking about and my parents have been more than generous in paying for everything and doing it pretty much how we – you – want.' She stared at him, her eyes glistening.

'She's right, Geordie,' said Flin.

'Oh come on – you know they've been difficult. You said so yourself. And it *is* a hell of a long way to Cheshire. I drive all week and so driving all weekend too is a complete bore.'

Flin wanted to kick Geordie; it was so clear Molly was upset, and he was unnecessarily labouring the point.

'You can be so fucking selfish sometimes,' said Molly, tears now running down her cheeks.

'Well done, Geordie – pleased with yourself?' said Lizzie angrily.

'What? What have I said? Come on, Moll, don't get all upset.'

'Oh shut up, Geordie,' Molly yelled at him, running out of the room.

Lizzie glared at him and followed her out.

'You idiot,' Flin told him after a small pause.

'What did I say?'

'If you really don't know, I'm certainly not going to tell you.'

Geordie sighed. 'Shit. Sorry.' He sighed again. 'You're right. But ... I don't know, Flin, it's just not how I imagined it to be. You'd have thought it was Molly's parents doing the marrying, not us.'

'Listen, Geordie,' Flin said, 'you're going about this all wrong. Remember that the wedding is for Molly and Molly's parents. Your role is just to turn up and say what you've got to say. Stop trying to take such an active role. If you release yourself of the responsibility, you won't have to get stressed out about it, will you? And then you won't end up bickering with Molly all the time.'

Geordie nodded glumly. 'I can't handle girls crying. I never know what to say.'

'Tell her you're sorry. Admit you've been selfish, that you

didn't mean what you said, and give her a big hug. And tell her that she's the most important person in the world to you and you never want to hurt her feelings again. Be contrite in a big way.'

Just then, Lizzie walked back in. 'I think she's going to pull through,' she told Geordie, 'but honestly, try not to be such a dick again.'

Following Flin's advice, Geordie managed to placate Molly. His friend was right: he should be more laid-back about it all. Whatever happened, he and Molly were going to have a wonderful day and he should not lose sight of what was really important. Their wedding day was just the first day of their life together. Spending numerous weekends with Molly's parents was a very small price to pay for the fun which would follow. It was odd how Flin could be so sensitive and sensible about other people's problems and yet found it so hard to sort out his own. Geordie was sure that would change. Flin had too much going for him to be in the doldrums for too long; as soon as he could see that for himself, Geordie felt sure Flin would be all right.

It may have been pure serendipity, or perhaps it was fate; but a couple of weeks after Flin returned to work, he found himself being headhunted. 'Can you talk?' said the voice on the phone and Flin, looking about him and seeing the department was quiet, said, 'Sure,' in hushed tones. One of the big four film distributors in town was looking for a divisional head of publicity – which meant having people working directly for him – and, the recruitment consultant told him, he had come highly recommended. Flin was more than delighted: the job on offer was a considerable promotion. He went for a first interview with the consultant and it seemed to go well enough. The consultant was obviously satisfied as to his delight he was asked to go and meet with the distributor's UK publicity director. This second interview turned out to be highly informal: more of a chat over lunch, in which Flin discovered that the producer of the film in Ireland had been a friend of the managing director and had suggested

302

they give him a call. The job was more or less his if he wanted it.

Flin could hardly believe his good fortune, and accepted the terms and conditions with alacrity. He was particularly triumphant to discover that his basic was quite a bit more than Geordie's, and what was more, his new job entitled him to a company car with a parking space beneath the Hammersmith offices. What a difference the extra money would make. At last he might be able to get through a month without having to borrow money and in any way scrimp and save. He could buy some clothes, and take weekend breaks without feeling guilty. Perhaps he would even start replacing all his old Beatles albums with CDs. He worried he might not be up to the new job and about telling Martina – and Tiffany for that matter – but despite these minor anxieties, his overwhelming emotion was one of huge relief.

'I can't believe you get a car! You jammy thing!' Tiffany had exclaimed.

'Nor me – I've never had a car in my entire life. It'll be very liberating.'

Tiffany smiled and gave him a nervous peck on the cheek. 'Congratulations – you really deserve it. Just don't forget your old workmates, OK?'

'Course not – just because I'm changing jobs doesn't mean we can't still see loads of each other. Don't worry, I'll be calling you all the time.'

Flin meant what he said. He'd taken the office companionship of Tiffany for granted, but in many ways she'd become one of his best friends. He would miss her; it was the one slight regret he felt in accepting the post.

Geordie and Jessica were delighted by Flin's apparent meteoric renaissance.

'It's wonderful, darling, because it was a real worry you being constantly down in the dumps,' Jessica told him.

'I know, it was a bad patch,' he admitted, 'and I'm sorry.'

'Think no more about it,' she pronounced, giving him an affectionate hug.

'I told you you'd be mad to give up your job,' Geordie told him later on in the pub.

'And you were right, as ever, old man,' Flin replied.

'So now you just need to meet your dream-girl,' Geordie continued, 'because you don't want to stay out in the wilderness for much longer.'

'I just don't see it that way,' Flin told him with satisfaction, 'someone will turn up when the time is right.'

Geordie laughed uproariously.

'No, I mean it: I've been far too uptight recently and I've been laying too much stress on having a girlfriend. It's ridiculous, so I've decided not to worry about it any more. If I fail with the pact, then so be it. I no longer care. I've spent nearly a year worrying about it and taking it far too seriously and it's got me nowhere. And anyway, I'm in a position now where I can afford to pay for a night of drinks.'

'Well, good for you,' said Geordie, still smiling. 'Another pint?'

'Absolutely,' Flin told him, 'and then tell me about the latest developments on the job front.'

Geordie's work situation had been developing fast. Burt had struck the deal with Contak, a big computer manufacturer. They demanded a stake in a new mice- and keyboard-making business, but also confirmed orders for a large number of monitors as well. However, these would all have to be built in the UK so that they could have a much faster turn-around on orders. As it stood, all FDU's parts were arriving from Taiwan, fully assembled, several months after an order was placed. By assembling the components in the UK, just for Contak, the process would be speeded up considerably. Furthermore, Contak had an empty assembly plant on the edge of Southampton. They would fund the setting up of the operation and FDU would run it. Or more specifically, Burt was suggesting, Geordie would run it.

'That's brilliant,' Flin told him, 'what a turn-around in just under a year!'

*   *   *

It was during his last week at work that Flin had his dream about Tiffany. He was aware he was feeling increasingly sad about no longer working with her and perhaps that was why she'd entered his subconscious. But this dream had been erotic – really erotic – and he'd woken up feeling an enormous sense of wellbeing. He'd never thought of Tiffany like that; she was just a work colleague, the department assistant for Flin and two other publicity managers.

Cycling to work that morning he thought about her. She was totally unlike Poppy. For a start, she was Australian and only about five foot three, but she did have a very sweet smiley face, her blonde hair usually pulled back into a bright scrunchy. He also liked her clothes sense: she was always wearing baggy trousers or lightweight skirts and plimsolls, her tiny frame hidden underneath oversized shirts and jumpers. He felt relaxed and easy in her company and she was always laughing at the things he said. 'You're so funny, Flin!' she would say and walk out of his cubicle still chuckling. It dawned on him that he fancied her hugely. Why hadn't he seen it before? How could he have been so blind? Perhaps he'd never thought of her in such a light before because she was a work colleague: Flin would never have been able to face the embarrassment of an office romance. But soon things would be different. Tiffany would not be working for him, she would be an equal.

All the same, Flin seriously doubted that the feeling was mutual; after all, he'd only realized his feelings towards her because of an erotic dream. There was no reason why she should miraculously change her opinion too. Or at least, that was what he thought until he overheard her talking to a friend on the phone on his last day. Having gone out of his cubicle for a meeting with Martina, he then forgot something and nipped back. Tiffany, talking just round the corner, clearly had not seen him.

'I dunno, I don't think he likes me that way. I don't want to ruin things,' she was saying. At first Flin's heart sank, but then he heard her say, 'I just think he's so gorgeous. You know we really connect and ... yeah ... yeah ... Flin, I know, it's such a cute name!' Slipping back out of his office again, he quietly shook his fist in triumph. It was hard concentrating during the debrief. He felt too excited.

When she next came into his cubicle, a bit later, he looked up and grinned.

'What are you so happy about?' she asked, smirking back at him.

'Oh, nothing, you know, um, life in general, I suppose,' he replied. He felt bashful and wanted to say something, but was not quite sure how. It was quite peculiar, feeling coy.

'You're still up for going to the pub after your drinks?'

'You bet.'

'Just checking – I don't want you wimping out on me.'

'Not in a million years.' She really did have the sweetest face, he thought to himself – and that smile of hers, it was enough to melt any heart. Everything seemed to be going right for him all of sudden. Astonishing to think that just six weeks before, he'd been flying to Ireland in a state of deep gloom. Why was he suddenly having this about-turn of fortunes? Was this his compensation for Poppy and Tommy and everything else?

By about nine o'clock that night, he and Tiffany were the only ones from work left in the pub. As he'd hoped, his farewell drinks in the office had been quite brief. Martina said nice things about him and presented him with a new fountain pen. A few of them had then gone to the pub round the corner, but one by one they'd gradually sloped off. It was the weekend after all, and Flin had never done much out-of-hours socializing with them.

'So,' he said emphatically to Tiffany, 'it's just us then.' Neither had eaten anything and the drink was taking effect. Dutch courage, in Flin's case. 'You know, I'd really like to see lots of you in the future.' He looked at her and added, 'Lots and lots.'

Tiffany flung her arms around his neck.

'Is that a "yes" then?' he asked her, laughing.

'What d'you think?' Her blue eyes appraised him mischievously, her smiling face dimpled. Did he fancy her, or what?

'Well, in that case,' he told her, trying to appear serious, 'let's go somewhere else and celebrate.'

'OK, where?' She was still smiling radiantly, and Flin felt his heart glow.

'The pub?' he shrugged. 'You're Earl's Court – that means we should go to the Atlas. That's halfway between us.

'We're going to have such fun, you and I,' Flin told her as they walked out of West Brompton tube.

'I know. Gorgeous, I can't wait.' She took his hand, hers so small by comparison. 'I'm so glad we sorted this out – I was really worried about you leaving.'

At the Atlas, they found an empty table and talked about things that require more than friendship in order to discuss them: the personal likes and dislikes, stories from when they were children. Tiffany told him about growing up on the farm with three much older brothers.

'One day, you'll have to visit. It's beautiful country, but in the middle of absolute nowhere.'

'I suppose you were spoiled something rotten when you were little.'

'You bet I was,' she laughed. 'God, I was such a little brat. They were all so protective of me. It was a nightmare for my boyfriends when I was a bit older.'

'Lucky for me they're not here then.'

'No, you'll be all right. They'll like you. As long as you look after me.'

'I promise.' Poppy had said something similar once, but now with Tiffany he felt he would be able to fulfil his vow. He trusted Tiffany, implicitly, instinctively, in a way he never could anyone else, least of all Poppy. What fun they would have together, and what opportunities suddenly lay ahead. Animatedly, he talked of taking her round England, romantically imagining all the weekends away they might take: to the Lake District, Cornwall, the Yorkshire Dales. He could think of nothing better. 'I think I'd like to go to Salisbury first,' she told him. 'When are you going to take me?'

'Tomorrow?' he suggested.

'Brilliant!' she exclaimed, clapping her hands together.

By ten o'clock they were both feeling rather drunk. They'd forgotten to order any food and the kitchen had long ago stopped serving.

'I'm starving,' Flin declared, 'let's go and get some food.'

'Good plan, I'm starving too,' Tiffany told him. Outside, she put her arms around his neck and said, 'Have I ever told you I think you're very handsome?'

'No, I don't think you have,' Flin grinned.

'Oh,' she said, 'well, I do.' Her mouth spread into a huge grin and then she reached up and they kissed. Flin thought he was in heaven, rather than standing by a collection of stinking black rubbish bags on Seagrave Road, and he felt a wonderful sensation swoop down his spine.

'You are so beautiful. I love it when you smile,' he slurred at her. 'If I saw you smile at me every day, I think I'd always be happy.'

'Now you've gone soppy on me,' she told him, squeezing his hand.

They wandered, very slowly, in the direction of Barons Court, looking in the window of every Chinese and Indian restaurant they saw and then moving on. 'No, I don't like the look of that one,' muttered Flin, as they paused at the Golden Dragon.

'I'm really not happy about that,' said Tiffany as they turned away from the Rajpooth.

'Nor that – too quiet,' at the Taj Mahal. They wandered on up the North End Road, giggling and swaying.

'Look, Flinders, are you going to find me anywhere to eat, or we going to just keep on walking?' Tiffany asked him.

'Almost there. Just round the corner,' he told her. He led her to Turneville Road and to his front door.

'Where's this?' she asked, leaning on him sleepily.

'My house.'

'You sly scheming fox!' she told him, turning and kissing him once more. 'I'm not hungry any more.'

Nor was Flin particularly. He led her into the house and up the stairs and for a while they just lay together on his bed kissing and laughing and talking nonsense. Flin felt ludicrously happy.

Not aware of ever falling asleep, he none the less awoke some hours later with the light still on and the spring dawn emerging outside. He looked at Tiffany, relieved to see she was still there and that he hadn't imagined the previous evening. Quietly slipping out, he went downstairs for some water and then crept back in again and lay next to her, watching her sleep, studying all her contours and features as carefully as he could: the smooth, precise line of her eyebrows; the perfect shape of her lips; the tiny little mole under her left ear. He wanted to know Tiffany in every detail, and to be able to picture her precisely whenever she was not with him.

At length, she started to wake. Without opening her eyes, he saw her mouth slowly turn into a smile. 'That'll teach you for getting me drunk, you rat,' she said, then yawned.

Flin laughed. 'Oldest trick in the book,' he told her.

Tiffany stretched and lifted herself off the bed. 'God, I don't even know where the bathroom is!'

When she came back she stood in front of him and peeled off her jumper, then stepped out of her skirt and pulled off her shirt and socks.

'Wow!' said Flin admiringly. She looked wonderful.

Tiffany smiled and said, 'Shush, you!' and then unclipped her bra and got into bed. 'Come on,' she said, 'get your kit off.' Flin, any inhibitions he may have had vanishing rapidly, happily pulled off his clothes. 'Phwoar yourself,' said Tiffany, rubbing his chest and then hugging him tightly. He could feel her naked breasts push against his chest and it felt wonderful. He kissed and caressed her from her head to her waist, while she lay with her arms behind her, grinning contentedly and occasionally murmuring with satisfaction. 'Oh, yummy, I feel like a purring cat!' she told him languidly as he carefully pulled her knickers down her smooth thighs and legs. What a fool he'd been over Poppy. His one-night stand with her a few months before made him feel ashamed – just sex and nothing more, no real affection, he realized with hindsight. Surely this was better – making love to someone as gorgeous and funny and sweet as Tiffany. He'd never connected so well with anyone before and as he slowly kissed her inner thighs and let her legs stretch apart he felt deeply, truly contented, as though all the ills of the previous year had been worth it because they had led him to this moment.

She confessed she was not on the Pill, but added, 'But I'm going to make sure I am as soon as possible, my gorgeous Flin.' He did not mind. He was happy to kiss her and touch her all over and to feel her light, delicate limbs wrapped round him.

'This is fantastic,' he told her.

'I know,' she agreed, 'we are going to have just the best time.'

'Tiffany, do you think this was meant to be?' he asked her as she lay with her head on his chest. 'Only I'm a bit more into fate and destiny than I used to be.' He was thinking of *Alchemy of the Gods*. Certainly he'd found it inspiring, but had no idea that, having read it, his life would improve so dramatically.

'I dunno,' Tiffany told him, 'but having found you, I'm not letting go, so there.'

They did go to Salisbury. Flin wondered whether they really should and that perhaps Tiffany had only suggested it in the heat of the moment. But, she assured him, she couldn't think of anything better to do, especially since she'd scarcely been out of London since she arrived.

'You still haven't taken me to see the dinosaurs – and you promised me that ages ago. But first I really want to see a bit of country – I'm getting withdrawal symptoms after all this

310

time in a city,' she explained to him, and added, 'So shall we stay overnight somewhere?'

By the sort of good fortune that was becoming a feature of Flin's New Life, he realized his parents were actually away that weekend. Not that he didn't want to see them, but at the start of this brand-new relationship, he wanted to be alone with Tiffany. And now that he thought of it, it would be good to take Tiffany to an old, listed, thatched cottage for her first proper visit to rural England. She thought it an excellent plan, especially as he talked of going to favoured pubs and sitting by the hearth in front of open wood fires. So they quickly tripped round to her flat, picked up some clothes, then hired a small car.

'Won't ever have to do that again,' said Flin, thinking of the freedom that would come with having his own car.

It was a magical weekend, two days where they were really able to get to know one another. During the drive down they had talked all the way without ever putting on the car stereo, moving from backgrounds to opinions, and discovering they shared similar views on many things. And they continued to make each other laugh. Stopping at the Radnor Arms for lunch, he then – since it was such a particularly fine spring afternoon – led her up to the old Iron Age fort of Clearbury above the Haverses' house.

'This is so beautiful,' said Tiffany, and they stayed up there for quite a while, talking and smoking. Flin was glad to be able to show Tiffany one of his most favourite places and was delighted she seemed so taken with it. To him, such places had taken on greater significance since he had moved away. He associated them with his childhood and growing up in the area, times when he had been happy, gay and carefree; it was sentimental of him, he knew, but he felt it important that Tiffany should see and appreciate the beauty of the place too.

He talked about Tommy, his friend whom he missed so much. But he was also aware that he thought about him much

311

less than he did; he was getting used to him not being around any more.

'You'll always miss him,' Tiffany assured him, 'but it's also inevitable that you'll get on with life. We're pretty resilient, you know.'

'You're right,' he agreed, 'but it was terrible at the time. Such a shock. I couldn't believe it. It still seems as though he's just gone travelling or something.'

'Well, I think that's quite a nice way of thinking about it,' Tiffany told him soothingly, 'and it should teach you to make the most of what you've got.'

'Yes,' said Flin, putting his arms around her and kissing her as tenderly as he knew how, 'I intend to.'

Flin took her to another backwater pub in the evening, and she adored it. There was no jukebox or fruit machine, and dangling from the walls were pots and saws and scythes and various other pieces of basic agricultural ironmongery. It consisted of just two tiny rooms, but was packed with locals, and Tiffany thought it was wonderful that not only did the landlord know Flin, but that he pulled pints of beer straight out of the barrel.

'Oh, Flin, why don't we just run away together and move down here. It would be bliss!' Tiffany said as they walked out into the still night. They could smell the damp grass around them. The night air seemed so serene and peaceful. Tiffany smiled up at him and squeezed his hand. He felt so happy, but worried his new-found contentment would any moment be taken away from him. His life was suddenly going too well. Could it really last?

A few weeks later, Flin was in his office, late in the afternoon, when the phone rang. It was Poppy. He hadn't seen her since the night Tommy died and not given her a moment's thought since Tiffany's entrance into his life.

'Darling, aren't I clever? I've tracked you down! I'm just round the corner and instead of chancing bumping into you,

I thought I'd ring this time,' she chirped down the line. 'Please say you can come out for a drink.'

'OK,' he said, 'that'd be great. You can tell me all your news.'

'And I want to hear all yours,' she told him. So, half an hour later, they were sitting together in the same bar in Soho that they had been to the previous November. Mark, she assured him, was by this time completely off the scene; rather, she'd just finished a relationship with a stockbroker called Glen.

'Honestly, Poppy, I'd have thought you'd have learnt by now,' Flin chided her, 'those City types simply aren't for you.'

'I know, you're right,' she sighed wistfully, 'really I should have stuck with you, especially now that you're such a hot-shot.' She was smiling at him, seeing whether he would rise to the flirt. Flin smiled back, not saying anything. 'You know, Flin, it's lovely to see you again. You seem a lot more self-assured – just like when I first met you.' Poppy was a very attractive girl, he thought to himself, and she was looking particularly good as she coyly made passes at him across the table. It was a warm spring day, still light; she looked sleek and, Flin thought, decidedly sophisticated in her trim, dark grey suit.

'Really?' said Flin, 'well, I suppose things are going pretty well at the moment.'

'I'm really glad to hear it,' she said with emphasized earnestness. They talked on and then she suddenly put her hands flat on the table and said, 'Look, I've got a topping plan – why don't we go back to my flat and I'll cook us supper?'

'I'd love to Poppy, but I've got plans.'

'Well, cancel them!' she told him brightly. 'Come on, it'll be fun and I hardly ever see you these days.'

'I can't, Poppy,' Flin told her. She pulled a comic-sad face. 'Sorry, but I really can't.'

He left her soon after and headed towards his wonderful Tiffany. In many ways, he thought, he should be thankful to

Poppy. After all, if he'd ended up going out with her, he would never have got together with Tiffany, and that would have been a tragedy. Poppy was very good-looking and he could completely see how he'd once fancied her so much, but to be honest, he thought Tiffany much prettier, far more naturally adorable. With Poppy, everything was a game, a matter of manipulation and flirtation and, although she'd kept him on his toes, he knew now that a relationship with her would never, ever have worked. He could see what Jessica had seen and he realized how blind and stupid he'd been. It made him cringe. And to think how distraught he'd felt just last November. What a waste of time that had been. No, Tiffany was better for him in every respect. He could be himself with her. There were no complications in their relationship, they simply had a lot of fun.

chapter twenty-six

May 24 and Back at the Atlas

The packing was nearly complete at the house in Turneville Road. Geordie had already moved most of his belongings to his new flat, and all that remained was his duvet, a few clothes and his washbag. His rural idyll was about to be realized. Burt had finally made the deal and had officially offered him the job in Southampton. It would not start until the end of the year, so in the meantime, he and Molly had decided to rent a flat in Chiswick. Being just that bit further out west would enable them to make easy getaways out of town at the weekends to look for a place to live. They'd feel a bit unsettled to start with, but both were so excited at the prospect of owning their own little cottage in a village somewhere that it seemed a small price to pay. It also meant they could go away on their honeymoon with a flat fixed up for their return and their immediate future resolved.

Geordie was so relieved that Flin had found Tiffany. He had to confess she was not exactly his type, but he certainly liked her well enough. It was obvious she adored Flin and he could see she was perfect for him; and in a funny sort of way, her arrival had stopped Geordie from feeling slightly guilty about leaving his friend in the lurch. He knew these were ridiculous thoughts, but they'd been such close friends all their lives that he hated the thought of leaving Flin behind in any way. As it was, he had never known Flin jollier, and felt sure their friendship would always stand the test of time. 'Our lives may be changing a tad,' Flin had told him, 'but that shouldn't make any difference to us being friends.' And then Geordie had suggested they go away on their own for a weekend at least once every year. 'You bet,' Flin had grinned, 'and when you're in the country, I'll be down all the time.' Still, it was sad to be leaving the house, and to be saying goodbye to Jessica and Flin as housemates. A chapter in his life was now over.

In both Jessica's room and the sitting room was an enormous pile of her suitcases and bags. It was only when she had to do a house-move that she realized just how many clothes she had. She'd been tempted to stay put and to get someone else in to take Geordie's room, just so she could avoid the upheaval of moving, but in the end had decided against it. Flin didn't want to live with anyone other than her, and when it came to it, she didn't want to live with anyone other than him. And, as Flin pointed out, they could now afford something a bit nicer. Turneville Road had never been especially aesthetically pleasing; in contrast, their new flat in Hammersmith was. Tastefully furnished throughout, it felt like a proper, grown-up flat. And she was looking forward to basking in the half-glass-roofed kitchen and sheltered garden at the back. All the same, if there was one thing in the world she hated, it was moving house. Such a performance and such a hassle.

Her mood was not improved by the quandary she felt herself to be in. She adored Titus and, to her huge relief, all her friends seemed to approve. The age-gap was not the issue she'd feared and Titus happily quaffed beer and yarned with Flin and Geordie. He'd even invited them up to Norfolk. Lucie was obviously envious, which pleased her, and Kim had to admit he seemed far less parochial than she'd imagined. He spoiled her, pandered to her foibles and had taken her for a romantic break to Paris. It was wonderful and Titus was lovely, and Manor Farm was everything that Jessica thought she had dreamed of. But Jessica was becoming increasingly aware that Titus had

316

reached a point in life when he wanted to think about settling down. He talked of 'wanting a family one day' but it was clear to Jessica that he meant sooner rather than later. She adored him and loved Norfolk and the house and everything, but did she want to leave London just yet? And when it came to it, did she really want to give up work? It sounded great on paper, but she knew she would quickly become bored if she had no job; what would she do all day? Feed chickens? Make breakfast, lunch and dinner? Breed? And day after day, for ever more?

And now she'd been headhunted by a rival firm and was being offered a very attractive package. What would Titus think? There was no way she could commute from Norfolk. Would Titus wait for her if she accepted the post? The thought of losing him was impossible to bear.

Lucie had not been able to see the dilemma. 'I thought that was what you always wanted, J,' she said, 'a rich husband with a large pad in the country.' Well, perhaps she might in ten years' time, but Jessica was not sure she wanted that right now, especially as her career was going so well. What *was* she going to do? She wished her own life was as seemingly straightforward and uncomplicated as Geordie's. She hadn't told Titus about the job offer, nor that she'd even been approached. In fact the only people she had told were Lucie, Flin and Tiffany. At least she liked Tiffany now. To start off with, she'd felt a bit mistrustful. Flin, as usual, had headed into this new relationship at full steam with his traditional romantic ideals intact and she worried it would be another Poppyesque disaster. And, she supposed, she had felt just the teeniest bit jealous as well. But Tiffany still seemed as devoted to Flin as ever, and she had changed her opinion. She and Tiffany were quite different, but they always had fun together, and she recognized that underneath Tiffany's ever-jolly exterior there lay a more serious and sensible side whose opinion on things Jessica grew to value.

'It's a bummer of a decision,' Tiffany had told her, in sharp contrast to Lucie, 'but feeling good about yourself is important.

If you think you'll be happy living Titus's life, then great, but if you think you'll start to feel worthless up there, you should stay put.'

'Well, I know I would be happy there, and I adore Titus, but I worry I'll always be saying "what if?" all the time. Or maybe I wouldn't. I just don't know.'

'I think you should read this,' Flin had said, handing her *Alchemy of the Gods*, 'and try to follow your heart.'

'Flin, darling, I'm not at all sure about this New-Age nonsense – it really doesn't suit you,' she told him firmly, but read it anyway. It just made her feel even more confused.

Flin's possessions seemed just as few and small as they had a year before. It had taken him little time to pack, and now having got used to the idea of Geordie moving out and getting married, he was looking forward to moving into the new place. Tiffany would be able to come over a lot and with Jessica around as well, they were all bound to have a great time. In fact, he felt as though life couldn't be better. Ahead of them that evening they had their promised night of drinks in the Atlas; if he felt any irritation at all, it was only in his impatience to get going and start drinking.

'Time to go!' he yelled to Jessica and Geordie for the third time. 'I'm feeling thirsty.'

'OK, then,' said Jessica, laying her hands decisively on the table and looking at Flin and Geordie in turn, 'we're agreed. Yes?'

Geordie looked at Flin, nodded, and looked back at Jessica. 'Agreed.'

'We all came equal first in the competition. No clear winner.'

'Absolutely,' said Geordie.

'So we all buy each other drinks in turn,' added Flin, 'but Geordie should get in the champagne because he took the pact one step too far by proposing marriage.'

'I second that motion,' laughed Jessica.

Begrudgingly, Geordie bought a bottle of champagne and,

carefully pouring three glasses, said, 'Here's to the two best mates in the world, to a great house and a highly successful year.'

'And here's to continued friendship,' said Jessica.

'And weekends in Geordie's house in the country,' added Flin.

They all raised and chinked their glasses.

'Cheers to all of that, darlings,' laughed Jessica, 'a pact made *and* fulfilled.'

postscript

Geordie looked anxiously behind him, only to be confronted by row upon row of people and hats seemingly staring at him. He quickly turned back again and, tapping his shiny black shoes on the cool, smooth stone of the church floor, said to Flin, 'Beginning to feel a bit twitchy.'

Flin, sitting next to him on the very front row, also started tapping his shoes on the floor. 'I'm feeling a bit twitchy too, on your behalf, old man,' he told him.

'D'you think she'll be on time?' Geordie asked. He sighed heavily and nervously.

'I'm sure,' said Flin. It was one minute to three. He glanced behind him. Jessica was looking fantastic in her wide-brimmed, black befeathered hat. She caught his eye and smiled happily. Titus smiled too, looking urbane in his double-breasted waistcoat. A few rows behind, he could see Tiffany, her face virtually covered by an enormous white hat. She was sitting next to Josh and he could see that they were laughing about something. Then the organ started playing and everyone stood up. Flin nudged Geordie. 'Here we go!' he whispered and they moved up to their positions.

Geordie could feel his palms sweating but felt incredibly proud as he saw the girl of his dreams walking slowly towards him. She looked beautiful. Suddenly he ceased to be aware of the people in the congregation: they seemed to blur and his anxiety about feeling ludicrously self-conscious disappeared. All he could think of was Molly and the fact that their moment had arrived. All the months of planning and preparation were over; his first twenty-five years finished, his next however-many about to start.

It seemed strange to Flin that finally he was watching Geordie saying his vows. Years before, as a child, he'd wondered what it would be like, seeing a best friend married, in the same way that he had wondered how it would feel to write a cheque or drive a car. Well, now he knew all these things. But he also knew that despite passing such landmarks of adulthood and accepting the responsibility that came with them, he was in essence the same person, and always would be. He was able to accept that growing older did not mean an end to having fun, or that the pleasures of youth could no longer be enjoyed. With Tiffany, he had every bit as much fun as he ever had, and more. The prospect of a committed and long-term relationship filled him with relief and joy. The pact Jessica had suggested the previous year had been fulfilled by all three of them, and Flin could finally look to the future with a glad heart.

Flin had felt very nervous about having to make his speech and was unable to eat his food properly. Sitting on the end of the top table next to Lizzie, he weakly smiled across at Tiffany for reassurance. Taking a few tips on how not to make a speech from Bomber the year before, everyone seemed to laugh at the right points. As he got into the swing of it, he even began rather to enjoy standing up there. Afterwards, people he both knew and did not know complimented him on his efforts, and he felt flattered and relieved that he could now get on with enjoying the reception.

'Bloody good speech,' Geordie told him and Geordie's father, agreed.

'Very revealing,' he winked.

At eleven o'clock, Geordie and Molly left. Everyone crowded outside at the front of the Duguids' house and then they emerged in their going-away outfits and made their way through the crowd to the waiting taxi.

'Thanks for everything, Flin – you've been brilliant,' said Geordie, clasping his friend in a rare act of open emotion. Then he hunted out Jessica and bid her farewell too.

'Have a wonderful time,' she sniffed, hugging both Geordie and then Molly. Then Molly threw her bouquet high into the air only for Jessica to catch it and everyone cheered. 'Bye! Bye!' said the happy couple as they strained to say final farewells to their families. Then they were gone.

The crowd waved as their car pulled out of the drive and then gradually dispersed back to the marquee in the garden. Jessica and Flin hugged one another and sighed. 'Well, that's them sorted,' said Flin and then seeing Tiffany said, 'Let's go and get another drink.'

'I feel rather emotional seeing Geordie and Molly go off like that,' Jessica said to Titus as they wandered slowly to the other end of the garden. 'All of a sudden it feels like the end of an era.'

'Or the beginning of a new one.' Titus smiled. 'Jessica,' he said slowly, 'will you marry me?'

Flin and Tiffany danced away until the disco finally stopped and then, hot and not a little sweaty, they walked out into the garden to cool themselves.

'What a day!' Flin exclaimed. 'Have you enjoyed it, Tiff?'

'I've loved it, just loved it,' she said, 'it's been a real happy day. And I felt so proud of you making that speech. Everyone's been telling me how brilliant they thought it was.'

'Ah,' said Flin happily. He sat down on a wooden garden bench and Tiffany lay down by him, her head on his lap.   'Flin?' she said.

'Hm?' said Flin, idly looking up at the stars.

'I love you more than anything in the world. Do you think we'll always be together?'

He grinned back at her, his heart brimming with love for this wonderful person who had come into his life. 'Course,' he said. She looked up at him again and her face broke into a wide smile. Flin leant down and kissed her. Life could be very sweet, he thought to himself happily.